DEAL TO DIE FOR

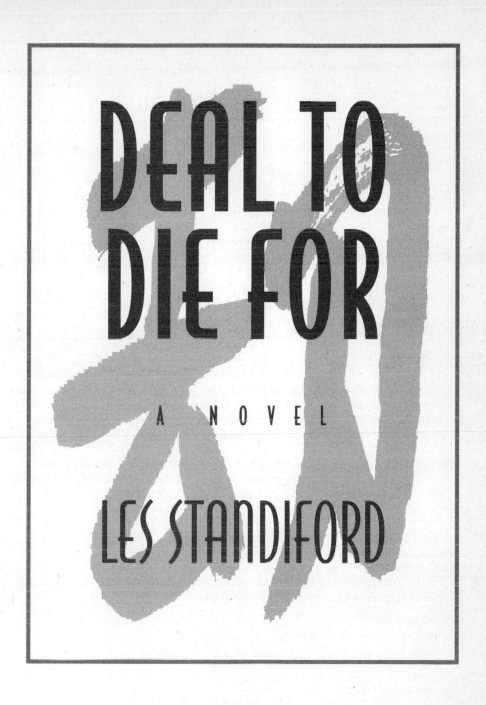

DEAL TO DIE FOR

A NOVEL

LES STANDIFORD

HarperCollinsPublishers

Author's Note: While I love South Florida just as it really and truly is, this is a work of fiction and I have taken certain liberties with names and places. May they please the innocent and guilty alike.

Designed by R. Caitlin Daniels
Calligraphy by Jamie Leung

Library of Congress Cataloging-in-Publication Data

Standiford, Les.
    Deal to die for / Les Standiford. — 1st ed.
        p.   cm.
    ISBN 0-06-017621-0
    I. Title.
    PS3569.T331528D43   1995
    813'.54—dc20   95-23174

95 96 97 98 99 ❖/HC 10 9 8 7 6 5 4

This one's for Ripley and Crumley
and the rest of the California gang,
especially Victor Lieberman and Leslie Lee,
who stayed behind to explain everything.

And, as always, for Kimberly
and the Three Muskatoots.

Deal and I would like to extend our heartfelt thanks to Professor Thomas A. Breslin, Stephen Lazarus, M.D., Eric Kurzweil, M.D., and Mitchell Kaplan for their help and advice on matters of medicine, Chinese history and customs, and international trade . . .

. . . and to Rhoda Kurzweil, James W. Hall, and Nat Sobel for their help in the shaping of this story.

Know therefore that the sword is a cursed thing
Which the wise man uses only if he must.
                            —from the *Tao Te Ching*

"You know how the Chinese like to have sex, Paco?" It was Richard Mendanian's voice, drifting up to him from the back of the limo. They were high in the Hollywood Hills now, Paco Edwards piloting the unfamiliar, bargelike limo along twisty Mulholland Drive.

Paco readjusted his grip on the wheel. "I hadn't much thought about it," he said, trying to get a better look at what was going on back there. The little guy, Mendanian, had dropped the glass that separated the main compartment so they could talk—or so that Paco could watch and listen, was probably more like it.

Paco had met Mendanian and the woman he was back there with at some bar his new landlord had directed him to—Larry's? Harry's? Gary's?—some hangout a couple of blocks up La Cienega from the Beverly Center, crowded little place between a limo service and a flower shop.

His landlord, guy with a shaved head and a stud driven through his tongue, looking him over: jeans, boots, an unconstructed jacket the clerk in the Beverly Center had sworn was the latest thing—finally nodding, "You should do all right in there," and it seemed he had.

"Exactly like we do," Mendanian said, finishing it, laughing at his own joke.

1

"You mean, while they ride around in big cars with other people driving?" Paco said, hearing the edge in his voice.

"You two be nice," the woman said. She'd started all this, he knew she had. Invited him to join their table in the crowded place, had laughed at Paco's Texas shtick, throwing back her head, showing her perfect teeth, baring the lovely curve of her throat. There were good-looking women in Odessa, he thought; this one would have them turning their heads in shame.

"Research," the little guy was saying, calling from the backseat. "You make a movie, you have to know what your audience wants, that's all. That's what a person like you needs to understand." There was a pause, and the sound of flesh scootching across leather. "You want to write for the movies," the guy continued, "I'm giving you that for free."

"Thanks," Paco said. He cut his eyes briefly to the rearview mirror, caught a glimpse of the woman's milky skin, her backside laid out in the dim sidelamps like a map of heaven.

"Richard just finished *Ghost Buddies*," the woman had told him over the din in the bar. "And he's going to do some work in China next year, the first American films ever to be made on the mainland?" She'd said it as if it were a question, an invitation for Paco to say he'd heard about these movies.

"It hasn't happened yet," Mendanian had said, his first recognition of Paco. "Goddamned Chinks are as bad as anybody else when it comes to putting up the money."

Once he'd found out what Mendanian's business was, Paco told him why he'd come out to California. Now he was beginning to regret it.

"You're not worried, pick up some guy you don't know, let him drive you around like this?" Paco said.

The guy was leaning back in a corner of the seat, still had most of his clothes on, his arms crossed behind his head as she worked on him. "Should I be worried, Paco? You told me you came from an old ranching family. I'm thinking salt of the earth and all that."

"That's right," Paco said. "Salt of the earth." Another mistake, telling him about his family, the ranch that had once covered ninety six sections of West Texas prime, now shriveled to a fraction of that, and what was left the subject of endless wrangling amongst the heirs.

Paco turned back to the road. Narrow road that ran along the very spine of the mountains. For two years, he'd never seen past the lip of a cement-block wall. Now, one second he'd have a breathtaking view of the L.A. basin, the next they'd swing around, give him an endless vista of the lights of the San Fernando Valley. On top of that, there was what was going on in the backseat. Though the edge of his own lust had fallen away—*too weird for a Texas boy, Paco?*—it was still something to behold.

Less than a week outside, out of Texas at last, look what he'd fallen into. *Material, Paco. View it as material.*

"So how does a fellow from the joint get into writing screenplays, Paco? How does that work?"

Paco glanced in the mirror. Something he hadn't brought up with Mendanian. The woman up on the seat now, atop the little guy and squirming in place, her eyes closed, lower lip caught in her teeth. Paco glanced away. Maybe his lust not all the way gone, after all.

"What joint are we talking about?"

"You don't want to discuss it, it's okay with me."

Paco heard some fleshy noises from back there. He thought about slamming on the brakes, see who yelped.

"Richard made *San Quentin Blues,*" the woman said, her voice breathy. "He researched it. By the time it was over, he'd spent more time in prison than Michael Milken."

Paco glanced in the mirror. He'd never heard of the movie, but he knew something about prison. Looking at it was one thing, living it another.

"It's the way you all walk," Mendanian said. "Always watching without seeming to, always ready for the next bad scene. Quite distinctive, really."

"You took me for a con? And you have me driving your car?"

"Some of us are amused by these things," Mendanian said.

"I don't think you're a bad person, Paco." The woman, her breathing labored. "When we saw you walk in, Richard said, 'There's a guy who's just come out of the joint.' I said you looked cute."

Paco shook his head. He'd heard it was strange out here, but no one had prepared him for this.

"Some guy came through the facility, did a weekend writer's

conference," Paco said finally. "He read my stuff, said there was grit. Said there was a movie in it."

"Do tell," the little guy said. "What did you do, anyway, stick up a 7-Eleven?"

Paco glanced in the mirror again. "This getting you off, grinding my ass, too?"

Mendanian laughed. "I'm just trying to find out what you're made of, Paco. See if you've got what it takes."

"Takes for what?"

"For whatever," Mendanian said.

Paco shrugged. What the hell, he could stand a little crap, was even getting used to it. He'd scored a few drinks, got the feel of driving a car again. How long before he'd be able to get a driver's license, after all?

"Let's go to the Watts Towers." The woman again, her voice in a different key. "I think he should see the Watts Towers, Richard."

"Smack," Paco said, ignoring her. "They caught me with a couple loaves of Mexican Brown halfway between Matamoros and Kingsville."

"Yeah?" the little guy said. "Running drugs when you had all that land to sell?"

Paco shrugged. Why had he told Mendanian about his family? But he knew why. Long as he'd been out of commission, find someone like her across a table, he'd have said anything to keep her looking at him with that dazzling smile, raising her arm to signal the waitress for another round, his gaze traveling down her slender fingers, her wrist, the milky hollows of her elbow and underarm.

It made him think of an old movie he'd seen a few months back, piped in for their Saturday night diversion. Spencer Tracy has a slug of a steaming drink, takes one look at Lana Turner, turns into Cro-Magnon man. *Sure*, Paco thought. Nothing fantastic about that. For all he knew, there were tufts of hair growing out of his own ears right now.

She was off the seat now, was moving in *his* direction, bent down, all the parts of her swaying with the motion of the car.

He leaned aside, trying to find the little guy's eyes in the mirror. "I got six brothers and sisters. You ever try to get six insane people to agree on the same deal?"

"Nearly every day," Mendanian said.

Not bad, Paco thought. Maybe he wasn't such a twerp after all. Maybe he and this guy had more in common than he'd assumed. So what if he wouldn't last a week in the joint. That wasn't the proof of a person's worth, was it? He was *outside* now, a normal person again. He had to start thinking like he was.

The woman was at the compartment window now, leaning through, her breasts brushing the back of his neck. "Wouldn't you like to see the Watts Towers?" she asked, her voice smoky.

Back in the restaurant, she'd excused herself from the table, he'd watched her go, soft black dress, medium spiked heels, every nudge of her body an erotic summons. When she returned from the bathroom, her eyes were glittering and a tiny tear of moisture glittered at one of her perfect nostrils. Paco had imagined what the drug was doing to her, how her blood had heated, what she might be thinking. He had stared back at her until he felt he had slid right inside the envelope of her skin, could feel her lungs swelling when she breathed, her blood pounding in his own veins.

"We're going now," she'd said, "but why don't you come with us?"

"Sure," Mendanian had said, sliding a set of car keys across the table at Paco. "Any friend of Lizzie's is a friend of mine."

Paco sensed a flash of light behind the limo, glanced in the outside mirror to see a car coming up behind them. He shrugged her off. "There's people coming." The glass of the driver's compartment wasn't tinted. Some other driver got a look of what was draped over his back, the guy would sail right off the cliffs.

"So what," she said, leaning heavily into him. Paco's head went down, came back up. He'd nearly missed a curve in the road. He dropped his speed, gripped the wheel tightly.

"I'm trying to drive," he said.

"Look, Richard doesn't mind. He'll drive a while, won't you, Richard . . . "

"Jesus Christ," he said, flailing at her, trying to shove her back into the compartment. The car behind them had swung out to pass, was clipping alongside them now. He'd caught the silhouette of cruiser lights atop the sedan, got a glimpse of a cop in the passenger seat glancing their way.

He held his breath, ready for it all to come down: first there'd be the spotlight in his eyes, then the bullhorn voice telling him to pull over . . . and then the film in his head collapsed into hyperdrive, a blur of familiar scenes, an instantaneous montage of the American judicial system that ended with the slam of a heavy iron door at his heels, Mendanian and the woman waving good-bye to him from the green, green grass of home.

He was ready for it, girding for it, trying to muster some story: "It's not my fault, officer. She pointed her breasts at me, forced me to drive . . . "

And then, miraculously, the cruiser sped on past. He didn't get a good look at the insignia. Maybe it was some kind of rent-a-cop, cruising the megabucks properties up here. Or maybe the uniforms just didn't fuck with stretch limos out here, no matter what might be going on inside. He took a deep breath, watching the taillights of the cruiser whisk on ahead, watched them grow smaller and smaller, until his relief was almost complete.

"You hurt my neck."

It was the woman, whining from the compartment behind him.

"He hurt my neck, Richard."

"You're lucky that's all that hurts," Paco said. "That was the goddamned cops just passed us."

He was about to turn, say something else, when he felt a stunning pain at his head, felt something splash across his face and neck. Brilliant sheets of light danced behind his eyes. He slammed instinctively on the brakes.

"You fucking ignorant hick," she was screaming. She was pummeling him with her fists now, deep into a serious mood swing. Paco had been there, lost in the chemical snowdrifts, where the least word crossways could put you crazy.

The limo slid to a halt across the opposite lane, its nose pointed out at the Valley lights. The bolts of pain had subsided and he blinked his eyes, grateful at first that he could still see, though what he saw made him catch his breath: A couple more feet, they'd have been over the side of the cliff.

He had one hand up to ward off her blows, the other at his temple, checking the knot that had already risen there. He felt a splinter of glass prick his finger, felt something wet trickling down his cheek. He smelled the sick-sweet odor of bourbon. She must have clobbered him with the whole decanter. At least he *hoped* it was whiskey that was dripping down his collar, soaking him.

"Calm down, Melissa." It was Mendanian, with a voice that wouldn't get an egg-sucking dog's attention. Melissa was halfway into the driver's compartment now, remembering she had nails, gouging him a good one across the cheek. If he hadn't been bleeding before, he sure as shit was going to be now.

Paco was retreating into the corner of the driver's seat, swatting her hands away, when he saw the brake lights go on up ahead of them. *Lord, Lord,* he thought. The cops had seen them.

The cruiser pulled into a driveway, briefly illuminating an iron fence and a pack of dogs snarling and lunging at the bars. Then it backed out, its headlamps washing over the limo as it hit the roadway and headed back in their direction.

There wasn't much time, but the cruiser would have to round a curve before it would be upon them, this road twisty as a bottomland creek. There was some justice in that, Paco thought, as his hand found the door lever and pulled. He rolled out onto the gravel shoulder of the road, into the cool crisp night.

He was up and slamming the door behind him in one motion, making his choices quick as the first con in the cafeteria line. Can't go forward, can't go back, there'll be another cruiser coming from behind them in a heartbeat. Far side of the road a steep embankment rising up, covered with brush that could hide him, maybe that way ... but then he saw some more of that spike-topped fencing running through the scrub oaks, and next thing there was the noise of things crashing through the brush.

At first it was snarling, then god-awful barking as the dogs he'd seen down the fence line a moment ago got close enough to catch his scent. Their growling changed to something that was more like gargling blood. Better to spend a month chained to a Crip and a Blood in isolation than go over that fence . . .

Which meant, with the cruiser slewing around the curve now, its lights bouncing high up, about to come down and catch him there with his thumb up his butt, he had but one way to go.

That's when he went out over the side of the cliff, his hand clutching some gnarly bush that poked from the dusty soil, praying there would be something soft to land on down below. Instead, surprisingly, his feet hit ground. He took one step, then another, picking up speed big-time, but was still beginning to think he'd lucked out.

Then the bush in his hand tore loose like it had never had roots in the first place and there was nothing underneath him but air. He went out into space, his breath gone, his stomach seeming to fly up through his chest, his arms and legs windmilling.

As he fell, he cursed his father for dying intestate, cursed his impossible, quarrelsome brothers and sisters, cursed the Kingsville cop whose job was so pitifully boring he'd pulled him over for a broken taillight and stumbled accidentally onto Paco's stash, he even cursed the member of the Lomos he'd had to cut with a converted butter knife he'd taken in trade for his old man's watch, for if that little Chicano jerk had been any kind of thug at all, he would have gutted Paco right there on the hardball court of the Permian Basin Correctional Facility and saved him from the terrible fate of falling off a California cliffside to his death.

He was trying to think of someone else to curse when he hit the tree. He felt something snap and rip through his side with an icy pain, felt another something shoot up under his shirt and jacket, trench the flesh along his spine. A jagged point of wood shot up through his collar, took out the lapel of his new coat, glanced off his jaw. His head snapped back as hard as it had the day Chico from the iron pile decided he didn't like some *gringo pendejo* walking around with a Mexican name, sucker punched him into another orbit.

But hey, Paco was thinking, screw Chico, screw the tree limb, screw his old man and his brothers and sisters and the horse they all rode in on, because the fact of the matter was, even if he was bleeding from several different places now, even if his side was ripped open and his jaw was kissing his own ear and his sphincter was shrunk to where he could crap through a straw, the main thing was, he was no longer falling. He realized, in fact, after he'd finally mustered the courage to open his eyes, that he was hanging like a scarecrow in the clutches of a tree, a tree that itself had defied gravity to grow nearly sideways out of the sheer cliff.

Beneath him, another thirty feet or so, was the backyard of an expensive house, a spacious area laid out in what seemed to be Japanese gardens, with a sizable grotto pool where great red fish lazed in the soft glow of hidden lights. He looked up, to the lip of the cliff where the limo sat, and saw that he couldn't have fallen more than twenty feet. It seemed to have happened years ago.

He saw the cruiser then, sliding to a stop on the graveled shoulder. Saw its passenger door fly open, heard the whine of its big cop engine dying down. He saw a cop approaching the limo, a flashlight beam dancing in his hand. Saw another beam from the other side of the limo, knew there was another cop over there somewhere.

There were voices, and muffled replies from inside the limo. Then, drifting down clearly on the sinking canyon breeze, "Open a door."

Open a door. What a weird way to put it, Paco was thinking, until he realized that the cop had some strange kind of accent.

Again the command, "Open a door." Then the sound of that very thing happening. A pause.

"Officer . . . " Mendanian's voice, commanding exactly nothing. "Hey, what is this . . . ?"

And then, the terrific explosion. The sound of shattering glass and steel. The biting stink of powder drifting down to him. *Shotgun,* he found himself thinking.

It took Paco a moment to understand, but when he realized what it was, what it had to be—it wasn't really cops up there at all—a fear swept him that made his tumble through the void seem something only good and true.

He heard the woman's screams, the sounds of footsteps running through gravel. More explosions. And the screaming stopped.

". . . where is driver?" Paco heard. Same voice, same accent. Paco was trying desperately to untangle himself from his ruined coat, now.

A second voice, this one in an Oriental language, someone shouting back to the other phony cop. The new voice much clearer, the guy probably right at the top of the cliff now, having figured out just what Paco had—only one way off this island, Dan-O.

Paco yanked wildly at his coat sleeve, felt the fabric give way, felt himself swing away from the limb that had nearly taken his head off. He was dangling by one arm now, some zoo monkey who'd escaped but lost his way.

He squinted when the flashlight beam swept across his face, tried to shield himself with his free hand.

His grip was slipping now, some kind of oddball California

tree bark peeling away beneath his fingers. One way or another, this would not take long. He imagined the big red fish down there, gazing up, their mouths popping open and closed, fins flapping them nowhere, unfazed and simply waiting.

"There," he heard a voice above him say. "In tree. In goddamn tree." Then the roar of the shotgun. Paco felt a stinging here and there, but nothing fatal yet. Then the blast of another weapon, maybe a handgun, but no pain, these guys apparently unequipped for anything that wasn't short-range.

Come on, hurry up, get lucky, Paco was thinking. Some guy as dumb as Chico from the joint up there, doesn't know what to do when the script changes. Then he heard another crack, realized that this time it was the sound of wood shattering . . . and finally, he felt a kind of relief, flying, going down to meet the great red fish.

"God in heaven," Janice was saying. She shook her head at something she was reading in the paper. "It happens everywhere, doesn't it."

Deal heard, but hadn't heard, not really. His mind was out there over the vast plain of sawgrass, twisting and turning lazily with a squadron of November buzzards riding the rising currents.

This was why Florida had been invented, he'd been thinking. A cold front had swept down the state earlier in the week, pushing a stubborn winter heat wave well out into the Caribbean, leaving behind bright skies and air that made you want to weep with gratitude.

Something had awakened him early that morning, some signal from the gods, that's how he saw it. Up before the sun, before Janice had even stirred, banging around the kitchen, brewing a pot of coffee thick enough to spoon into the thermos, laying out a phalanx of his special avocado and tomato sandwiches, sourdough bread on the bottom, slabs of hand-cut whole wheat on top, lemon pepper and a drizzle of vinaigrette dressing for Janice, Captain Rick's Caesar for himself, then fruit yogurt, juice bottle, and any number of snack things for their daughter Isabel, all of it packed and their bikes loaded into the back of the pickup they called Big Red, and the sun still just a hint at the horizon.

11

Janice had been grumpy at first, but was finally game—it was an annual trek, after all, their first foray into the Everglades with the mosquitoes gone into hibernation and the park empty, the crowds of snowbirds still massing up North, shining their Winnebagos and white shoes and dreaming of a paved spot in the Florida sunshine.

The tradition had begun when they were courting, a dozen years ago, two rent bikes tethered to the trunk of his car, and a bottle of wine, out the Tamiami Trail past the dikes and the last tendrils of urban sprawl to the shuttered visitors' center at Shark Valley, over the chained barricades with the bikes to the loop road, and a seventeen-mile circle through corridors of sawgrass and hammock. They had ridden past alligators, raccoons, ibis, and anhingas, all the creatures still too stunned with the rhythms of a solitary summer to pay much notice to a single pair of humans cruising through.

That first trip they'd found the observation tower at the halfway point closed, but Deal had jimmied the door to the stairwell with the awl point on his Swiss Army knife. They drank the wine on this same shaded stairwell landing and made love there, their first time, while the sun sank steadily and the air grew cool, almost as cool as the air on this day, and had to ride the bikes back flat-out in the gathering dusk, dodging the rousing gators all the way.

That's where his mind had been on this day, twelve years later, while Janice lounged in a sunny spot on the landing, reading the copy of the *Times* they'd picked up from a box in a strip mall on the way. Isabel, no early riser, even at three, had stayed at home after all, watched over by Mrs. Suarez, their neighbor. "Let her sleep, Deal," Janice had said. "Let's do this, just you and me."

And now they *were* doing it: Deal was sitting with his legs dangling in space, his arms hooked over a part of the stair railing, his chin resting on the cool metal. He lay his cheek on the rail and watched her as she read, her brow furrowed, her head still shaking in consternation. He thought that she hadn't changed much in the intervening years, not in physical ways, at least. She was a little leaner maybe, her hair shorter, with a fleck of gray here and there; if anything, her soft, pleasant features had acquired an underlying edge, a character that only intensified her beauty. *Here is a woman who might be great-looking but has never let it get in her way,* he thought. He was still a bit in awe of that.

And in awe of what she'd overcome. Two years since the fire that had destroyed their home and nearly claimed her life. Two years of painful surgery to soften the scars and restore the flesh the flames had stolen from her. It made his own skin feel taut and fiery just to think about it. And yet, looking at her now, it seemed almost as if it hadn't happened. There were places below the line of her jaw where the grafts below showed lighter, some tell-tale scarring if you were looking for it, but makeup could very nearly erase those traces. It was, in fact, a miracle.

"You remember the first time we came here?" he said.

She looked up from the paper, her eyes seemingly unfocused. "What?"

"The first time we were here," he said. "I was just thinking about that."

She stared at him, her gaze coming into focus. It was as if he could see her thoughts rearranging themselves, leaving whatever had held her in the paper and moving to a consideration of him.

"You always think about *that,*" she said.

He wasn't sure if she was joking. "Not just the sex," he said, trying to protest. "I was thinking about all of it, what a great place this is. In fact," he added, "I think we probably owe our relationship to the fact we started out, more or less, I mean, right here, right in the middle of all this. Just look at it. It *looks* like a place for beginnings, right?"

He swung his arm enthusiastically out into space, over the vast expanse of sawgrass below, where a breeze they hadn't felt cut a sinuous pattern of waving green off toward the horizon. It was as if a huge, invisible hand were smoothing the nap on a giant rug.

She gave him an odd stare. "That was a long time ago, wasn't it?"

He nodded, a little deflated. That was Janice, all right. You couldn't count on her to lock up with your own train of thought. She was probably still thinking about whatever it was she'd been reading about, was only giving him the appearance of her attention, even now.

That was something she'd been better about, though, especially since Isabel had come along, being *here,* in the world. In their first years together, there were times when she would drift away so completely, become so self-contained, that he worried she would never come back. More properly, he worried that she would not need him in the same way he needed her.

But that was silly, she assured him. She did need him, he had no idea how much. "You come from one of those touchy-feely Walton kind of families, Deal," that's what she told him once, laughing. "Popcorn on the Christmas tree, everybody kissing under the mistletoe, all that. My mother's idea of affection was a handshake." She claimed never to have seen her parents kiss, could not fathom the very intercourse that had brought her into existence. "I guess they tried it at least once," she'd said, shaking her head. "But they couldn't have enjoyed it much."

Janice herself had no such reservations, though. They'd both been oozing blood from their concrete-raw knees and elbows the night of their first ride back through the Everglades, and that aspect of their relationship had never cooled. Still, there had been times, even after the most stunning, exhausting sex, when he'd sensed her slipping away, drifting off to that place where he could never go, even though he'd hold her as tightly as he could.

Although he assumed the episodes had something to do with growing up in such a frigid household, Deal had no way of knowing how accurately Janice had described her parents' shortcomings. Long before he'd met her, they'd both died, killed in an automobile accident, a head-on collision with a tractor-trailer on an icy Ohio two-lane while Janice was away at college. And that was reason enough, he had long ago decided, to allow her those moods, to try to understand them, and most important, to not be threatened by them.

Given what they'd been through the past few years, she was entitled. And, he told himself, they were tiny blips, more a reflection of his own insecurities than anything else. He had a beautiful wife. Their life together was good. They could talk about things that mattered. They had a lovely child. DealCo, his contracting business, was finally on solid ground again. He had a lot to be thankful for.

She was staring out toward the horizon now, her face drawn in thought. He felt a flood of warmth wash over him, a mixture of desire and gratitude. He found himself thinking of their first visit again, felt a sudden wave of arousal. Maybe Janice was right. Maybe he *was* always thinking of that. Still, nothing wrong with the way he was feeling, was there? Perfectly innocent. Not what had been on his mind when he was getting ready for this trip. He'd been the one willing to wake Isabel, after all.

"What were you reading?" he asked. He could be patient. They could have conversation. Just be together. And be patient. See what happens.

"What?" she said, turning to him. Her eyes blinked again, refocusing, coming back. She glanced at the paper, which ruffled in a momentary updraft, then waved, as if to dismiss the memory. "Just another killing," she said, wearily. "A man and his wife shot in their car."

"Here?" Deal said. It was a fact of life now. Murder in paradise, a wrap-up of the prior day's slaughter part of every breakfast newscast. Tourists blown away on the interstate, 7-Eleven clerks macheted to pieces at the till, cops picked off by snipers passed over for promotion at the post office. He wondered what South Florida atrocity had been remarkable enough for the *New York Times* to pick up on.

She shook her head. "In Los Angeles," she said. "The man was a movie producer and his wife was an actress." She glanced away, again, shaking her head. "It happened on Mulholland Drive." Her voice had grown faint, almost pained.

Deal looked over at the paper, curious. "Did you know these people?"

"No," she shook her head. "But I was on Mulholland Drive once," she said. He saw a tear break from the corner of her eye, slide down her cheek. There was a tiny scar there, near her chin, nothing anyone else would have noticed, only enough to shift the course of the tear a fraction. She gestured out at the scene before them. "It *is* pretty here, Deal. That's what got me thinking. And that was the prettiest place too . . ." Her voice was faltering.

"Janice . . . " he said, reaching out for her. *Not again,* he was thinking. *Not now . . .*

She turned to him, held her hand up, turned her head, a gesture that said *stay back.* A chill swept over him. It was a stranger's expression on her face, come over her in an instant. Even her posture, the cant of her body, seemed wrong. Flashes of a dozen bad science fiction films ran behind his eyes: *"She looks like my wife, but she isn't. She isn't!"*

"I can't do this any longer, Deal," her voice strangled. "I'm sick of pretending."

"Do what?" He reached for her again, but she lurched back, toward the railing, which looked suddenly very frail to him. "What's wrong, Janice?"

"This is not your fault, Deal," she said, her eyes jittery. She took a breath, gathering herself, avoiding his gaze now. "You've tried. I know you want me to think that I'm still attractive . . . "

He stared at her, felt his mouth working dumbly. "Stop fooling around." She backed further away at the sharp tone of his voice, and he stopped, then began again. A knot of pain had formed in his chest. "You *are* attractive. You're goddamned gorgeous . . . "

"Don't lie to me, Deal. We've always been honest with one another." She ran her hands along the line of her jaw, tracing the thin scars, then abruptly clenched her fists, pulling back her shoulder-length hair. "You can't deny this." She swung her head to one side, then the other, like some petulant child. The tissue of both ears was still gnarled, much of it angry red, but that was normal. The process of reconstruction was nearly complete. Another operation, possibly two. And meantime, with her hair worn down, who would even see what scarring remained?

He felt stunned, even nauseous, with helplessness. At the time of the accident, the doctors had cautioned him that burn victims often experienced bouts of depression over the course of reconstructive surgery, but Janice had seemed immune. She'd weathered the worst times without a whisper of complaint. And suddenly, now that she was, by anyone's measure, nearly back to her old self again, she was suddenly falling apart, disintegrating, before his eyes.

"Janice, I know it's been tough on you, but you're fine. You look wonderful . . . "

Her scream cut him off. Froze him. Her eyes clenched tight, the tendons jumping from her neck. She threw back her head and screamed until her breath gave out. The sound echoed off the steel and concrete, splintered the pristine silence about them, worse than any sonic boom or airboat engine could have. A flock of ibis who'd been foraging in a soggy meadow at the foot of the tower rose and soared away, their wings slapping the air a dozen

16

feet from where Deal sat, as stunned as Lot looking at his wife.

Finally, she opened her eyes, took a breath, turned toward him. "Don't *ever*," she said abruptly, as the sounds died away. "Don't *ever* say that again." Her voice had regained that same desperate note. She'd drawn her legs up under her body, staring at him warily, as if she were ready to spring backward, out into space.

Deal locked his gaze with hers and nodded. "All right," he said, forcing his voice to sound calm, the apotheosis of reason. "I won't. I promise."

She seemed to relent then, sagging as if all her energy were suddenly spent. He leaned forward, caught his arms about her shoulders, pulled her close, away from the landing's edge.

"Janice," he said. She was sobbing now, her body shuddering as she gasped for air. He had one arm locked about her shoulders, pulling her steadily from the edge, using his free hand to stroke her hair. Far out of the Everglades, the buzzards were still soaring, and the ibis had fluttered down to another, quieter meadow. He held his lips to her forehead and rocked her in his arms. "Dear Janice." Where would they go from here?

"Fish pond? What the hell do you mean, *fish pond*?" The big man stopped himself, glanced around the outdoor terrace of the Griffith Park clubhouse, worrying that his voice had carried.

He shouldn't have bothered. It was misting lightly and most of the golfers were huddled inside, swapping lies in the grill room. Just one old fart at a table across the way, adding and re-adding his scorecard, frowning, wouldn't have budged for an atomic blast.

"Just like I told you," the Chinese guy sitting across from him said. "Man fall in fish pond"—he lifted his hands in a gesture of helplessness—"get away."

"Sounds like fucking Confucius," the big man said, fuming, drumming the table with his fingers. Next thing, someone would walk outside, recognize him, want to know what was going on, never mind the sunglasses and Lakers cap he had donned. Not much chance of that, it being a city course and far too déclassé for most of his associates, but look what had happened already. If *Chinese* gangsters could screw up, where did that leave you?

"Sorry?" the Chinese guy said, not sure if he was being insulted.

"Forget it." He sat back in his chair, drumming the table with both hands now. His gaze lit on the old guy across the terrace, who was furiously crossing something out on his scorecard, penciling something else in. The guy's face had grown beet red, and he seemed to be talking to himself.

A mess, the big man was thinking. *A big freaking mess.* That's what he got for bringing in someone like Richard Mendanian in the first place. Offer a bottom feeder a nibble, he's going to try and take the whole chunk, every time. He turned back to the Chinese guy, tapped the newspaper that lay between them.

"Here's what I don't get. Your people try to take this chauffeur out, but he gets away. How come he doesn't go straight to the cops?"

"Maybe has something to hide."

He thought about it a moment. He'd met some of the hangers-on in Mendanian's orbit. Sleazewads following a bigger sleazewad, champing down the chunks that fell off. Sure. It would make sense, the driver being some kind of criminal. Who'd believe some guy who probably looked like he stepped out of a pirate picture: "No sir, I had nothing to do with killing my employer. It was two Chinese guys in cop suits that did it."

The big man nodded, pointing at the paper again. "So now this chauffeur is a suspect," he said. "At least there's that much in our favor."

"You worry about nothing. Man turn himself in, talk all he want to. Knows nothing in the first place."

"He's a loose end," he said. He stared glumly out over the golf course. Four guys in rain suits walking down a fairway, looked like they were ready to clean up radiation. What a fucking game.

The Chinese guy shrugged. "Nothing to worry about. Cops think he in on it." He tapped his finger on the paper between them. "Forget this man. Are bigger fry to fish."

He stared. "It's 'bigger *fish* to *fry.*'"

The Chinese guy thought about it. "Make more sense the other way," he insisted. He was quiet for a moment, then moved on. "Who going to make our movie now?"

"There's a zillion guys where Richard Mendanian came from," he said.

"Need someone to trust," the Chinese guy said.

"Don't worry," he said. "I'll take care of it."

"You say don't worry about this Mendanian. No problem. Look what happens."

"*I'll* do it if it comes to that," he said. "I'll move to fucking Show Dog and set up shop myself."

"Guangdong," the Chinese guy said, patiently correcting him. "Lot of money riding along this. Lot of movies, lot of money."

"Riding *on* this," the big man said, correcting in turn. "Like riding *on* a horse."

The Chinese guy shrugged. "Maybe need to see somebody else after all."

"Don't get your bowels in an uproar," he said.

"Lot of dollars involved," the Chinese guy said. "Don't need any more mistakes."

"Don't worry," he said. From the Chinese guy's expression, he wasn't sure he was being convincing. Then he thought of something else. "I'm getting a little low on that fish oil you've been sending me," he said. "I like to keep stocked up."

The Chinese guy waved his hand. He hoped that meant something positive, but it was always hard to be sure.

He might have pressed him on the matter, but there was a noise across the way then and they both turned. The old guy who'd been adding and re-adding his score had slumped backward in his chair, knocking his carry bag over with a crash. His head was flung back, his mouth open to the sky. His face had turned the color of old sheets, his hands splayed limp at his sides. It occurred to the big man that whatever the old fart had done to his score, he was already in the process of explaining it to some higher authority.

"Man not look so good," the Chinese guy said. "Maybe ought to tell someone . . . " he added, turning back.

But by then he was speaking to air.

"Well, *I* think that when people think of Paige Nobleman, they think *poise.*"

Actress and reporter, they were sitting at a table in a corner of Outré, the newest in the ever-evolving series of industry hot spots. Paige had been staring at the one empty table in the place, a definite *power* table, the ultimate see-and-be-seen spot, wondering idly who would command the post on this day.

Paige turned back to the smiling magazine reporter, trying hard to keep her coffee cup from sloshing over as she raised it toward her lips. *Poise,* she thought. Focus on the concept. Bring it in to the core of yourself, fix it, let it radiate back out. First principles of the profession.

"It's all an act," Paige said, mustering an equally mindless smile. This girl across from her was clearly a rookie, twenty-five, twenty-six tops. Thick mop of blonde hair, flawless skin, jaw-dropping figure inside—more or less inside—those swathes of Banana Republic cotton. What could such a person know about the need to maintain poise? And she'd just used the same word three times in one sentence. Paige hoped there was a good copy editor somewhere in the chain of command.

The reporter laughed in a good-natured way. "That's hard to

believe," she said. "The kind of men you've played against and all."

Paige saw a young man in a sleek three-piece suit cut a glance across the room. Attorney-turned-producer flanked by two others in similar suits, combined age under a hundred, they'd come to Outré to settle all the important business of the entertainment world amid the linen and the china. His gaze flittered across Paige's features—was there a flicker of recognition there?—then settled in on the bosomy young reporter. Paige wanted to call out to him: *Poise, ace. Give some thought to poise.* But instead, she took a sip of coffee, returned the cup to the saucer. Deep breath. No spills, no rattling of china. Yet.

The reporter gestured at the empty table then. "That's Richard Mendanian's table, you know." She said it in a hushed voice, no need to startle any fellow diners.

Paige glanced over, a bit surprised. Richard Mendanian, king of the sleaze pic, when there had been such a domain. He'd offered her a part once, in the early days. She'd turned it down, not necessarily because of the nature of the film, for she'd been too hungry at the time to be fussy about questions of art. She wouldn't even have minded taking her clothes off in the film Mendanian was making. It was just that she refused to take them off there in Mendanian's office, *before* the shooting started.

But now Mendanian was dead, shot to death in the hills. Robbery was the official motive, though one of the trades had speculated that it had been some kind of drug deal gone bad. In any case, Richard Mendanian was dead. And she was dying, too, careerwise, at least.

"I didn't know," she told the reporter at last, surprised he'd have the king-of-the-table locked up.

"He was spreading the word around he was back in the fast track, that's what I hear. He took a *lease* on that spot from Albertine. I guess everybody's too freaked out to want to sit there now. Or maybe his rent's not up."

Paige shrugged. "They'll put some tourists there soon enough," she said. The reporter laughed in agreement, took the cue to get back on track. She checked her notes, then glanced up at Paige.

"I watched *White Dungeons* again yesterday? That nude scene with De Niro? I mean, you just blew him away. And he got to wear a towel through the whole thing. How did you manage to stay so cool?"

A towel and a beige Speedo underneath that, Paige wanted to add. Instead she smiled. "It helps when you have a good script," she said. She was wondering when it had happened, when it had come to be you could ask a question without actually posing it, just add a rising inflection at the end of your line.

Not *line,* she corrected herself, *sentence.* This was real life. This girl was interviewing her, a retrospective piece, she'd said. For Christ's sake. What did it mean, someone doing a "retrospective piece" before you'd even turned forty?

"It's more than that," the reporter insisted. "Garbo had it, and Hepburn . . . and you," the reporter said.

Paige did some quick calculations, figuring that the reporter had just removed her at least two generations from her own peers. But hey, Garbo, Hepburn . . . and now Nobleman. They could tear down the Hollywood sign, carve their poised likenesses into the side of the mountain in its place.

"I've got some work to do before I enter that company," she said mildly.

"Oh, that's what I *mean,*" the reporter said. "You're always so together!"

"Lori . . ." Paige began, feeling the onset of a massive headache about to claim her.

"Jorie," the reporter corrected her. "Jorie Hubbard."

"I'll tell you something, Jorie." She paused, her gaze holding on something over the reporter's shoulder. She was staring now, across the crowded main room, through an elegantly framed archway, into one of the many secluded nooks provided by Albertine, Outré's famed chef and owner, for the patrons more interested in privacy than in proving their place in the industry pecking order.

A waiter had drawn aside a curtain that shielded the alcove in order to flambé something for his customers. It was a couple, the young woman—dark-complexioned, her hair twisted into a braid that wound exotically about her neck—facing outward, the man with his back to Paige.

The light was dim, and Paige would be damned if she was going to fish her glasses out of her purse in front of Jorie Hubbard, but she'd lived with the same man for a half-dozen years, knew the shape of his movements as well as the shape of his nose. When the man in the alcove reached his hand out to stroke the cheek of the woman with the dark braid, pulled her close and kissed her, Paige felt her stomach turn over.

"What were you going to tell me?" Jorie Hubbard asked.

Paige blinked. The waiter had withdrawn, the curtain had fallen closed. She turned back to face the reporter. She couldn't say she was surprised. Not with the way things had been going lately with Paul, but still . . . having to *see* it . . . her lover with another woman in the very restaurant . . .

"You were going to say something," the reporter prompted again. She had a pen in her hand, a tiny leather-bound notebook on the table open beside a bowl of chilled summer blossom soup.

"Yes," Paige heard herself saying, her eyes still on the swaying curtain.

"And . . ." Jorie Hubbard staring at her, a little puzzled now.

Paige forced her gaze from the curtain, forced herself from what might be going on in there now—sea scallops flying this way, seared duck salad that, all fangs and claws and dark braids in the cactus spine soup . . .

"I grew up in Miami," she said to Jorie Hubbard. "It was a different place back then. A small Southern town, really. I was the most awkward, gangly, unprepossessing kid you ever met."

Paige heard the sound of her own voice clearly, was herself impressed with the breezy, carefree tone. Jorie was scribbling furiously, still shaking her head in disbelief.

Paige's gaze fell upon the knife that was part of her place setting. There seemed to be a fairly sharp point there. She'd prefer a saber, of course, something she could use to hack down those curtains over there like De Niro had in *White Dungeons,* slicing in half the two thugs hiding behind them in the process, but a steak knife would do. She'd be able to make her point in the alcove, wouldn't have to face a life sentence.

"In high school," she was saying, "I went to this citywide debate tournament?" There. She'd got it, rising inflection, asking the question, Jorie Hubbard nodding encouragement. "No one knew who I was, of course, and there we all were in this big auditorium?" More nodding. Paige picked up the knife. A satisfying heft, but why be surprised? This was Outré, after all, and Albertine was no piker.

"Anyway," she continued, "When it came my time to speak, they called my name and I was too scared to answer."

"What happened?" Jorie Hubbard asked.

"Nothing," Paige said. She had the knife turned around in her hand now, held it like a seasoned assassin, point digging into the soft linen tablecloth. She leaned forward, rested her chin atop her fist, felt the knife point sink a bit further into the several layers of linen below.

She smiled again at Jorie Hubbard. "I listened to them call my name again and again, until finally they gave up and went on to the next person. I waited out in the hall until it was all over and then I rode the bus home. I told my mother I lost."

"That's a great story," Jorie said, shaking her head. She'd left off scribbling for a moment. "It's hard to imagine you getting all choked up like that."

"I suppose it is," Paige said, sighing. She was doing her best to keep her smile propped up. She glanced at the curtained alcove again, laughed miserably to herself, put the knife back in its place as their waiter arrived with lunch.

"If you'll just excuse me for a minute," she said to Jorie abruptly.

The waiter had to step smartly out of the way as she pushed herself up and brushed past him. The buttery fragrance of the shrimp dish she'd ordered had overpowered her, threatening to send whatever it was she'd had for breakfast all over the trio of power brokers who were staring at her as she hurried out.

She'd barely made it into the hallway leading from the main dining room when the tears came, blurring her vision so that she had to make her way toward the ladies' room by feel. She fumbled along the narrow passageway, past the maitre d's station, unoccupied, thank God, and no one in the foyer, just give her a few minutes to herself, she could handle this, she had *poise*, she could cope . . .

. . . when she felt a hand at her elbow, someone guiding her back toward the front.

"Ms. Nobleman." Dear God. Albertine himself. His cultured voice, soft, solicitous, discreet. But tomorrow it would be all over the trades: "What aging, ultra-poised lady of the silver screen was seen weeping her way toward the ladies' room while her significant other held court with a pasha's daughter elsewhere in the same glitter dome . . . "

She turned to face him, wondering if a sufficiently poised expression might divert his attention from the otherwise ruin on her face. "I am sorry," he said, before she had a chance to say anything. He'd given her his little bow, kept his face averted. It took her a moment to understand he was only apologizing for disturbing her.

"I told the party, no phone calls, but they say it is emergency."

She stared at him, her mouth working, shaking her head. "Phone call?" she repeated.

"Your sister," Albertine nodded. "From Florida. She say it is about your mother."

And then she knew. The call she'd been dreading for months now. "Oh God," she said, forgetting about the state of her career, about Paul, about gossip and everything else. And followed Albertine to the phone.

"So tell me, what do you think, my friend?"

Deal glanced at Emilio, but said nothing. He was standing outside the body shop entrance, watching idly as the metal door to one of the bays clattered up its track. A chrome-sided lunch wagon pulled into the courtyard of the warehouse-cum-cottage industry complex, tootling its horn outside a furniture maker's place: lunch at ten-thirty in the morning.

Emilio was standing beside him, one hand on the key-operated door opener, the other sweeping grandly at whatever was behind the door. Emilio, who'd insisted he come right over, grinning, waiting for his reaction like some Latin Pat Sajak, spin the wheel and win *this* baby, Deal thought.

Other than that, Deal wasn't thinking much at the moment. In fact, he'd spent the last few days trying not to think at all, just moving around where he had to—checking in on the endless restoration work at Terrence Terrell's mansion, overseeing the construction of a small strip center in Perrine—just keeping it going, like one of the pod people. Like they said in that old movie, life was so much simpler that way. Yesterday, he'd shown up at the Terrell site, taken a nail apron away from one of his workers, launched into two hours of frenzied hammering, nailing partitions together until his arm seized up with cramps. He'd dropped the hammer, clutched his arm, looked up to find the whole framing crew watching him, concern etched on their faces. *El jefe es loco,* that was the consensus he drew from their expressions, and they were probably right. Maybe not crazy, but crazed, sure enough.

When the door had risen high enough, Emilio ducked under the frame and flipped a light switch on the wall inside. A couple of banks of fluorescent tubes flickered to life, and Deal, who thought he'd become impervious, felt his stomach lurch. There, gleaming in gunmetal flake under the bluish-white lights, crouched like some dream out of the distant past, sat the Hog. As impossible, as real, as terrible in its dumbness as the Sphinx itself.

"It's the very same car, my man. I hauled it out of the impound yard myself."

Emilio clapped him on the shoulder, his eyes pinpoints, his grin manic. "I been spending nights and weekends on this since I don't know how long."

Deal knew Emilio was waiting for him to say something, but it didn't seem possible. Where to begin? Just a car, on the one hand, that's what he was staring at. An '83 Seville, its rear seat and trunk chopped away, the whole thing transformed by Cal Saltz, his long-dead friend and car junkie, into a gentleman's pickup, an El Camino of a higher order. The last time Deal had seen it, a police wrecker was winching it up from a full-fathom-five parking spot at the bottom of Biscayne Bay. It had nearly cost Janice her life, and his as well.

"My cousin did the mechanic work," Emilio said. "He's been through it top to bottom. Also, we dropped a '67 V-8 in there, runs like a sonofabitch without all that emissions crap."

Deal glanced up at the sign above the bays, still speechless: "EMILIO AND RODRIGUEZ, FINE COACHWORK," the sign read. Four years before, it had been "EMILIO AND SON, FINE CABINETWORK": Emilio's father and Emilio, who'd built kitchens and bathrooms and dens full of bookshelves for DealCo, for Deal and Deal's father before him.

Then, after the hurricane, with Emilio Sr. retired, had come "EMILIO AND RODRIGUEZ, BACKHOE SERVICE": Emilio and his cousin with the big machine, down from Tampa to work four hundred days straight, big money, clearing deadfall and debris from shattered homes. Now, with that work long gone, the pair were in the body shop business. If he lived long enough, Deal thought, maybe he'd see the two cousins in advertising, or maybe banking: "EMILIO AND RODRIGUEZ, FINE SAVINGS & LOANS."

"What are you going to do with it?" Deal managed finally. He felt the silent chirring of the phone pager in his pocket, but ignored it.

Emilio stared at him, an odd expression on his face. "Do?" He turned and swept his hand at the car again. "I'm *giving* it to you. This is my gift to you, man, make up for that fuckup on the Terrell job." Deal nodded. Emilio was referring to the cabinets that had never been delivered, one last job, a favor to Deal, forgotten when the body work beckoned.

Rodriguez had come out of an adjoining bay, paint mask pushed down around his neck, wiping his hands on a cloth. He came to stand beside Emilio, and though he was not smiling, Deal knew Rodriguez was just as eager to see his reaction. Emilio tall and lean, with his boyish good looks and grin that made it hard to be angry with him, no matter what the screwup—and there had been many; and Rodriguez, short and stocky, a bushy handlebar mustachio and a bandit's tough stare—both of them with the coppery skin and high cheekbones of the Indios. Deal felt a wave of affection sweep over him, and for a moment he thought he might weep. All the effort he'd expended to wall himself in about to be swept away at the sight of two charming bandits and the car they wanted to give him.

"It's a great job," Deal managed. "Unbelievable." He found himself moving forward, his hand tracing the curve of a fender. The acrylic paint was luminescent, flawless beneath his touch. God knew how many coats were on there. He glanced back at the two. "But I can't take it, Emilio. Really."

"The parts didn't cost us nothing," Rodriguez said. "We put in a little time, that's all."

"You got us a lot of jobs, man. You had your share of trouble. We wanted to do something for you."

Deal took a deep breath. How could he explain it to them? That what they thought was a prize seemed more like a portent of disaster. *Hey guys, I got my wife back but now I've lost her again and somehow it seems it's this car's fault?* The beeper was going off in his pocket again, vibrating like an angry insect.

"What I told Emilio was, a man loses his ride, his *special* ride, it's like he loses part of himself, especially if it's somebody tried to *take* it from him, you know?"

Deal nodded. He'd never heard Rodriguez approach philosophy before.

"This is a special car," Emilio nodded. "We wanted you to have it back."

Deal looked back at the Hog, found himself kicking a front tire like a buyer on a used car lot. New Michelins, he noticed, mounted on oversized chrome rims. He pulled the beeper from his pocket, still angling for the right words, then stopped when he saw the number on the readout: it began with 911, then gave a number with a Broward exchange. Only one person up that way who knew his code for an immediate callback.

He glanced at Emilio. "I have to use the phone, okay?"

"Use the one in there," Rodriguez said, pointing at the Hog. Deal stared, puzzled, then noticed the little antenna poking out of the roof for the first time. Emilio tossed him a set of keys. "Some guy drove a 'Vette into a pillar on I-95. The wrecker guys said he still had this phone in his hand when they scraped him up."

"He must've paid in advance or something," Rodriguez said. "I used it to talk to my mom in Colombia a *couple* of times."

"Go on," Emilio said. "You have to start the engine, though."

Deal was about to protest, then felt the beeper go off again, this time in his hand. He sighed, got in the Hog, searched for the ignition key. Surprising how comfortable the leather seat felt, as if he were dropping into it again with hardly a day gone by. He turned the key and the engine came alive with a rumble he felt more than heard, a throb that made the car seem capable of flight. The phone, mounted on a little console pedestal, beeped to life. He shook his head, picked the thing up, and dialed the number.

"Barbara?" he said, when she picked up.

"Deal?" she said. He heard it in her voice, knew it was bad before she told him a thing. Some things you never forget, he thought, even as she explained what it was about. She was on her way out the door, she said, could he meet her somewhere down his way in an hour. Then she broke off, fighting her tears to tell him how sorry she was for presuming. She was being silly. She'd understand if he couldn't make it. It wasn't that important. Sure.

After he'd hung up, Deal sat silently in the car for a moment, his hands gripping the wheel, staring out the windshield down a road trip from the sadder past. For the first time in years, his life had seemed in order, disaster far at bay: business on the upswing, his wife on the mend, his daughter happy and thriving . . .

And then, Janice—stalwart, impregnable Janice, who'd weathered more physical trauma than any dozen people should have to without so much as a whimper—had suddenly caved in. Even this offending car had come back into his life. And now, there was Barbara, Miss Tough-as-Nails herself, sounding like she was ready to go off like a rocket. It had to be a dream. In a moment, he was going to wake up, laugh it off, go back to his real life.

He heard a tapping noise and realized that Emilio was at the passenger's window, trying to get his attention. Without thinking, his hand found the controls, sent the window gliding swiftly down. Deal smelled fresh paint, lacquer thinner, a trace of male cologne.

Emilio was pointing out into the courtyard. Startled, Deal saw his own pickup speeding off, banging over a speed bump and into the street.

"My cousin, he had to run over to the bus station for some parts," Emilio said. "I didn't think you'd mind."

"Goddammit, Emilio," Deal said. He was trying to force the door of the Hog open, then realized he'd somehow locked himself in. He was searching now for the control buttons, but, because he was actually looking for them, didn't have the slightest idea where they were. "I have to go somewhere, Emilio." Deal heard the whine of his voice in his own ears. "I've got to *go!*"

Emilio nodded, his good-natured grin in place. "Well, why don't you drive your car, man?"

Deal stared back at him, fuming, ready to explode. But what good would it do? He'd seen Emilio suffer the outrage of the most apoplectic contractors and homeowners: threats, harangues, pleas, they all washed over placid Emilio like heavy surf against the rocks. What chance did he have of thwarting the intentions of this man who wanted to do a good deed?

Deal sighed then, and mashed the accelerator down. Emilio was still grinning as Deal took the Hog out of the bay, chrome-clad Michelins squealing all the way to the street.

*   *   *

31.

Deal idled at a traffic signal, waiting to swing onto Ocean Drive at 5th Street, noting a Santa mannequin in one of the corner shop windows. Christmas, he thought. He'd forgotten that holiday was coming up. But then, given the state of his life, he could be forgiven, couldn't he?

He did notice that the Santa in this particular window wore his big white beard and red cap, but very little else that was traditional. His red suit was gone, his boots replaced with sandals that laced up his skinny plaster legs. His chest was bare, his big gut hanging over a thong bikini that barely concealed his anatomical correctness. *Christmas on South Beach,* Deal thought, as the light changed and he piloted the Hog easily through the turn.

And how the Hog had changed. If Emilio had performed a miracle of coachwork, Rodriguez had done an equally amazing job on the car's infrastructure, Deal had to admit. Not only was the engine responsive to the slightest touch of the accelerator, the old-style suspension had been beefed up as well. Now the old boat cornered like a sports car, and, if he wasn't careful, snapped his head back as he moved off every light. The Hog had become, in the words of its original owner, "an automobile."

He was well up the boulevard now, spotting The News Cafe, then a parking space opening up just in front of him. A lucky break, he thought as he eased into the spot. A sandwich sign across the street advertised valet parking for only $8.

He got out of the Hog, marveling at the solid clunk of the automatic door locks falling into place. From the time he'd taken it over from Cal, he'd never been able to lock the thing, automatically or otherwise. Even the door seemed to shut in a satisfying way, more the sound of a meat locker closing than the crash of metal he remembered. Maybe Rodriguez should go to work for Cadillac, he thought, lay his magic touch on all that big iron.

He fished a couple of quarters out of his pocket, stepped to the curb to plug the meter, had to dodge a pair of bikini-clad girls in Rollerblades whizzing down the sidewalk. He watched them go, thinking that the last time he'd been on South Beach, most of the foot traffic had been using walkers.

He glanced around the stretch of grass that separated the boulevard from the broad band of beach. A long-haired guy tossing a Frisbee to a tireless mutt, a lemonade cart tended by another girl in a microscopic bikini, a person of indeterminate sex bundled in what seemed to be several coats asleep beneath one of the palms.

He'd heard about it, of course, how the Beach had become hot, the crumbling Deco hotels given a coat of paint and a new set of room rates, the dodderers shoved off the porches where once they'd sat in rows, elbow to elbow, and stared out across the boulevard at the Atlantic. Now the porches and the shaded colonnades and the fanciful terraces had become sidewalk cafes and bars and restaurants of note, and glitterati from New York and Los Angeles crowded onto weekend flights just to schmooze along this ten-block strip where a dozen years ago you couldn't have given away the property.

Another business opportunity he'd failed to foresee, Deal thought, as he stepped lively across the boulevard. There was a red Testarossa bearing down on him from the right, a bargelike Buick convertible from the fifties, meticulously restored, lumbering up from the left. He squeezed between a Bentley and a gleaming '65 Mustang parked on the opposite curb, thinking, *there is a serious car thing going on here,* and took a backward glance at the Hog. It seemed to fit right in. Maybe someone would make him an offer, he could go home in a taxi.

He was also worrying that he had made a mistake in suggesting The News. The cafe was another facet of the "revived" South Beach that he had heard about but never seen. The place was a madhouse, tables spilling out onto the terrace, an adjoining courtyard, the sidewalk, all of the places filled, waiters and waitresses edging frantically through the throngs and the gauntlet of customers who waited under the front awning and clamored for a seat.

Deal glanced around, thinking that he'd collar Barbara when she arrived, take her somewhere where they could hear themselves talk. There was a Newberry's over on Washington, in the old downtown, had been there since he was a kid. That was the ticket. Orange soda in a paper cone plopped in a silver holder, BBQ beef sandwich that was really a Sloppy Joe, grease-dripping fries in another conical cup.

He could taste it, suddenly, smell the tang of the ketchupy sauce, see the waitresses in their hair nets and starched white uniforms, feel his mother taking time out from the weekly shopping trip to wipe his mouth with a handkerchief she'd wet with her tongue . . . and thought for a moment that he was going to lose it, maybe just sit down on the curb and break into tears in front of all these pretty people and their automobiles.

"Deal," he heard then. "Deal!" And looked up to see Barbara, standing on tiptoes at the door of the restaurant, as pretty as an angel, elbowing a guy in mirrored sunglasses aside, and waving him her way.

"I got here early," she said, staring at him from across the wooden table. They were tucked away inside, in a rustic diner-styled booth, another world from the madcap scene outside. Although all the inside booths were full and the kitchen doors whipped steadily open and closed, the hubbub and the chatter seemed to be soaked up by the dark beams and paneling. Across from where they sat was a tiny library of books and newspapers—"feel free to browse," the waitress had told them—which Deal assumed gave the place its name.

He took the intensity in her gaze until he was the one to turn away. When he'd met Barbara, she'd been coming off a years-long affair with her boss, one of Miami's movers and shakers, a lawyer with more money than Croesus and an unshakable arrangement with his equally prominent wife. The guy had eventually gone down in flames, and Barbara had professed gratitude at the turn of fate that set her free. She'd moved to Boca Raton, found a job she liked, dated, lived like a normal person, as she put it. Still, Deal thought, *still* . . .

He turned back, uncomfortable with his own presumptions. Barbara had saved his life, Janice's, too. She wanted him to walk on water, he'd walk. Never mind the way she looked at him. "So how's your mother?" he said as the waitress brought them coffee. "How's she doing?"

She glanced down at the table, shook her head slowly. "It's not good, Deal." She took a deep breath. "That's why I got here so soon. I stopped at the hospital, but they wouldn't let me in to see her." She paused, trying to gather herself. "The doctors were doing some kind of tests . . . trying to find out whether her brain was still functioning . . . "

She swallowed, her voice starting to clutch. " and I thought, my God, what if they walk out and tell me my mother is a vegetable and do I want to pull the plug . . . "

34

She stopped, tears spilling from her eyes now. She wiped them away with a napkin, fought to get her breathing under control. "I just couldn't handle that, Deal. Not by myself. I just couldn't. Do you know what I mean?"

He nodded, squeezed her hand, tried to think of something to say. The waitress was back suddenly—*too soon,* he was thinking, she'd just brought their coffee and why didn't she buzz off . . .

"Chicken soup," the waitress said, putting a steaming bowl down in front of Barbara, along with a thick wad of napkins.

"I didn't order soup . . . " Barbara began, but the waitress put a hand on her shoulder, shushing her.

"On the house," she said, giving her a little smile. And then she was gone, whisking back into the kitchen.

Barbara picked up a fistful of napkins, blotted her cheeks. "That was nice," she said, trying for a smile. She paused, glanced about the room. "I must look like a wreck."

Deal shook his head. "You look great."

"Such bullshit," she said, patting his hand. She checked her reflection in the window, swiped at a smear of mascara. She turned, crumpled the soggy napkins away, tossed her hair. Giving it her best to conjure up the old, carefree Barbara, he thought.

"I knew I'd be happy to see you, Deal," she said. She gave him her brightest, perkiest look. "I'll get through this." If it hadn't been for the red circles around her eyes, the fieriness at the tip of her nose, he might have bought it.

"Now how about you?" she continued. "How's things in big-time contracting?"

"You'd have to ask a big-time contractor," he said.

"Okay, I walked into that," she said. She regarded him for a moment. "Tell me, does Janice ever get tired of gay repartee, push you to open up?"

He felt a twinge, felt himself nodding. "All the time."

"And do you?"

Like a book, he was about to say, but somehow he couldn't get the glib phrase out. His mind had emptied suddenly. There was a flash of bright light, like the moment before a projector cranks in the film, and then he was seeing Janice again, that day hardly a week ago, running from him down the steps of the Shark Valley observation tower, flailing at him, crying, stumbling, pounding the rough concrete with her fists and her face before he could get to her, her wails rending the wilderness with the essence of human misery.

"Hey . . . are you all right?"

Deal blinked. Barbara had reached across to take his hand.

"You just blanked out there. Did I say something?"

Deal looked about the room. He had the impression that he had screamed himself, but if he had, no one seemed to have noticed. People eating, drinking, chatting. One fellow pulling a thick book down from a shelf of the library.

"Janice is in the hospital," he said.

"What?" She shook her head. "Another operation?" Her face filled with distress. "And I dragged you out to hold my hand . . . ?"

"Not that kind of hospital," he said. "She's . . . " he wiped his face with his hands, massaging feeling back into the flesh there. When he looked, Barbara was still staring at him, concern etched on her features.

"She's in the *home*," he blurted. He shook his head. *Open up,* he thought. It was supposed to make you feel better. He felt like he was chewing broken glass. "She's in a private clinic in the Gables."

"I don't understand, Deal."

The waitress was back, and they both fell silent as she set down their plates. Deal stared down at the massive sandwich in front of him. Toasty bun, buttery lettuce, tomato, thick wedge of meat, the sort of hamburger you see in menu pictures all the time but never, ever get. He thought he might throw up.

He glanced at Barbara as the waitress disappeared. "She's . . . " He broke off, started again. "She's been having some trouble. All the surgeries she's had since the fire." He threw up his hands. "I don't know. The doctors say it's some post-traumatic stress reaction. They *think,* anyway. She's not communicating too well right now." He broke off. All the opening up he could manage.

Barbara stared back at him, stunned. She noticed the salad in front of her, pushed it aside, along with the soup. "You want to go someplace?" she said gently.

Deal nodded.

"Me too," she said. And rose and took his hand, pulling him up after her.

*   *   *

36

"So it's just you, handling all the stuff with your mom?" Deal had to speak louder than normal. They had walked south along the beach, sharing their miseries, until he sensed that they'd both come down a bit from the jagged peaks of tension. They'd found an abandoned lifeguard kiosk atop a dune. They were sitting on its little porch now, staring out to sea, their legs dangling free above the sand. The wind had kicked up a bit, and the surf boomed in a way that seemed satisfying. It meant the world was still working, Deal thought. Part of it, anyway.

"There's not that much to do," Barbara continued, "not really. My mom was a real control freak. Once she found out she had cancer, she spent most of her time getting ready for the end. She packed up most of her apartment, made her own funeral arrangements . . . " She broke off and gave Deal a wistful smile. "Sometimes I think that makes it worse. There's none of the bullshit left to deal with. Nothing to do but wait."

Deal nodded. "Still, being all by yourself, that's not good . . . "

"I called *you*," she said, striving for the old perkiness. Then, just as abruptly, her smile fell away and she turned back toward the ocean. She took a deep breath. "And I called my sister."

Deal stared, puzzled. "Your sister? I didn't know you had a sister."

Barbara shrugged, staring out to sea. "Paige Nobleman," she said after a moment.

Deal shook his head, puzzled. "Paige Nobleman? What's she have to do with it?"

Barbara turned to him, her face a mask. "Her real name is Cooper. She's my sister."

"The actress? Come on, you're kidding." He'd seen Paige Nobleman in a half-dozen films. She was usually cast as the obligatory love interest to some action-hero cretin and was unfailingly the most interesting aspect of the proceedings. Deal had even considered shifting his movie-star crush over from Debra Winger.

"I'm surprised you know of her," Barbara said, her voice suddenly arch.

"Because I don't hang out on South Beach? Jesus, Barbara, Paige Nobleman is your *sister*?"

Barbara shrugged. "I didn't think it was such a big deal. She's not famous or anything." She glanced at him as if she'd read his mind. "You want an introduction?"

"Come off it, Barbara. I don't even know you have a sister, then you tell me it's Paige Nobleman, for God's sake." He broke off, staring at her. She glared back at him, her jaw set, her lips compressed.

"So you called her?" he asked, changing tacks. "What did she say?"

She took a deep breath, her gaze turning inward, as if she were making up her mind about something. She glanced out to sea, where a pair of freighters had appeared on the horizon, and, finally, began to talk. "Look, Deal, I haven't seen my sister more than two or three times in the twenty years she's lived in Los Angeles. Maybe my mother saw her half a dozen times all that while. A day or two here and there while she was on her way to or from some frigging movie location, basket of fruit on the holidays, gift certificate to Macy's at Christmas. That's about it, okay? She was too busy, too good for us. She left us and never looked back, and I don't care anymore. I was going to wait till Mom was gone, send her a frigging telegram."

She whirled upon him, her eyes flashing, and for a moment he thought she was going to take a swing at him. Then she relented. "But I just couldn't do it, you know. Even if she ran out on me, I figured she deserved that much, to know she was dying." She turned away abruptly, and he wondered if she were hiding her tears.

"Is she going to come?" he asked gently.

Barbara nodded her head almost imperceptibly, mumbled something.

"I couldn't hear you," he said.

"Tonight," she said, turning to him. Her face was a ruin once more, and she swabbed at her nose with the sleeve of her jacket. "I got to the hospital this afternoon, there was a bouquet of flowers bigger than Kennedy's hearse at the nurse's station." She swallowed, continuing.

"You can't have flowers in intensive care, goddammit. The nurses couldn't even move around. *What should we do with these, Ms. Cooper,*' they were asking me. You want to know what I told them?" She broke off, shaking her head angrily. "That's how much they know in the frigging movies," she said.

Deal took a deep breath of his own. "You going to talk to her when she gets here?"

Barbara shrugged, her eyes still flashing. "I haven't made up my mind."

He stared at the expression on her face. Something odd there, something she was holding back, he thought. "What did you mean, she ran out on you?" he tried.

She glanced at him, then away again. "Nothing," she said. "I've told you what's important."

He looked at her skeptically. "You're going to talk to her, Barbara. You have to talk to her. You wouldn't have called her otherwise."

She swung about, her eyes flashing. "If you're so damned smart, what put Janice in the hospital?"

It took him like a punch to the chest.

Barbara saw it at once. "I'm sorry," she said immediately, reaching her hand to his shoulder. "I didn't mean that. You know I didn't."

He eased away from her touch. "It's all right. I didn't have any business butting in."

"Oh God," she said, biting her lip. She glanced around the deserted beach as if she were looking for someone to help her. "I screw everything up," she said. "Everything."

She picked up her shoes and socks from the floor of the station, hopped down to the sand.

"Thanks for coming," she said, looking up at him. "I can't tell you how much."

"Barbara . . . " he said, starting after her, but she held up her hand to ward him off.

"I have to go, Deal, really." She started off over the dunes, then turned back. "I'll pray for Janice," she called.

Deal raised his hand, watching her walk away. *Way to go, Deal,* he was thinking. She was in distress to begin with and he had added to her misery and she had only struck out in reflex. *Wait,* he wanted to call after her. *Wait!*

But he didn't. He only sat and watched her form grow smaller and smaller and finally disappear into the crowds on Ocean Boulevard. On one count, she was right, he found himself thinking. He wasn't very smart at all.

"Well, what kind of things *do* they like?" Mahler was speaking into the phone, his sizable feet propped on the window overlooking Westwood as Paige Nobleman came into his office. "I need to know, for Chrissakes."

He glanced up, waved her in.

"Yeah, that's the whole freaking point," he said.

Mahler was her agent, had been since she'd come to Los Angeles. Since before she'd come out, really. She'd been doing summer stock in an Orlando dinner theater when Disney World was still in its infancy, had won "Most Photogenic" in the Miss Florida pageant. A week later, there'd been a call from Marvin Mahler: She was being offered a "New Faces" acting internship with Universal, ten thousand dollars for a year as a contract understudy for various television series. Could she get on a plane? When she'd told him warily that she couldn't afford the ticket, Mahler had laughed. They'd flown her out first-class.

"Well, at least they understand that much in Hong Kong," Mahler was saying. "It's a goddamned business, first, last, top to bottom. As in bottom line. Uh-huh. Okay. Well, I can't get into that right now," he said, giving Paige a welcoming smile. He pointed into the receiver, rolled his eyes to let her know the caller was impossible.

Paige smiled back, despite her mood. She'd come off that

plane twenty years ago sure that it was all a hoax. Marvin Mahler was some slavering sex fiend, or worse, a white slaver who preyed on Miss Photogeniae from around the country. Never mind the official-looking letter from Universal, the plane ticket that had arrived by messenger, her calls to the Westwood Better Business Bureau, which assured her there had been no complaints filed against the Marvin Mahler Agency.

She'd graduated from the University of Florida *magna cum laude* in English and had read her Nathaniel West. She'd scraped enough money together for a return flight, had it wadded in her purse, ready to bolt right back onto the plane at the first hint of drool. Then Marvin Mahler, shambling bear that he was, had shown up at the airport with his boyish grin, a bouquet of flowers, and an entourage that couldn't have been better designed to disarm her fears: a secretary older than Paige's mother, and, most surprising of all, Rhonda Gardner, no stranger to the cover of *Life, Look,* and *Photoplay,* who had just finished a picture in Italy with Cary Grant. Rhonda Gardner, as it turned out, was not only Marvin Mahler's client, but also his wife. "He gives you any trouble, just come to me," Rhonda said to Paige, and the rest had become history.

"Right. We'll deliver. Just tell them to get their yen together." He heard something, made another face for Paige's benefit. "Okay, *fen, renmibi,* whatever. Exactly. I'll get back to you."

He hung up the phone, swung his feet down off the window ledge, turned his famous smile on her. Same sparkling blue eyes, the unruly mane of hair—peppered with flecks of gray now—same eager pose: hard to believe it had been twenty years since he'd thrust those roses into her hands and bowed theatrically: "Welcome to your town, Miss Nobleman."

Now as then, she was feeling better immediately. All the sharks in this city, she had to be grateful she'd fallen in with Mahler. Despite his lumbering carriage, he was a terror in a business meeting, of course, had certainly done plenty to maintain a steady if unspectacular career for her, but what she valued most was that sincerity. Maybe Mahler could cut a studio boss's heart out, but he was always happy to see her, that much she knew, and right now, that seemed like plenty.

"I didn't mean to interrupt," she began. "Jean said . . . "

He waved away her concern. "Are you kidding? The day I

don't have time for you, schwee-taht . . . " He was into his Bogie role then, hunched down over his desk, teeth set in an overbite, his eyes darting nervously back and forth.

"That was the Chinese on the phone, see. They're very clever. Turn your back for a minute and wham . . . " He smacked his big palm with his fist. He kept up his mugging until he got the smile he was playing for.

"You should have been the actor, Marvin," she said.

"Right. And who would have taken care of the store, huh? You, Rhonda, all my lovelies out there at the mercy of the wolves?" He waved his arms theatrically at the tall windows. It was a corner office, high enough up to afford a view of the UCLA campus to the east, the Century City complex to the south. On a clear day, you could see all the way out to the beach. Right now, the sky was leaden, the air thick with haze. Nothing you wanted to breathe, she thought, though she'd been doing it for half her life.

"How is Rhonda?" she asked, sobering.

Mahler's face reassembled. He raised his hands in a gesture of helplessness. "The same." He shook his head. "She sits. She eats. She stares at the goddamned wall like they hung the Mona Lisa there." He glanced out the window, chewing on his lip. "God-damned doctors."

Paige felt a pang. Rhonda Gardner. She'd been a rock for Paige from the moment of her arrival. She'd insisted Paige stay in the guest house on their Bel Air estate for more than a month while she settled in, found her own apartment. And while Mahler had handled the business aspects of Paige's career, steadily moving her up the rungs of a solid if never spectacular career, Rhonda had been a foun-tain of more practical advice. Do this, sweetie, if they ask, but never that. Make them want you, but above all, make them respect you.

Presents on her birthday, holiday gatherings at the big house in Bel Air, long notes after every set of reviews in the trades: "A lady knows how to step through crap as if it were a field of vio-lets, sweetie. Don't worry. Quality will out."

Dear Rhonda. In her day she'd knocked the socks off every stud-muffin in Hollywood: Sinatra, Cary Grant, Warren Beatty. She was in her sixties now, but looked a dozen years younger. She should still be out there, kicking butt and playing all the roles they'd once had Barbara Stanwyck for. Instead, she'd been sitting like a ghost in her home in Bel Air for the past year or more, tended to by nurses and physical therapists who called her by her name and waited endlessly for a response.

She thought of something then, turned her attention back to Marvin. "I heard something the other day, about this new drug they're trying for Alzheimer's," she began. "Something on the news . . ."

Mahler swung back from the window, cutting her off. "You want to know something," he said. "I'm talking to her doctor the other day—the *'lead'* doctor," he added, making little quote marks with his fingers, "because I been hearing about these things too. So this putz—who is the head of neurology at UCLA, by the way—he tells me, 'Mr. Mahler, we're not so sure your wife suffers from Alzheimer's after all.'"

"What?" Paige shook her head. "What is it, then?"

"That's what *I* said." Mahler threw up his hands. "What? What are we talking about? What marvelous development have you guys made here? And he tells me, they don't know. It's *like* Alzheimer's, he says. It might even *be* Alzheimer's. But they don't know for sure." He threw up his hands. "Guy knocking down a couple of mil a year, tells me he doesn't know why my wife's off with the walking dead."

He pushed back from his desk, sat staring at her in frustration.

"Marvin . . ." she began, trying for words of solace.

"A story," Mahler said, interrupting. "Guy goes to his doctor, wants his yearly checkup. Doc looks him over, takes some blood, runs some tests, comes back in the room, says he's got good news and bad news, which does the guy want first."

"Marvin . . ."

"I'm trying to clarify something, all right?" he said, holding up his hand.

Paige nodded, feeling sadness about to overwhelm her.

"Guy thinks about it, says, 'I dunno, the bad news, I guess,' and the doc says, 'Okay, you got cancer.'

"So the guy looks at him and says 'Gee doc, what could the good news be?' and the doc points out the door at this knockout blonde over by the X-ray machine. 'See that nurse over there?' the doc says. The guy is puzzled as shit, says, 'Yeah?' The doc whacks him on the back and says, 'Well, I'm bopping her.'"

Paige stared back at him.

"You don't think that's funny?"

She bit her lip, searching for words.

"Okay," he said. "You're right." He raised his hands in surrender. "Maybe this is more to the point: Guy takes his wife to a doctor, she's been acting strange, the doctor looks her over, says he doesn't know if she's got AIDS or Alzheimer's . . . "

"Stop it, Marvin," Paige said, her voice rising sharply. She felt she was about to scream.

He dropped his act as if she'd flipped a switch. "Sorry," he said. He stared at her, contrite, slumped like an old circus bear in his seat. "It's not a lot of fun, that's all."

"I want to come see her," she said.

"Sure." Marvin nodded. "Anytime, you know that. It'd be good for her."

"Maybe this afternoon," she said. "I'm on my way out of town. That's what I came by to tell you."

He stared at her, puzzled. "Out of town?" He glanced at his desk calendar. "Don't we have something this week? Friday or something? With the idiots at CMA?"

"My mother's in the hospital," she said. "My sister called this morning. She's dying." Paige heard the words come out of her mouth. Flat, she thought, flat as she felt inside. If it were a reading, she'd never get the part.

Still, Mahler was out of his chair, shambling around his burnished desk to throw his arms about her. "Ah, sweetie. Jesus. I'm sorry!"

She wanted to fold into his arms, draw some warmth from his bearish hug—she was desperate for warmth from somewhere—but it was hopeless. She'd spent a lifetime shielding herself from what was happening to her now. What she needed would take more than a hug to fix.

"It's okay, Marvin," she said. "Really." She patted his shoulder until he eased his hold on her, stepped back to grip her shoulders.

"Look, what can I do? Anything you need . . . "

She shook her head. "Nothing. I'm fine. I've known this was coming."

He shook his head. "And you didn't say anything?"

She shrugged. "We're a tough bunch, the Nobleman clan," she

said. *Oh yes,* she was thinking. *I'd like to take a flying leap out of one of those big broad windows, show you just how tough.*

She tried to work up a smile. "Can you cover for me at the meeting? I know I'm letting you down . . . "

"Are you kidding? Forget about it. I'll kill them. There's nobody else they can use for that picture."

Paige nodded. "It would mean a lot to me, Marvin. It's a different kind of film for me, and . . . "

"Sweetie, it's not the Schlock Brothers we're talking about. This is a British company." He jabbed his finger at her. "The Brits! They asked for you in the first place. They want you in their movie. You got nothing to worry about."

Her smile, when it came this time, was genuine. "Thanks, Marvin. I'll call Jean with my phone numbers when I get in."

"Go," he commanded, holding up his hands. "We'll take care of things on this end. How about Paul—he going with you?"

She bit her lip, shook her head. "He's got a shoot." *And hasn't been home for two days,* she thought.

"You need a car?" Mahler was already reaching for his intercom.

"I'll get a cab," she said. "My plane's not 'til six . . . "

"Jean," Mahler barked into the intercom. "Call down, tell Eddie he's taking Ms. Nobleman to the airport."

He released the phone button in the middle of the secretary's acknowledgment, turned back to Paige, checking his watch. "You want to, tell Eddie to swing by the house. You have time."

Paige nodded. "Thanks, Marvin."

"Are you kidding? Ask me to kill somebody. Then you can say thank you." He gave her a sorrowful look. "I'm sorry about your mother, sweetie." He reached out for her again. "Real sorry."

Paige nodded once more. She didn't trust herself to speak. She stood on her toes, gave Mahler a kiss on the cheek, then hurried out of the room.

"Who do we know in Miami?" Mahler said, the phone tucked against his shoulder. He was standing before one of the tall windows of his office, staring down a dozen stories at the entranceway of the building. The limo was just coming up from the underground, making its turn onto the circular drive.

"What Miami?" the voice on the other end replied.

"The one in Florida, for Chrissakes," Mahler said. "Palm trees. Oranges. Guys with guns."

There was a pause. Mahler imagined the pages of an atlas being turned. "Nobody there," the voice said. "Have a cousin in Fort Lauderdale, own a restaurant. *Real* restaurant. Pretty good."

"That's not what I had in mind," Mahler said, still staring down at the scene below. Eddie was out of the limo, holding the door, Paige scooting inside.

"What wrong?" the voice asked after a moment.

The limo was moving off now, joining the ribbons of traffic curling down toward the boulevard. Mahler glanced out at the horizon, where the airport might have been visible were this a normal town. He could see a mile, maybe less. What passed for air was getting thicker as he watched.

"Probably nothing." Mahler ran his hand through his hair. "Weddings and funerals," he said. "They make me nervous. You never know what might happen."

"Uh-hah," the voice said. Not agreeing. Just letting Mahler know he'd been heard. That was one thing he appreciated about dealing with the Chinese, the lack of extraneous bullshit. The stuff he spent most of his life wading through.

"I like to be prepared, that's all."

"You need somebody go to Florida, say so," the voice said.

"Yeah?" Mahler said. "That's good to know."

"Whatever," the voice said.

Mahler nodded to himself. His mind was already drifting, back to more pressing matters. *Other fry to fish,* as his little friend would say. "Hey—on that other thing. The films we been talking about. What about ponies, dogs, that kind of stuff?"

"Animals?" the voice said, rising in disbelief. "Animals not good."

"I was just thinking," Mahler continued. "Year of the dog, year of the monkey, all that."

"No animals," the voice said angrily. "Not good."

"It was a thought," Mahler said, feeling defensive. "That's all. We got plenty to choose from. I'll get back to you on the Florida thing."

"That what phone for," the voice said. And then the connection broke.

 "I don't get it," Deal said, shaking the slip of paper under the doctor's nose. "Why didn't anyone call me?"

The doctor glanced about the posh waiting room as if he were hoping for reinforcements. In one corner there was a television carrying a canned tape of supposed-to-be-soothing nature images with a New Age soundtrack, in another, a gleaming reception desk the size of a yacht, currently untended. It was the kind of place that suggested that psychological illness was a function of the privileged class. By the door stood Driscoll, craning his neck in an agony of embarrassment, looking anywhere but at the two of them, the doctor and the outraged husband.

"Mr. Deal, your wife admitted herself to this facility. She doesn't need your permission to sign herself out." The doctor's tone was reasonable, but firm.

"But I *brought* her here," Deal said, trying to control the anger in his voice. "She's not . . . " He broke off. What was he going to say? *She's not in control of her senses?* He glanced over at Driscoll, who seemed to be looking for flaws in the weave of the thick carpet at their feet.

"She's not well," Deal finished lamely.

"Your wife has been under a great deal of stress," the doctor said, agreeing without really agreeing. Something in his tone told Deal that *he* was the one under suspicion. A couple more outbursts, they'd find a safe place for the agitated Mr. Deal.

Deal took a breath, turned back to the release form he'd been holding. "This was at eight o'clock last night, right?"

The doctor nodded warily, as if it were something that might be litigated. "If that's what it says on the paper," he added.

"And she didn't say where she was going?"

The doctor shook his head, tight-lipped.

"You know," Driscoll's voice cut in, booming around the sizable waiting room, "the man's just trying to find out what's happened to his wife. You might show a little compassion."

They both turned to stare at him.

"How'd you feel, Doc, show up with flowers and candy, find out your wife left the place where they were supposed to take care of her?"

The doctor started to say something, took another look at Driscoll, who'd sucked in his gut, seemed to grow a couple of inches as he came toward them. The doctor turned back to Deal, his voice softening.

"I'm sorry, Mr. Deal. Your wife has been depressed, but she is, in my opinion, fully in control of her actions. She cares very deeply for you and your daughter. I'm sure she will be in touch with you. I'd stake my professional career on it."

Deal nodded. *His professional career.* The guy couldn't wait to shoo him and Driscoll out of the waiting room, get back to the other troubled souls in the back. So what if one of his charges had flown the coop. She'd used her insurance ID, signed the right name, everything was hunky-dory, next patient, please.

"You could call us, couldn't you," Driscoll had his arm around Deal's shoulder, testing the anger there, just being ready, Deal thought. At the same time, the ex-cop extended a card to the doctor in his thick fingers. "If Mrs. Deal should get in touch with you, you could tell her that my client is worried about her, wants to talk to her, you could do that much, couldn't you?"

His *client*? Deal was thinking. Driscoll was his *neighbor,* just come along to say hi.

The doctor took the card. "Of course." He turned to Mr. Deal. "And I am truly sorry, Mr. Deal."

Deal glanced at him, nodded. For a moment he thought the doctor was about to add, "And if you feel in need of a little tune-up yourself . . . ," but instead they simply shared a glance, and then Driscoll was guiding him out the double doors of the clinic.

They hadn't gone a half-dozen blocks, on their way back to the fourplex, were about to turn off Le Jeune and join the river of northbound traffic on US 1, when it struck Deal. Nearly overcome, he began jabbing his finger out the passenger window toward the gas station on their right.

"Stop the car," he said abruptly.

"What?" Driscoll said, swerving to the curb. He glanced toward the station pumps, where a burly guy was gassing up a landscaping truck. "Janice? You see her?"

Deal didn't bother to answer. He was out the door and across the sidewalk before it closed behind him, on a gallop toward the pay phone he'd spotted. He dug frantically in his pockets, spilling his keys, a mass of pennies, his battered Swiss Army knife, until finally he found a quarter and managed to guide it into the slot. As the coin dropped, he jabbed in Mrs. Suarez's number so hard his finger ached.

He had to wait what seemed like minutes for the connection to complete, then fumed again as the ring signals mounted in his ear. Driscoll had made it out of the car and had nearly joined him at the phone stanchion by the time Mrs. Suarez finally picked up.

"*Si, Señor* Deal," she said, cutting into his torrent of fractured Spanish.

"*La señora,*" he repeated. "If my wife . . . " He broke off, then began again. "*Cuando mi esposa . . .* " He glanced at Driscoll, but what help did he expect there? Driscoll had learned to say *cerveza,* could buy a beer anywhere in South Florida. Thirty years living in a bilingual community, that was the extent of his language studies.

"*Cuando mi esposa es eya . . . ,*" he tried. Deal had a reasonable vocabulary, but tenses, conditions, all the subtleties remained beyond him. And it was only worse trying to speak on the phone, with none of his trusty sign language to help him out.

"Si, si, si," Mrs. Suarez cried enthusiastically. "Your wife was here. Ten minutes when you leave."

Deal felt dread sweep over him even before he had fully registered the words. It was what he'd feared, the very thing he'd thought of the moment he'd seen the phone, ordered Driscoll to stop.

Mrs. Suarez meant Janice had turned up ten minutes after he and Driscoll had left for the clinic. As if she'd been sitting somewhere, watching, waiting . . .

"She was there? *Mi esposa?*"

"Yes. You wife," Mrs. Suarez said, enthused. "So happy. *Su niña. Juegó con la niña . . .* "

"She played with Isabel?"

"Con mucha gusta . . . very happy," Mrs. Suarez said.

"Let me talk to her," Deal said, practically shouting now.

"Su esposa?" Mrs. Suarez said, surprise in her voice. "Is not here. She go."

"Isabel?" Deal said, and he was shouting now. "Where is Isabel?"

"Con su esposa," Mrs. Suarez said. *Gone. With your wife.* And the way she said it made it sound like the most natural thing in the world.

8

"I've had some bad news, Rhonda," Paige said softly. She was sitting in a floral print wing chair, a twin to the one in which Rhonda sat a few feet across from her.

Rhonda said nothing, of course. She sat gripping the arms of her chair in the posture of someone expecting an airplane takeoff. But her eyes were the tipoff. The eyes. *You've got to get the eyes,* Paige thought automatically. The cinematographer's commandment, the reason why close-ups had been invented. Rhonda's eyes were as opaque and lifeless as any glass beads in a taxidermist's mount.

They were in a small study, a cozy place off what had been the Mahlers' bedroom until recently. Paige had caught a glance in there, through the open doorway, as the nurse left them. She glimpsed a motorized bed, a hospital tray on rollers, some strange exercise equipment she supposed was used to keep Rhonda's unused musculature from atrophying. But no sign of Marvin's presence—not these days—in what looked more and more like a hospital ward.

The day had turned chilly and a gas fire hissed in the study's fireplace. This had always seemed a cheery spot to Paige. The walls were covered with pictures: young Rhonda in pith helmet

51

with John Ford, somewhere in Africa; bosomy Rhonda in a sundress, shrieking with laughter as Frank Sinatra labored to sweep her up in his arms; an older Rhonda cutting the ribbon of some public place, a phalanx of men in suits and a youngster in a wheelchair looking on. Nothing of Marvin on the walls though, at his own insistence. It had always been that way.

Rhonda's head was bobbing slightly, as if to some ghostly music only she could hear. Or, Paige thought, it could just as well be permission to go on, to talk about distress, of which there seemed plenty in the room already.

"My mother," she said, drawing a breath. "She's in the hospital back in Florida. She's dying." Paige thought she saw a flicker in Rhonda's eyes, but passed it off as some reflection of the flames.

"My sister had the decency to call, at least," she continued. She had no idea why she was going on like this, she thought, as a phone rang somewhere in the distance.

Rhonda had known for years how strained things had been between Paige and her family. She'd been a mainstay, always counseling patience, understanding, endlessly going more than halfway to stay connected. "Your family, they're all you have, sweetness. Stay in this town long enough, you'll see." That was Rhonda's constant refrain, no matter how many rebuffs had come Paige's way. "Do your best. Do whatever it takes."

So maybe it was no surprise, then, her rattling on to Rhonda as though she could hear, as though any moment now she might unbend from that frozen attitude, come and curl her arms around her and hold her tight, tell her how much her mother loved her, even if she could never show it, how much it would mean to have Paige at her side . . . and it didn't matter one whit to Paige how transparent it all was: her wanting the mother she'd never had, Rhonda playing mother to the child who had never been.

A soft moan escaped Rhonda's lips and, though she sagged a bit to the side, her face remained impassive, a mannequin unhinged by a quirk of gravity. As Paige leaned to settle Rhonda back in her chair, the door to the bedroom opened and the nurse looked in.

"That's Eddie," she said to Paige. "He says you'd better be going if you want to make your flight."

Paige nodded, her hands still on Rhonda's frail arms, and the nurse withdrew.

Paige felt the skin, papery beneath her fingers, sensed that the bones were as fragile as twigs. This woman had been the toughest, fiercest, most fearless creature in a town where standing nose to jaw with men generally meant disaster, or at the very least, banishment, and she had come through forty years of confrontation unscathed. And now look what had happened. Look.

Incongruously, she found herself smiling, wistfully of course. She drew Rhonda carefully toward her and hugged her, trying not to notice how sharp and angular everything about her body had become. She breathed in a scent of perfume and thought, *That's good,* and promised herself to mention it to Marvin, how good the nurses were being to Rhonda, how thoughtful.

"Take care of yourself. I'll come and see you soon," she said to Rhonda, her lips at her ear, her hand patting her softly on her back. "I love you."

She gave her one last hug. And though she knew it had to be an illusion, some casual shift of inert weight, some chair spring dutifully responding to the laws of physics, she could have sworn she felt Rhonda give the slightest nudge in return.

"What the hell do you mean, Driscoll? It's kidnapping." Deal stood in the middle of Mrs. Suarez's living room on the second floor of the fourplex where they lived, a flannel jacket of Isabel's in one hand, a portable phone in the other. Mrs. Suarez stood in the doorway to the kitchen, her face a ruin. Deal knew she felt responsible, that he should take a moment to reassure her, but he couldn't. The fact was, he did blame her. Her, the doctor at the clinic, the entire *world,* for that matter. He thrust the phone at Driscoll, another candidate for blame.

"Call somebody. You've got friends. *Someone* will listen to you."

Driscoll eyed the phone, glanced up at him wearily. "Sure, I can call. But they'll just tell me what I'm telling you. Your wife went somewhere with your daughter, there's no crime in that." The ex-cop shrugged. "It's only been a couple of hours. Why don't we wait and see what happens."

Deal stared at him. He could see it in Driscoll's manner. His old buddy Deal overreacting, going over the edge himself. And maybe it was true. You're cruising along, life in order, you're happy, therefore everybody's happy, you love everyone, everyone loves you, good old Deal. Good Deal. Good boy. Wag your tail around the world. And then, out of nowhere, someone, though not just anyone, but someone you know, and love, and trust, gives you this sudden, vicious kick, something so brutal and inexplicable that the world turns inside out and you wonder how you could have been so mindless and happy in the first place.

He'd read about people so whacked-out they saw conspiracies in cloud formations, heard trees saying nasty things behind their backs. Bad weather was a personal affront. But this was something different. He had reason to fear. Didn't he?

"Driscoll," he said, struggling to keep his voice calm. "My wife checked herself out of a psychiatric clinic without letting anyone know, spent the night who knows where, and turned up here the next day, the minute she saw me leave. Now she and my daughter are gone." He took a breath. "If you were me, what would you think?"

Driscoll sighed. "I'm not arguing how you *feel.*" He started to say something else, then stopped, throwing up his hands.

"What if you just had them looking for the car?" Deal said. "I could report it stolen . . . " His mind was already racing ahead. There couldn't be another such vehicle in all of South Florida. The police would have her pulled over soon enough, Driscoll would get the word . . .

"That ain't the way it works," Driscoll was saying, shaking his head. "You're just gonna have to wait . . . "

"The hell with that, Driscoll." Deal had already punched in 911, had tucked the phone under his chin, was cursing himself for not having installed one of those antitheft homing devices they advertised on the radio all the time. Hide this little transmitter under the hood, then if someone steals your car, it sends out this little signal. The cops go out and pick up your car, haul the bad guys away. Except who were the bad guys in this situation, he wondered? A chill had descended over him, chasing away whatever satisfaction he'd gained with his little scheme.

"Dade County Police. May I help you?" The female voice in his ear, curt, professional.

"Yes," he said, glancing at Driscoll again. He had to stay focused. Someone had to get the job done. "My car. Someone's taken it . . . "

Driscoll threw up his hands in disgust. For a moment, Deal

thought the ex-cop was going to come after him, snatch the phone away.

He was starting to back away when he heard Mrs. Suarez's voice behind him. *"Madre dios!"* she cried, and Deal turned to see her pointing over his shoulder, out the living room window.

"Someone's stolen your car?" the voice repeated in his ear.

Driscoll was already at the window, staring down at the street. "Put the phone down," he called, disgusted.

Deal's gaze traveled out the window, feeling a lurch in his gut. There it was: The Hog, in all its resurrected glory, gliding to a halt below.

As he watched, one wheel climbed awkwardly onto the curb, the passenger door swung open, Isabel's tiny feet popped into view. In moments, she was running across the lawn, clad in some bulky furred jacket he'd never seen before, a massive ice cream cone aloft in her hand like a pink torch.

He felt a flood of relief wash over him, felt himself break the phone connection, cutting off the police operator in midsentence. The driver's door was open now, and Janice was getting out, coming around the nose of the clumsily parked Hog after Isabel.

At least it seemed like Janice. It took him a moment to realize something was wrong. This Janice—this *woman*—who wobbled over the curb in tall spiked heels was also clad in a fur jacket, a stylish waist-length model of fox, maybe, wearing huge sunglasses and a scarf around her head. As Deal stared, she undid the scarf and shook her hair free, unleashing a mane of blonde curls.

A *wig,* Deal thought, stunned. A *wig??!!*

She stood on the sidewalk, adjusting a handbag that hung from her shoulder, reaching inside her coat to straighten her clothes. What there were of them.

"Jesus God," Driscoll breathed beside him.

Deal stared, still trying to make sense of what he was seeing. A wisp of gold lamé blouse, a black leather skirt that barely reached midthigh, black fishnet stockings.

She removed the sunglasses, flicked at something on an eyelash that seemed even at this distance to droop with the weight of mascara. She replaced the sunglasses, pouched her bright red lips into a smile, and started unsteadily toward the building.

Down below they heard the workings of the front door, the

sound of Isabel's feet on the tiled entryway. The portable phone had begun to chirp and Deal handed it dazedly to Driscoll. He pushed away from the window, moving like a man in a dream toward the door.

He was out into the hallway then, had made it to the head of the stairs as Isabel, halfway up the flight, caught sight of him. *"Papi!"* she cried, her face lighting up.

She took the rest of the stairs two at a time, throwing herself into Deal's arms. He pulled her close to him, closing his eyes, breathing in the smell of her—the tingle of cool air, woolen tang of fur from the new coat she wore, little girl flesh basted in ice cream—savoring for a moment her precious weight in his arms. It was all he cared about for that instant, never mind that Driscoll had thought him crazy, Driscoll whose voice even now carried out into the hallway as he explained to the police operator: "No ma'am. It was a mistake. No. He *found* the car. That's right . . . "

Never mind, for that one moment, that he was going to have to open his eyes back to the world and wrestle with all its demons. For in that one instant he had his daughter back, squealing in his arms, dribbling pink ice cream down his neck and back—and for the brief eternity that it lasted, it was all that mattered.

Finally, though, he had to give it up, let the moment pass, set her down, let her run her carefree way inside to Mrs. Suarez, dispenser of milk and cookies, of care and all things good. He had to turn then, face this woman who came unsteadily up the stairs toward him, tottering on the impossible heels, her mouth moving askew beneath the lipstick caked crookedly there.

"Hello, sailor," she said, smiling as she clutched the handrail for support.

"Janice," Deal said, feeling his heart clench inside him. "Oh, Janice," and his woe filled the hallway to the brim.

 Paige, who rarely used alcohol, had a drink while the plane was still on the ground, another before dinner, a split of wine with the pasta she barely tasted, a brandy afterward. By the time the plane landed, she was reeling.

She moved unsteadily down the broad concourse of the Fort Lauderdale airport, sensing the onset of a headache with the potential to blossom into a full-blown screamer. Her legs felt flaccid and heavy beneath her, as if she'd disembarked on a planet with stronger gravity.

She scanned the faces of the small crowd lining the concourse exit, not really expecting to see her sister's among them, but unable to keep herself from hoping. She'd phoned ahead, left her flight numbers and itinerary on Barbara's machine, left a message about her message at the restaurant where Barbara worked.

But despite all that, there was no familiar face as she walked out into the lobby. That was all right, she reasoned, it was nearly midnight. Barbara would be at the hospital, or somewhere doing something important. She couldn't expect her sister to drop everything and rush to the airport, could she? Not when they hadn't exchanged a dozen words in the past several years, the most recent phone call discounted.

Paige had swung away from the knot of people gathered on the other side of the metal detectors, headed toward an escalator labeled "Baggage Claim—Ground Transportation," when she noticed the man with the sign.

"NUBBLEMAN" was the name scrawled in magic marker on a piece of cardboard, and at first she paid no attention. The man who held it was short and thin, and wore a chauffeur's uniform that engulfed him, too large by a couple of sizes. He held the sign in one hand and consulted something in his other palm, scanning it and the departing passengers with intensity.

Paige had almost reached the escalators when he caught up with her. "Miss Nubbleman," he said, thrusting the sign in her way.

She turned, noticing that he was Latino, that his mustache and sideburns were peppered with gray, that even his hat seemed too big to stay on straight. He was holding a facsimile of a still picture the studio often used for publicity releases. "Es you, right?"

She stared at him, uncertain.

"Mr. Mawlul send me," the man said.

Paige shook her head, still puzzled . . . and then it dawned on her. "Mahler," she said. "Mr. Mahler."

The little man checked something on the back of her picture, then nodded. "Right," he said. "Mawlul."

Paige shook her head in disbelief. He was so painfully thin she felt the urge to guide him to a restaurant.

Just like Marvin to arrange a car for her. For a moment she wished he were there with her, and then, as she tried to imagine Marvin with his smile and his can-do attitude, one arm around her shoulders, another around her sister's, "Hey, let's just sit down and talk this out, ladies . . . ," it all came crashing back upon her, every aspect of her life that she had tried to push away during the long flight, and she sighed, feeling as weary as she ever had.

"I'm Paige Nobleman," she said to the little man, finally.

"*Bueno,*" he said. He tossed the sign into a trash can, wadded the photo in his hand. "Car is outside," he added, smiling.

"Let me just get my bags," she said, and motioned toward the escalators, which, coming as no real surprise, she found to be closed for repair.

*   *   *

"In Miami?" the driver said, when she gave him the name of the hospital. She'd tried Barbara's house again from a pay phone, then the restaurant, too. The hospital was her best guess, but no one was answering at Patient Information at this hour and she didn't have a room number. At least she'd find her mother there, that much seemed certain.

"Miami Beach," Paige said.

"Long way," the driver said. He glanced into his outside mirror, tossed his wobbling hat aside, then cut the limo through a line of traffic onto a freeway ramp.

Paige wondered, the way he said it, if the guy were paid by the mile. He was good behind the wheel, though, unlike some of the drivers you'd get with a service, gunning the accelerator, then slamming the brakes, goosing you along. This one was as smooth as L.A. Eddie, and any other time she'd have laid her head back, tried to rest.

Instead, she found herself staring out the window, lulled to a zombielike trance by the gentle motion of the car. She noted an exit for "Hollywood," and wondered briefly why there were no hills in the distance, why her clothes were sticking to her despite the fact that it was December, and then she remembered where she was, that this Hollywood was a collection of high-rises on the ocean . . . and with great weariness, she remembered what had brought her here.

Odd that she'd keep blanking out like that, or not so odd, maybe. Maybe it was like a mind fuse. You could take just so much and then—pop—the circuits would overload and you could sink into the zombie zone. Fine with her. She'd be happy to take a nice long nap, wake up and find everything behind her like some awful dream, some part she'd played in a grade-Z film.

The limo was snaking through a gauntlet of barricades now: little yellow lights everywhere, a quick glimpse of men in hard hats caught in the glare of some portable lights, and a great boiling of dust about some unearthly machine, two idling police cars with their flashers turning—it looked more like a disaster zone than a highway, she thought.

Barely was all that behind them, the road back to itself and humping high over some ribbon of darkness below—a river, a chasm?—when a pair of cars roared up, passing the limo on either side. There was an instant of deafening motor thunder that vanished as quickly as it came, the taillights shrinking into nothing as she watched. How fast had they been going? A hundred? Maybe more? She'd never seen cars go that fast before.

"Was that the police?" she called to the driver.

"Race," the voice came back, crackling over an intercom speaker at her ear.

It took her a moment to understand. She sat back in the spongy seat, feeling disoriented again. What was this place she had come to, anyway? Hollywood without mountains, drag races on the freeway, no one answering the phones at the hospitals . . . maybe she *was* in a dream.

They were turning again, looping toward the east, it seemed, toward the water. The freeway rose up, giving her a brief view of the broad Intracoastal Waterway, red and green buoy lights, the glitter of Miami Beach beyond.

She found herself in memory, suddenly, one happy Sunday from her childhood, or at least it *seemed* happy: her father appeared in his normal form then, at the wheel of some ungainly houseboat, chugging down that same broad channel of water, she and her sister tossing bread off the stern to a crowd of wheeling gulls, her mother asleep in a chaise longue in the sun. One shining moment when they were still pretending to be a regular family, she thought with a pang . . . and then her mother was awake and shouting, at them for the noise they were making, at their father for permitting it, or maybe at them all, just for just being alive . . . and the image fell apart.

"Is over there," the driver's voice crackled at her ear. Paige blinked out of her reverie to see the massive hospital complex looming up on their left. The limo wound through a series of turns, past another long line of traffic barricades, ended up on a broad entryway to the main building.

The driver stopped under a brightly lit awning, turned to her as the compartment window slid down. "I am waiting for you here," he said.

"It's not necessary," Paige said.

"Here," the driver repeated, his voice firm.

"You can go on," she said. "I don't know how long I'll be. I'll get a taxi."

The driver shook his head, his face twisted in concern. "Is all taken care of," he insisted. "All the time while you are here." He smiled at her and tapped a picture ID on the visor above his head. "I am Florentino. At your service."

Paige sighed. "All right, Florentino," she said finally. "Right here." Then she turned, gathering herself for more important things, and stepped out into the humid night.

She should have prepared herself, she was thinking. She should have tried to picture the worst. But even then, how could she have conjured up anything like what lay before her now?

"Just for a moment," the ICU nurse at her side was saying.

Paige nodded, her mind numb. If the nurse had not led her to this bed, she would not have recognized her mother. The person who lay there inert, hair fallen away in patches, innumerable lines and tubes trailing from her body into the darkness, was a stranger, a wraith. Her mouth was open as if she'd been felled by a stunning blow, her yellowed, nearly transparent skin stretched tightly across her cheekbones, like some ghoulish decoration for a death's head.

Paige felt her legs give, had to steady herself against the foot of the bed. Machines sounded out the shallow rhythms of her mother's breath; another electronic thrum kept erratic time with her heart. A heavy line snaked out from beneath the sheets, draped itself across her mother's exposed feet like some power cord left behind by workers at a building site.

Paige reached out, gently moved the cord aside, the urge to scream vying inside her with an equally powerful impulse to weep. Her fingers carefully found her mother's feet. There seemed no hope of finding her way further around the bedside, past all those lines and tubes, past the pulsing machines and printouts that tumbled like failed streamers to the floor. Her mother's feet were like cool, featherless birds in her hands. The bones were hollow flutes, the skin the thinnest of membranes.

"Oh, Mother," she said, forgiving everything in that moment, feeling a flood of guilt for all the years she'd kept herself away. She could have come back long ago, when there was still time, when they might have set things right, or at least made a stab at it. But now . . .

"Oh, Mom," she said, staring at the pitiful form in front of her, at the bank of machines and monitoring equipment. "We've got to let you go."

"She's not your mother," the voice came from behind her, bitter, accusatory.

Paige turned, startled. Her sister had appeared in the doorway to the room, her face drawn and haggard, but a mask of fury now.

"Barbara," Paige managed. "You scared me . . . "

"You don't breeze in here from California, tell us what we're going to do," she said. "That's not the way it works."

Paige shook her head, confused. "Barbara, I just . . . "

"As long as my mother can draw a breath, she's going to live," Barbara said, biting the words off, her voice rising dangerously.

"I just meant . . . "

Barbara strode forward, her eyes glittering as if she were ready to strike. "She's not your mother!" Barbara said again, and this time her voice had risen to a shriek.

"I don't . . . " Paige began, her words seeming to stick in her throat. Her heart was thudding in her chest. Her sister, she was thinking, her own sister. The hatred. The venom. "What are you talking about?" She swallowed, tried to get her breathing under control. She saw nurses bolting from the central station, hurrying down the hallway toward the open door.

"This is my mother, too," she cried, staring at her sister in disbelief, in fury, in dismay. Her sister's words were incomprehensible. Impossible. But there was something inside her that was also crying *"What? Explain yourself."*

And then, before she could continue, the machines and monitors left off their measured beeps and pings, and joined the screaming chorus.

**11** "Most of our office temps are women," the guy behind the desk was saying. *Carl Cross,* his name-plate read. Paco seemed to remember that the out-fit was called Cross Employment. Middle-aged guy, a little gray in his good haircut, a little soft around the gut. Paco noted the soft drape of the guy's suit, the Rolex on his wrist.

So that meant he'd gotten right to the top. Ten days holed up in his apartment, picking buckshot out of his hide, eating delivered pizza and Chinese food, he'd finally decided he was safe, mustered the nerve to go out, get his life in gear. Maybe this was an omen, getting to talk to the boss.

Cross was staring thoughtfully at the form the secretary had left on the way out of the room. "You did a heck of a job on the typing test, I'll have to give you that!" He looked up from the form. "What kind of a name is Paco, anyway?"

Paco shrugged. Might as well make it easy. "My mother was Mexican," he said.

The guy nodded, scanning Paco's broad face, his fair hair, looking for some sign of the genes.

"From Spain, originally," Paco added.

Cross gave him a closer look.

"My father was a diplomat."

Cross raised his head in acknowledgment. He still looked hesitant. Paco wondered if he'd overdone it. They probably didn't get a lot of diplomats' children applying for these jobs.

"He died before I was born," Paco said.

"I'm sorry to hear that," Cross said. He looked like he might be ready to say something else, then changed his mind. He turned back to the form Paco had filled out. "You didn't put down your Social Security number."

Paco nodded. "I was telling the secretary. Somebody stole my wallet. My license, my Social Security card," he threw up his hands, "everything." The guy had his thoughtful look going again. "I wrote off for a new card, though. They said it takes a couple of weeks."

"You can't get paid without a Social Security number," Cross said.

Paco nodded, glum.

"And no employer in this state is likely to hire you, either. This isn't Texas, Paco."

Paco blinked. There was no mention of Texas on the application form he'd filled out, he was sure of that. For the purposes of this interview, he was Paco Edwards, from Columbia, Missouri. And in a way it was true. He'd spent a few nights in that college town, when he was still in the recreation enhancement business, and he'd used that very name while he was there.

He gave the guy a wary look. "Who said anything about Texas?"

Cross leaned forward in his chair, dropping his managerial facade. "Paco, I've been in this business for ten, twelve years now, *and* I came out here from Dallas before that. Give me some credit."

Paco nodded. "I had a roommate from Texas."

"You mean cellmate?"

"Excuse me?" Paco was on his way out of his chair.

"That's where you polished up your typing, that's what I'm thinking," Cross said. "In the joint. Tell me I'm right."

Paco waved his hand in the air, on his way out. "I've got another appointment . . . " What was it? Somebody had tattooed "jailbird" on his forehead, he'd never noticed?

"Sit down, Paco."

Paco hesitated. It wasn't an order, more an invitation.

Cross was leaning back in his chair now, his palms raised in surrender, a let's-be-friends smile on his face. "Look, you can be straight with me," he said. "The fact you did time means absolutely nothing to me."

Paco stared at him. "I came in here looking for work, that's all."

"Of course you did," Cross said, his voice mild. "And I believe everyone deserves that chance."

"You want to jerk somebody around, wait for the next guy," Paco said.

"Paco, I have no intention of jerking you around." Cross put his palms down on the table. "I'm sorry if that's what I seemed to be doing."

Paco shook his head. "I get the Social Security card, I'll stop back."

Cross waved it away. "Don't worry about that, Paco. I was just making a point." He stared up earnestly from his chair. "The fact is, there's plenty of work around this town," he paused, gave Paco his shit-eating grin, "for a man of your experience."

Paco knew it was time to get out, knew he should just turn on his heel and leave Cross and his how-do-you-get-rich-running-a-temporary-employment-agency-anyway far behind. But he also knew that the guy had marked him and, instead of tossing him out on his ear, had decided that in some way Paco might be useful. Which meant, of course, that a proposition might be on its way. And given the state of his finances, Paco figured that he owed himself that much, at least. Whatever he decided to do, stick it out in la-la land or kick it on back home, he was going to need some bucks. Just hear the guy out, he reasoned. See what he had in mind. What harm could there be in that?

"You're not a bad-looking guy, Paco," Cross was saying. "Ever do any acting?"

"Acting?" Paco said, altogether bewildered now.

"Well," Cross said, "It's something *like* acting, anyway." And then he filled him in.

12

"Hey kiddo!"

The voice in Paige's ear seemed impossibly bright, entirely out of kilter with the dream she'd been having. She'd been standing in the middle of a misted field, the soft grass about her filled with rabbits, hundreds of them, it seemed, all of them sitting up on their haunches like dogs, begging for little Milk-Bones she was tossing from the newsboy's sack she wore, no sound but the sigh of an unseen breeze.

She struggled groggily with the bedcovers, the rabbits vanishing, the field vanishing, the phone sliding away in the tangle. She didn't remember hearing the phone, didn't remember picking up, though the room still seemed to vibrate with the ring. She swallowed and tried to blink her eyes into focus, though there wasn't much point in it—the room was still pitch-black. When she was sure she could speak, she groped about the bed until she found the receiver.

"Marvin?" Her head felt like it was stuffed with batting. She'd felt such peace in her dream. And now this. "What time is it, Marvin?"

"Must be about seven on your coast," he said.

Seven, she thought. She'd come back from the hospital, taken a couple of Xanax around five. No wonder she felt so out of it.

"Why are you calling me at 4:00 A.M., Marvin?"

There was a pause on the other end. "Sweetheart, I don't know what time it is in Florida, but it's four in the afternoon out here. *Friday* afternoon," he added.

She swung her legs over the edge of the bed, rubbed at her throbbing temples, vaguely aware of the burning of her bladder and an ache in the small of her back. "Just a minute," she said, dropping the phone on the bed.

She fumbled her way to the curtains, drew the fabric back. The room was fairly high up, with a view to the north—or so it seemed—the inky expanse of ocean on her right, the lights of the city off to the left. It was dark outside, all right, but there seemed to be a lot of traffic on the streets for 7:00 A.M. And there was no sign of the sun coming up over the Atlantic, just a deep red band out there to the west.

She thought about it. Rises in the east, sets in the west. Right. She stood there until she had comprehended it, knew for certain that she had slept fourteen hours straight, then made her way slowly into the bathroom. She sat, relieved herself, stood, found a cold cloth for her face. Then she remembered, and went back to the phone.

"I'm sorry, Marvin," she said when she'd found the receiver again. "You were right."

"You okay, kiddo?" Marvin's voice seemed extraordinarily clear, as if he might be calling from the next room.

"I'm fine," she said. She snapped on the bedside light, stared down at her feet. She knew that she was having a telephone conversation, but it seemed impossible to concentrate. Her feet, for instance, seemed far more interesting.

They really were the oddest-looking appendages, she thought. And then realized she had begun to speak.

"My mother died, Marvin." Her voice sounded hollow in her own ears. Cruel to say it just like that, wasn't it? But what was the choice?

"Oh, shit," Marvin said. "I'm sorry. I'm really sorry, kiddo."

She listened to the empty silence on the line. She wanted to say something in response, but what?

"When did it happen?" Marvin asked finally.

She paused, making sure she could do this. "This morning," she said, dully. "Early this morning."

"This morning," he said. "Jesus. I'm sorry, kiddo. It's awful." Another pause. "I wish I could be there for you."

"It's okay, Marvin," she said. "It wasn't like we didn't expect it." She finished the water she'd left on the nightstand. Warm. Vaguely sulfurous. She wriggled her toes. No doubt about it: *her* feet. Dark green carpet, odd white feet. She tried to reclaim her dream, but all she could see was the carpet, flecked with lint, and those terrible, blue-veined feet.

"I got there in time to see her before she went," Paige said, letting her breath out in a sigh. "I got to say good-bye."

"Oh, sweetie," Marvin said. "This is tough. Just really tough."

"It *was* tough," she said, feeling her head begin to nod. Though every fiber in her being rebelled against it, she felt herself being reclaimed by the reality of her life. Toes, feet, legs. She was going to have to accept it. She was absolutely who she was.

"But you know what, Marvin?" she said, hearing a note of gaiety in her voice. But it couldn't be gaiety. More like hysteria, about to erupt. "Her dying, that was bad, but that wasn't even the worst thing."

"Look, Paige, are you okay? You sound a little funny."

"I'm fine," she said. "You want to know what the worst thing is or not, Marvin?"

"I'm here, kiddo. Talk to me." His earnest, I'll-do-anything-for-you voice. Good old Marvin.

"She wasn't my mother," Paige heard herself saying. She hesitated, feeling giddy, as if she were swept along by a rush from the drugs. But that had been a long time ago. And it had been just two Xanax, hadn't it?

"It's what my dear sister told me, anyway. They hadn't even taken my mother out of the room, Marvin. And there she was, telling me I'd been adopted."

Her own sister saying those things, hissing at her, following her out into the hallway, impossible, of course, but of course it explained so much.

"You see," she told Marvin, "My mother couldn't have any children, or so she thought, so they adopted me. And four years later, Barbara came along. What do you think of that, Marvin?" It sounded positively logical. And her voice echoed *Blithe Spirit* in her ears. *I could play any part,* she thought. *Any part at all.*

Only hissing, crackling noises at the other end of the line. Three thousand miles of amazement whispering back at her.

"Jesus God," Marvin said finally. "Is it true?"

"So my sister says," Barbara answered. "Or should I still call her that?" She took a deep, shuddering breath. Though she had not smoked a cigarette in more than fifteen years, she longed for one now.

She pulled her hair back in one hand, stared at herself in the mirrored wall. She noted that she'd gone to sleep without wearing anything, something she rarely did. Breasts, belly, pubic hair. There'd been men who'd found these things attractive. Now she felt like a stranger in her own body. "So why were you calling me, anyway, Marvin?"

Another major hesitation. Actors *used* these moments, she thought. Civilians gave themselves away.

"Just calling." he said. "To check in, see how you were doing."

"Marvin," she said. "Don't bullshit me. This is not the time."

"You're not as tough as you try to be," he said quietly.

"It's the Brits, isn't it?" she said.

"Paige . . . "

"I know, being the kind of people they are, it tore them up, having to tell you."

"The deal's not dead yet, Paige."

She couldn't hold back her laughter. Not really laughter, of course. A harsher, more bitter, sound than that.

"You know how these things go," he said. "They brought a new partner in . . . " He trailed off. "Tomorrow it could turn around again. They'll be begging."

"It's okay, Marvin," she said, glancing in the mirror again. Who was the woman there, wild-eyed and naked, squatting on a rumpled bed? "I'm doing fine down here."

"It's lousy timing, I know," he said. "And this thing with your sister. It sounds pretty strange to me . . . "

She laughed again. "That makes two of us, Marvin."

"I think you need to get right back out here after the funeral," he said. "Get your feet on solid ground," he said. "We'll talk. We'll get you together with the new people . . . "

"I'm going to take some time away, Marvin," she said. She was up and off the bed now, the phone set in her other hand, while she traced the cord to its source. "I think I'm going to need that."

"Sure," he said. "I've still got the place in the desert. A couple of weeks out there, you'll be raring to go."

"*Away*, Marvin," she repeated. "I'm going to be away for a while. But I'd like to feel I could call you. If I had to, I mean." She'd found it now, a little plastic plate hidden behind the night stand, the cord snaking in there, snugged by a plastic clip.

"Paige," he said. "I don't like the sound of this . . . "

"I'll call you, Marvin," she said. "I'll call you when I can, okay?"

Her hand followed the cord down behind the stand until her fingers found the clip. Marvin was still talking, his voice imploring, his words wafting out into the ether. Good old Marvin. Dear Marvin. She tugged once, then twice, at the cord, and finally she was on her own.

"I heard from Paige today," Mahler said. He was at the sideboard of the sitting room, pouring a scotch. He was about to settle for half a tumbler, then added a little more. End of a trying week, he deserved something extra.

Rhonda sat unmoving in her chair. He couldn't see her face from where he stood, but he knew she would have shown no reaction. He could have told her anything: the Academy had voted her an honorary Oscar, Rodney King had used his settlement to buy the house next door, she'd have sat there like a cigar-store Indian.

He took a healthy sip of the single-malt whiskey, made a face. Something his new partner had told him about, hundred and twenty bucks a bottle, engraved picture of quail and country houses on the label, tasted like battery acid. He poured it down the bar sink, reached for the Dewar's. He dropped in a couple of fresh cubes and filled the glass without hesitation this time, came around to sit in the chair opposite her.

Nice little fire, wifey with her afghan over her lap, papa bear in a cozy chair with his end-of-the-week drink. Pretty picture. Except wifey had turned to stone.

He took a drink of the Dewar's, grunted his satisfaction. Something around here still worked.

Rhonda had her thousand-mile gaze pointed in the direction of the mantelpiece, her eyes as clear and crystal blue as the day they'd met. Eyes you could spot across a room, or an airplane hangar, for that matter. Eyes that would bore into you until you'd have to look away, if you had any bullshit on your agenda, that is. There'd never been anything hidden in Rhonda's agenda, that was for sure. He'd appreciated that. The same thing that drove most men in this business batty, he'd loved about her from the first minute. And why not. You spend every waking hour dealing with people who make Richard Nixon seem forthright, it was a tonic to come home to Rhonda. Or had been.

He had another slug of the scotch. Keep yourself off the hootch all week, didn't it taste good when you finally gave in. He glanced at her, shook his head, sat back in the leather chair with a sigh. To tell the truth, even healthy, Rhonda probably wouldn't mind if Rodney King were her next-door neighbor. And she'd have to be dragged kicking and screaming to pick up any Oscar. Popularity contests, she would grumble every year. Or any time one of the special lifetime statuettes was given out, "pity awards."

"You're a case, Rhonda." He smiled. "A real case." He lifted his glass.

"I was talking about Paige," he continued after a moment. "She called to tell me things were okay, she's holding up just fine. It was a blessing her mother went so quick, all that." He noticed the quiver at Rhonda's hand, the slightest movement, like some feathery aftershock that touched only her. The first time it had happened, everyone had taken it as a sign of hope, that she was tuned in, trying to communicate. But the doctors had set him straight: just a nervous tic, they assured him. A galvanic response to some transitory quirk of body chemistry. Remember those frogs from high school biology? Still, what could it hurt to talk to her, treat her as if she could comprehend? Who could say she didn't, after all?

"The upside is, it's given her and her sister a chance to reconnect. Be girls together. Talk. That part's going so well, she's going to stay a few more days."

He turned to her, shaking his head. "It's a shame, isn't it? Takes a tragedy to make you appreciate what's really important." He made a waving motion with his hand, sent a little wave of his drink onto the carpet. "Family. Tradition. Roots."

He glanced up at the array of pictures above the hearth. "Something we're in short supply of out here, huh?" He gave a humorless laugh. "Nothing rooted deep enough in the whole state of California," he said, "that won't slide right into the Pacific when the big one comes. That's our problem, when you think about it."

He was about to settle back in his chair when he noticed that a thin line of spittle had inched from the corner of Rhonda's lips. He took a Kleenex from the box on the table between them, dabbed it away. "So out here you just have to do your work, play the game, count your beans at the end of the week, see how you're doing."

He sucked up one of the cubes from the glass, crunched on it. "But we're doing okay, Rhonda. Okay in that regard. Big doings, in fact. Deal of a lifetime. We'll be set." He looked up from the fire. "It's going to take everything I've got to get this thing off the ground—everything *we've* got, in fact—but it'll pay off in the end, you don't have to worry about that."

He swung his gaze away from her vacant stare. "And don't worry about Paige. I have people keeping an eye on her down there."

He sat quietly for a moment, then checked his watch. "Medicine time, kiddo." He put his drink down, opened a drawer in the table. He withdrew a syringe, a med bottle, flicked the needle cap away with his thumbnail, stabbed through the seal, loaded up. Something one of her attendants could have done, of course, but what the hey, he could shoulder some of the burden, couldn't he?

He held the syringe between his teeth, turned Rhonda's arm in one hand, chafed the dry flesh inside her elbow with the other. He found an unscarred spot—a blessing, given the number of times she'd been stuck—jabbed, shot, tossed the works into the special disposal bag they were supposed to use—no needles washing up on the beaches anymore, thank you very much—all of it done in less than a minute. At first he'd been squeamish, but it was a daily routine: one does what one has to do.

He picked up his drink when it was over, saluted her. "You're a trooper, Rhonda." He noticed the needle guard on the carpet, bent, and tossed it into the can. Not a can, really, but something fashioned from an elephant's foot. She'd brought it back from Africa, in the pre–endangered species days, before the whales and the owls had become their friends. Rhonda had wanted to get rid of the thing, but he'd held fast. He wondered if it might still bother her.

He glanced up at her. "Paige said she sends her love, sweetheart. Kiss-kiss." He made smooching motions with his lips as he stood. He brushed her cheek with the back of his hand as he started away.

"I'm going to hit the shower," he said. "There's a screening at the Directors' Guild tonight. Some remastered print, tribute to Gregg Toland. Bobby Wise, the ghost of Orson Welles, they'll all ask about you." He nailed the last of the scotch in his glass, glanced at the sideboard, decided against another. There was a picture on one side of the alcove, an old publicity still, Rhonda on the set— something vaguely borderlands seedy—with the big man himself. Orson, smiling and handsome, before he'd started to bloat, Joseph Cotten looking stern in the background, Rhonda spilling plenty of cleavage from an off-the-shoulder Carmen Miranda getup.

"I ever tell you about the last time I saw Orson?" he asked absently. "It was a party the winery he worked for got up out in the desert, at the Annenbergs. He was immense by then, took two guys to lower him into a chair, two more to get him up." He shook his head, smiling at the memory, his head swimming a bit with the scotch. "Sonny Bono, who wasn't the mayor yet, comes over to shake hands, Orson reaches up, grabs hold, then he loses his balance and falls back, all the time still holding onto Sonny. Looked like some kung fu movie," he said, laughing. "Threw the little shit clear over the couch."

He put his empty glass down, wiped a tear from his eye. He glanced over at Rhonda's deadpan profile. *Jesus,* he thought. *You couldn't get a laugh out of something like that, what was the point of living?*

"I'll have Wesley look in on you," he said finally, and went out.

He found her in the dressing room off the bedroom. She was bent over, rooting around in the small refrigerator they'd installed there, sorting through the trays of medications, vials of this and that, several bottles of Pellegrino, a Pilsner Urquell, a can of Slim-Fast. Her white dress had risen high enough to expose the tops of her hose, the snaps of a garter belt.

"Is that a nurse thing?" he said after a moment.

She started, banging her head on the edge of the refrigerator. She stood up, rubbing the top of her head as she stood. "I'm a physical therapist, remember?"

He liked the pout of her lips. "I didn't know anyone still wore garter belts, that's all."

She rolled her eyes. "Another turn-on," she said. "I'll tell them to make a note on your chart."

He moved closer, hooked his finger inside the front of her crisply starched dress. "God," he said. "There's just something about women in uniform."

She smiled, rolled her hips into him, made little wriggling motions with her shoulders that helped ease his work with the buttons. "Probably that they tend to be women," she said. She was moving on him now, the hem of her dress riding toward her hips, her breath quickening. *Get to a certain station in life,* he thought, *so many things were simpler.*

He struggled with the last button, then gave up and yanked it free. "The sound of ripping cloth," he said. "That's not bad either."

"You're an animal, Marvin," she said, her voice flat. Another twist of her shoulders and she was out of her bra, a wisp of wire and lace.

"It looks like Victoria's Secret in here," he said.

She had her hands on him now. She leaned back, her hips levered against the tiny refrigerator. "Exactly like that," she said. Her breath was coming in gasps.

Another tiny pane of lace that seemed to dissolve at his touch, then he was driving himself against her, hearing the crashing of glass from inside the refrigerator. "Wesley," he managed, one hand grasping a coat hook, another braced against the wall, "have you ever thought about acting?"

She was matching his rhythm, a little song coming from somewhere deep in her throat, more like a growl, in fact. "All the time, Marvin," she said. "All the time."

He liked that. He meant to check the expression on her face, but it was a fleeting thought. Besides, he could picture it. Tough girl. Bored to tears. But she had her arms around him. In fact, she had everything around him. "Just say the word," he told her. He was breathing hard enough for several people.

Somewhere glass was shattering, shelves of it crashing into ruin. *He* was ruined, of course. Utterly, morally bereft.

He bared his teeth, drove himself deeper.

And what she said was, "Now."

* * *

"Do you have any idea, the size of the porno industry in this country?"

"In inches?"

He glanced over at her, her face illuminated by the silent flicker of the big-screen TV. It was late, she'd tucked Rhonda into bed hours ago, they'd been eating some Chinese food he'd dug out of the refrigerator. She glanced down, flicked a pearl of rice off one of her breasts. The picture of boredom. Absolute, total insouciance. But just get her started. The combination drove him crazy.

"In dollars," he said. "American dollars."

She turned to him. "Is this your way of getting it up again?"

He brushed the remark away. "Say somebody was to walk up and offer you every frigging McDonald's franchise in the U.S."

She shrugged. "If it were Saks, I might get excited."

He waved the air with a chopstick, a professor with his pointer. "Throw Saks in, too. Plus Citicorp, and every airline ticket sold in a year from every carrier there is."

"I know this is leading somewhere," she said.

"You go to acting class, right?"

She shrugged, turned away.

"Come on," he said. "Admit it. You've been angling to be discovered from the first day you showed up here."

She gave him a sour look. "I'm happy being a physical therapist. I just do acting to express myself."

"Sure." He nodded with satisfaction. "So you'll comprehend this figure. Total gross of the motion picture business last year was five point one billion."

She sighed and turned her eyes to the television screen, where a Japanese couple writhed about a swaybacked double bed. He'd switched the singsongy Cantonese dialogue off but the subtitles were clear, one set in classical Chinese ideographs, another in English: "*Ooooooo . . . feel good . . . feel good!*"

"Does that count the six thousand I spent on lessons?"

"Maybe," he said. "The record industry does about twice that. Legitimate publishing is about eighteen billion."

"No wonder she went batshit, she had to listen to this in bed all the time."

He rolled over on his elbow, stared at her in profile. "Porn is worth nineteen billion dollars, sweetheart, and that's just what the bean counters know about. Some say it's more like forty billion a year."

She glanced down at him. "Jesus. This kind of talk *does* turn you on."

"Last question," he said.

She was up, reaching over him for something on the bed tray. "Shoot," she said, her voice muffled.

"What's the population of the United States?"

She found what she was after, worked her way on down the bed. "We didn't have geography in therapist school, Marvin."

She was crouched over him now, fussing with some tiny packet in her hand. Surely she wasn't bothering with a condom, not after all they'd been through.

"Population of China, then. Take a guess."

"A lot," she said. She was smearing something on him, something cool and wet and slick. "Line them up four abreast, start marching them into the ocean, they'll never stop coming." She turned, grinned. "I saw it in that Ripley's Believe It or Not place, down on the Boulevard."

"One point three billion," he said, suppressing a groan. Whatever had started off feeling cool was turning warm with the steady motion of her hands. "Five times the population of the U.S. You want the upside of doing business in China, multiply those figures I gave you by five."

"Would I find that number on a stress monitor?" Her voice went one way, what she was doing another.

"If it reads out in green," he managed. It was true, he'd had a point to make, but things were getting out of control. He was digging his heels into the bedclothes.

"Oooooo," she said, mocking the wretched dialogue on the screen. "Feel *really* good!"

"Yeah," he said. "But it's getting a little hot." He caught a tangy scent in the air. A familiar, spicy scent. Something he knew, something he rarely used . . . but dear God, the way she moved, maybe she *did* have a future in his films . . . then it came to him.

"Hey," he said suddenly, struggling onto his elbows. "Is that mustard?" He tried to wriggle from her grasp. "Did you put *mustard* on there? *Chinese* mustard?"

She pushed him back. "A little mustard, a little sweet and sour," she said, then flashed a wicked smile. "But don't worry," she added, bending down. "It won't be on much longer."

"Yeah, that's it. That's right." Shanalee Braxton murmured the words with soft urgency, as if she were peering down into clear water off the Haulover Docks, pole in hand, urging some dumb sheepshead to take her bait. Just like fishing, when you thought about it. And the people they dealt with not much smarter than some dumbass fish. She smiled, watching with satisfaction as the red Lincoln Town Car up ahead of them edged to the curb, its interior dome light blinking on.

She glanced at her driver—Anthony, this trip—but she didn't have to say anything. Anthony had killed the van's headlights the moment the Town Car turned down this lonely street. Now he was smoothing the van over to the side, a good fifty feet behind the Lincoln, people up there wouldn't even know the three of them existed.

Anthony had some brains. That's why he was driving and Pencilhead was riding shotgun in the back. Pencilhead had a big jones and an itty-bitty head, about size five and a half, with a brain the size of a pea rattling around inside of it. She didn't know anything about the size of Anthony's jones and she didn't care. Some men were good for one thing, some for another.

Take the way she'd seen Anthony flinch last week when she'd had to shoot the woman they'd run off to the side of the road, wouldn't let go of her purse. Anthony's looking at her like, "Why did you do that?" and Pencilhead had just laughed and shot the bitch again, even though the old woman was way past being able to hold onto anything ever again. Shot her and the old fart with her, while the guy was crying, gibbering some language she'd never heard before, trying to crawl down under his steering wheel and hide.

Pencilhead was seventeen, which might have something to do with it. Anthony was in his twenties, already spoiled for some things by the time she'd got hold of him. Still, he had brains, and was quick. He'd wired the van they'd stolen from a tile company's lot in less than a minute, had them on the job by midnight. They'd waited a little over an hour down the block from the Avon Agency before this pair had turned up to rent a red Lincoln. Two Chinese guys in a luxury car, Shanalee thought. Almost like they'd hit the Lotto. Good as five numbers out of six, at least. And a lot more certain.

Anthony had kept them in sight through six lights, four turns, one stop at a 7-Eleven, and now this detour. He was good, all right. He was sitting there this very moment, ready to deal, holding his foot over the accelerator like he should be.

She glanced around the deserted street, a warehouse district near Miami International, but it was a waste of time. Only person who'd be crazy enough to come down here this time on a Friday night would be some other tourist, lost, wondering where were the palm trees and the beaches. Uh-huh. That should happen, Shanalee would be glad to help them out, too.

The two men inside the Town Car had a map out now, holding it between them, the driver, the great big guy, gesturing angrily at the little guy in the passenger seat.

Shanalee could imagine what was being said: "How so you get us lost, motherfucker," or however the Chinese talked. Who cared what they were saying, anyway. They thought they had problems now, just wait a minute, here comes Shanalee.

"Hit them," she said to Anthony then. Anthony nodded, and pressed the pedal down.

The impact was enough to send his partner, Wayne Chan, flying against his seatback, then forward, on the rebound, against the dash. By the time Wayne Chan stopped bouncing around the cabin of the Lincoln, his eyes were rolling back in his head.

Gabriel Tan fared better. Although he'd sent the power seat all the way back to its limits, he'd barely been able to squeeze his bulk behind the wheel as it was. Still, the sudden shift of three hundred and forty pounds just one inch into the steering column was enough to inflate the airbag on his side of the car.

It wasn't exactly panic that Gabriel felt as the fabric billowed up against him, smothering him momentarily. Surprise, possibly. But panic was allied with fear, an emotion that Gabriel had effectively extinguished from his repertoire.

Of course, he *had* spent the better part of his early years in Bangkok experiencing fear, a by-product of the endless teasing about his size from the other alley children, the ensuing fights that had everyone piling on, always leaving him on the short end in those days. There was also the matter of his home life, if you could call it that, recoiling from one beating or another at the hands of the men his mother brought home. Afraid to go out during the day, afraid to come home at night.

Then, one evening, he'd made the mistake of walking incautiously into the shack they called a house, caught his mother in the only room, in the midst of some paying entertainment. His old lady still screaming for him to get out, Gabriel had held up his hand to ward off the roundhouse hook of an American master sergeant wearing unbuttoned skivvies and his pecker still waving free, Gabriel catching the man's fist in midair. Gabriel had been scared, all right, was just acting out of instinct.

He could still see the look on the guy's face. Fourteen-year-old fatso from gooktown got his hand in a grip that feels like a vise, it's a whole new world.

When the guy brought a knife up with his other hand, Gabriel had still been scared, petrified in fact, was only acting out of instinct. He flung the guy against the wall so hard, the guy had to pull one arm out of a hole he made in the plasterboard. If the guy had left it alone after he'd gotten his hand loose, taken his knife and his offended manhood out into the steamy night, Gabriel might still have been able to reach down and find fear somewhere deep inside. But the soldier had come back, had meant to kill him, and somewhere in the process of defending himself, Gabriel discovered the rage that he'd been bottling up all those years.

He took a few cuts on his arms and shoulders, still had a zipper visible on the side of his neck, but for all that, he had beaten the man until he was unconscious, until his mother had run screaming into the night, until he had broken every part of a person he knew there was to break. He had been stomping the soldier's manly manliness into something resembling a strip of beef jerky when the MPs arrived and the real show began. The series of places they kept him after that, even fear was afraid to go.

Given all that, what could an airbag do to frighten him? Or the things that happened next in that strange place he and Wayne had brought themselves to?

Gabriel was still swatting at the limp fabric of the airbag when he felt his door fly open.

"Hey, man," the voice was calling. "We didn't see you. We're really sorry."

Gabriel didn't think the man sounded sincere. When he saw the pistol in the man's belt, he became certain of it. He heard the passenger door opening, caught sight of another man pulling the dazed Chan outside.

"Yo, Anthony," the second man called. "This guy's all messed up."

"Fuck, Pencilhead, why don't you just tell them our names?" the first man shouted back, across the top of the car, then bent down to Gabriel.

"Better step on out, take a look at the damage," the guy was saying to Gabriel.

Gabriel glanced out through the windshield, where Wayne Chan was now lying across the hood, groaning, starting to come around as the second man watched warily, holding something out of sight behind his back. The second man had an unusually small head, Gabriel noticed, wondering briefly if it had brought as much abuse as his size had in his own childhood.

Gabriel swung his feet out onto the pavement, hauled himself up by the doorframe. He affected exhaustion at the effort.

"Why do you have a gun?" he said ingenuously, wiping his face on his sleeve.

The one who had been called Anthony glanced down at his belt, as if he was surprised to find the pistol there. "Hey, it's a bad neighborhood," he said. "Come on, let's have a look at your car, man."

Gabriel glanced at the van that had plowed into them, saw a vague movement at its rear. "It is okay," he said, "No harm. It is not my car."

"Hey, we fucked up your ride," the one called Pencilhead shouted. "Now do what the man says."

Gabriel heard the tone of that voice and turned. There was a security lamp at the rear of one of the warehouses. It threw off a wavery light, enough to illuminate the boxy-looking pistol that Pencilhead had taken from behind his back and trained upon him now. Wayne Chan had stopped groaning and lay motionless across the hood of the car. That was either a bad sign or a good one, Gabriel thought.

"We do not want trouble," Gabriel said.

"Neither do we," the man in front of him said. He reached down for his own pistol.

Gabriel took two mincing steps, shot out his left hand. His fingers caught the one called Anthony beneath the chin, his hand plunging like a dull spade into the soft flesh of the man's throat. Gabriel felt a dull pain as his fingertips drove all the way to bone. The man stumbled backward, a look of astonishment on his face. He was making strangled, mewling sounds, one hand clawing desperately at his crushed voicebox, the other clamped on the pistol he'd tried to draw.

The pistol had not quite come clear of his belt when the gun went off. There was a muffled sound as the fireball erupted into the man's leg. Something hit the concrete at their feet, splintering concrete fragments against Gabriel's shins.

Gabriel strode forward, driving the butt of his palm up under the man's nose hard enough to lift his feet off the ground. As Anthony went over in a heap, Gabriel heard an explosion behind him. He wheeled to see the one called Pencilhead backpedaling, his pistol flying away, across the roof of the Lincoln.

Wayne Chan had come alive and was advancing, firing a series of fist blows against Pencilhead's slender frame. Pencilhead took a solid shot to the chest, gasped. He fell against the side of the Lincoln, then tumbled sideways toward the pavement. Wayne Chan moved in, sent a kick that Gabriel only heard as it landed, with the sound of a soggy gourd splitting open. Another kick, and another awful sound, something bursting inside a burlap bag.

Gabriel was thinking it was over when a new voice shrieked behind him:

"Kung fu motherfucker," he heard, and spun toward the sound, cursing himself for forgetting the shadowy form he'd spotted by the rear of the van.

There was a blast that he felt as much as heard, and a flare of scorching fire from the mouth of a shotgun erupting a few feet from where he stood. The first load threw Wayne Chan against the fender of the Lincoln. The second took off the top of his head and sent him sprawling across the hood where he'd lain moments earlier. Gabriel did not imagine that Wayne Chan—tough enough for Hong Kong streets, maybe, but this was Miami—would be getting back up this time.

That is in fact what he found himself thinking as he vaulted over the trunk toward the woman who had killed his partner. He was also thinking that he was advancing toward this woman not out of any misguided sense of revenge, nor because he was brave, nor because he had any desire whatsoever to go up barehanded against a crazy woman with a stubby pump shotgun in her hands. He was doing it because there was no real choice left open to him, because he knew that were he to try to run—and fear had nothing to do with it, either—she would cut him down before he made it halfway across the deserted street.

The woman turned to him, her feet spread wide like some badass gangster from a chop-socky film. She raised the shotgun toward Gabriel, jacked another round into the chamber. "Karate sonofabitch," she cried, and fired again, at the very moment that Gabriel came down, his foot cracking solidly against her temple.

The blast went wide, taking out the windshield of the van. The shotgun flew from the woman's hands and clattered onto the pavement. She was still tottering upright as Gabriel landed, then began the execution of a whirling pirouette, a movement as smooth and graceful as a ballet dancer's twirl, Rudolph Nureyev in an offensive tackle's shape.

Shanalee was thinking how impossible it seemed, how unfair, for someone so big to move so fast. She was also wondering what the problem was. She *thought* she had this man dead to rights, could have sworn she was still pumping and firing, pumping and firing, and yet, somehow, he was still standing and there was her shotgun somehow on the ground.

The big guy wasn't exactly standing, of course. The way he was moving was more of that jackoff judo, and what was it about that stuff, anyway, him dancing, her standing like she was paralyzed, like she was a bird in front of a snake, and wasn't it supposed to be the other way around?

Thinking this, she was bending—or was it actually falling—toward her weapon when the big man finished his pretty spin and caught her with his foot a second time, his heel burrowing into the hinge of her jaw.

The force of it froze everything for one electric moment. The pain was ecstasy. The night around her turned glorious, every star a brilliant diamond light. Distant sirens became the cries of angels. For one brief moment, she knew what all this meant, knew why she'd gone wrong so many years before, and was sorry, and wondered if she'd be saved. And then she heard a sharp cracking sound that echoed off the cement-block storefronts around her, and her head fell back into an impossible pose, and all that was left of her went down.

Gabriel landed in a crouch, blood roaring in his ears, ready now for anything. He glanced down at the inert form of the woman who'd been ready to kill him, swept his gaze about for the thin man whom Chan had battled. But that one lay now with his cheek driven into the pavement, his jaw opened improbably wide, a dark pool circling his head like a halo. Gabriel swung his gaze to the van, which sat motionless, its engine creaking in the suddenly stilled night. There had been three, so caution dictated that there might easily be four. Somewhere jet engines roared, but whether the plane was landing or taking off was impossible to tell.

He waited in his crouch, ready to spring, until finally he knew that it was finished, that all this was over. Already he was calculating, assessing the damage: too bad about Wayne Chan, but Gabriel could manage on his own. The important thing was, who had known they were coming? Who could have sent out these people to kill him and Chan? And why send such amateurs, unless they were all that could be found on such short notice—in which case, would it not have made more sense to wait?

Gabriel was still wondering these things when a shriek of tires sounded and he stood up to see the street filling with cars: three, four, five of them, squad cars, their lights painting the streets and storefronts red and blue, their sirens blaring. Then, careening behind them, a pair of brightly painted television vans, one with a tiny satellite dish sprouting from its top and pushing toward the sky like something from a fairy tale even as he watched.

He glanced at the Lincoln, considered making a run for it, but gave up the thought immediately. Even if the car were not damaged, where would he go in this box canyon of a street?

The cruisers were bearing down on him now, their spotlights criss-crossing, fixing him in their sights, blinding him. He heard a series of commands blaring from the grill-mounted speakers, each blasting over the next, the result a cacaphony that Gabriel could not decipher but had no problem understanding and even less obeying.

There were five squad cars screaming to a halt about him. Which meant that ten weapons were being trained on him by an equal number of frightened and angry policemen. Had the loud-speakers commanded him to defecate in the street and howl at the Miami moon, he would have been glad to comply. Instead, he did what he knew they actually desired of him: he raised his hands high, and turned very, very slowly, and, in the way of a man bracing himself for the worst, leaned up against the the big American car.

"Five thousand, seven hundred dollars," Deal was saying, holding up the printout for Driscoll to see. He'd found it, along with the credit card receipt, in Janice's purse, which itself had been tossed into the open bed of the Hog, along with several shopping bags full of merchandise.

Driscoll glanced at the printout, shook his head in commiseration, then took a swallow of his beer without saying anything.

It was late on a Saturday, and Deal had just returned from the hospital where he'd had to readmit Janice. Her physician couldn't be bothered to come in, but after hearing Deal's account of things and a brief conversation with the doctor on duty, they did agree that Janice would not be permitted to leave again without Deal being notified. Deal rubbed his hands over his face, feeling exhausted. If it weren't so sad, it would be funny.

He and Driscoll were sitting in the kitchen of Driscoll's apartment, which sat across the breezeway from his own. The apartments were identical in layout: each had an eat-in kitchen with a tiny bay window at the breakfast nook, a sizable family/living room, and two bedrooms, each with bath, down the hallway.

The only difference was that it looked like people actually lived in Deal's unit. In the case of Driscoll's apartment, it was more difficult to tell. There was furniture, of course, and food in the refrigerator, and clothing in the drawers and closets. But you'd have to open something up to be sure. Then you'd find socks rolled and nested like eggs, sorted by color, boxer underwear in neatly ironed stacks, and in the closet, three starched white shirts next to three blue shirts next to three yellow shirts, all short-sleeved with buttonless collars, each with a color-matched mate in an adjacent line of slacks . . . and on and on.

It didn't matter that the moment Driscoll put any of these things on they seemed to wilt and rumple into immediate disar-ray—for the time that they stayed separate from the man himself, his things were absolutely in order. Deal thought of the morass his place had become in the last few weeks and thought briefly of hir-ing Driscoll to come in and take charge. Then he caught sight of the printout again.

"How could you spend that much in one day," Deal said. "Not *even* a day, really."

"My wife bought a hundred-dollar set of pillowcases once," Driscoll said, shrugging. "I saw that, I knew the world had passed me by. My first car cost a hundred bucks."

Deal was scanning the hotel printout again. "I didn't know you could still do this," Deal said. "Charge clothes and jewelry to a hotel room."

Driscoll nodded. "It's the Grove. Lot of Brazilian millionaires come down to the Grand Bay Hotel. People'll do anything to help them spend."

"I guess they do," Deal sighed, tossing the paper aside. Maybe he could take the Rolex back—he'd found the box and paperwork after all. The fox coat was another story. There was makeup all over it and it reeked of whatever overpowering perfume she'd been wearing. He shook his head sadly.

Also, there was the matter of the boxes and boxes of expen-sive children's clothes from Kidding Around, a place where the very sight of the display windows caused Deal to clutch at his wal-let. He could take all that stuff back too, of course, but the thought of it, one of those supercilious salesladies staring him down while he tried to come up with a story . . . "I'm sorry, I don't want my kid to have these jodhpurs . . . "

He left off the vision, glanced at Driscoll with resignation. The big man shrugged again. "You know what my old man used to say?"

"Should I?" Deal said.

"Any problem that money can fix iddn't a problem."

Deal stared at him, then at the hotel bill. "Maybe your old man would like to pick this bill up."

Driscoll shrugged. "I dunno. He was broke when he died."

"Christ, Driscoll."

Driscoll shrugged. "It's all right. I didn't mean to criticize. I don't suppose he ever had to put up with anything like what you're going through, pardner."

Maybe so, Deal thought. Janice's disintegration had come so suddenly, he wasn't sure *what* he was going through. At first, the doctors had assured him that hers was a natural reaction, but something that would respond to treatment. Now she seemed to be getting worse, far worse.

Driscoll had been studying him, Deal realized, waiting for some response. All he seemed able to do was shake his head.

"I'll be right back," Driscoll said finally. He stood and shambled away toward the bathroom.

Deal watched him go, thinking that Driscoll was right, of course, that the money was the least of it. Though thank God he'd been able to pull them out of the hole somewhat. At least there was something in the bank. If this had happened four years ago, he'd have bankruptcy to face, along with everything else.

Four years ago, he'd been studying a whole set of printouts like the one on the table beside him, and every one of them assured him that the company his own father had founded—a company that had built two of the major hotels on Miami Beach, a series of condos down Brickell, a half-dozen office towers in the financial district and the Gables—was doomed. His father was dead and the business was hollow, the cash gone like water fled from a sinkhole lake, all the DealCo assets tied up in boom-or-bust joint ventures that had failed spectacularly.

Too stubborn to let go of the last piece of property that the company held, Deal had designed and built the fourplex where they sat, a project that was to anchor DealCo's resurrection from the ashes. And it had happened, he thought, just as he had promised Janice it would.

He'd finished the fourplex, they'd moved into one unit and rented the rest, he covered the payments with income to spare. He'd created *assets* again. Then there'd been all that rebuilding work following the hurricane, and just when that was tailing off, he'd fallen into a job rebuilding an old Coconut Grove mansion for Terrence Terrell, owner of baseball's Florida Manatees. That, in turn, had led to a number of commercial projects, and Deal had begun to believe that there really was hope for restoring a once-grand operation to prominence. He and Janice had been talking about getting out of the fourplex at long last, finding a house with a backyard again, with a good school nearby . . .

He heard the toilet flush, watched Driscoll reappear, moving through the living room toward him. "Maybe you could claim the person who bought the coat was an impostor," Driscoll said.

It brought an involuntary laugh from Deal. "It's not that far from the truth, is it?" he said. He sighed again, thinking it was time to go upstairs and gather Isabel from Mrs. Suarez's place, though he didn't relish having to wake his daughter up, go through all the explanations again about where Mommy was staying . . . and then the little phone on the table began to ring.

"Deal?" The voice that came as he picked up was slurred, so faint that at first he'd thought it was Janice.

"Deal," she repeated. "'S me, Deal. Old buddy."

"Barbara?" he said finally.

"Sorry," she said, her voice rising momentarily. "Very sorry."

Deal heard a crash, the sound of something breaking. "Barbara, what's wrong?"

"Glass," she said. "Old glass. No problem."

Deal felt apprehension, and, almost simultaneously, an intense wave of weariness. More trouble. The world full of trouble and heartache. "Barbara," he said. "Is it your mother?"

"Did a bad thing," she said, ignoring him. "My sister . . . " she trailed off, leaving a silence on the line. There was another, similar crash.

"Barbara," Deal called. Driscoll was staring at him, trying to fathom what was going on.

"Told my sister the truth," Barbara said, her cadences rising drunkenly. "Told her the whole thing."

"The truth about what, Barbara?" He did not have time for

9 1

this, Deal thought, then corrected himself. He did not have the energy. Most of all, he did not have the desire. He had a full plate of his own right now, thank you very much.

"A bad thing, Deal. Did a real bad thing."

"Where are you, Barbara?" he said wearily. "What's going on?"

"My mother died, Deal." It was if the static had abruptly cleared from a bad radio broadcast. For a moment, her voice was clear and matter-of-fact, as lucid as if she'd never had a drink. "She died."

"Dear God," Deal said. He glanced at Driscoll. "I'm sorry, Barbara."

"Yeah," she said. He heard something close down in her voice. "Too bad, huh." He heard ice cubes clattering into a glass.

"Barbara, listen to me," he said. "You have to take it easy . . . "

"Sure, Deal." There was a pause, and he imagined her filling her glass, knocking back another drink.

When she spoke again, her voice was falsely bright, struggling for control. "Sorry I bothered you, okay? Just wanted you to know."

"Barbara, listen . . . "

"Sorry," she said again. He thought he heard a curse as she broke the connection.

Deal fell back in his chair.

Driscoll was at the refrigerator now. He'd pulled out a beer for himself, held one up for Deal. Deal shook his head.

He took a deep breath, turned back to the phone, punched in Barbara's number. He was not surprised when the busy signal came. He still had the picture vividly in his mind, her stalking away from him out there on South Beach, stung at his rebuff. How she must have fought herself before she made this phone call, he thought. Her mother dead, God only knows what kind of blowup with her sister, now she'd heard the tone in his voice, giving her the brush-off.

"What's up?" Driscoll said, dropping back into his seat.

Deal massaged his face with both hands now, trying to bring back feeling, rub away the fatigue . . . or maybe, he thought, he was trying to rearrange his features. Maybe he could mold and massage long enough, then drop his hands, he'd have turned into someone else, someone who could smile, head down to Leo's Tavern with Driscoll, pop a few, walk away from calamity without a care.

"Barbara," he said. "Her mother died."

"Aw, Christ," Driscoll said.

"Then there's something with her sister, she wouldn't tell me what." Deal looked away. "It doesn't sound like she's holding up too well."

"Drunk on her ass, you mean?"

Deal gave him a look.

"Hey, I'm not criticizing," Driscoll said. He raised his beer. "Just wondering."

"I gotta go to Fort Lauderdale," Deal said. He was staring out the window, had made no effort to move.

Driscoll nodded. "Course you do. She thinks the world of you, Johnny."

"Yeah?" Deal said. He stood, patted his pockets for his keys. He felt an unreasoning anger rising within him. "Why is that, Driscoll? Why in the hell should anybody think I have what they need?"

Driscoll gave him an odd look. "That's a heck of a thing to say. You don't want to drive to Fort Lauderdale, then don't."

Deal stared back at him a moment, then nodded. "I'm just tired," he said.

"Yeah," Driscoll said, "we all get tired." He took a swallow of his beer. "Go on, then. And tell her I'm sorry about her mom."

**16** A light rain had drifted in off the Atlantic, slowing traffic so that it was nearly an hour before he found his way to Barbara's place. She rented a cottage on the back end of a once-grand property on Commercial Boulevard in Fort Lauderdale. What must have been one estate among many was flanked these days by a strip shopping center and a series of used car lots. The former main house had been converted to a set of offices that held an insurance agent and a direct-mail advertiser. The broad lawn had gone bare in spots, the ancient fruit trees were scraggly, the driveway crumbling.

Deal swung the Hog around a fender-bender that seemed to have involved a pickup and an ancient VW van, then made a right into the drive. A wrecker lit up like something from a flying saucer movie had arrived at the scene of the accident behind him, and Deal spotted the lane that led off to the rear in its glare. As he moved further along, he noted that the back end of the property had maintained some of its original charm. The drive changed from asphalt to crackling white shells and curled under a thick canopy of banyan limbs and ficus, giving out in a leaf-strewn parking area beside an old Florida cracker house with a wraparound porch and a steep-pitched tin roof, a dim yellow lamp burning at the entry, another alive in one of the inside rooms.

Despite the questionable neighborhood, Barbara felt safe. "Nobody even knows there's a house back here," she'd told him more than once. And the rent, by South Florida standards, was a joke.

Deal got out of the Hog and stood in the shelter of the great trees, hesitating, listening to the hiss of the rain in the leaves. Except for that sound, and the distant crackle of the wrecker truck's CB, it was quiet, the essence of peacefulness. Maybe she'd fallen asleep, he thought.

He swung the door of the Hog closed and kicked through the shoals of fallen leaves to the front stoop. He knocked firmly on the wooden screen of the porch, listened to the sound die away, knocked a second time. He called her name then, feeling the first stirrings of concern.

The screen gave at his touch, as did the inner door. He was inside the living room then, his eyes drawn toward the lamp that tilted crazily in a far corner. He saw the streaks on the walls first, and found himself thinking someone had started to paint. Then his feet caught on something beneath him, and he stumbled. He tried to catch his balance, but the floor seemed as though it had been greased. His feet flew out from under him, and he felt a painful crack as his elbow landed on something hard.

It seemed, as his eyes adjusted to the dim light, like a series of terrible snapshots slowly fitting together into one awful whole: one hand reached beneath him, groping for the thing he had fallen upon—some rock, some bookend, something tossed aside—and, finding it, raised a pistol into view; at the same time, the paint-splattered walls, lit in random shafts from the tumbled lamp, came into focus as the blood-drenched backdrops that they were; and the last, of course, was the worst—turning, knowing, even before his eyes confirmed it, the awfulness of what had thrown him to the floor.

**17**

She *could* do this, Paige told herself as she stepped out of the rental car into the damp Florida night. She *had* to do this. She had spent the better part of her life running away—now it was going to stop.

She had spent all day Saturday running over the possible scenarios. Finally, when she had decided she was prepared for almost any response, she'd called for a rental car and arranged for a pickup at the hotel next door.

On the way out she'd had to dodge Florentino, who'd been waiting faithfully for her, attired in a fresh but equally blousy uniform and lounging against the fender of the limo at the end of the taxi line. That was the last thing she needed, a faithful retainer sitting outside in a limo while she tried to connect with a sister who despised her for being too good for the family. She did not think for a moment that she and her sister could ever have anything approaching a normal relationship, but by God they were going to treat one another like human beings, Paige was going to see to it. And she would find out just how much truth there was in that mind-numbing accusation that her sister had made.

Yes, her sister might insist, it is true, and in a way, every miserable aspect of Paige's childhood might be accounted for. No, it was a lie, though it was what her sister had always fantasized, and Paige would be left to wrestle with the same cruel conundrums she had lived with all her life. Or, Get out of here, I have nothing to say to you, her sister might say. Only the last would Paige refuse to accept.

She felt a moment's hesitation when she saw the strange car parked outside her sister's cottage. Paige had not considered the possibility that her sister might have company. She had thought about phoning ahead, had even dialed the number before she'd left her room, but her nerve had left her when she heard the receiver lift, and she'd slammed the phone down quickly.

She'd driven quickly, almost recklessly, given the slick streets, but once she had known her sister was at home, she'd been overwhelmed with the urge to arrive here. It was as if she realized that any hesitation would be fatal. If she did not confront her sister while her courage was at its peak, she feared she might never manage it. After all, she'd had a lifetime of practice in denial, in self-deception.

She raised her hand to knock, then realized that the door was open, the wood frame pushed inward, wedged against the uneven slab of the porch. She stepped inside, ignoring the warning bells that had begun to ring the moment she'd spotted the strange car outside. She was far too wrought up to pay attention to something as feeble as common sense.

She heard a sound inside and hurried forward, through the entryway, where the door also stood ajar. She had enough of her wits about her to be concerned, of course, had even managed to get her mouth open, ready to call out for her sister . . . when she came through the foyer and saw it, illuminated in the crazed glare of an unshaded lamp:

The stark white walls splattered with gore. A kneeling man, disheveled and wild-eyed, the front of his shirt and slacks covered in blood. He knelt above her sister's body. One of his hands was pressed to her throat. A gun lay on the floor at his feet.

The man stared up at Paige with an expression that seemed to mirror the shock she felt in her own. He held up his hand toward her, his mouth open as if he was about to say something but couldn't get it out. She remembered thinking how odd it was that he hadn't reached for the gun. It looked as if he meant to entreat her, not kill her.

Whatever had caused him to do that, it surely saved her life. She screamed once, in pure terrified reflex. And then, as he was still struggling to stand, she was outside and running, praying she could make it to the lights.

 Even as he ran, Deal felt the craziness of it all. Were any sane person to observe it—a wild-eyed man covered in blood pursuing a terrified woman across the grounds of a darkened estate—that observer would be perfectly justified in thinking the worst. Were that observer—a policeman, say, or a typical South Florida homeowner out walking his dog—to have a weapon in hand, there was no doubt in Deal's mind what it would be used for. Another reason why he redoubled his speed, ignoring the fiery protest in his lungs, the lashing of the banyan tendrils at his face, the sudden jolt of pain when his foot twisted on an outcrop of coral rock and doubled under him.

He went down hard—his shoulder and cheek slamming against the damp bare earth—then rolled to his feet as if it were something he'd practiced. He paused for a moment, light-headed and staggering. Bright lights pinged behind his eyes, brilliant pinpricks that danced across his vision, along with the flickering blue and yellow flashers of a tow truck somewhere out there on Commercial Boulevard.

He saw that she was struggling, too, caught for the moment in a noose of the dangling, vinelike roots of the enormous tree that spread a hundred feet out from the cottage. She was screaming for help as she fought the vines, clawing her way toward the flashing lights, and all that Deal could think of was to stop her before she got there.

He started on, gasping when the pain shot up his leg. He took a second stride, willing himself to ignore it, felt his eyes roll back, but kept going. By the third or fourth step he could bear it, and by the time she had fought loose of the vines, he was moving in a hobbling, short-legged run.

Her screaming had stopped, transformed to ragged gasps and whimpers as she ran.

"Wait," Deal cried. "Please!" Knowing even as he spoke how ridiculous the words would sound.

She was gaining ground on him now. No way he'd ever stop her before she made it to the street. And then what? Limp out to the curb, smile, explain everything to the bystanders in a calm voice . . .

"I'm a policeman," he cried then, surprised at his own words.

She faltered.

"I'm a cop, goddammit!"

She turned, uncertain. She still hadn't stopped, but it slowed her just enough.

He hit her about waist level. He'd expected more resistance, was surprised when she went down like a breath of air. Holding her was another matter, however. She was squirming wildly in his grasp, kicking, one knee driving like a piston into his chin.

The stars were dancing before him again, but he ignored them. He rolled atop her, his weight smothering her kicks, his hand clamping down on her screams. He waited until she'd calmed, then raised himself above her, trying to find her eyes with his own.

"It's all right," he said. "Listen to me. I didn't hurt your sister."

She squirmed frantically in response.

"You're Barbara's sister. I know that. It's all right." She was staring at him now, her eyes frozen wide.

"I didn't hurt her. I found her, just before you came in." She shook her head violently. "I'm not going to hurt you," he said. "I'm going to let you go now."

He took his hand from her mouth and rolled aside. She sprang up into a crouch, ready to bolt, her gaze still wild. She glanced toward the street, still a hundred yards or more away. The wrecker and its flashing lights were gone. A soft drizzle had sprung up again, and the traffic whizzed along the boulevard in a spray that would have sounded lush, even pleasant, in another life.

She turned warily back to Deal, still panting. "What did you do to my sister? What did you do to her?"

Deal shook his head, his gaze locked with hers. "She called me, about an hour ago." He swallowed, trying to bring his own breathing under control. "When I got here, she was lying there, just like you saw her."

She glanced toward the house, then again toward the highway. "Please," she said. "Let me go. I have to get help." There were sirens sounding in the distance now.

Deal held up one hand in a conciliatory gesture, reached to his belt with the other. She flinched, as if she were expecting him to produce a weapon.

"I called them," he said, holding up his tiny phone. "The EMS. They're on the way."

Surprised, she turned toward the boulevard, where the sirens were already growing louder. She glanced back at him, her expression transforming like the ripplings of some filmic special effect: fear gradually eroding, shading back into uncertainty, then into anguish.

"You called for help?" she repeated, and he watched as she internalized the meaning of his words. Maybe that's what made her an actress, he found himself thinking. Every emotion registering, molding her whole outward self.

"Go," he said, gesturing toward the cottage. "Stay with her." He felt his own anguish welling up suddenly. "Go on," he said. "I'll go out to the street for the ambulance. They'll never find the place otherwise."

The sirens were blaring now, no more than a block away. Swirls of red light slashed across the top of the huge banyan.

The woman hesitated. "Is she . . . ?"

"Just go," he said, unable to meet her gaze. And then he was running toward the street.

"She saved my life," Deal said. He watched helplessly as the attendants wheeled Barbara's body out of the airless room toward their van. The technicians had tried CPR, had tried their injections, had tried to start a pulse with their electric paddles, but Deal had seen the looks on their faces. All that effort had been by rote. They'd taken one look at the pulpy mass where the back of her head had been, at the dark scorched cave of her mouth, at the terrible burns that seared her cheeks, and they had known, as Deal had known from the moment he'd found her.

The detective he'd been speaking to nodded, not discourteous, but not sympathetic either. Did that mean he was a potential suspect, Deal wondered. A cacophony of emotions crowded his skull: grief, disbelief, outrage, self-loathing.

Barbara was gone, and nothing would ever change that. Yet his grief and disbelief were tempered by his anger, that she would do a thing like this. It was a suicide, clearly. Clear to Deal, at least. And he'd heard the coroner, a young Indian or Pakistani, mumble the same thing in his accented English to an aide a few moments ago.

But here was someone else suggesting, however subtly, that no possibility would necessarily be discounted. He would have felt an even greater sense of outrage, but the worst of it was, Deal did feel responsible, as if he were some kind of ghoulish accomplice. *If* he'd arrived a few minutes earlier, *if* he'd been gentler with her on the phone, *if* he hadn't been so goddamned arrogant and self-centered when they'd met out on the beach . . .

He realized he was staring at the dark pool of blood where Barbara's body had been and forced his gaze away, his stomach knotting. Another detective huddled outside on the screened porch with Barbara's sister. Paige Nobleman, he thought. The actress. The irony of it. Leaves Hollywood and all those made-up concoctions of violence to come to another, lesser Hollywood and find this very real and awful thing.

Deal found himself starting for the porch, felt the detective's hand on his arm.

"I'm not through here," the detective said.

Deal turned, an unreasoning anger sweeping through him.

"What else do you want?" he said. "We've been through it half a dozen times."

The detective gave Deal an appraising look, as if his response was tantamount to a confession. "My colleague tells me that Ms. Nobleman declines to press assault charges . . . "

"What?!"

"Don't get yourself worked up," the detective said. "We advised her of her rights, she declined." He shrugged, as if the matter were of no consequence. "I'd like to see your driver's license," he added.

Deal stared at him, ready to explode. "You want to give me a traffic ticket?"

The detective raised his eyebrows in a weary gesture. "Do you have a driver's license, sir?"

Deal fumed, dug in his pocket, fumbled through his battered wallet until he found the license, stuck to the back of a Publix check-cashing card. He handed it, with its photo of a weary man startled by the operator's flash, over to the detective, who glanced at it, then jotted a note on his clipboard.

Deal found himself drifting. He'd had that picture taken back in the glory days, when Janice had first come home from the hospital, her burns all tended to, turned to shining pink ribbons of grafted flesh. Had he looked that worn to her, too?

"This your current address?" the policeman asked.

Instead of nodding, Deal repeated the information aloud, clipping off each syllable. The cop looked up. "Maybe this is uncomfortable for you," he said. "Maybe you'd like to come on downtown, sit in a quiet little room for a while, go over all this again with one of my colleagues."

Deal stared at him, tight-lipped. He felt his fists clench, unclench. He wouldn't give this jerk the satisfaction.

"My very good friend has killed herself," he said evenly. "I walked into this room a couple of hours ago and found her. Now unless you have further business with me, I'd like to leave." He felt his rage rising up again, struggled to keep his voice even. "I'd like . . . to get . . . the hell out of here."

The cop stared at him impassively for a moment. Finally he screwed up his face in a "who knows" expression and handed his license back.

"You drive home carefully, Mr. Deal," he said. "We know where to get in touch with you."

Deal accepted the license wordlessly, tucked it away, turned to go. Paige Nobleman and the second detective stood together on the porch, facing his way. He hesitated, then stepped through the open doorway into the cool air outside. He was past them, halfway down the steps, when he heard her voice.

"Mr. Deal?"

He turned. There was a moment as they regarded one another.

"I'm sorry," she said.

He hesitated. "So am I," he said.

She glanced back inside the open doorway. From this distance it looked as though someone had thrown dark paint in random swatches on the stark white walls. She turned, closing her eyes briefly. She took a deep breath, then looked squarely at him.

"The detectives told me they found powder burns on my sister's hands . . . " she faltered, her jaw working hard to hold everything in check. "They told me . . . " She broke off then, turning away.

"You don't have to apologize to me," he said.

She nodded, her face still averted. After a moment, she calmed and turned back to him.

"Had you known my sister a long time?" she asked quietly.

"A few years," he said. He paused. She was waiting for something more. "We met more or less by accident. She did me a very big favor once."

She nodded. "My sister and I weren't close. I don't know if she told you . . . "

"I didn't even know she had a sister," Deal said. "Not until a few days ago."

She nodded, glancing down at the ground. "I see."

Something occurred to Deal then. "Look, Ms. Nobleman, I don't want you to have the wrong impression. Your sister and I were friends, but that's all there was to it. There were a lot of things I didn't know about her life."

She nodded, but whether she believed him or not was impossible to tell. The two detectives had moved out onto the porch together, glancing at Deal and Paige while they conferred.

"She killed herself," she said, her face twisting into an awful, mirthless smile. She threw up her hands. "My sister was so goddamned angry with me, and she killed herself." She turned to Deal. "That makes a lot of sense, doesn't it?"

Deal stared back at her. It occurred to him, despite her anguish, her exhaustion, her bafflement at her sister's act, that she was beautiful. No, more than that. Stunning. Drop-dead, impossibly, flawlessly beautiful. And yet she'd never seemed so on screen. Attractive, yes. Well above your run-of-the-mill pretty, to be sure.

But here, her face a few feet from his own, she seemed the apotheosis of female beauty. How was that possible, he wondered? Did they make up some women to seem less than what they were? *"Hey, she's not a star yet. Sly says to ugly her up a little."*

"I don't know," he said finally. "She had her moods, she was upset about your mother . . . "

He broke off when he saw her wince, then went on more gently. "But I don't know," he repeated. He was thinking of Janice now, wobbling up that flight of stairs on those impossible heels, her lipstick smeared, that thousand-mile stare in her eyes. "What I think is that nobody knows anybody, not really." He gave her a sad smile. "You know what I mean?

She was watching him closely, nodding slightly with his words.

"Why did you chase me?" she asked. "Why didn't you just let me go?" She gestured wearily at the house. "It would have all come out, sooner or later."

Deal studied her. "The cops asked me the same thing."

"What did you tell them?"

He shrugged. "I told them I didn't know."

"I was certain you were going to hurt me," she said.

He nodded. There was a pause.

"I saw the look on your face," he said at last. "I knew your sister was . . . gone. I knew what you were thinking." He broke off, shaking his head. "Maybe I really don't know why I went after you. It just seemed important to me that you understand. I had to explain. Does *that* make any sense?"

She was staring at him intently, her eyes reflecting the dim yellow light from the porch. A drizzle was falling again, spangling her hair with droplets. Earlier he'd seen her in terror, in anguish. He'd seen her on screen in other guises: tough, breezy, seductive. At this moment, she was vulnerable. Totally, utterly vulnerable.

"Yes," she said finally. "I think so." She seemed to sag then, as if the weight of the events had finally caught up with her. "Anyway, thank you for talking with me, Mr. Deal."

"John," he said as she started away. "John Deal."

He found himself fumbling with his wallet again, searching for one of his business cards. Finally he gave up, scrawled his number on the back of one of Driscoll's. "Here," he called after her. "If I

can help . . . I mean, I don't know if there's any other family . . .
with the arrangements and all . . . "

She stopped and turned, accepted the card. "Thanks," she
said. "I don't know, either. I guess there will have to be something." She gave him a wan smile then and was off, moving
unsteadily, as if she'd just suffered a beating, to her car.

Deal watched until she had driven away, then went for his
own car. The two detectives were still standing on the porch, still
talking, still staring at him as if waiting for him to grow claws and
fangs and shriek his guilt. He knew they were watching him,
could feel their eyes on his back. But he was goddamned if he
would give them the satisfaction of looking back to make sure.

**19** Deal awoke in his bed, still in his clothes, Isabel nestled against his chest. His arm, where her head lay, had gone numb, and it took him a moment to ease it away without waking her. He sat up, swinging his legs over the side of the bed, still groggy with sleep. He'd been dreaming, and it took him a moment to sort things out. It was just growing light outside, which meant that he couldn't have slept for long.

Just moments ago, he'd been a film director, sitting in a chair that swiveled at the end of a huge crane, looking down at the death scene in Barbara's house. Only it had been Paige Nobleman kneeling over her sister's body, her face twisted in anguish.

The tableau was that of the famous shot from the Kent State massacre, the coed looking up from her fallen comrade, and Deal the director had been calling out film imprecations: "Cut. Print. Wrap," but no one was paying any attention. Janice was there in her tart's getup, her face a mad sprawl of lipstick, huddled in the corner with the two detectives, who scribbled notes furiously as she shouted, pointing accusations at Deal, who hovered in his silly chair. Driscoll seemed to have been there, a surly grip, maybe, as was his old friend Homer the Dwarf, who had been running about like some lunatic court jester. It was when Deal realized that he

107

was strapped into the chair, and that the thing had begun to whip about on its mount like a car from a carnival ride, that he came awake.

He shook away the memory of the dream, turned and put his hand on Isabel's shoulder, then bent to press his face against her tousled hair. Her little-girl smell—shampoo, and sleepy flesh, and some indefinable essence of innocence—was a necessary elixir, and he found himself lying that way for several minutes, as if inhaling her very goodness.

If she hadn't been there, he wondered, would he have been able to find the will: Stand up, Deal, move into the bathroom, face the wreckage that your life has become.

He stood under the shower for what seemed like hours, the hot water pounding on him until it became a hypnotic roar in his ears. He would not read the paper, he thought, he would not turn on the television. He could not stand one more iota of sadness. He could not.

And then there was a tapping at the shower door, and he opened it to find Isabel standing there with her nightgown around her ankles, her shy, sleepy smile turned up to him. "Wanna be with you, Daddy," she said, holding out her hand. And he smiled, and drew her inside, feeling that maybe, just maybe, he could endure all this after all, and he was grateful for the water that hid his tears.

**20** To Mahler, who had been watching the weekend edition of the morning news show with an ever-increasing fascination, ever since the words "Miami" and "incredible story" had caught his attention, the entire proceedings seemed surreal, some kind of colossal, ghastly joke.

Just coming awake, he'd been confronted with any number of angles of the remains of the "Miami Freeway Bandits," as the press had dubbed them. A trio of thugs who'd robbed and killed half a dozen tourists in the last month, they'd been making national headlines ever since they'd shot a Canadian woman, left her dying in the middle of the freeway with her baby strapped in the back seat.

Now, it seemed, it was over. There had been a series of mug shots worthy of any post office wall, interspersed with other, more vivid images: pools of blood on a darkened street, bodies covered with sheets, more bodies being trundled into a series of meat wagons. A local news standup with the mayor, another with an embattled-looking police chief. "We're saddened, of course. But we're happy it's over."

Mahler found the phone at his bedside, punched in a number.

"Tell me this is all a dream," he said when the connection was made. "Tell me it's just a coincidence, it's some other Chinese tourist."

"What dream?" the voice on the other end replied.

"Turn on your goddamned television," Mahler said. "Look what they're talking about in Miami."

"Don't have to turn on television," the voice said calmly. "Know all about it."

"Jesus Christ," Mahler said, groaning. The weekend version of Joan Lunden was staring into a big monitor on her network set. The monitor displayed a live shot of a huge man with vaguely Oriental features. *Big Daddy Lipscomb meets Mr. Moto,* Mahler thought. The man was standing on a brightly lit beach, a pair of coconut palms forming a waving X behind him.

"Mr. Chin," the female host was saying in a loud voice, "how does it feel to accomplish something that the entire police force of a major American city has been unable to do?"

The big man stared back at the screen as if he hadn't heard. A hand reached into the picture, fiddled with something at the big man's ear. Mahler heard fierce whispering, watched the network host squirm.

Finally the big man seemed to understand. He shrugged, his face impassive. "Am being very good fortune," he said in atrocious pidgin English. "My good friend discover them all. One, two, three." He made fierce jabbing motions with his hands.

The host winced, but she was game. "Mr. Liu-Chou was an expert in martial arts, I understand."

The big man stared blankly for a moment. Then, as if there were some light-years' delay in the transmission of her words, he nodded soberly. "Is knowing the computer very well, Liu-Chou."

It took the weekend host a moment, but she managed. "Well, sadly, your companion, Mr. Liu-Chou, was not so fortunate as you have been. What do you have to tell other Chinese citizens who might be planning to come to Miami?"

More fierce whispering. The big man looked puzzled, then seemed to comprehend. He turned back to the camera. "Renting a big car," he said solemnly. "Big red Lincoln."

Mahler switched off the television as the scene cut away to a commercial.

"Tell me he's not yours," he said into the telephone.

"*Ours,*" the voice said. "Everything fifty-fifty on this deal."

Mahler sighed. "It's true, then?"

"Sure, is ours," the voice said. "Pretty good, huh?"

"Tremendous."

"I mean, sound like a dummy, got better English than me."

"Now that's an accomplishment," Mahler said.

"English here better than Chinese there," the voice said, rising ever so slightly.

"Okay," Mahler said. "You've made your point."

"Anyway, you worry about nothing," the voice said.

"That's me," Mahler said. "See a few bodies strewn over the pavement, I tend to overreact."

"Is local hero now. What more you want? Perfect cover. Do job, get key to city the same time."

"What if something goes wrong?"

There was a silence on the other end, a major inhalation of breath, an impatient release. "One thing about Chinese," the voice said. "Something to understand. No matter what. Beat. Shock. Cut one thousand times. Never say anything to anybody."

"This guy?" Mahler said. "He's pretty tough. Is that what you mean?"

"Is of Hung Mun," the voice said. "Once of Hung Mun, never talk. Die first."

"Whatever that means," Mahler said.

"Means go back to sleep," the voice said. And then the connection broke.

"I am thinking that I know you," the little man said, peering at Gabriel over the glare of the propane lantern he'd pulled close between them. He'd been working on a snag in his fishing reel, had finally cleared it, guided another shrimp onto his hook, dropped it back down off the pier into the water.

Gabriel shrugged. "I come here sometimes." He gave his own fishing rod a shake—the rod he had borrowed from a man who would no longer need it, that is— and glanced down into the murky water as if he knew what he was doing. He had in fact fished, more than a few times, with his grandfather, back in Thailand, but that had seemed more ceremonial than anything else.

His grandfather, originally a seafaring man from the Chinese province of Fujian, had refused to eat anything they'd pulled from the foul-smelling canals of Bangkok. "These are not fish," he would tell Gabriel haughtily, tossing whatever they had pulled up back. "And that is not water," pointing at the scum-laden surface beneath them. Puzzling words for an eight-year-old boy. But then his grandfather had always been a strange one.

Gabriel glanced about the deserted fishing pier, a former bridge that had been shorn in two, was comforted to see that the

broken roadway opposite them was empty. It would make things
that much easier.

The sundered halves of road paralleled a much newer causeway that arched high over the bay waters a half-mile to the south
of them, but it was still early, the sun yet to climb from the ocean
to the east, and only one pair of headlights inched silently along
the new bridge from the mainland out to the island and its parks
and beaches. To the west, the sky reflected a hint of dawn to
come, but the tall buildings of the city were still decked in artificial light, their towers winking red warnings that reflected in the
waters almost to where he and the little man sat, at the end of a
road to nowhere, tending to their lines.

"Not here," the little man said, shaking his head. "Somewhere
else."

Gabriel shook his head. "I don't know you," he said firmly. The
fact was, the little man reminded him in an uncomfortable way of
his grandfather. The slight build, the shock of white hair, the insistent, intrusive stare that would not let you go. Even though this
one was Latino, with a healthy dose of Indian, there was a certain
resemblance to his grandfather's swarthy Oriental features.

"I will think of it," the little man said. He tapped the side of
his head and smiled. "Once it is inside here, it always comes out."
He cackled. "Sooner or later."

Gabriel shrugged. The international brotherhood of madness,
he thought. His crazed grandfather, who would take him to the
banks of the Bangkok canals, their only refuge from that hovel of a
home, where they would sit, overwhelmed alternately by the stench
from the garbage scows that drifted by, then by the sickly-sweet perfume of flower barges piled high with cut blossoms on their way to
market. They only pretended to fish, while the old man chattered
endlessly in the unfamiliar Minnan dialect, filling Gabriel's head
with tales he only half-understood, most of them spinning the fabric
of a glorious, impossible past, before, as he was always reminded,
the Communists had come to drive them from their homeland.

Gabriel turned to the little man, gesturing back down the
abandoned roadway. To get to this place, you could only drive so
far. You came around a barrier at an entrance far out on an island
that was likely locked up in foul weather, and drove along a road
that marched on pilings over the bay and had started to crumble

and crater at the urging of the sun and salt water until you were a mile out from any land and had reached another barrier, this one welded fast. There you were forced to walk another quarter-mile or so to the place where the road fell away into darkness and, presumably, the most worthy of the great fish lurked.

"You have a very great car," Gabriel said. The shape of the man's limousine nosed against the welded barrier glowed vaguely white in the distance. Beside it loomed the darker shadow of the truck that Gabriel had borrowed from the same man who had provided him with his pole for fishing.

The little man gave his cackling laugh. "It is mine for as long as I use it," he said. "I am just the driver of that machine."

Gabriel nodded as if it were news to him, working carefully. "You're a chauffeur, then."

"At eight o'clock I am a chauffeur," the little man said, glancing up at the sky. "Right now I am a fisherman."

Gabriel raised his chin to recognize the man's cleverness. More and more like his grandfather, he thought. He wondered briefly what tragedies, if any, might have befallen this one. Like his grandfather, this man had the look of a person starved for understanding, for the barest glimmer of companionship.

In his grandfather's case, perhaps such cravings had been understandable. If the tales he told were to be believed, his grandfather had been a dashing figure in his prime, no fisherman where the seas were concerned, but a merchant sailor, and finally a gunrunner, a Chinese pirate with a red bandanna to cover his closely shaven head. At times, even a dagger clenched in his teeth.

"We were the only Chinese who did not fear the sea," his grandfather would proclaim, thumping his bony chest with his aging fingers, no bandanna, no knife, no boat, a pathetic figure on the bank of a stinking sewer, a thousand miles from his home. Still, he told the stories. He did not fear the sea, he insisted, and he had not feared the men who did, especially the cowards hiding behind a red star and the fear of living a life on one's own behalf. A group of those men had come one night, expecting to find Gabriel's grandfather, who had taken up the work of supplying arms to the small pockets of long-suffering loyalists in the distant mountains beyond Zuangping.

His grandfather had, by good fortune or bad, depending upon

how one interpreted it, stolen away to the docks of Xiamen, to supervise the offloading of several crates of rifles made in Russia, shipped to Japan, and brought by fishing boat from Taipei. When he came home at dawn, he found his family slaughtered: his parents beheaded, his wife hacked to pieces and thrown to the alley dogs, his two sons with their brains dashed out against the door stone, his fourteen-year-old daughter given the torture of one thousand cuts and left for dead. None had talked, that much was clear.

His grandfather had fled Xiamen that morning with his daughter, her wounds bound and packed with what herbs and medicines he could find, had cradled her in his arms inside a crate in the stinking, airless hellhole of a junk's cargo hold for twelve days and nights, and, miraculously, she—the woman who would become Gabriel's mother—had survived. With nothing but his words to soothe her pain and fever, he held her fast until they'd rounded the horn of Asia and come to Bangkok, to join the thousands of other Chinese refugees in the place they'd called home ever since.

How many times had Gabriel heard it, each time the account growing more fervent and lurid, until it would have been impossible to take it for truth, unless you were to come home and find your mother undressed for her work, plunging a needle into the flesh of her arm, between her toes, wherever she might find a vein, and you could trace those scars that crisscrossed her body like some drunken mapmaker's misplaced tracings.

"Put-together Girl" the other Asian girls at Jack's American Style Bar called her. As if she'd been made up from random scraps of flesh. But her face, save for one long line that traced the furrow of her brow, was unmarked, and lovely, and her breasts were larger than was usual among Asian women, and, perhaps most importantly, she had inherited something of her father's brazen disdain.

Until the dragon had consumed her, she had been a favorite of the American GIs who came to Thailand—and to Jack's—for rest and recuperation, in increasing droves as the Vietnam war heightened. Some of them called for the Put-together Girl, and some even called her by her name. But still they called, and often. Maybe there was something in her scarred body that comforted as well as excited them, that gave them hope, those men who were likely to return to their jungle war and fly into scraps themselves,

Gabriel thought. But that was just a thought and one he'd come to long after he'd left Bangkok.

"We're lucky to have this place to ourselves tonight," the little man on the other side of the lantern said, and Gabriel roused himself to nod his agreement. He was wasting time, he thought, and yet the past seemed to lay some spell upon him.

He glanced around their deserted spot. There was really no point in telling this little man that the gate at the island entrance had been closed and blocked, was there? Nor that there *had* been one other fisherman trying his luck a bit closer in toward shore.

Instead Gabriel said, "But where are the fish?" Thinking as he spoke the words, how many times had he asked his grandfather the same thing?

The little man laughed. "They will be along." Gabriel felt a chill hearing the words, his grandfather's familiar reply.

His grandfather, who had told him other stories, tales of mystery and magic, at the same time less terrible but far more strange. Of Mazu, the little girl who died to save her fisherman father at sea, and whose spirit lived on, to come to the aid of shipwrecked sailors everywhere. Of the *Tiatong,* the one possessed by the spirits of the departed, and the *Fashi,* who listened to their strange-tongued discourse and translated the messages for the living.

Once his grandfather had taken him deep into the Chinese quarter of Bangkok, where they stood on the curb of a narrow street and watched, amid clouds of incense, the yearly procession of the *bai-bai,* a pagan ceremony much older and far beyond the ken of the Tao, of the Buddha: crowds of men bearing strange godlike figures aloft on divans, bands of flute and cymbal players fore and aft, and most disturbing of all, the two messengers from the King of Hell, a tall thin man on stilts, all in white, and a short fat man in black, so round and full he seemed ready to burst.

The pair surrounded Gabriel and buffeted him back and forth, waving their arms, squawking in their strange language like cranes, until he screamed for help and his grandfather waved his arms and the two finally went on their way. Though no words passed between him and his grandfather, Gabriel knew why he'd been chosen by the pair.

His mother, fair-skinned, and lovely, until the drug had taken her beauty, even her very self, away. His father the huge black man the GIs called Sergeant Snow. His bar. His women. His drugs, which came across the border from Burma in the form of opium to be transformed into the drifts of white powder that sustained so many American troops and gave the man his name. The big man had never acknowledged Gabriel as his son, had never so much as given him a kindly glance, but his mother told him the truth.

"So you cut the trees," the little man was saying.

Gabriel roused himself again, saw that the light was growing now in the east, that the looming shape of the truck he had borrowed had grown into an orange immenseness there by the limousine, that the big letters that explained its function were clear, even at this distance.

The little man was waiting for some response, staring at Gabriel as he turned down the feed on the gas lantern between them. As the artificial light fell away, a shadow seemed to cross the little man's face, transforming his features momentarily, and Gabriel felt another chill.

"Right now I am a fisherman," Gabriel said.

The man cackled and his face rearranged itself, and Gabriel felt reassured. Nothing had changed. Not really.

"It is the way you must think about it," the little man said. "When you work for them, you might be theirs, but when you do what you want, you are yours."

Gabriel nodded. It was growing light, and he had wasted enough time. He turned to the little man. "Your work is not so difficult, though?"

The man shook his head, agreeing.

Gabriel kept his voice casual. "And you meet many interesting people."

The man shrugged. "Some rich people. Some famous people." He smiled. "Some good people." He tapped something in his pocket. "The lady I have now, she is one of the good people."

Gabriel glanced at the limousine again. He had the car now, and he needed just one more thing. If he were lucky, it would come to him easily. If not, he would have to take measures, and he hoped that he would not have to. "Is she famous?" Gabriel asked.

"She is an American actress," the man said. "I suppose that she is famous."

"And she stays at a fabulous hotel?" Gabriel asked.

The man shrugged. "She did. Then she wished to move. She was not happy there."

Gabriel nodded. That much he knew already. "The rich are very difficult to please," he said.

"It wasn't that," the little man said. "She wanted someplace to be that was more comfortable, more like . . . " He broke off to think of the proper word.

"A home?" Gabriel ventured.

The little man smiled. "Exactly. A home. She was feeling of great distress, you know. And she was wanting a home."

"Your home?" Gabriel asked, feigning surprise.

The little man cackled. "No, no. Of course not. She is a famous actress, after all. I was taking her to a little hotel. One place I know about not even so far away. My friend from Santo Domingo has. She is much happier there." He reached into his shirt pocket and withdrew a Polaroid photograph, extended it to Gabriel.

Gabriel held it close to the dim lantern. A small hotel, its fanciful bands of stonework and bright colors shadowed by some glass and steel monster in the background. The actress standing on a patio, one hand trailing on a balustrade, a pool tiled in a black and white checkered pattern just behind her. She had managed a smile, but her eyes were saying something else. Beside her, half a head shorter, stood the little man, chauffeur's cap cocked back, delighted that this good and lovely person had placed her other hand on his shoulder. One neon letter, an "R," part of a neon sign from another era, in the upper right-hand corner of the shot, the rest cut off at the margin. One dark blurred hump at the picture's bottom—most likely a Santo Domingan thumb.

"What is the name of this hotel?" Gabriel tried.

The little man looked at him, almost sadly it seemed, and shook his head. "I mustn't say," he told Gabriel.

Gabriel nodded, as if he understood. "It's all right," he said. "This will do," he added, mostly to himself.

"I have it," the little man said, at the same time. He was pointing at Gabriel now, his face a mask of excitement. "I am sitting here thinking, 'A certain goodness is in this man,' and then I remember. The television. Those people who tried to kill you and your friend. The robbers!"

Gabriel stared back at him, expressionless. The little man so pleased to have remembered. And then his expression abruptly shifted. His smile fell away, replaced by puzzlement as he glanced again at the big orange truck, at the strange contraption that angled out from behind it.

"But you don't work here," the little man said. "It said you were from China. You were coming here to . . . " He turned back to Gabriel, a question on his face.

"To fish," Gabriel said. He had tucked the photograph into his own pocket. In the same motion he leaned swiftly forward, focusing all his might into the point of his fist, into the knuckles that drove like rock against the man's frail chest.

The little man's eyes widened sightlessly, his mouth forming an unspoken "O," his breath rushing away.

Gabriel took him by the hair as his head fell forward, drew his arm back in an instant, sent another blow, a piston's invisible movement, to the man's temple. Freeze the heart, freeze the head, he thought, clutching the slumping man by the folds of his shirt front. The little man would have felt little pain, not much more than an instant's surprise. Gabriel knew no more merciful way.

Hardly how his grandfather, who'd been too foolish—or too brave—had left this world. His eyes pleading, his hands clawing toward the surface of the filthy water as he sank, the stones in his pockets, the massive bricks tied to his bound feet, the weight pulling him forever down. Two of Sergeant Snow's thugs standing at the bank until his grandfather's face had disappeared, until a festering garbage scow had passed over the spot and its wake had wiped the water clean.

Gabriel had stayed hidden in the bamboo thicket where he'd watched it all, until long after the men had gone, until the sun had gone, and the night-feeding insects had bitten him into submission and his weeping had finally stopped forever. He found a soggy scrap of flower fallen from a barge at the shoreline and tossed it out into the middle of the water where he thought was the proper place, and watched it sink, and then walked home. He had been ten years old before that night. After, he had had no age.

He stood, pulling the little man's arm over his shoulder as if he were a friend who had overindulged, then kicked the lantern, and the tackle box, and the fishing rods, one of which had begun to buck with something alive, into the water below. The lantern winked into darkness with a hiss.

He walked back toward the barrier, hardly conscious of the weight of the little man at his side, or of the sound of his shoetops dragging over the rough concrete that had once been a road.

Gabriel paid scant attention to the work that was required now, feeding the last of the branches at his feet into the maw of the hopper. He had had little difficulty in starting the big truck's engines, or in operating the massive grinder tethered at its rear. The language stamped on the machinery might be strange, but its levers and buttons spoke a universal language.

The machine whined with every chunk of wood he fed it, roared and spat a pulpy mulch into the truck, layers and layers of shredded tropical wood already beginning to steam and reek in the early morning heat: striations of green leafy banyan, of feathery Australian pine, bold cordovan streaks of mahogany, spikes of Brazilian pepper, and the broken tendrils of a pencil tree, weeping its deadly white sap down the lip of the tailgate. On the top of the pile he noticed what seemed to be a shoe, but he didn't think that was possible. By the time he had finished with the last of the branches, that apparition had vanished.

When it was over, he unhitched the grinder and backed the truck to the edge of the abandoned causeway. He found the lever that raised the bed and pulled. The shredded cargo cascaded out, most of it plunging into the water past a clamor of wheeling, screeching gulls, some of it drifting in a fine scree like a rain squall driven by the morning breeze.

The tide had gone to work before he'd finished, had hitched the chipper back to the truck, tossed the truck keys into the water. He saw, as he turned the limousine around, that what hadn't gone under right away was already streaming off in bands that were headed out to sea. He paused, thinking of it as ashes being spread, and wondered for a moment if the goddess Mazu might be appeased.

And then, thinking briefly of his mother, and of the man who had been his father, and finally of the old man who called himself a pirate, he drove the limousine away.

"Hell of a night, John." Driscoll was shaking his blocky head in commiseration. He swallowed the chunk of Cuban toast he'd been working on, washed it down with the last of his coffee. A green-aproned waitress wearing a hair net came by to give him a refill before his cup had hit the saucer.

That was one thing about having breakfast on *Calle Ocho,* Deal thought. No ferns, no frills, no fooling around. People came to the *Rincon Norteno,* the Northern Corner, to eat.

The waitress eyed Deal's plate uncertainly. *"Es problema? Quieres otra cosa?"* She'd scaled her Spanish down to Deal level, wanting to know what was wrong, if he wanted something else. He managed a smile, picked up a forkful of eggs, shook his head. She nodded and bustled off, he dropped the eggs back on the plate. He'd been hungry when he ordered, still was, in fact, but the moment he'd start for the food, the images from the night before would rush back upon him.

"You think this is your fault or something?" Driscoll said, watching him.

Deal glanced up at him. Driscoll had his no-nonsense face on, was pouring an inch or two of sugar into his coffee. He was trying to think of the right response when Driscoll went on.

"Like, this lady who saved your life once, as you put it, you might have said something different to her on the phone that night, like maybe if you'd got to her place a couple minutes earlier it wouldn't of happened?"

Deal was about to admit it, say yeah, I guess, something like that, when Driscoll held up his big paw to stop him.

"Let me tell you something, my friend. You remember twenty, twenty-five years ago, while the Republican Convention was going on out at the Beach?"

Deal nodded. That was Driscoll, a story for every occasion.

"Yeah, well, I was still in uniform then, and me and my partner, guy name of Ray Robertson, we're on the way out to help keep the Huns off Tricky Dick and Tricia, like every other cop in the county, when we get this call: there's some jumper on top of the County Courthouse."

Driscoll shook his head at the memory of it, went on before Deal could cut in. "So we have to turn around, go down to the old tower, ride those ancient elevators that take forever, climb a little catwalk up to the very top, it's hot as shit because it's the middle of the summer and they don't air condition that part of the building, of course. But anyway, we finally find the door the guy's jimmied open and look out, and sure enough, there he is, Cuban guy in his early twenties, sitting on the edge of the parapet in the middle of about fifty tons of buzzard shit, because that's the only other living thing that's been out there for about ten years, and this guy is giving us this pissed-off look like who in the hell invited us to the party, right?"

Deal nodded. It wouldn't have done any good to do anything else. He could get up and walk away, or erupt in spontaneous flame right there in his seat, robbers could storm into the place, make off with the till, the coffee machine, the green-aproned waitress, it wouldn't matter. Driscoll was intent.

"Of course, by this time we have received a little background on the matter. The guy out there is of the gay persuasion, he's still living at home, him and his mother get along just fine, but his old man has come to the realization that his son's macho index is seriously out of whack."

"Driscoll . . . " Deal began.

"So naturally the old man called him in for a discussion and you can still see where the kid's face is swollen up from this little talk: couple of black eyes, lip all busted up, nose over sideways," Driscoll shook his head again, "just a real pretty picture."

He held up a finger then. "Which is compounded by the fact, as we come to find out, that the kid has dropped a bunch of acid and is higher than a very large kite." Driscoll leaned across the table. "You can grasp this, can't you?"

"Very clearly, Vernon."

"So we try moving out onto the ledge after this guy, but it makes him understandably nervous, not to mention the fact that buzzard shit is extremely slippery and we're looking to skate right out into thirty floors of air if we're not careful . . . " Driscoll broke off, raising his hands in a gesture of helplessness.

"So?"

"So I'm suggesting to Ray, why don't we just wait in the doorway where there's a nice draft, decent view out over the bay, pretty soon somebody with a better idea is going to show up to help, when my partner figures that we should talk to the guy, get inside his head, you know, convince him this is not the way to deal with his problems."

The waitress came by, hit Deal's coffee, gave him another look about the eggs, but he ignored her this time.

"So Ray starts in like, 'Hey asshole, your mother's down there on the street, your sisters, all your friends. Is that what you want to do, splatter yourself all over the sidewalk in front of them because you can't handle your problems?' or words to that effect."

Deal stared in disbelief.

"Hey," Driscoll said, "maybe Ray saw it in a movie or took a psychology class or something, I don't know. The point is, he goes on like that for a while, figuring that he's going to shame this guy in out of buzzardland, and all of a sudden the kid just bursts into tears, puts his face in his hands and bawls like a baby. I'm thinking maybe Ray is a genius after all, I can just sneak out there and put a comforting arm around the kid and we'll all go home together . . . "

Driscoll broke off, a quizzical expression on his face.

"And," Deal said.

"The 'and' is, I'm about two steps out along the ledge when the guy stops crying long enough to glance over at Ray and say 'Fuck you' in some kind of Spanish and kick himself right off of the side."

Driscoll gave his characteristic shrug. "What I will never forget," he said, "is all those people down there screaming, running for cover like there was an atom bomb coming down." He pursed his lips. "I guess in a way it was. Turns out his mom and sisters *were* down there, after all."

He stopped then, lost in the memory, lifted his coffee cup absently.

Deal shook his head. "It's a terrible story, Vernon. But . . . "

"I'm not finished," Driscoll said, putting his coffee down. "The point I'm trying to make has to do with Ray."

"Ray," Deal repeated.

"That's right. Because this whole thing shook Ray up pretty bad. He'd been having a rough time of it anyway. His old lady had left him a couple of months before, he had a shitpot full of bills, he's trying to figure out where he made his wrong turn in life, then this happens. Two or three weeks later, he starts telling me how he's having dreams, this kid hanging onto the ledge by his fingernails, Ray is stomping on his hands until he screams and lets go, takes a header to the sidewalk . . . "

"Wait a minute," Deal said. "Did your partner get in trouble over this?"

"Naw," Driscoll said. "There was an inquiry, of course, but I didn't bring up what Ray said to the guy." He shrugged again. "I didn't see the need. But Ray couldn't get it out of his mind. 'I did it to him,' he started telling me. 'I might as well have pushed him off the side.' Didn't do me any good to try and convince him otherwise."

"So I'm Ray, and Barbara is this guy who threw himself off the County Courthouse," Deal said. "Where does that get us?"

Driscoll made a noncommittal gesture with his hands.

"So what's the point? Ray finally goes for counseling, Deal should too? I don't get it, Driscoll."

"Well," Driscoll said, "Ray did seek help, as a matter of fact. He contacted Doctor Smith and Doctor Wesson, had an intimate conversation with them. He hadn't called in for a couple of days, I was walking up the stairs of his apartment to see why, when it took place."

Deal stared at him as it sunk in. "Jesus Christ, Vernon."

"The *point* is, that it wasn't Ray Robertson's fault that kid took a header off the buzzard perch, and it wasn't my fault or any-body else's fault that Ray Robertson redecorated his place with the inside of his head. The *point* is," Driscoll thumped the table with one of his thick fingers, "you got troubles of your own to worry about. Barbara hadn't done what she did last night, she would have done it some other time and it wouldn't have had a damn thing to do with you. She had big-time problems, Johnny. You were just a blip on her screen."

Deal stared at him for a moment, then turned away.

"Go ahead," Driscoll said. "Grieve for her. But don't start thinking this was your fault."

Deal stared out at the traffic on 8th Street, already bustling, never mind it was still early on a Sunday morning. The kind of morning where he ought to be in bed, cup of coffee on the night-stand, Sunday paper strewn all over the place, Janice at his side doing the crossword, maybe a chance he could distract her for a little fooling around while Isabel watched cartoons in the den. That wasn't asking for the moon, was it?

And Barbara. What had she wanted? How much would it have taken to make her content, to allow her to want to wake up in the morning, at least? Was it her job? Her love life? Some weird chemical, or the lack thereof, in her brain? Some or all of that taken together and then your mother dies and your only friend pisses you off so bad you decide to teach him and the rest of the world a lesson once and for all? He supposed that was the way it worked, but something seemed wrong.

He forced himself from his thoughts and turned calmly to Driscoll. "She didn't do it, Vernon." The words were out before he realized he was going to say them.

"Excuse me?" Driscoll had turned back to his neglected break-fast, had a sausage patty speared on his fork.

"That's what's bothering me," he said. "Barbara. I just can't believe that Barbara killed herself."

"Is that right?" Driscoll said. He took the sausage down in a gulp.

"This detective I was telling you about," Deal said. "He doesn't think she did it, either."

"What makes you think so?" Driscoll said. He'd cleaned his plate, was eyeing Deal's plate now. "You going to eat those eggs?"

Deal pushed his plate across the table. "The way he looked at *me*, for one thing," Deal said. "Like I was a suspect."

"That's what cops do," Driscoll said. "It's their nature. It doesn't necessarily mean anything." He took a sizable forkful of Deal's cold eggs.

"Listen to me, Driscoll. A minute ago, you were giving me a life-and-death sermon, now all you care about is your breakfast."

"A minute ago I was worried you were going off the deep end. Now I see you're just deluded."

"It's not funny."

Driscoll sighed, put his fork down. "A cop gives you a fishy look, that means Barbara didn't kill herself?"

Deal shook his head. "He took me through it a half-dozen times: what I was doing before she called, who I was with, what I did when I got there . . . but the way he was going over the details, it was like he was fishing for the slightest discrepancy . . . "

"Sounds like SOP," Driscoll said. "Anyway, the guy already called me. He's not on your case."

Deal gave him an astonished look. "This detective called you? Why didn't you say anything?"

Driscoll shrugged. "I'm telling you now," he said.

"Jesus Christ, Driscoll." An old guy with an unlit cigar in his mouth glanced over from his place at the counter and Deal lowered his voice to a hiss. "How do you *know* he isn't on my case?"

"Giverty?" Driscoll laughed. "I know Buzz Giverty from the time we used to drive a patrol car up and down this street right here, before he joined the white flight up to Broward." Driscoll nodded out the window that gave onto 8th Street. A low-rider had pulled up to the light, its windows smoked to obsidian, the bass from its throbbing speakers pushing enough air to rumble the plate glass at Deal's elbow. "I told him the whole thing, how you met Barbara in the first place, what you told me about her mother and sister and all . . . " he broke off to signal the waitress for more coffee, then turned back ". . . and that you're basically the squarest, most law-abiding citizen that it has ever been my pleasure to rent an apartment from." Driscoll opened his meaty palms on the table, resting his case.

"I guess that's a compliment," Deal said. He considered things a moment, then turned back to Driscoll. "But the point is, he seemed to think there was something worth following up on."

"Giverty's just doing his job. The ME says it's a suicide, it's a suicide."

"That ME's just off the boat. He could hardly *pronounce* suicide," Deal said.

Driscoll paused, giving Deal a look of concern. "Something does occur to me," he said finally.

"What's that?" Deal said.

"That you're doing just what I was talking about earlier."

"Come again?"

"This whole guilt thing," Driscoll said. "You don't want to accept that Barbara did herself in because that gets you all screwed up thinking you could have prevented it." He gave him a look. "So if Barbara didn't kill herself, you're off the hook."

Deal stared back, dumbfounded. "Terrific, Driscoll. You should forget the private eye business, go into psychiatry."

Driscoll raised his hands in innocence. "I'm just trying to figure out why you're having these feelings."

"Goddammit, Driscoll. Even her sister said it. Barbara just wasn't the type. She was too pissed off to kill herself."

Driscoll feigned surprise. "Aha, now *there's* your proof."

Deal stared at him for a moment, then turned away. "Forget it, Driscoll. You're right. She blew herself away, let's forget about it and eat." He raised his hand to signal the waitress. "What do you want," he said over his shoulder. "Couple rashers of bacon? A roast pig? How about a side of beef to go with that?"

Driscoll pulled his hand down, gave him a weary look. "Look, Deal, somebody gets killed, there are usually reasons. Robbery, jealousy, fit of rage, stuff like that." He ticked off items on his fingers as he continued. "We know that nothing was taken from Barbara's place. Do you have any knowledge of anyone who was angry with her, anyone who would have wished her harm?"

Deal turned back to him. It was true—all logic argued against his feelings. "No," he admitted. "*She* was angry with her sister."

"But the sister—this actress with a life, and money, and all that—she wasn't angry with Barbara?"

"It didn't seem like it to me." Deal stared at him.

"Okay," Driscoll said. He threw up his hands in surrender. "I don't have anything to do. You want to leave Isabel with Mrs.

Suarez a couple more hours, I'll ride with you up to Broward, take a look at what they got."

Deal looked at him. "It's Sunday. Is anybody going to be around?"

Driscoll laughed. "You think the ME's office takes the weekend off? That's when the crazies go into high gear." He sighed then, as if he were recalling the weight of thirty years of such weekends.

"Let's do it, then," Deal said, and the big man heaved himself up out of his chair.

"Real pretty," Driscoll was saying, flipping through the photographs the medical examiner had provided. He dropped the stack back into the manila envelope, handed it to Deal with a dour glance.

Deal caught a glimpse of the first of the stack, had to turn away. There were three of them in a tiny third-story office that suddenly didn't seem to have enough air in it for breathing. Block walls painted beige, industrial carpet worn to the thickness of a handkerchief. Deal checked the window, but he knew it was the kind that would only open with an axe. He fought the feeling of claustrophobia, glanced out at the intersection below, empty except for one sun-blistered hawker sitting on a stack of Sunday papers piled high at the curb.

"Suicide is a terrible thing," the ME said. It was the same earnest young man from the night before—Mekhtar, according to his desk plate. The way he said it, the way he sat, his lips pursed in a disapproving way, it made Deal want to open the window by tossing him through it.

Driscoll motioned at the envelope in Deal's hand. "You mind if I borrow these for a while?"

Mekhtar's eyes widened. "Mr. Driscoll," he said. "I am truly sorry. As you are no longer . . . " He broke off, trying to avoid any conception of insult. He shook his head in consternation. "Yes. This would be a thing that we could not allow. The property of the department as it is being. Yes, I am very sorry about that."

Driscoll stared at him for a moment, astounded by the locution. He glanced at Deal, then swept his gaze about the office, considering things. Something seemed to catch his attention and he made a gesture out Mekhtar's open office door. "Fenderman's finally out of here?"

Deal followed the ex-cop's gaze. Across the hallway was the entrance to a much bigger office. He got a glimpse of a couple of flags behind a barren desk, dark-paneled walls, some mostly empty bookshelves. Even Deal had heard of Irwin Fenderman, until recently Broward County's Chief Medical Examiner. He was a flamboyant figure, always on the scene where foul play and any measure of celebrity converged, face in front of the cameras, ready to offer an opinion of what had happened on the spot. The run-and-gun school of journalism loved him, but he'd been less than popular among his peers in law enforcement.

Mekhtar too followed Driscoll's gesture, nodding. "Oh, he is gone, all right." He turned back, pointed at the computer screen on a metal credenza behind him. "He is gone, everything is gone." Deal saw a series of green lines crawling up an otherwise blank screen.

"What are you talking about?" Driscoll said.

"The files, the computer program, everything," Mekhtar said, gazing mournfully at his blank monitor. "The chief installed our system, you see." He glanced up at Deal. "And when he had his . . . " he hesitated, searching for the right words ". . . *falling out* with the city council, he decided to take what he felt was his." Mekhtar threw up his hands.

Driscoll nodded. "It sounds like Fenderman," he said.

Deal placed the photographs back in the manila envelope, returned the envelope to the file and handed it to Mekhtar. "I guess they should've given him the raise he wanted."

Mekhtar smiled in agreement. "Yes. Things are in much disarray here," he said. He glanced at Driscoll, holding up the envelope. "I am sorry about the photographs. Perhaps if the Chief were still here, something could be done . . . "

"Forget it," Driscoll said, motioning to Deal.

"And I am sorry about your friend," Mekhtar added as Deal brushed by him.

They were in Driscoll's Ford now, waiting on the light at the intersection Deal had looked down upon a few minutes before, Deal still so steamed about Mekhtar and his eagerness to dismiss Barbara's death as a suicide that he'd almost forgotten.

"You wanted these?" Deal said to Driscoll. He reached into his jacket pocket, withdrew a wad of photos he'd palmed from the coroner's envelope.

Driscoll glanced over, saw what Deal was holding. "Well, I'm a sonofabitch," he said, his scowl rearranging itself into a grin. "I'm proud of you, Johnny-boy."

Deal shrugged. "I've been spending too much time around you, I guess."

Driscoll clapped him on the shoulder, tucked the photos into his own pocket. "Things get tough in the construction racket, you come see me."

Deal nodded absently, still focused on Mekhtar. Anal-retentive little guy, it probably made him feel better to account for every messy death as quickly as possible. On the other hand, maybe it was an unavoidable consequence of the job. Given the murder rate in South Florida, there were plenty of demands on his time. Who needed to manufacture a case when you needed a computer to keep the victims straight? And, he had to admit, there didn't seem to be much to go on here, not if logic was your measuring stick. Just Deal's vague hunch, her estranged sister's chance comment that Barbara was too angry to commit suicide. He turned away from his thoughts then, fighting the sneaking suspicion that the real reason he was up here, running around Broward County on an otherwise beautiful Sunday afternoon, was because the alternative was to be at home, face to face with the calamity of his own life.

He rolled the window down, no chance of a power window in a car that Driscoll owned, noticed that the newspaper hawker he'd seen from above was heading their way, a copy of the Broward paper held before his chest. From the vantage point of the third floor, the guy had looked like a surfer: cordovan tan, sun-bleached hair, T-shirt, baggy trunks, and rubber flip-flops—a kid picking up a few bucks while the tide was slack. Down here, though, Deal could see the guy was pushing fifty, his face a mask of creases, his eyes leached by the tropical glare to the color of concrete.

"*Sun Sentinel,*" the guy said in a rasping, singsong voice. "Get your *Sun Sentinel.*" He had to be talking to them, but his eyes were locked on something far away. "MORE RAFTERS WASH ASHORE," Deal read the inch-high headlines. A color photo of bodies tumbling in the surf, more people who'd died trying to get to the promised land. More people who'd died.

"Hold it," Deal said as the light turned green. He put out a hand to stop Driscoll, dug into his pocket with the other. He held out a bill for the guy, took the paper.

"Go," Deal said to Driscoll.

Driscoll hesitated. "That's a ten you gave him," he protested.

The hawker stood there uncertainly, turning the bill over and back in his hands.

"Keep it," Deal said.

The guy looked at him. "You want some more papers, Mister?"

"Go," Deal said again, and finally the ex-cop hit the gas.

They drove in silence for a few blocks, Driscoll obviously troubled as they cruised down Las Olas past a long string of fashionable shops, past a sidewalk cafe jammed with Sunday brunch-eaters, then into prime residential territory that bordered the Intracoastal Waterway.

"That guy you gave the money to," Driscoll said finally, his eyes on the road ahead. "He's just gonna go get juiced."

Deal nodded. "So I saved him a couple hours in the hot sun."

Driscoll glanced over at him, started to say something else, then gave up, shaking his head. At the next light, he swung off Las Olas, heading down a tree-lined street that alternated antebellum-style mansions with modern glass and stone estates, each place sitting on an acre or so of jade-green lawn.

"Detective Giverty lives out here?" Deal asked.

Driscoll snorted. "Giverty lives in a crackerbox down in Davie," he said. "Place on a couple of acres, where he can keep a horse. That's one reason why he wanted to move to Broward. So he could keep a *horse.*" He rolled his eyes.

"Then what are we doing here?" Deal said. In one way it was all right, cruising aimlessly along the streets of a strange city. Pretty Sunday afternoon, pretty houses. But why wasn't he with his wife, his daughter, on some happy family outing, burgers on the beach, everybody arm-in-arm on Daddy's day off . . .

"I thought we'd go see Irwin Fenderman," Driscoll said, breaking into Deal's thought. He tapped his jacket where he'd put the photos. "See what he thinks of these."

"You think there's something in them that Mekhtar doesn't?"

"Let's just wait and see," Driscoll said. He pointed up ahead, then abruptly swung the Ford through a break in the lushly planted median. They crossed the opposite lane and entered the long driveway of what looked like an abandoned house. In contrast to the neatly manicured lawns on either side, this one had run riot: the St. Augustine grass rose up in knee-high clumps, wild redleaf vines dragged at the low-lying branches of live oak and ficus seedlings, a lamppost with its glass blown out leaned like a drunk fighting into a gale.

"Welcome to the Fenderman estate," Driscoll said dryly, using his jaw as a pointer.

Deal stared up the cratered driveway, a pale tongue of crushed limestone pocked with outposts of weeds and bahia grass, which circled around in front of the house. The place *had* to have been something, once upon a time. A big two-story white clapboard with a green-shingled gabled roof, lots of gingerbread trim, and broad overhangs to ward off the sun. On one end, the place was anchored by a massive brick chimney with a number of flues peeking from the top. On the opposite end, the easternmost, was a glassed-in tower with a widow's walk. Deal didn't doubt that you could actually see the ocean from up there. It looked like a shore house picked up by a big wind off Chesapeake Bay and dropped perversely down in the tropics.

On the downside, it didn't look as if the place had been painted in a dozen years. Mildew had turned the eaves nearly black, and elsewhere the sun, salt air, and rain had eaten at the paint in big bites. Some of the shingles had come away from the main roof near the widow's walk, exposing the crumbling underlayment. A long tongue of tar paper had worked loose and lolled out over one gabled end, working in what breeze there was like a listless tongue. Still, the old character of the place shone through, and Deal found himself automatically running repair estimates through his head. Whatever it would take would be worth it.

"Looks like the servants took the week off, doesn't it?" Driscoll said, grunting as the Ford bottomed out in a pothole.

"You've been here before?" Deal asked.

"A few times," Driscoll said, guiding the Ford around a fallen limb that jutted into the roadway. "Fenderman used to throw a big bash once a year, big political fundraiser."

Deal gave him a look, trying to imagine Driscoll as a guest on the political fundraising circuit.

Driscoll caught the expression on his face. "I worked off-duty security," the ex-cop said.

Deal shrugged. "I was just wondering."

"Yeah," Driscoll said. He pulled the car to a stop in the weed-pocked parking area near a fountain, an impressive double-decked affair with carved figures scalloped at its edges and a leaping dolphin for a main font. Improbably, the thing was operational, a steady stream of water spurting up from the dolphin's mouth.

As Deal got out, something hit the ground near his feet. He glanced down to find an emaciated cat crouched in the gravel, eyeing him intently. He sensed another movement and glanced up at the fountain, brim-full of greenish water. As his eyes adjusted to the glare, he realized that what he had taken for stone carvings were actually cats: maybe a dozen similarly marked creatures perched on the stone ledges in various poses.

When Driscoll's door slammed, the cats sprang away, vanishing into the overgrown shrubbery like smoke.

"Fenderman knew how to throw a party," Driscoll was saying, oblivious to the cats. "That whole yard'd be full of cars," he said, sweeping his arm out over the untended grass. "We'd fill that up and have 'em up and down the street all the way out to Las Olas."

Deal nodded. All the humps and swales in the vast yard, there could be whole cars still hidden under the grass. "So what happened?" he said, following Driscoll toward the front steps. A pair of stone lions guarded the entrance, more or less: one had shifted off its base and had slid snout-down into the gravel drive. The other had lost half its face to a blow of some sort: cement teeth in a snarl gave way to a tangle of rusted wire mesh waving in the air.

"I dunno," Driscoll shrugged. He pushed at an unlighted doorbell, paused. He pushed again, then turned to Deal. "You hear anything?" he asked. Deal shook his head.

Driscoll studied the bell button, picked at it with one of his stubby fingers. Finally he gave up and hammered at the door with the side of his fist. The sounds echoed hollowly inside the place. Driscoll turned back to him, ready to fill him in.

"When Fenderman's wife died—she came from money, by the way—that's when he started to go weird. Not to say he wasn't colorful before . . . Hey, what the shit!"

Driscoll cried out as a sudden flood of water cascaded down upon the stones of the entryway. Deal threw up his hands instinctively, dancing back down the crumbling steps. Another wave of water descended, breaking over Driscoll's head, soaking him altogether. Deal backpedaled into the graveled parking area and stared up at the pristine skies, dumbfounded by what he saw.

A wild-eyed older man in shirtsleeves, bow tie, little wire-rimmed glasses, the picture of a dithery scientist, leaned from a second-story window of the Fenderman house, clutching a yellow plastic bucket in his hands. He glared at Deal, who must have seemed out of range, then turned his attention back to Driscoll, who stood gasping, water still pouring off him.

"Vernon . . . " Deal shouted, but he was too late. The wild-eyed man, whom Deal had recognized by now as Fenderman, upended the yellow bucket. Driscoll glanced up in time to take the next wave squarely in the face. He staggered backward, under the cover of the door overhang, swiping wildly at his face.

"Get out," Fenderman shouted. "Get off my property." He glared at Deal, hand suddenly raised to hurl the bucket down. Deal sidestepped as the empty bucket caught a gust and sailed wide, bouncing harmlessly off the side of the fountain.

When he looked up again, he saw that Fenderman had ducked inside and was leaning well out of the window once more, a new bucket in his hands, green this time, little sloshes of water splatting to the steps below as he angled for another bombs-away on Driscoll.

"This could be boiling oil," Fenderman shouted. "You think about that the next time." He nearly lost his grip on the bucket and had to claw wildly to hold it. Deal thought for a moment that he was going to tumble out of the window, bucket and all.

Finally, Fenderman regained his balance, steadied himself against the frame. "Who do you work for?" he shouted at Deal, who was backing away, his palms upraised. "The mayor?"

Fenderman's eyes blanked out as the sun reflected off his glasses. Now it was a mad prophet up there, a man with glowing silver disks where his eyes should have been, the bucket upraised like an idol about to be dashed to the ground.

"Did Mayor Bream send you over here?" Fenderman shouted again. He shaded his face with one hand, and his eyes turned abruptly into eyes again.

Deal shook his head, staring up warily. Even though the paint on the siding had faded into a dingy gray, the sun reflected off it brutally. It was hard to keep a fix for long.

"Are you from the papers, then?" Fenderman fairly shrieked. "Is that it? You want *my* side of the story?" He laughed, a short lunatic's bark, then heaved the bucket Deal's way. Deal danced back as the water thrummed across the hood of Driscoll's Ford.

"Are you finished now, Irwin?" It was Driscoll. He'd emerged from the protection of the overhang and stood swiping at his face, calling up at Fenderman. "Is the show over?"

Fenderman hesitated, then glanced down at Driscoll. He leaned out further, squinting, grasping the window ledge with both hands. A smile broke across his features. "Is that Vernon? Vernon Driscoll?" His voice had changed quality entirely. The mad prophet had become an elderly schoolmaster, surprised by the visit of a favorite student.

"We going to cut the crap, Irwin? That's all I want to know." Driscoll stared up at him, soaked, water still dripping off his chin.

"Mayor Bream didn't send you, did he?" Fenderman asked, still cautious.

"Irwin . . . " Driscoll said in an aggrieved tone.

"Well, why didn't you *say* it was you?" Fenderman said testily. "I'll be right down," he added, and ducked back inside the window.

"Interesting," Fenderman said as he fanned through the photographs Driscoll had handed him. "Who handled the case, one of those dreadful sand jockeys they've been hiring?"

They were in Fenderman's study now, a room jammed with mismatched furniture, unpacked boxes overflowing with books and printouts, and enough battered computer equipment to start up a secondhand store: a dozen or more processors were stacked precariously in a corner, some trailing plugs and ripped wires.

There was a row of monitors lined haphazardly nearby, one with its screen shattered. In another corner was an enormous tangle of cable and wire, mysterious little boxes and switches dangling within the strands here and there as if the whole thing had been deposited by some huge technological spider.

The back wall was a bank of windows that overlooked the broad Intracoastal and the pristine lawns of the estates opposite Fenderman's place. Fenderman had seated himself at a cluttered library table, where he'd cleared a swath among tumbled books and papers, some dirty dishes and pizza crusts. There was no air conditioning, no fan, no open window. The place smelled of mildew and damp clothing, of locker rooms that festered in school basements, of old books dissolving in soggy cartons, of rotting mushrooms and wet concrete. Deal knew it well—it was the scent burned into his memory from trekking through scores of ruined houses after the hurricane had pounded Miami.

But this place was well north of the damage zone. There'd been no shingles lost to storms here, no rain driven through the jalousies by freight-train winds. This rot came from the inside. A pigsty with a million-dollar view, Deal thought, his skin prickling.

Driscoll finally looked up at Fenderman from under the towel he was using to dry himself. Fenderman had taken it from a closet, delivered it without apology.

"The name was Mekhtar," Driscoll said. "He's a Pakistani."

"What the hell's the difference," Fenderman snorted. He glanced at Deal. "You ever see what those people bring in for lunch?"

Deal stared back, beginning to have some sympathy for Mekhtar. He tried to imagine what it must have been like, working for Fenderman. Likely the whole office staff was still celebrating the man's departure.

Fenderman turned his gaze to Driscoll. "I sense your partner finds my remarks offensive, Vernon."

Driscoll shrugged, tossed the towel over the back of a wicker chair, startling a big gray cat who'd been sleeping there.

"Don't worry about it, Fenderman. He votes in Dade County."

"Well, in *that* case," Fenderman said, giving Deal an ingratiating smile as he went back to the photographs, "he's welcome to his opinion."

He peeled one of the damp photos from the back of another,

then took a closer look. "Mmmmm-mmmmmm," he said, tapping it with the stem of an unlit pipe he'd come up with. He glanced up at Deal again. "Take a look at this, young man."

Deal gave him a look, took a step closer. The photo Fenderman was holding was a close-up of the lower half of a face—*Barbara's* face, he thought.

"You see these discolorations here," Fenderman said, using the pipe stem as a pointer.

Deal willed himself to stare at the dark streaks that radiated outward on her flesh. Only the fact that he could not see her eyes allowed him to hold his gaze there.

"They're what you would call powder burns," Fenderman was saying, his voice as disinterested as a don's. "From the muzzle flash. That's *one* thing."

He slipped the photo back and flipped rapidly through the packet. "Then there's *this*," he said, extracting another shot.

Deal took a quick glance, caught sight of Barbara's sightless eyes, her matted hair, the dark fan of blood that spread out from her skull.

Fenderman was watching him, his jaundiced eyes glittering behind his glasses. "How long have you been a detective, if I might ask?" His voice was chiding, faintly amused.

Deal stared back. Gray stubble on Fenderman's chin, stains on his outsized teeth, knots of untrimmed hair boiling out of his nostrils. The man looked like something that had crawled up out of a drain.

"Have you always been an asshole," Deal said, "or did it just happen after you got old?"

Fenderman blinked a few times, his jaw working.

"He's not with the department, Fenderman," Driscoll said. "He's a civilian. Leave it alone."

Fenderman's gaze switched from Deal to Driscoll, then back to Deal. It took a moment, then something seemed to register with him.

"Aha!" Fenderman said, triumphantly. "You *knew* her." He actually smiled at Deal. "*That's* why you're here." He touched his forehead with his fingertips and nodded. "My apologies, sir."

"You were going to say something else," Deal said, fighting back his anger. He gestured at the picture, but kept his gaze averted. Nothing could make him look at it. Ever again.

Fenderman had turned to Driscoll. "Not a good idea, Vernon," he said. "Involving an injured party in an investigation. You should know better than that."

Deal started forward, but Driscoll pulled him back. "I'm not on the force anymore, Fenderman. This is a private matter. You want to help us out, or you want to sit there and choke your chicken?"

Fenderman, apparently oblivious to Deal's anger, seemed to think about it for a moment. Finally he shrugged. "Well," he said primly. "Since you've gone to all this trouble." He laid the photo he'd been holding on the table, then went searching through the pack again.

Deal exchanged looks with Driscoll, who made pacifying motions.

Fenderman found more photos that he was interested in and laid them on the table beside the first. He glanced up at Driscoll. "You say they found gunpowder residue on the woman's hand and her fingerprints on the weapon itself?"

Driscoll nodded. Fenderman took it in, turned back to the photos, shaking his head as if something bothered him.

"You've seen enough shooters in your time, haven't you, Driscoll?"

Deal watched Driscoll closely. The ex-cop nodded, his eyes opaque.

"So you know what happens when someone swallows a gun," Fenderman continued.

Again Driscoll nodded, grudgingly. His face seemed to be aging as Deal watched.

A cat had leapt up onto the table to pick its way through the crusted plates. When it put a paw on one of the photographs, Fenderman scooped the animal up with one hand and tossed it casually aside. The cat bounced off a carton, landed on its feet, skittered away silently.

Fenderman turned his gaze on Deal then. It was a helpful expression, even solicitous. "We're not talking about the effects of the bullet itself, you see. It's the force of the explosion which propels it. Try to imagine these hot gases, caught in a small chamber, in this case the oral cavity, searing, raging, trying to expand at an incredible rate and searching for some outlet, any outlet, eye sockets, nasal passages . . . "

"You asshole," Deal said. He was moving toward Fenderman when Driscoll caught him.

"Just hold your horses," Driscoll said, wedging his body between the two of them. Deal wasn't going to hold anything, except Fenderman's neck, but banging into Driscoll was like colliding with a pillar of lead.

"It's what he likes to do," Driscoll said, his voice harsh in Deal's ear as they struggled. "He likes to piss people off."

"Well, he gets the blue ribbon from me," Deal said, still trying to fight his way around the ex-cop.

"You need to calm down," Driscoll said. "Now."

Deal registered the tone of Driscoll's voice and finally relented.

"You okay?"

Deal pulled himself back, straightened the front of his shirt. "Sure," he said. "I'm fine."

He shot a glance at Fenderman, who sat calmly at the table, pipe poised before him now, watching the two of them like a professor contemplating an interesting problem.

"There's the possibility she didn't do it, that's what you're saying," Deal said to Fenderman after a moment.

Fenderman glanced at Driscoll before nodding. "As I was attempting to point out, if *she* were the one holding the gun in her mouth, the trauma would have been much worse, characteristically speaking." He pointed at one of the photos with his pipe stem. "One could theorize that this woman was shot while she was trying to pull away from whomever held the weapon. If her mouth were open and she were trying to scream, let's say, that would account for the facial burns you see there and the absence of secondary trauma elsewhere . . . "

"We get the picture," Deal said, feeling his hands clench.

Driscoll gave him a last admonishing glance, then turned to gather up the photographs. He squared them on the table and replaced them in his jacket pocket, then turned back to Deal.

"How about the gunpowder on her hands, her fingerprints on the gun?" Deal said.

"What do you say, Fenderman?" Driscoll said.

Fenderman raised his pipe. "She could have been forced to hold the weapon by someone much stronger."

"Or the killer could have put the gun in her hand afterward, squeezed another round out the window," Deal said. He yearned to be out of this awful room, to draw in a breath of decent air.

Fenderman shrugged his assent.

"The point is," Deal continued, "there's a chance that Barbara didn't put that gun in her own mouth. There's a chance that somebody else did it, somebody who wanted to make it look like suicide."

Fenderman raised his hands as if to say it was a reasonable guess.

Deal nodded slowly, taking it in. Finally he turned to Driscoll. "The shame of it is, we had to come to this dickwad to hear it," he said finally.

Fenderman's mild expression did not change.

Driscoll turned his gaze to Fenderman. "Well," he said, giving his customary shrug, "he's a smart dickwad. Aren't you, Fenderman?"

"None finer," Fenderman said. He raised his pipe stem in acknowledgment, gave Driscoll a little bow.

He was still beaming at them from behind the filthy table as they made their way out.

Deal sat with his head back on the headrest, his eyes closed, trying to bring his breathing under control. Driscoll was behind the wheel, easing them down the potholed lane to the street, when there was a strange whining noise and a sudden slamming of the brakes.

"Jesus Christ!"

Deal opened his eyes to see Driscoll clawing at his shoulders, where one of the scrawny fountain cats had leapt from the back seat to attach itself.

"Fucking-A!" The ex-cop caught the whining cat by the scruff of its neck and flung it out the open window in one motion. He glanced at Deal, then turned awkwardly, trying to see over the seat. "Any more back there?" he grumbled.

Deal looked, too, saw nothing but a couple of beer cans and a wadded-up sack from a fast food restaurant on the dusty carpet. Part of the corner of the sack had been torn away, probably what had drawn the cat into the car in the first place. He looked up at Driscoll, who stared back with something approaching apology in his expression.

"I'm sorry about Fenderman . . . " he said, letting his voice trail off.

Deal waited a moment before he spoke. "You already suspected something funny, didn't you?"

Driscoll's mouth twitched, a little tug at one corner of his lips that was a tiny reflection of his typical shrug.

"Why didn't you say something back at the ME's office?" Deal persisted.

Driscoll stared at him. "What I *thought* is one thing," he said. "And what good do you think it would do to get into a debate with a guy like Mekhtar? He saw the same photos I did. Hell, he was on the *scene*. Guy like him, he's just concerned about saving face. Once he's made up his mind, it's all over." He nodded back in the direction of the house. "So we came out to see Fenderman and now we have some corroboration."

There was a silence as Deal considered Driscoll's words. That was one of the differences between them, he supposed. Deal the hothead, an all-or-nothing kind of a guy, one moment everything is copacetic, the next he hears something and he's ready to take off some heads. Then there was Driscoll, the methodical one. He might have a hunch, but he'd check it three ways from Sunday before he acted upon it.

"Okay," Deal said, feeling the steady idle of the Ford beneath them. "So forget Mekhtar. But somebody may have killed Barbara. What are we going to do about it?"

"We could still give it a shot with Giverty," Driscoll said. "But there's no apparent motive, nothing to make him doubt it's suicide. He could always say she changed her mind at the last instant, tried to pull away . . . " Driscoll broke off when he saw the look in Deal's eyes.

"Hey, it's possible," he said.

"She didn't do it," Deal said stubbornly.

Driscoll threw up his hands. "Okay, I've got another one for you: Even if Giverty was to think it was murder, guess who his prime suspect would be."

Deal met his gaze. "That's not funny, Driscoll."

"I'm just telling you how cops think. Somebody kills themselves, who knows why? There could be any one of a million screwed-up reasons and none I know of makes any sense when you get right down to it. But murders happen for obvious reasons, nine times out of ten. You want to figure out who killed somebody, you consider the simplest possibilities first."

There was a soft *thump* as the cat Driscoll had flung through the window reappeared on the hood of the car. The thing sat down in front of the windshield and began to groom itself, pausing now and then to glance through the window at them.

"Love and money," Deal said.

"What's that?"

"Something you said to me once," Deal said. "The two simple reasons why people kill other people."

"Yeah, so?"

"I was just thinking about Barbara, that's all. She wasn't in love, or at least I don't think she was. She'd have said something."

"How do you know that?" Driscoll said.

"I just do," he said.

"You seem to know an awful lot," Driscoll said.

Deal paused. "You trying to piss me off, Vernon?"

Driscoll shrugged. "Force of habit," he said.

Deal turned away, still angry.

"Say it's true, no involvements whatsoever," Driscoll said. "That leaves money."

Deal laughed mirthlessly. "She was a hostess at a family restaurant."

Driscoll nodded. "But her old lady just died. Maybe there was an estate."

Deal looked at him skeptically. "Nothing that I know of. Her father had been dead a long time. Barbara said the hospital bills had taken just about everything that was left."

Driscoll nodded, watching the cat toy with one of the windshield wipers. "That leaves the sister."

Deal glanced at him. "What do you mean?"

Driscoll shrugged. "You said they weren't getting along."

"I said Barbara was pissed at *her*."

"You think there's only one side to these things?"

"Come on, Driscoll. Paige Nobleman got to Barbara's house after I did. She thought *I* had killed Barbara. She was running for her life when I caught her."

"Uh-huh," Driscoll said. "She *is* an actress, as I recall."

"What are you trying to say? That she shot Barbara and then hid someplace, waiting for me to show up?"

Driscoll sighed and turned to roll up his window. "I dunno. Still, it wouldn't hurt to have a talk with Paige Nobleman," he said.

Deal sighed.

"Something bothers you about that?" Driscoll said. He was distracted, staring at the cat, which had somehow snagged one of its claws in the rubber windshield blade.

"First, I had to convince her I hadn't hurt Barbara," Deal said. "Now we're going to show up and tell her she's a suspect." When Driscoll didn't answer, Deal followed Driscoll's gaze out the windshield. The cat was trying to jerk its paw loose from the wiper, but the blade would only move so far before the spring mechanism slammed it back against the glass.

"Yeah," Driscoll said at last, "but that's not what's worrying me."

Deal glanced at him, curious. "Okay. What *is* worrying you, Driscoll?"

Driscoll pointed. "I'm sitting here wondering who's going to go out there and get that goddamned cat loose from my car."

"Beyond ecstasy, huh?" the lady cop was saying. She dangled a Baggie full of bright green pills the size of M&M's before Paco's eyes. "Do the nasty all night long behind these, can you?" Her face seemed as hard as the West Texas landscape he'd left behind.

Paco shrugged, trying to suppress a grimace. His hands were cuffed behind him and the top rung of the wooden chair they'd sat him in was digging painfully into his back. How the world turns, he was thinking. Come a thousand miles, find yourself right back in the same little interrogation room, only it was a hard-assed woman with an LAPD shield grinding him this time.

"And this," the cop said, nodding at several powder-filled bags on the battered table before them. "You don't have to tell me what this is."

Paco managed a tough-guy shrug. "Fuck you," he said through battered lips.

The lady cop laughed, shot a glance at her partner, another woman, who stood at Paco's shoulder, patting the truncheon she'd been using on him in her palm.

The first cop reached for one of the bags, dipped her hand inside, raised two powder-coated fingers to her nostrils. The sound she made snorting it up sent a chill down to Paco's toes.

"How about you?" she said, offering the bag to Paco, wiping her nose with the heel of her hand. Her face had flushed red, and moisture glittered at the corners of her eyes. She was pretty good, he thought. Or she was using the real thing.

Paco shook his head. The cop gave him a sympathetic look. She tossed the coke back on the table, shook the Baggie of pills in front of his face. "Maybe a couple of these, then?"

Paco shook his head again, and the cop laughed. She gave a signal to her partner, who snaked an arm around his throat and squeezed. He felt her fingers go up his nostrils, jerk his head back savagely.

His mouth was open, gasping for air, and the first cop was on top of him, forcing pills down his gullet as if he were a goose.

"Now let's see what he's got," he heard the first cop say, and felt a hand jam roughly against his crotch.

He had about as much chance of getting an erection as a palace eunuch, he was thinking, when the sound of a cellular phone's chirring echoed across the set and Cross's voice boomed, "Cut!"

Paco felt the hands leave him, heard one of the actresses mutter an obscenity. He spat out the candy pills, brought his head down, his eyes away from the bright spots at last, twisted his shoulders to ease the pain. What had ever possessed him to suggest inserting this scene into the action, he wondered? He should have just gone along with the script as it had been written, let the dealer character he was playing sweet-talk the cop who'd pulled him over and take her right there roadside, in the back seat of the car.

He glanced into the darkness that surrounded the brightly lit set, watched Cross in his tall canvas-backed chair speaking earnestly into the phone. ". . . middle of a shoot, goddammit," Paco heard, before Cross saw him staring and turned to shield his conversation.

The two actresses lounged on the neighboring set, a mocked-up car Paco was supposedly driving when arrested by two lady motorcycle cops. The first cop was jittering about, tapping her nails on the hard Ford paint, sucking furiously on a cigarette, further proof to Paco's mind that the stuff she'd hit from the bag wasn't just baby laxative. The second cop stared off into the nether reaches of the North Hollywood warehouse they were using, spinning her truncheon idly, her leg cocked up on a fender. He could see that the leather jodhpurs she was wearing had been cut out at the crotch.

Any other time, the sight might have sent toots of steam out his ears. Deliver her to the facility dressed like that, he'd have popped the cuffs on his wrists quicker than the Bionic Man could've. He'd been fairly bionic as it was, the first several days of his new acting career, four years of pent-up urges having pretty much carried him through all manner of undignified sexual behavior. On top of that, the very baseness of the actions on the set had appealed to Paco's innate appreciation of depravity, and he'd been able to carry on just fine without recourse to the range of drugs most of the other actors made use of. It was also some comfort to him that the editing techniques he'd had a look at were able to make even the most jack-rabbity of his encounters seem endless when the various angles were spliced.

But now, it seemed, he had finally spent everything he'd stored up in the Permian Correctional Facility, and Cherise, who was playing the first cop, had quickly expended her store of winsome entreaty.

The phone call, in fact, was the second interruption of the morning, and a welcome interruption for Paco. He had already stopped the shooting once, pleading for a short break to get his head together.

"Your head?!" Cherise had fairly shrieked, all her cop brass glittering. "Who gives a shit about your head? That's not the problem here."

Maybe it seemed that way to her, Paco thought, trying to console himself, wondering how anyone could blame him, the temperature in the place somewhere in the fifties at best, even under the lights, Cherise now about as come hither as a longshoreman. He glanced down at his offending member—nobody'd bothered to zip him up again—and wondered if it might be worth it, just take a couple tiny snorts from the bag, get through this scene, go right back to the straight and narrow where drugs were concerned, at least . . .

. . . but broke off, knowing he was trying to bullshit the chief bullshitter himself, a couple snorts and he'd be off to the races, have Cherise doing things with him and the other cop and the truncheons and the motorcycle, stuff even she had never dreamed of, soon enough he'd be back in the facility, and there'd be no cutout crotches in any of the jodhpurs there, you could bet your Tony Lamas on that.

He glanced up then, cutting short his reverie, about to call for someone to come and zip up his pants, for Chrissakes, when he noticed that Cross had finished his phone conversation and was walking across the set his way.

"How's it going?" Cross called to him in his hearty way. They could have been a couple of guys saying hi on the golf course, the way Cross acted.

Paco glanced down at himself, then back up at Cross, who had come to stand in front of him. The guy was rubbing his hands together, staring off distractedly at the two women like there was suddenly something on his mind.

"I'm doing all right, Mr. Cross," Paco said. "It's just a little cold in here, is all. Just give me a couple of minutes."

"That's okay, Paco," Cross said. He made placating motions with his hands, his eyes still on the actresses. "We may be putting this project on hold for the time being, anyway."

"On hold?" Paco tried to envision himself in an unemployment line.

Cross gestured at the two actresses. "How about Cherise over there? You think she looks Asian at all?"

Paco glanced at Cross, craned his neck for a better look across the set. "Asian?" Paco echoed. Cherise was probably 5'10", had red hair, huge breasts, the face of a trailer-park queen.

"Yeah," Cross said, shaking his head. "It's going to be a challenge for makeup, all right."

Paco stared up at him. "We're going to start a new film?" he said hopefully.

"We may be onto something big, Paco," Cross said.

He turned, then clapped him on the shoulder. "You're a college boy, aren't you?"

Paco was wondering what he should say when Cross continued, his gaze traveling back to the actresses, his voice contemplative. "You know anything about how the Chinese like to screw?"

"Where is Florentino?" Paige said, hesitating as she approached the limousine. She'd had to swallow a couple of times, uncertain she could still speak. In the dimly lit hotel room, with its cool currents and muted colors, she'd felt capable, as if she might deal with a world that had turned inside out.

Outside now, into a tropical midmorning that seemed to hum with energy, she felt herself wavering. Her head was suddenly stuffed with batting, her tongue thick. It was as if she were insulated from actual sensation by a thick layer of invisible foam. Even the mighty sun had become a watery disk, its heat a barely perceptible caress. She had to will herself to put one foot forward, then the next . . . it was as if she were moving through a dream, a nightmare really, where nothing made sense, where the only way to survive was to move. She had no idea whether she was moving forward, of course, but she knew that without putting herself in motion, she would be sucked into a vortex of forces that would pull her so far down she might never see light again.

Despite what she'd said to John Deal about her sister being too angry to kill herself, Paige knew that the very despair that tugged at her was the same force that had claimed Barbara. Given the chance, it would sing its siren song to her, too. Career teeter-

149

ing, lover gone, mother dead, sister a suicide . . . dear God, where did that put her on the potential-to-end-it-all charts?

Her mother was gone, there was nothing to do but accept that. Until her death, she'd been able to suppress all those ancient feelings, pretend they were just a mother and daughter "who did not talk," as if that explained something. She'd met other women, a number of them in her profession, of course, who'd become disaffected from their families. The reasons were myriad, and exacerbated by the gulf that separated life as an actor from any normal existence, but she'd taken some comfort in knowing that others had been able to survive without that mythic mother-daughter connection.

She'd even drawn some perverse strength from the fantasy that her reasons were "better" than others', reasons that she had never been able to share, of course. But with her mother gone irrevocably, she'd had to confront the truth. No reasons made up for the absence of a mother. She, Paige, had run away from the possibility of that bond a long time ago. And now there was nothing that could ever be done about it.

Then, with all that swirling in her mind, had come her sister with her mind-numbing assertion. "She's not your mother." Impossible. The sort of insult a jealous four-year-old might hurl at her older sister. But they weren't kids anymore, not by a long shot.

Paige's thoughts drifted, seeing herself catching up to Barbara outside her mother's hospital room, her sister standing grimly at the nurses' station, grimly signing the necessary paperwork, Paige sidling up to her, trying to keep her voice under control:

What had Barbara meant, saying such a thing?

"It's true," Barbara had repeated, never taking her eyes from a form in front of her.

Paige shaking her head, searching for words. Had their mother *ever* said such a thing?

"She didn't have to," Barbara had said, scrawling her signature across the form. She glanced through the wad of paperwork, then pushed everything across the counter to a nurse who sat with her gaze averted from the confrontation.

When the nurse confirmed that everything was in order, Barbara nodded curtly and started toward the elevators. Paige caught her by the arm. "Barbara, please, tell me what you're talking about."

Barbara paused, turned, her eyes icy. "She adopted you," she said. "*They* adopted you. And now they're both dead." The elevator doors opened and she shook her arm free. "So what does it matter?"

"For God's sake, Barbara . . ." Paige came after her, but Barbara whirled upon her, hand upraised, warning Paige away.

"You left me alone a long time ago," she said, venomous. "But it's all over now. There's nothing more to worry about. You can go back to your real life now," she said. "Go back to California." Then she was inside the elevator and the doors had closed . . .

. . . Paige heard the blast of a horn on the street, shook herself from the memory. Here and now, she told herself. Here and now.

Her new driver smiled, pushed himself easily from the front fender where he'd been resting. "Florentino is become sick, Ms. Nobleman," he said, extending his hand. "I am Gabriel."

She wavered then. Through the open passenger's window, she spotted the plastic Virgin on the dash, the tiny Manatees helmet dangling from the rearview mirror. Baseball and Catholicism, Florentino had happily explained to her: the two spiritual forces in his life.

She felt her hand enveloped in Gabriel's massive one. He closed his other hand atop hers and bowed. "I am pleased to be of service," he said.

She withdrew her hand—like taking it from a giant clamshell, she thought, her head still reeling—and nodded. "Gabriel," she found herself saying. "Like the angel?"

The man's face lit up behind his dark glasses. "Very much like the angel," he agreed.

She studied him for a moment, forcing her eyes to focus. From a few feet away, she'd taken him to be Samoan. Now, she wasn't so sure. His features were unusual: Mongol, she might have guessed, an Asian Cossack in a chauffeur's uniform . . . but he was so huge. And something else stirred in those high cheekbones and sallow skin, something she couldn't be sure of.

"You're not Cuban," she said.

Gabriel's smile was thin but steady. "No," he said. "Not Cuban."

She waited for him to continue, then realized he had finished with the subject. He stood with his hands crossed before him, his smile undiminished, staring at her. She felt embarrassed momentarily, as if she'd been caught prying. And she had begun to feel the heat, the press of the sun.

"I hope Florentino's all right," she said.

"Just something like the flu," Gabriel said, waving a hand. "They called me only this morning."

She nodded. The flu, she thought. Maybe that's what was happening to her. Florentino had come down with the flu, and he had passed it along to her. The flu on top of everything else. "Well," she said, "I'm pleased to meet you, Gabriel."

She started a bit unsteadily for the door then, and Gabriel was there in a flash. He ushered her in like it was something he'd been born to do all his life, and she fell gratefully into the car.

Once inside, the quiet rush of the air conditioning began to revive her. And if she'd had any doubts about Gabriel's driving ability, she soon put them aside. Though somewhat heavier of foot than gentle Florentino, no sooner had she given him the address than he had them out of the maze of South Beach streets, and within minutes they were onto one of the causeways stretching across the bay.

She sat pensively in the plush seat, wondering now if she were doing the right thing, staring out sightlessly at the coruscated surface of the water, the glitter of the sun dimmed by the heavily smoked glass, the gulls and pelicans turned to shadows, the sailboats and cabin cruisers blanked into silhouettes. When she realized that she'd chewed her thumbnail nearly to the quick, she pulled it away from her lips in disgust.

"Great," she said, staring at a drop of blood that welled up from her cuticle. "Just great."

"Excuse me?" Gabriel called through the open interior window.

"Nothing," she said. "I'm sorry," she added. "Would you mind closing that?"

She saw him nod into the rearview mirror and lean to push a button that sent the tiny window closed, but his eyes were hidden by the dark glasses. Anger had energized her. If she'd offended him, too bad. Why was she worried about everyone else's feelings all the time, anyway? It was high time she started taking care of Paige Nobleman. All these years of swimming with the sharks, and she was still behaving like some kind of wimp fish.

She saw her reflection in the mirrored glass: staring back at her was a too-thin woman in oversized sunglasses, her face drawn, complexion pasty, the lips thin and chapped, the pale blonde hair lifeless and unkempt. The woman staring back at her needed sun, rest, a bit of food, a good laugh or two. A few weeks ago, Paige had been reading for the part of an accomplished attorney. Now she could be a barfly, a harridan, swell the chorus of the *maenads* . . . or weep at a graveside, she thought, turning away from her own gaze.

She forced herself back against the seat with a sigh, ruling out any more forays into self-pity, and began to replay the real conversation she'd had earlier that morning with her mother's attorney. *Her mother,* she thought, interrupting herself immediately. Loretta Cooper. Loretta Cooper *had* been—no, strike that—*was* her mother. *Wasn't* she? Loretta Cooper had raised her, that much was fact, despite everything that had happened between them, despite the things Barbara had said, despite the gnawing uncertainty that had come to plague her. And today, she had told herself, she would do what she could do to put those doubts to rest.

Her discussion with the attorney had begun with the basics: She learned that what little cash there was—a smallish bank account and the proceeds of the sale of her mother's home—most would be consumed by the medical bills. With luck, there'd be enough to cover the funeral costs, which would be minimal. Her mother's wish had been to be cremated. No service, no interment. Her ashes to be scattered to the winds. Nothing for Paige to worry about, the attorney assured her, no hurry, she could contact the mortuary at her convenience.

That would be like her mother, Paige thought while the attorney blathered on, to be unsentimental and self-abnegating to the very end. No surprise that she wouldn't want to spend her eternal rest next to Paige's father, of course. He'd been dead a dozen years, and even though they'd continued to live together, even after the things Paige had disclosed on the eve of her departure for California, it had been at best an uneasy coexistence. She and her mother had never had another conversation that you could term intimate after that day, but still, Paige was aware of how things stood between her mother and her father. There had been a few years when she and Barbara still functioned as sisters, at least at long distance. She'd heard enough to know that something had sunk in, despite her mother's fervent denials.

"I don't know what it is," Barbara would say. "But ever since you left, what little bit they had just disappeared, Paige. It was never great, but now they're at each other's throats all the time. Or what's worse, they just circle each other, snarling, and everybody's always got a drink in hand."

And each time her sister had said those words, or passed on similar dreary news, Paige had felt a pang. She knew that Barbara, who'd barely reached her teens when Paige left, had gradually come to blame Paige for her parents' disaffection, to resent her older sister's absence from what had come to be the familial battlefield.

And it was no mystery, was it? Surely, in Barbara's mind, Paige had run off to fame and fortune, sharing very little of either, never mind the long letters to her baby sister that so often went unanswered, nor the checks her mother had always returned uncashed. It was as if Barbara had condemned herself, had chosen to tend the hearth like some Cinderella whose prince had never come.

Every time Paige had tried to explain the truth about why she had had to leave, to tell Barbara what had really happened, it was Barbara who had shut her off, who had refused to listen, who could never believe. And despite her unwillingness to believe, despite her natural resentment at Paige's fleeing the scene, which Paige could well understand, how could Barbara have said what she had said the night of their mother's death? How could hatred have grown so deep, and so venomous . . .

And then she felt it and stopped herself. That same blessed warning that had saved her all these years. A chill rushed upon her like a blast of air risen from a tomb and when she felt it, she shut down her thoughts as utterly and completely as if they had never begun. Those things had never happened. That life was not her life. Paige Cooper had ceased to exist many, many years ago. She had become Paige Nobleman, person in her own right. Her very survival depended upon it. And every time she was tempted to remember, the chill winds swept over her and warned her away from the real grave, where only rottenness and decay existed, and to draw a breath was to end her life.

Paige felt the tears began to well in her eyes and realized that she had once again been tearing at the cuticle of her thumb. Dear God, she thought, swallowing her revulsion. Next she'd be rending the flesh of her cheeks, or whipping herself with a cat-o'-nine-tails. She tucked her hand under her hip and shook her head violently, vowing to be strong, to do what she had to do. What else was there? Sit in her hotel room and stare at the walls until those terrible winds howled up through the floorboards and took her off once and for all?

So she had forced herself up, into the shower, out of the room in the South Beach hotel, which tiny though it was, seemed ever so much more human than the mausoleum where Marvin had put her. Hardwood floors. Blonde maple furniture. Oxblood tile, with matching toilet, and sink basin in the bath. Rounded chrome fixtures that looked like they'd been constructed from pieces of old Buicks and Chryslers. Things that had been new the day she'd been born, and that gave her a certain comfort even in the calamity that her life had become. When she saw Florentino, she would have to thank him for saving her. Had she stayed on in that other place, she doubted she would have found the energy to even draw the thick curtains back, much less take this little trip.

This little trip. Something the attorney had said gave her the idea. Her mother's personal effects were to be divided equally between her two daughters. Her two daughters. The attorney had been very clear on that. Paige had asked him to repeat the language of the will's codicil. Of course, the attorney pointed out, all of her mother's personal effects had been moved to Barbara's cottage when her mother's home had been sold.

Paige had felt her hand go slick on the old-fashioned phone handle. "Let me be frank with you, Mr. MacLayne," she'd said. "Is there any indication in my mother's will that I . . . " she had broken off, then finished in a rush ". . . that she and my father had adopted me?"

There had been a moment of silence on the other end and then a mildly astonished response. No. Absolutely not. Paige had been referred to by both her parents' surname and her stage name, of course, but there was certainly no mention of anything like an adoption. The attorney's voice pronouncing the word as if it were something both preposterous and shameful.

"I just wondered," she said. "I mean, I'm not sure, but something Barbara said . . . " She trailed off, feeling foolish.

"I've handled your mother's affairs for a number of years, Ms. Nobleman," MacLayne said. "Our dealings are privileged, as you must know . . . " He paused. "But under the circumstances, I'm comfortable in saying that nothing of the sort was ever made known to me."

Nor to me either, she'd wanted to shriek at him, but she'd held her tongue, thanked him for his trouble, wondering at the same time how much of her mother's pitiful estate was going to wind up in his hands and in the next instance telling herself she didn't give a damn, he was welcome to, if not deserving of, anything he got.

She'd hung up with MacLayne, cutting him off as he was launching into an explanation of the Florida statutes bearing on inheritance and Barbara's standing in these matters. Her whole family gone in a weekend, save for one infirm aunt in an Atlanta nursing home so senile the nurses couldn't promise she'd understand the message, though they'd try, what did she care about how long it might take to sort out the details of her mother's effects, and had her sister possibly made out a will, blah, blah, blah . . .

She'd called her home in Los Angeles twice, once hanging up before the second ring, the next time hanging on through a dozen rings, each one stabbing a little deeper as she tried to imagine Paul struggling to the phone, picking up on the very next ring, his voice sleepy, "Yeah, babe, when you coming home?" on the next, the next . . . She let the rings drone on until her answering machine finally reset itself. She'd hung up in the middle of her own perky recording, some mindless version of herself implying to callers just how wonderful it was to be rung up, how terrific it would be to get a message.

"We are here, Ms. Nobleman." The voice cut into her thoughts, startling her, and she blinked herself back into the real world, where Gabriel's Buddha smile mirrored itself to her through the reopened passage.

She glanced out a side window and saw that they indeed had come to a stop beneath the massive ficus that shrouded Barbara's cottage. She'd been so lost in her thoughts that she hadn't even noticed the turn off the busy street out front, the bumpy drive down the lane that twisted and turned through the overgrown trees and impossible tropical shrubbery.

Gabriel had turned off the engine, she realized. The heat was already seeping in through the door seals, osmosing through the very steel and glass as well, she felt. She'd nearly forgotten about that, how different the desert heat was from the tropics. She'd lived for so long in a place where desiccation was the threat, it was hard to imagine there being such a thing as humidity. But that's what carried it, what gave the Florida heat its special character and strength: It was like some creeping dread, she thought, and when she opened her door and stepped out, a roach the size of her thumb scuttled across her shoe top and vanished just as quickly into the cover of the fallen leaves.

"OK?" Gabriel asked. He waved his hand at the cottage, deserted behind its strands of yellow crime-scene tape.

She stood surveying the place for a moment. Somehow she'd imagined police technicians still being here, tidying up, or at least some patrolman with his feet up on his dash, keeping away the curious and the ghoulish. But that had been a foolish thought, hadn't it? Her sister had committed suicide. Who would care about the site? Who would care if Mongol hordes stormed through? What could she have been thinking of?

She gathered herself, strode through the crackling drifts of leaves toward the cottage. She brushed a veil of banyan tendrils aside, saw as she got closer that the yellow porch bulb was still burning. She saw vivid images from the night before: herself approaching that same doorway, the sudden jolt of seeing her sister's body, that man—John Deal—kneeling beside her . . . and then she'd been running, sure she was about to die herself . . .

The screen porch door gave at her touch and she pulled it open, moved resolutely to the wooden inner door . . .

. . . she was ready, she told herself. What she would see would not take her by surprise. She would not be overwhelmed. She reached for the knob and turned. And found that the door was locked.

She turned to see Gabriel at the porch steps behind her, staring in at her from behind the disks of his glasses. His smile had faded at last and he seemed only curious at her intent. She came back outside, walked around the back of the cottage, tried a door that apparently led to a kind of pantry off the kitchen. The knob gave in her hand, and for a moment she thought she was in, but the door groaned inward a fraction, then stopped. She cursed silently, and swung away from the door in frustration, stopping short when she saw that Gabriel had followed, and stood watching her with the same detached curiosity. She gave him a look, then turned back to a window, tested it with her fingers. It was one of the crank-up–style windows indigenous to Florida, four wide panes that opened out horizontally like airplane flaps when you turned the handle inside. Maybe if you pulled hard enough, she thought, the force would get the crank spinning on its own, and she actually thought she felt the bottom pane give with her effort . . . but then her fingers slipped loose abruptly and she staggered back from the side of the house.

"You forgot your key?" he said at last.

She glanced up at him, her lips nursing a nail she'd torn loose. "I don't have a key," she said, hesitating. "It's my sister's house."

He raised his head as if that explained everything. "You want to go in?" he said.

It took her a moment to understand. It was an invitation, not a question. "Yes," she said finally.

"Come on," he said, motioning her to the front of the house.

She followed him onto the screen porch, stood as he tested the front door for himself. He gave her a look, then withdrew his wallet from his jacket pocket, found something she couldn't see, and turned back to the lock.

"I should tell you something," she said.

Gabriel paused, cast a glance over his shoulder. "Your sister," he said. "Maybe she doesn't know you are coming." When she hesitated, he shrugged. "It is all right with me."

She stared at him, jimmying the lock, annoyed that he'd taken her for some kind of interloper. She took a breath, then blurted it out. "My sister's dead," she said. "She shot herself in there, last night. That's what all the yellow tape is about."

Gabriel raised his head in acknowledgment, but he did not turn to her. She might as well have told him her sister was on vacation.

"You still want to go in?" He was still working on the lock.

"Yes," she said after a moment. "I just wanted you to know. It's not very pretty."

"It is all right," Gabriel said, nodding. He turned away, did something sudden with his hands. She heard a clacking sound, then a shuddering noise as the heavy door swung inward, and she was in.

She'd prepared herself for the sight of the bloodstains, which had dried and darkened into streaks that might have been something else if she willed it so in her mind. But she hadn't been prepared for the smell. The police had switched off the groaning wall-unit air conditioner before they'd left, had cranked every window in the place down tight. What hit her as she moved inside had the force of a blow: the air, cooking for hours without release, was laden with heat and moisture; the odor that it carried was a mixture of aging plaster and paint, damp plasterboard, sodden carpet, bug spray, and sour milk, all of it underlain by the rancid tang of something left standing too long in the sun.

She reeled backward, out of the doorway, staggered out into the yard to heave until her stomach was empty, and still she could not rid herself of the feeling that she'd breathed her sister's very essence inside herself. When she was finally able to straighten, she saw that Gabriel was still standing inside the screened porch, his hands folded before him, watching with his implacable gaze.

"Maybe you want to go home now," he suggested. His voice seemed muffled, slightly distorted by the screening.

She shook her head, rummaged briefly in her purse for a handkerchief, finally gave up and wiped her chin on the back of her hand. Her legs were still trembling, but her stomach had calmed and she willed herself to move back onto the porch.

"I'm all right," she said, brushing by him. She was ready when she entered the cottage this time. Although some of the pent-up heat seemed to have escaped through the open doorway, she held her breath as she made her way across the room, intent on reaching the air conditioner before her resolve gave out. She randomly punched unlabeled buttons on the ancient wall unit until it finally groaned into life, then stood there, her face close by the dusty vents until the air that issued was cool against her cheeks and she felt that she could breathe again.

She heard the sound of the latch closing and turned to see that Gabriel was inside now, holding his undertaker's pose by the doorway. "I might be a while," she said. "It's all right if you want to wait in the car."

He answered with a shrug, his heels moving a fraction wider as if he'd settled into a position of rest. Although the room was gloomy, he was still wearing his sunglasses and she found herself revising her image as she regarded his massive, inscrutable form: not an undertaker so much as a palace guard. So be it, she thought. Despite his oddness, it was not the worst thing in the world, having someone with her in this dreadful place.

She found her way into the tiny kitchen, glanced about. There was a green-flecked Formica table with one matching chair, a gas range with a chipped top, an incongruously new refrigerator beside it. The counter held a toaster, a blender with a cloudy glass container, an empty plate with a few crumbs scattered on it.

Paige moved to the sink, splashed some water on her face, rinsed the sour taste from her mouth, dried herself on a dish towel that carried the scent of old food and grease. She felt her stomach start to rise and turned back to the tap quickly, rinsed her face again, let the water drip from her chin this time until she found a roll of paper towels tucked under one of the wooden cabinets.

There was a small window over the sink that gave a view out onto a back porch, a smaller version of the type that served as an entryway to the front of the house. She could see furniture stacked out there, a mahogany bed frame, a matching dresser, a chest of drawers, all of it carrying heavily carved rosettes and scrollwork that she suspected were really molded of plastic. There was a pale green sofa with a matching easy chair upturned on top of it, along with a Naugahyde recliner, its webbing frayed and dangling. A sheet of milky plastic that she supposed had covered the couch and chairs had worked loose and had come to rest against the screening, where a corner of it flapped in a listless breeze like a signal from a lost and dismal world.

Paige gripped the edge of the counter, fighting for strength. There had been times, years ago, shortly after she'd left home, when she was still struggling for parts, still wondering where her next month's rent was going to come from, still wondering what on earth a little girl from Florida was doing thousands of miles from home, pretending to be a grown-up actress in the most ruthless town on earth; those were times when, friendless and essentially alone, she'd felt a similar desolation and despair. But she'd been young then, and even in her darkest moments she'd been buoyed by the mindless optimism of her youth, by the gut-level understanding that she was following her dreams.

But what on earth, she wondered, was going to get her through this? Staring out at that pathetic clutter of furniture that constituted her mother's "personal effects," she felt suddenly depopulated, abruptly and utterly defenseless, as though everything that might have lent her strength or comfort had been taken.

Then something happened. She felt a wetness growing at her hips and glanced down at the counter, where she saw that water she'd spilled from the tap had collected in a pool. If she hadn't been standing up against the countertop, it might have simply dripped on over the edge to the floor. As it was, however, she stepped back from the sink to stare at the broad band of wetness that had wicked up from the counter into the fabric of her khaki slacks.

"Shit, shit, *shit!*" she hissed, snatching another wad of paper towels. She was well into blotting herself dry before she realized how much better she felt.

Anger, she thought, remembering the same buoyant moment she'd felt earlier, in the car with Gabriel. She vowed to make a note this time. If anger was the tonic it seemed to be, then she was going to stay pissed off for a very long time. She wadded the towels, tossed them into the sink, and strode back through the ruin of the living room, her jaw set. Her pants were going to dry, she was going to get through this, and she was going to find out once and for all if there was any truth to what her sister had said.

She cast Gabriel a dark look as she passed, but whether or not he registered it was impossible to tell. For all she knew, he was asleep behind those obsidian lenses.

She tried the tiny closet near the entrance, found it empty except for a raincoat, a faded golf umbrella, and a nylon windbreaker with a wrinkled hood slung over its shoulder. She swung the closet door back and moved down the musty hallway that led off the main room toward the back.

The first door she tried led into what must have been Barbara's bedroom. It was a small room, as airless as the rest of the house, but a window gave onto a pleasant if shadowy view under the spreading branches of the huge ficus in the front of the place. She struggled with the window crank, wondering if the thing were locked somehow, until she put both hands on it and the panes sprung loose with a popping sound.

The rush of air, warm as it was, made being in the room just bearable. She stood at the foot of the bed, noting the inexpensive floral spread, the mismatched rug, the pale green paint on the walls. No paintings, no prints, no posters. A chest of drawers, a small dressing table on spindly legs, exactly two small bottles of perfume—one Opium, one Charlie—on a mirrored tray, a tiny clock radio blinking 12:00 in frantic repetition. Set in motion by the breeze from the window, a flotilla of dust balls jittered over the hardwood floor beneath the dressing table.

Paige shook her head, trying to imagine bringing a man into this room, but the notion seemed impossible. She moved to the dressing table and pulled open its single drawer to reveal a scattering of cosmetics and makeup tools.

She turned away and opened the closet, which had the same musty smell that seemed to pervade the entire house. As she surveyed Barbara's wardrobe, surprisingly stylish in contrast to the decor around her, Paige wondered idly how long it would take the odor to disappear once you'd put something on and left the place.

In the top drawer of the dresser she found some costume jewelry and a silver bracelet with a chunk of turquoise that she remembered as a favorite of their mother's. There were also a few hints that Barbara had not lived an entirely nunlike existence: there was a diaphragm in a plastic case that had gone yellow with age and a small box of condoms that advertised the benefits of exotic colors. Tucked under a stack of scarves she came across a photograph of Barbara smiling, almost slinky in a red cocktail dress, her hair done in a French twist, clutching the arm of a distinguished-looking older man in a white suit. The two of them were standing on a pier that stretched out over the water toward a glorious sunset somewhere. On the back of the photo, her sister had scrawled something in pen: "Thornton and Jezebel, Key West," along with a date.

Paige hesitated—"Thornton and Jezebel," she wondered, her eyes misting over, then put the photo into her purse. She scanned the rest of the drawers quickly: panties, stockings, and socks in one, T-shirts and shorts in another, a sheer nightie all alone in the last that sent a vague wave of shame through her when she held it up to the light. She replaced the garment and left the room, sure there was nothing she was looking for in here.

The doorway across the hall led to a small bath, where Paige was surprised to find the same oxblood-colored fixtures that graced her hotel room. How could such a color have ever been popular, she found herself thinking, wandering on down the hall to the last door.

This one led to a second bedroom that seemed to have functioned as a storeroom. There was an exercise bike set up before the window that gave out onto the withered backyard, but the seat of the thing tilted forward at an unlikely angle and there was a coating of dust on the handgrips. The rest of the room was buried under a welter of boxes, each of them labeled in scrawled felt-tip pen, the same hand that had scrawled the note on the back of the photo. There were several labeled "Books—Mom," and a number of others that said "Linens—Mom." Also "Bric-a-brac—Mom," "Bath Stuff—Mom," and two that said "Kitchen—Mom," one with an oily stain spreading ominously up its side.

Beneath the box labeled "Bric-a-brac" was another that said simply "Papers," and Paige decided to try that first. She eased the "Bric-a-brac" box to the floor, her teeth going on edge at the sound of broken china jiggling inside.

The "Papers" box was heavier than she expected, and it almost fell from her hands as she wrestled it to the floor. The thing had been bound up with multiple layers of packing tape, and Paige bent her thumbnail double trying to pry it open. She was sucking her injured thumb, cursing herself silently, when she spotted an old butter knife lying on the window sill.

The tape gave easily before the knife and she lifted the flaps to find the source of much of the weight piled on top: six thick copies of the North Beach Panther, the high school yearbook, one for each of the three years she and her sister had done time in that place. Paige piled the books aside. Under no circumstances, she thought. Under no circumstances whatsoever.

In one large manila envelope just beneath the annuals was a clutch of insurance policies in her father's name, all of them long since redeemed or canceled. Why on earth would you keep such things, Paige wondered, tossing the policies aside. In another envelope, she found a wad of warranties and instructions for an array of lawn tools and household items, including a bicycle that Paige remembered getting for her twelfth birthday. Fighting a wave of sadness, she tossed that packet aside as well. There was a folder full of contest entry stubs and tickets: Publisher's Clearing House Sweepstakes, new home giveaways from the local papers, car and boat raffles, none of which had ever borne fruit; and another envelope crammed to overflowing with old photographs, many of which Paige could remember flipping through as a girl: there was the same set of black-and-white snaps of her mother and her father on a cross-country jaunt they'd taken before they had children.

Paige didn't have to look to remember: her mother in shorts and halter top, her hair done up in a modified Aunt Jemima scarf, holding onto her handsome father's arm in front of the Washington Monument, the Statue of Liberty, Niagara Falls, Mount Rushmore, the Grand Canyon. The first time she'd seen the old snapshots, she'd been overwhelmed with the romance of it all. Her beautiful mother and her perfect father living out the ideal life. The photos had seemed to embody everything a girl might want, at least in her innocent, post-toddler's mind. But that was before things had started to happen. The terrible, unspeakable things.

Paige felt a chill take her, despite the heat that filled the room, and she hurriedly shoved the photographs aside, looking for the next find. That seemed to be it for the keepsakes, however. She stared down in disappointment at the newsprint that lined the bottom of the box, then scanned the rest of the stacked-up boxes for hints of other memorabilia, but unless her sister had been less than systematic in her labeling, Paige had scanned the sum total of what paperwork her mother deemed worthy of saving.

Jesus Christ, she thought. Her mother could save phony give-away certificates and instructions for plugging her goddamned vacuum into the wall, but when it came to her kids there was nothing but some high school annuals, the testaments to the dumbest parts of their lives. She couldn't believe it. Surely there was more here somewhere. She'd find it if she had to go through every box, sort through every piece of insignificant trash that marked her mother's time on this earth.

She stood up then, feeling the stiffness in her legs from the unaccustomed posture, and gave the emptied box in front of her a solid kick of frustration. Instead of flying over the pile in front of her as she'd expected, however, the box barely moved. She tapped the side of the box again with her toe, then rocked it with the pressure of her sole.

An awfully heavy cardboard box, she was thinking, at the same time she realized that this particular carton *was* different from the others. It was much sturdier and apparently older than the others, its fibers crumbling away at the edges of the flaps. The faded logo stamped on the side touted the virtues of long-vanished Ipana toothpaste. There was a picture of a beaver holding a toothbrush aloft beside the logo, and suddenly the ridiculous jingle of her youth was running through her mind: "Brusha-brusha-brusha, it's goooooo—d for your teee—eeeth!"

As Paige bent down again, she saw something else, something that her sister's heavy scrawl, "Papers–Mom," had nearly obliterated. There, in dim ballpoint that had faded almost to nothing, was her mother's neat script: "Things to keep," it said, and Paige reached inside the box, realizing that what she had taken for an old newspaper laid in to line the bottom of the box actually formed a kind of divider.

She carefully removed the yellowing newsprint and glanced at the headlines. An ancient *Miami Daily News,* with nothing of particular importance to note, she thought, "IKE TO KHRUSHCHEV: BALONEY!" Then she noticed the date on the masthead and realized it had been published on her sister's birthday. Beneath that paper was a copy of the *New York Times,* dated nearly five years earlier. Fighting still raged in Korea. President Truman defended his dismissal of Douglas MacArthur. And though it said so nowhere in those pages, on that day, Paige Cooper, now Nobleman, had been born.

Paige lay the papers aside carefully, noting that her hands were trembling. There was one more moldering newspaper in the box, another issue of the *News,* but neither the date, somewhere in between the date of her birth and her sister's, nor anything on the front page—"KEFAUVER HEARINGS OPEN," "BOY WAITS FOR PASTOR TO LEAVE, KILLS DAD"—meant anything to her. She lay the third paper aside, meaning to scan it more thoroughly later, and turned back to the box.

With the newspapers removed, a faint aroma, some ancient sachet perhaps, rose from the objects on the bottom of the carton. She found two pairs of bronzed baby shoes, her sister's and her own, and two framed certificates from a beauty salon in Miami Beach, each with a lock of hair pressed behind the glass, attesting to the fact that she and her sister had in fact had their first cuts. Inside a yellowing envelope with a return address for a Dr. Earle Conaway of North Miami Beach, she found a paid receipt for "Delivery, baby girl: $120." Her heart had begun to thud by the time she realized that the date was wrong—the delivery referred to would have to have been her sister's.

She put the receipt aside, pawed through the rest of the loose papers there, looking for some similar envelope, but though she went through them twice, there was nothing. There were a pair of slim baby books with cardboard covers, one for her and her sister, each with the pertinent details filled in: date and time of birth, city—Miami for herself, North Miami Beach for her sister; their height and weight, hair color and eyes; the requisite entries for first word, first step, etc., along with a few photos, of birthday parties, beach trips, new puppies, and the like. To her mother's credit, each book seemed equally well kept.

Paige sat back on her heels with a sigh. Why was she doing this to herself? She could see the proof of the matter before her: the four of them at some tourist trap in Central Florida, posed behind a silly cutout sign that made them all appear to be buxom bathing beauties: her and her sister, her mother, and her father, Paige with her father's dark features and her mother's fair hair, Barbara with her mother's round face, the same pinched look passed from mother to younger daughter already. This was a family, Paige told herself. Or at least it had been. Why had her sister said otherwise?

She flipped the books shut and added them to the pile she'd begun with the newspapers, then scanned the few things that were left. Two baptismal certificates, one Presbyterian, the second Methodist, marking a cataclysmic argument between her parents that Paige could still remember; two kindergarten registration forms (Paige could still feel the splinter she'd picked up, sliding on her bottom across the wooden floorboards of that cavernous room—her first day at school and her mother had had to come take her to the doctor to have it removed); she rubbed the back of her thigh absently, eyeing the two official envelopes that remained. She'd known they were there, of course, had spotted them right off. Both bore return addresses from the Dade County Department of Public Health; both had been cut neatly open; both held bulky paperwork that edged its green engraving out of their pouches.

Paige felt her mouth go dry as she reached for the first. She checked the postmark to be sure, then withdrew her sister's birth certificate, scanned all the pertinent data, which matched precisely with everything Paige knew. She returned her sister's paperwork to its envelope, then reached with trembling fingers for her own.

She held her breath as her eyes flew over the entries: "Certificate of Live Birth" . . . Paige Lee Cooper . . . October 31, the year correct . . . the name of the attending physician, not Doctor Earle

Conaway but one Emma Kane Rolle . . . the place Rolle's office on Flagler Street, far to the south, near the city's center, an "emergency birth," at 12:15 A.M., all that information typed in smudged lettering, as if the typewriter keys had been made of fur . . . and then, added in pen, in the same hand that had signed the certificate, she found what she had been looking for: "Father: Bertram Wayne Cooper, 27, Salesman/Auto," "Mother: Loretta Rose Richardson," as if in those days it was taken for granted that mothers had no other occupation worthy of mention. She read and reread the entries until they were burned into her consciousness. Strange that she'd never known the doctor who delivered her was a woman. And odd that she'd never heard about the "emergency" nature of her birth. Paige shook her head. Hadn't her mother always referred to "taking her home from the hospital"? Or was that something Paige had simply imagined? In any case, here was the proof she'd been looking for. No reason to have doubted the foundations of her very existence. No reason at all, Paige.

But still the relief she had expected to sweep over her would not come. And why not? What obstinacy was this? What new proclivity for self-negation? What more do you want, Paige? What more could you ask for?

She closed her eyes, squeezing out tears, unable to shake the picture of her sister's face as she stood at the nurse's station that night. Her sister unable to meet her gaze, her fury leaked away like gas from a tired balloon, as if she were sorry she'd ever brought it up.

"Did she tell you I was adopted?"

"She didn't have to."

She let the certificate slip from her fingers, watched it flutter onto the pile of jumbled photographs. Her hand wandered to one of the packets of old black and whites, a little booklet of the type they hadn't made in years: "Precious Memories" stamped on a thin yellow cover, a series of shots stapled together, this group of photos tracing her parents' progress up the West Coast: a pier in Santa Barbara, gnarled pines and surf in Carmel, cable cars in San Francisco, her mother's tan golden by this stage of the trip, her father's hair longer, her mother vamping on Fisherman's Wharf in shorts and high heels like some Betty Grable wannabe, and Paige had to admit she had some figure in those days . . .

. . . and suddenly she stopped, giving a little cry, her blood freezing inside her. She reached again for the birth certificate— though God knows why, if she didn't know the date of her own birth, what did she know—and held it up beside the photograph of her slender, stylish mother.

Her mother—or so she had always thought—smiled coquettishly back at the lens, while the bushy-headed shadow of a man with a camera—her father, wasn't it—fell across the wooden pier in the foreground. In the margin of the photograph was stamped the date, heavy black type that was hard to mistake, September of the year Paige had been born. Her mother would have been eight months pregnant at the time. Eight months pregnant, Paige thought, staring at the photograph of vampish, flat-bellied Virginia Rose Richardson Cooper. Not a teaspoon of fat on that body, not the slightest telltale swelling in that bronzed belly. Paige felt her defenses crumbling like a series of pitiful, little-pig-built walls that had been trying to hold back a hurricane. What she had sensed from the moment the words came out of her sister's mouth was finally undeniable. The flood of emotions took her with physical force. Astonishment. Anger. Bafflement. A sadness as deep as that which had gripped her with the deaths of her mother and her sister. And yet somewhere deep within that maelstrom of feelings it flickered, nothing more than the dimmest of sparks, but it was there just the same; it was the tiniest dot of relief she sensed, and along with that came its handmaiden, the most slender thread of hope.

She had begun to weep when she heard a sound behind her. She whirled, staring up at Gabriel's massive form in the doorway. He stared down at her impassively from behind his opaque glasses.

"You are all right?" he said.

She nodded, wondering how long he'd been standing there. "I'm fine," she said. She wiped at her eyes with the back of her hand, tucked the birth certificate into her purse.

She glanced up at Gabriel again, feeling another odd wave of emotion, and this time, she realized, it was shame. This enormous, inscrutable powerhouse of a man staring down at her like someone who could read minds . . . she had a sudden flash, a terrible old movie Paul had kept her up for once, *The Man with X-Ray*

Eyes, Ray Milland, all puffy and gone to seed, wearing sunglasses the tint and thickness of welder's glass . . .

She shook away the vision, her feelings irrational to say the least, for why should she care if some person she didn't even know were to grasp her secret. But that was it, wasn't it? Her secret. Every orphan's shame.

She got to her knees, began to toss things back into the Ipana carton: newspapers, photos, baby shoes, all the detritus of a suddenly uncentered life. Gabriel bent down to help when she snatched a sheaf of photos from his hand.

"I'll do it!" she snapped at him, and he held his hand away as if it had been burned.

She stopped, shocked by her own anger. She closed her eyes momentarily, and pinched the bridge of her nose with her fingers, forcing herself to calm. She would not let this happen. She would not allow herself to be controlled this way.

She opened her eyes and stared back at Gabriel. "I'm sorry," she said evenly.

She took a breath, gestured at the box, then looked back at him. No shame, she told herself. No more shame. "I was adopted," she said. "I just found that out."

Gabriel's mouth opened into a silent O, and his chin lifted ever so slightly in recognition. He turned aside for a moment, as if he were considering the fact. Or perhaps, she thought, she'd simply embarrassed him.

She tossed the rest of the items that she'd discovered back into the box, then stood, brushing the seat of her pants.

"I'd like to take that," she said, pointing to the box. Gabriel was still sitting on his haunches, still staring off into some other place. After a moment, he turned, registering her words with an absent nod. He picked up the box with one of his massive hands and followed her into the hallway.

"I don't suppose Ms. Nobleman said where she'd be going?" It was Driscoll talking to a desk clerk, a young man in a stylishly short haircut who gave him a bored shrug in reply.

Driscoll glanced around the ornate lobby. Late on a Sunday afternoon, high season a month away, things were pretty quiet. He turned back to the clerk. "What do you say I have a look at the phone records for her room?"

The clerk, who'd been picking at lint on the lapel of his dark blazer, glanced up at him. "You must be kidding."

Driscoll leaned across the counter, his meaty hands clasped together. "No," he said. "Not really."

Something in Driscoll's tone got the kid's attention. "What happened to your hands?" he said after a moment.

Deal glanced at the angry red cross-hatchings that scored the backs of the ex-cop's hands. Some of the scratches were still oozing blood. Driscoll glanced over his shoulder at Deal, then back at the kid. Deal saw the scene in his mind again, Driscoll grabbing for the cat, the cat tearing into Driscoll with the three paws it could use, the windshield wiper thudding against the glass in triple time. They'd finally had to throw Driscoll's soggy sport coat over the thing, Deal holding it wrapped up in a ball, while

Driscoll worked its claw out of the wiper.

Driscoll stared at the desk clerk, flicking a white cat hair off his cuff. "Some asshole I was talking to gave me a hard time," he said mildly. "I had to address the matter, take him downtown in a bucket."

The kid edged back a bit, wary. "Are you a cop?"

Driscoll gave a stare of his own, reached into his jacket. He produced a joke shield he'd gotten as a gift at his retirement— Sonny Crockett, Chief of Police—flipped it open and shut in an easy motion, put it back it in his pocket.

The kid nodded, but he was still hesitant. "Don't you need a court order, something like that?"

Driscoll turned, gave Deal a glance. Deal raised a finger, making a face as if the kid had reminded them of a major oversight.

"He's absolutely right, Vernon." Deal pointed at a sideboard that held a house phone and a stack of stationery for writing notes.

"Hand me one of those envelopes, would you?"

Driscoll looked at him, then went for one of the envelopes and brought it back.

Deal took the envelope, laid it on the marble counter, glanced around the deserted lobby again. He reached into his pocket, took out his wallet, deftly withdrew a hundred-dollar bill. He paused just long enough to let the kid see what he was doing, then slipped the bill into the envelope, licked it, pressed it shut with a thump of his hand and shoved it across the countertop.

"There it is," Deal said. "Signed by Judge Franklin. Everything in order." He smiled. "Now let's have a look at those phone numbers."

The clerk's attitude had undergone a complete transformation. He smiled, palmed the envelope smoothly, tucked it into his blazer pocket, turned to the computer, and punched up some numbers. There was a whining sound as a printer coughed out information. The kid bent, tore off the printout, handed it to Deal, who handed it to Driscoll in turn.

"Let's go," Deal said.

"Hold on a second," Driscoll said, already scanning the printout.

"I think we ought to go," Deal insisted.

"What's with you?" Driscoll said. He'd found something on the sheet, called out to the desk clerk, who was on his way into a back office. "Does that phone ring out?"

The kid turned, saw Driscoll pointing at the house phone. He shook his head. "Pay phones are around the corner," he said.

"I don't have any change," Driscoll said.

"Couldn't we do this somewhere else?" Deal said, but Driscoll ignored him.

The kid made a sighing noise. "Pick it up when it rings," he said, turning to a phone panel set in the wall.

Driscoll walked briskly to the house phone, waited for the signal, picked up. "Yeah," he said. "Try this number, okay?"

He read off a number from the printout, then stood listening as the connection was made. "What?" Deal heard him say to whomever had answered. "Slow down, will you?"

Driscoll listened for a moment, then cut in again. "Jesus Christ, use *syllables.*" He covered the mouthpiece, turned to Deal in exasperation. "You'd think somebody in the service industry, they'd learn the English language, wouldn't you?"

Deal nodded absently, his eyes on the desk clerk, who was working the phone connection with one hand, holding the envelope Deal had given him with the other.

Meantime, Driscoll's conversation had resumed. "Give me the name again, okay? Uh-huh," he said finally, scrawling a note. "He was one of our greatest presidents. That's right, *American* president. You're on South Beach, correct? That's okay, hoss, we'll come have a look."

Driscoll hung up, glanced at his note again, then motioned to Deal. "Let's go," he said.

Deal held his gaze on the desk clerk, who had hung up the main phone, was tearing into the envelope.

"I'm ready," Deal said, backing quickly toward the door.

"It's the Grover Cleveland Hotel," Driscoll was saying. "Little place down on South Beach." He dangled his note in front of Deal's eyes.

"That's where Paige Nobleman went?" Deal said absently, hurrying them along.

"Maybe," Driscoll shrugged. "You okay?"

"I'm fine," Deal said, swinging the lobby door open. "Why

didn't you just ask the person you were talking to if she'd checked in?"

Driscoll's eyes flared. "Because the guy couldn't speak English, for Chrissakes."

The clerk was bustling around the counter now, his face red, the envelope Deal had slipped him held high above his head like a summons.

"Come on," Deal said. "We gotta go."

"Hey!" Deal heard the desk clerk calling as he pulled Driscoll through the door and toward the waiting Ford. "Hey you!"

Driscoll gave Deal a questioning look as they piled into the car. Deal answered with a hiss. "Hit it, Driscoll!"

By the time the kid made it outside after them, the Ford had roared away.

They were whisking down Collins Avenue now, the road snaking a path through banks of towering condominiums, eight lanes of pavement cutting a narrow canyon of glittering glass and steel. Climb high enough to see it, a hundred yards east would be the broad white beach and the sturdy surf of the Atlantic; a hundred yards west there'd be the broad blue ribbon of the Intracoastal Waterway. In between were more luxury apartments and moneyed owners per square inch than anywhere else on earth.

If Hurricane Andrew had veered north twenty miles, a mere blip in meteorological terms, Deal thought, what had already turned out to be the most costly disaster in history would have racked up figures beyond all imagining. He had a sudden image of all these buildings, opening up their glass sides like so many human beehives being blown clean: sofas, credenzas, pianos, who knows what, all of it hurtling out, along with a number of stubborn owners, no doubt, to cascade down from twenty stories and more over the Miami landscape. That's exactly what would have happened, what very easily *could* happen the next time around, he thought, as Driscoll's voice broke in.

"So what did you put in the envelope you gave the desk clerk?" Driscoll asked. He swung their car around a Cadillac that was creeping along in the right lane at just above dead stop.

Deal gave him an innocent look. "I'm not sure," he said. "Looked like a hundred, but maybe it turned out to be a one."

Driscoll smiled, shook his head.

"Hey," Deal said. "The guy did a public service, got a dollar for his trouble."

Driscoll laughed. "I'm telling you, you got a future in this line of work."

"Spend a lifetime as a contractor," Deal said, "you get used to handling payoffs."

Driscoll laughed again.

"Besides," Deal continued. "You let him think you were a cop. Suppose he calls up and complains. You could get in real trouble."

"Right. He's gonna call up the station house, say some detective whose name he doesn't know asked him for a look at some telephone numbers." Driscoll affected a look of concern. "They'll probably put out an APB for me, right after they finish scraping the day's body count off the sidewalk."

Deal smiled. "I'm not criticizing, Vernon."

"I'm glad to hear it," Driscoll groused. "The day I start telling you how to build houses, we're all in big trouble."

They both laughed then, and Deal clapped the big man on the shoulder. "I appreciate your help, Vernon. Really."

Driscoll nodded, rolling his shoulders stiffly as if the words embarrassed him. "You'd do the same for me," he said finally.

They rode in silence then, under the flyover that led west to the Arthur Godfrey Road, where Collins changed from a broad thoroughfare with synchronized lights and a carefully tended median into a cramped four-lane bisecting a business district, with ten times the traffic and signals guaranteed to shift to red within fifty feet of any driver's approach. They had pulled up to an intersection where an older man in brogans, black socks, powder blue shorts, short-sleeved white shirt, and porkpie hat was negotiating the crosswalk. The light turned green when he was still half a dozen slow steps away from the curb: the old guy turned suddenly and pointed an accusing finger at Driscoll, who threw up his hands.

"Take your time, pop," Driscoll called through the windshield. A horn sounded behind them and the old guy shook his finger at Driscoll once again.

By the time the old guy reached the curb, the signal had turned red again. The driver behind them revved an engine that sounded like it had been taken out of a Donzi. Driscoll checked the rearview mirror.

There was a screech of tires as the car in back of them popped into reverse, another as it swung into the lane abreast. It was a black Honda Accord that had been chopped down to ride about a dime's thickness off the pavement, its windows smoked nearly to the darkness of the paint. Driscoll turned to stare as the passenger window of the Honda slid down. There was a pimply kid in a muscle shirt sitting shotgun, a surly look on his face. His clone behind the wheel, a kid with what looked like hieroglyphics carved into his skull-cap haircut, gunned the motor again and sent an equally challenging look at the Ford.

Driscoll nodded, reached into his jacket pocket, produced his shield for the pair to see, holding it out the window without a word. The decibel level of the Honda's engine dropped off by a factor of ten and the smoked window seemed to rise much faster than it fell. In seconds the Honda had hung a left and disappeared down a one-way cross street.

Driscoll looked at Deal and gave his little shrug. "It's a weakness," he said. "What can I say?"

"Maybe you should have stayed on the force," Deal said as they pulled away from the light.

"It'd have been a steady paycheck," Driscoll said. "But then look what I'd be missing out on."

Deal nodded, his eyes ahead, his thoughts turned glum again. "I have this really sick feeling, Vernon. If you'd seen what Barbara's place looked like when I walked in there last night . . . " He broke off, shaking his head. He turned back to the ex-cop. "You really don't think her sister could have done something like that, do you?"

Driscoll was shaking his head. "I try not to think that way," he said. "Not the way you mean, anyway. If you're asking me, do I think someone's sister is *capable* of sticking a pistol in her loved one's mouth and pulling the trigger, then the answer is yes, because I have spent considerable time in the presence of guys who'd think sodomizing Mother Teresa was an act of generosity."

He paused, as if he were considering such matters for the first time. When he continued, his voice had taken on an earnest quality Deal had rarely heard. "You have to understand what being around people like that does to you, Deal. But if you're asking am I *guessing* that she did, then the answer is no. I think we ought to talk to her, though, and my main reason for selecting her is she's about the only person still alive who had much of a connection with Barbara."

It was as long a speech as Deal had ever heard from the ex-cop. Even Driscoll seemed a bit awed by it. "There's no science involved here, Deal," he continued in a softer tone. "You go around, you ask enough questions, sometimes you get lucky. A case like this—if there *is* a case, mind you—where there's no apparent motive, all you can do is troll."

Deal nodded glumly as they pulled to the curb in front of a small hotel. They had turned onto a narrow side street running east off Collins toward the water. This far south, the ancient reef widened and Collins no longer fronted on the beach. Here that honor went to a street called Ocean Drive, a dozen or so blocks crammed with tiny hotels that had once been dives and oldster havens, where sidewalk cafes had materialized on every available inch of what had been until recently nothing more than sidewalk.

When people talked about South Beach, this short stretch was what they meant; and what the words connoted was more than geographical. Fashion and photography center for the world; international hot spot; place to see and be seen . . . and to somehow become.

Uncounted trillions of tiny marine creatures had come to stack their shells one upon another from the very beginning of time so that one day their distant air-breathing cousins could congregate on dry land here, to eat, drink, dance, wear Spandex pants and tops that made a crease around every body part, and drive automobiles which, converted to cash, could feed a Third World tribe for a lifetime.

Far down on the corner, just short of where the late-afternoon breeze tussled with a couple of coconut palms in the dunes, Deal saw the green flapping awnings of the News Cafe, where he'd met Barbara for lunch. He and Barbara, come together for commiseration and comfort in the midst of all the moving and shaking and desire not just to be but to glow. And look what had happened since.

As he had any number of times already, his mind traced the

events of that day, trying to recapture the tone of her voice, the look in her eyes, to see if there was something that might have suggested the mind-set of a person teetering on the edge, ready to pack it in. But despite her anguish, and her anxiety, and her anger, there was nothing that suggested she had been beaten down.

There was the other possibility that Deal had considered, of course: that he was willing to involve himself this way, to undertake this half-baked investigation, because the alternative was to be at home wrestling with his own demons, but he refused to be that cynical. A woman who cared for him, who'd saved his life and Janice's, had died. If there was the slightest suspicion that someone else was responsible, then he owed Barbara that much, didn't he? He turned back to Driscoll, who'd been waiting, watching him closely.

"So," Driscoll said, waving his hand at the facade of the Grover Cleveland Hotel. It was a tiny place that looked more like a rooming house than a hotel, but it was freshly painted, with the requisite canvas awnings and gaily decorated umbrellas and patio furniture lining its porch and patio. "Do we go see what's brought Ms. Nobleman here or not?"

Deal glanced at him and nodded. "Sure, we ought to do that much, Vernon," he said.

And they got out into the gathering twilight together.

"Rich or poor," Carl Cross said, sweeping his arm expansively over the view before them, "it's a hell of a lot better to have money." He smiled and raised his third Bloody Mary of the afternoon in salute.

Mahler smiled back, tipped his iced tea in return. He and Cross were sitting on the veranda of a hotel bungalow high in the hills above Santa Barbara. The air was pristine, the temperature in the low seventies, the afternoon sun just strong enough to counteract the cool breeze that rolled up the canyon from the Pacific that sparkled far below.

They looked down on a nearby tennis court where a bronzed young couple in white, Cross's traveling companions apparently, whacked balls back and forth. The red tiled roofs of other cottages poked up through the canopy of pines here and there like angular banks of flowers, a young woman pedaled an adult-sized tricycle laden with fresh linens down a geranium-lined path, a sprinkler fired jets of water over a swath of emerald lawn. Cross had a point, he supposed, obvious as it might be. And Rhonda would like it here, he thought. She always had.

"I spent my honeymoon here," he said absently.

Cross considered that a moment. "Which marriage?" he asked.

"I've only been married once," Mahler said.

"No kidding," Cross said, clearly amazed.

"Rhonda is quite a woman," Mahler said. "I never saw the point of screwing things up." He shrugged, staring out at the horizon where the Channel Islands popped in and out of view like huge whales sounding in the surface haze. "We've been very lucky all these years."

Cross grunted, shaking his head. "I'm on my fifth," he said, "but it doesn't look good."

"I'm sorry to hear that," Mahler said. "How long has it been?"

"Going on two months now," Cross said.

Mahler stared at him.

"What the hell," Cross said, oblivious. "This deal goes through, I can afford to get divorced again."

"Don't worry about that," Mahler said. "This deal is solid." He took a drink of his iced tea. "Hard as it may be to believe, these are men who actually keep their word." He paused and gave Cross a significant glance. "And expect us to as well."

Cross nodded. He was watching as the woman on the court nearest them bent to pick up an errant ball. She revealed formidable cleavage, then stood and waved gaily up at the terrace. Tall, red-haired, careful makeup job. *A Rockette comes courtside,* Mahler thought.

Cross smiled and waved back at the woman like some kindly uncle. "It's a fixation," he said to Mahler. "I'll be the first to admit it." His eyes were still on the young woman who tossed, stretched her perfect body, and served to her playing partner, a far less graceful young man with his shirttail flapping.

"You know how Jack Valenti used to say he never saw a movie he didn't like?" Cross turned to Mahler, still shaking his head. "Well, I never saw a *set* I didn't like."

When Mahler didn't respond, Cross shrugged and finished his drink. "Anyway, you and your Chinese friends won't have to worry about product. The kind of money you're talking about, we can have these kids bopping one another twenty-four hours a day. The thing I don't understand is why your guys just don't buy up a bunch of dupes of what's out there now, take it back home to China, and be done with it. Why screw around with guys like you and me?"

Mahler sighed. He'd gone through it all once before, had

taken the trouble to explain things thoroughly to Richard Mendanian, and look what had happened.

Before he knew it, there was Mendanian going straight to the Chinese, trying to cut Mahler out of the loop. The only thing that had saved him was the rigid sense of propriety that his new business partners maintained. And it wasn't like Mahler had suggested they go whack Mendanian in retaliation, for Chrissakes. The matter had simply been *handled.* Maybe a little intimidating the way they went about it, but at least Mahler could take heart: He had partners who would actually look out for his interest, a rarity in this industry. And as for himself, if he'd ever considered chiseling on these people, well, one look at the picture the *Times* ran of the backseat of Mendanian's limo had cured him.

So what the hell, he thought. Go ahead and give Cross an idea of what he was getting into. Guy like Cross who'd been just smart enough to turn a failing temporary employment agency into something that actually paid off, using the agency to attract enough industry wannabes to turn out porn for twenty years running, he had sense enough to know his boundaries, didn't he? In his case, maybe a little knowledge would keep him from getting any dangerous ideas.

"You remember that industry trade mission to China last year?"

"Sure," Cross said. "It was all over the papers."

"That's right," Mahler said. "I particularly liked the *Variety* headline: KLONDIKE!" He broke off to make little quotation marks with his fingers. "A Communist country of one and a quarter billion opening itself to foreign trade at last. Including the movie business."

"So?" Cross said.

"I was part of the group that went over there—studio execs, some of the bean counters, a couple of directors and technicians, and just one agent. Did you know that?"

"You're telling me," Cross said, shrugging. "How was the food?"

"The food was fine," Mahler said, impatient.

"But the hotels were lousy and the women are flat-chested," Cross said gloomily. "Some junket, right?"

"It's not why I went," Mahler said.

"Why else?" Cross said, his eyes fixed on the court, where the young woman had bent over to retrieve another ball.

"Because it sounded *interesting*," Mahler sighed. He sat back in his chair, stared up into a thicket of bougainvillea that lapped over the terrace. He was speaking more to himself than to the man next to him. "Because I was sick and tired of furthering the careers of idiots. Because I was flattered to be asked. It suggested to me that there was some merit in all the years I'd put into this line of work."

Cross glanced up. "Tits and ass," he said flatly.

Mahler stared at him. "What?"

"Tits and ass," Cross repeated. "That's what we do out here. At the end of the day, that's what it all comes down to."

"I don't know . . . " Mahler said, feeling a headache coming on.

"Hey, it's nothing to apologize for," Cross said. "The way I see it, it's the meaning of life. Everything anybody does, Henry Kissinger, Arnold Schwarzenegger, Joe Blow from Kokomo, it gets around to tits and ass: how big's your whanger, how big are your boobs, who wants to hang onto 'em." He shrugged. "Any time I get stressed out with the business, I just remind myself: Tits and ass, Carl, you're playing an essential part."

Mahler sighed, covered his face with his hands. In a way, talking to Cross was like talking to his former self, the Marvin Mahler who thought small and fed off the eddies of greater creatures, glorying in evanescent victories of dealmaking and pleasures of the moment. He'd spent most of his life that way, but now he had the opportunity to put Marvin Mahler front and center. What he was putting in place might not make him famous, but it sure as hell would make him rich. No more kowtowing to nincompoops whose greatest asset was playing make-believe, no more treadmill of tedious parties and handshakes and back-claps, no more second fiddle. And after the man had fulfilled his "essential part," as he put it, no more morons like Carl Cross to deal with.

"I was going to tell you about China," Mahler managed.

"Take your time," Cross said, amiable.

Mahler nodded, forcing himself to be patient. "I have to be honest with you, Carl. At first, I was looking at the trip just as you say— a chance to get away from the phones, see the Great Wall, all that. But then it occurred to me, this is a real opportunity, Marvin. You're getting older, you're sick and tired of what you've been doing, maybe, just maybe, you can cut yourself a slice of this new pie."

Cross nodded. "Midlife crisis," he said. "Hits most guys a little earlier. Like me and the employment business."

Mahler nodded. "I did some reading before the trip," he said. "I didn't know a damned thing about the Chinese economy."

"Who would?" Cross said.

Mahler waved it away. "I discovered some interesting things," he said. "The way the Chinese have prepared themselves for the transition to capitalism, for instance: where the European Communists tried to switch over from an agricultural economy directly into heavy industry, steel, automobiles, all that, what they got was instant rust belt. The Chinese, of course, did it the smart way. The last twenty-five years, they've been slowly phasing out rice paddies, phasing in light industry: toys, clothing, computers, consumer electronics, the kind of things that people working in the factories want and can afford. Forget steel. Nobody's wearing armor these days. But give a guy a job sewing shirts, pay him enough to buy one of those shirts, pretty soon you have a billion happy campers."

"Sounds good to me," Cross said.

"There's an actual growing middle class over there. They have eighteen thousand Avon ladies in the province of Guangdong, for Chrissakes. Up on the Mongolian border there's still people living in caves, families with one pair of pants, so that they have to take turns going to town . . . "

Cross stared at him on that one, but Mahler pressed on. "But in the coastal cities alone, there's three hundred million people with an average ten percent increase in their economic growth. That's more people than the entire U.S.," he said. "People who'd like to entertain themselves—among other things, to go to some movies that didn't look like they were made in the basement of the Ministry of Communist Culture."

"What did I tell you?" Cross said. "Tits and ass. All they have to do is set up and start cranking them out. Klondike, just like you said."

"The Chinese would like to do a lot of things," Mahler said patiently. "The problem is, they lack the expertise *and* the dollars. They're looking for technical advice, of course, but more important, there's still no hard currency, not nearly enough for all the start-up costs, anyway. We weren't two days into the trip before we started hearing it. What they really want is partners with wherewithal. Joint ventures. In simple terms, we put up the cash, and they'll take it from there."

"You can't blame them for that," Cross said. "It sounds like a pretty safe bet: all those people ready to see some movies."

"Maybe," Mahler said, "but the governmental interference is a nightmare. They've got a million restrictions and conditions and they're hellbent on running the actual businesses themselves. That might be all right if you're bottling Coca-Cola, but can you imagine sitting around listening to Mao Tse-tung's grandson telling you how to make movies?"

Cross shrugged. "Couldn't be any worse than Louie Mayer."

Mahler ignored him. "Besides that," he said, "you're looking at a period of long, slow growth and return on capital. It's great if you're Met Life or some outfit like that, but once I began to see what Klondike really looked like, the whole prospect was boring me to tears."

"You're not doing a bad job on me," Cross said. His eyes were following the tennis players. "I still don't see how this gets to you and me doing the deal of a lifetime here."

"I'm getting to that," Mahler said. "I just want you to have the whole picture, just so you'll appreciate how it finally developed."

"Can we get another one of these?" Cross said, holding up his empty glass.

Mahler nodded, and pulled a cord that would run a little blue flag up a pole on the peak of the bungalow. In a minute, there'd be someone there on one of the trikes, ready for orders.

"Watch out!" a voice called. It was the young woman on the tennis court, staring up their way in concern. A moment later a tennis ball landed by Cross's foot.

"Sorry," her playing partner yelled.

Cross waved and tossed the ball back.

"I hope that guy acts better than he plays tennis," Mahler said.

"He doesn't have to *act*," Cross said. "Paco's from Texas. He's got a lot of energy. That's what's important."

Mahler was trying to think of some response to that when a young man in the hotel's service outfit—blue shorts and white polo shirt—appeared on the path, guiding a trike to a stop near the terrace. Mahler signaled for another round. "And see what they want down there," he added, pointing to the courts. The young man nodded smartly and picked his way down the bank to where the tennis players were taking a breather. The woman had her leg hiked up on a net pole, retying her tennis shoe. Even from this distance, Mahler could see that her bloomers were sheer, hardly the sort of thing he was used to seeing on tennis courts. She smiled, watching the young man approach, making no shift in her posture.

"He'd better watch out," Cross said. "Cherise there'll have him in a new line of work if he's not careful."

Mahler turned away. He cracked a cube of ice in his teeth, asking himself again if he had the patience to endure the Carl Crosses of the world. But it was necessary for now. He'd assured his partners. Later, with the pipeline open, product quality assured, a mutual trust established, Mahler could step away, let things take care of themselves, virtually retire if he wanted. Right now, it was essential that he be involved.

"We were getting to the interesting part," Cross reminded him.

Mahler turned back grudgingly. "Well, there I was," he said, "sitting in some karaoke bar in Guangzhou with one of our hosts—a guy who imports refrigerators—and I'm thinking that this trip has been one colossal waste of my time, when the guy points at something on one of the video screens that runs with the lyrics of the songs—it's a couple holding hands on a beach—and he says that a couple of years ago, you could get arrested for showing something like that in public . . . "

Mahler broke off then, snapping his fingers. ". . . and just like that, bells start going off in my head. We get onto one thing and another, about how for the Chinese orgasm is this terrific mystical union of the yin and yang that the religion even celebrates, all that, and the guy goes on to say how the Communists tried to wipe all that out because it was screwing up their population control efforts and so on."

"So the Chinese like to screw just like the rest of us," Cross said.

"Exactly," said Mahler. "The only thing is, the Communists come in . . . " he paused, searching for words that might reach Cross, ". . . they come in and tie a knot in everybody's whanger."

Cross was nodding as Mahler went on. "No more Tao talk about the mystical orgasm. No more sexual subjects in painting or the arts. Public kissy-face can get you thirty days. Premarital sex or adultery carries a minimum mandatory."

He broke off, savoring the look of disbelief on Cross's face. "That knot's been there in the national whanger for fifty years. You have any idea the force behind what's been knotted up in a billion or so people for fifty years?"

Cross was enthusiastic now. "Tits and ass," he said softly. "Just like I told you."

Mahler nodded. "So by now I had begun to sense a vacuum in our trade talks, you know? I take this so-called importer of refrigerators who wants to get involved in the movies aside, and we get down to the nitty-gritty. Like how important is the artistic motive, I ask him, this guy whose production office is a cubicle you have to walk to through a warehouse full of shitty Polish refrigerators leaking freon all over the Chinese ozone layer, right? And when the guy tells me the summit of his ambition is to make a chop-socky movie that'll net him out of the refrigerator business, I ask him about porn . . . "

"We're in business with an appliance salesman?" Cross cut in.

"Just listen," Mahler said. "I ask him about porn, and he gets this look in his eye and calls over the manager of the karaoke bar who in turn calls up *his* business partner, who is a connected sort of a guy if you know what I mean, and he comes down to join us and we're up into the wee hours going over what presently exists, which is either soft-core stuff from Hong Kong or this awful Japanese material dubbed in Cantonese—and finally we got onto discussing the possibilities of what might be."

"Chinese gangsters," Cross said. "I don't know. I've spent twenty years dancing around the mob . . . "

"It's not the same thing in China," Mahler said. "These people are just businessmen. They had to organize to survive the goddamned Communists, that's all."

"I read about these triads," Cross said, glumly. "These people like to use hatchets to settle their differences . . . "

"That's gang stuff, and it's just what goes on over here," Mahler said. "Chinese-American kids a long way from home, and out of control. We are dealing with men of substance, people I have met. They are the ones who are going to put the Chinese economy back together again. Even the Reds know it, for Chrissakes. The ones who haven't turned in their party cards and signed on for capitalism are sitting back ready to rake in the bribes for looking the other way while business goes back to work. The whole country is dying for a taste of the twentieth century. Who's going to give it to them, Mao's ghost?"

"I still don't see where we come in," Cross said. "Seems a lot easier just to go buy Johnny Wad's backlist."

"Carl," Mahler said, "I am trying to be patient with you, but I'm beginning to wonder. I'm starting to think that you don't have the necessary enthusiasm for this project."

"I didn't say that," Cross protested. "I'm trying to see the angle, that's all."

"The angle is simple. First of all, you're talking about shipping *our* idea of eroticism over to another culture, and that doesn't necessarily work. You ever see any Japanese porn tapes?"

Cross shook his head.

"Well, I have," Mahler said. "Nothing against the Japanese, but something gets lost in translation."

"So?"

"So it works the same going the other way. Marilyn Chambers begging for it in Mandarin just isn't going to work for the Chinese, nine times out of ten. They have different fetishes, positions, attitudes." He broke off, giving Cross a look. "There's much more interest in what they call 'the blissful portal' than there is in breasts, for instance. There'll be a little bit of curiosity factor about your brazen Western slut, of course, and we'll supply what's needed. But what we have to offer is unprecedented, Carl. We are going to bring all the technological resources of the West to appeal to the erotic impulses of a billion people who haven't had a suitably forbidden orgasm in fifty years. This is going to be the biggest union since yin and yang, and we have got the franchise. The exclusive distributorship. It is Klondike, after all."

"Uh-huh," Cross said. "What about this studio on the Chinese mainland you were talking about?"

"It'll exist eventually." Mahler said. "These men have been in touch with a couple of legitimate Hong Kong studios. We'll let them crank out a kung fu film on the mainland every so often, just to keep up appearances, but that studio's real function will be to simplify import and distribution, at least at first. Porn is like any other product, Carl. We can do it better. That's where we come in."

Cross nodded dolefully, as if Mahler's enthusiasm had over-whelmed him. He gave a bloodhound's sorrowful look toward the tennis courts, where Cherise had engaged their waitperson in a lengthy conversation of her own. "I'll never get that drink," he said sadly. He turned back to Mahler. "So who puts up the money for this first run of films—your gangster partners?"

"The money's in place, that's all you need to know," Mahler said.

Cross nodded. "So it's your ass on the line, right?"

"It's a matter of demonstrating the proper commitment to these men," Mahler said, feeling defensive. "Just make these movies the way I tell you to, Carl. That's all you have to worry about. Make the movies and keep your mouth shut."

Cross shrugged. "You can count on me," he said. "I'll have to tell the wife, though."

"I don't understand," Mahler said. "Why would you want to involve your wife in this matter?"

"Involve Cherise?" Cross laughed, and pointed down at the tennis court. "Where do you think I met her? If she's going to screw a Chinaman, she's going to have to know about it up front."

Mahler followed Cross's gesture to where Cherise was stand-ing, demonstrating a tennis stroke to the young waiter, one hand on his arm guiding the path of the racquet, the other at the small of his back. Mahler was still staring in surprise when the phone rang. The moment he answered, the familiar voice began its famil-iar, article-free delivery.

"What are you telling me?" Mahler said finally. He was gripping the receiver tightly by now, his stomach constricting into a knot.

"Not me," the old man's voice rasped. "What Gabriel say."

Mahler turned away from Cross, holding his hand to his other ear.

"Say she find something, her mother *not* her mother," Mahler heard, and he understood it perfectly this time. He held the phone down from his ear, staring out at the horizon, where the sun was slipping into the steely Pacific. He shook his head, fighting the feel-ing that his heart was going under with the purple sun, then picked up the phone and cut into the voice that was still droning on.

"Okay," he said finally. "Let me get right back to you." He hung up the phone.

"A problem?" Cross asked. The young waiter had given Cherise her racket back and was headed toward his tricycle, something that seemed to lift Cross's spirits.

Mahler stood, motioned that he'd have to go inside the bungalow for privacy. "Just this business," he said. "Always one more fire to put out."

"Ain't it the truth," Cross said, affable, settling back in his chair to await his drink.

28

"So that's about it," Deal said. "Her sister wasn't at the hotel she'd moved to. That's about as far as we could take it."

Janice nodded as he finished his recap of the previous twenty-four hours; her hand was at the collar of her housecoat, her expression neutral as she listened. After they'd discovered that Paige Cooper was registered at the Grover Cleveland but hadn't been seen since the morning, they'd left word for her, and Deal had Driscoll take him back to the fourplex. He'd picked up the Hog and driven quickly to the clinic in the Gables, spent a few minutes convincing the receptionist to bend the rules and call Janice down after visiting hours.

They were sitting in a spacious visiting "parlor" now, a kind of sun porch you might expect to find in a comfortable country house. There was a fireplace against the back wall, some tasteful fabric wall hangings flanking it, a number of softly burning floor lamps scattered about, artful *objets* on the side tables. Windows ran around three sides of the place, giving a view out onto a well-tended yard, its flower beds and shrubs and trees illuminated now by discreetly placed floodlights. There were a couple of round tables in the room, ready for bridge or mah-jongg players, he supposed, and several groupings of overstuffed furniture arranged for

189

some degree of privacy, though Deal hadn't seen another soul since he'd arrived.

He sat forward in his chair, uncomfortable with the way Janice eyed him. "I don't know why I'm doing this," he continued. "But it seems Barbara deserves that much."

"She cared about you, Deal," Janice said, her voice distant. "I always said that."

He glanced at her. No edge in her voice, no accusation in her gaze. Just that gut-sapping matter-of-factness, a neutrality that made Deal feel he could be anyone sitting here, passing the time of day. But at least she was willing to recognize him, he told himself. That was some kind of step forward.

"She's responded well to the medication. But don't press her, Mr. Deal," the doctor's voice echoed in his ears. "Don't make any demands of her. Be the kind, supportive husband you've always been. And be patient. Try your best not to take this personally."

Deal thought it was a mark of his own progress that he hadn't snapped at the doctor over that one. *Don't take it personally.* Your wife looks at you with all the feeling she'd give the change attendant at the tollbooth and you're not supposed to take it personally. Okay, Doc. No problem.

He shook his head, gave Janice a buck-up smile. "A hell of a day, all in all," he said.

"Paige Nobleman," Janice said absently, gazing out at the night. "I don't remember seeing any of her pictures. Does she resemble Barbara?"

Deal shrugged. "I don't know. I guess she does. I mean, I never thought about it. She looks like Paige Nobleman to me."

Janice nodded. "I always thought Barbara was your type," she said.

"Jesus, Janice," he began.

"I'm not saying you two were running around behind my back, Deal. I'm just stating a fact. Chemistry is chemistry. If I hadn't been there, if you'd met her first, who knows . . . "

"A lot of things *might* have happened, Janice. The woman is dead." He heard the exasperation in his voice, saw her eyes going blank.

He softened his voice, and tried again. "The way I see it, Barbara not only saved my life, she brought you back to me. That's worth everything in the world to me, Janice. There's nothing more to it than that."

She stared down at her hands, picked at a nail as if she hadn't heard. She glanced up at him after a moment. "They said I could see Isabel," she said. "Why didn't you bring her?"

As if they hadn't gone over that already, he thought. He passed his hand over his face, took a deep breath. "She was already asleep when I got back. I'll bring her with me tomorrow."

"Good," she said softly. "I'd like to see my daughter."

"Of course you will," he said. He felt as if he'd swallowed broken glass. He put his hand out to hers, but she drew away.

"I'm tired, Deal," she said, pushing up from her chair. "I'm going to go back up now."

He stood, watching helplessly as she moved toward the doorway to the wards, the rooms, whatever they called them in this place.

"We'll see you tomorrow, then," he said, his hopefulness ringing hollow in his ears.

She nodded, moving quickly on. At the doorway she paused. "And Deal," she said, a question in her voice.

"What?" he said.

"You shouldn't be so quick to dismiss suicide," she said.

He stared at her dumbly. "What are you talking about?" he said.

"It's what happens when people think there aren't any choices," she said.

"Janice . . . " he started toward her.

"Don't worry," she said. "I don't feel that way. All I meant was, maybe Barbara did."

"Janice . . . " he repeated.

"I'm all right, Deal," she said. "I'm going to be just fine. You go home now." She turned then, slipped through the door.

He heard a lock snap shut behind her.

"I'm telling you," Deal said, fighting to keep his voice even, "she mentioned suicide." He was at the receptionist's desk, phone in hand, just as he'd been for the last half-hour, waiting for Janice's doctor to respond to his calls.

"I understand." The doctor's voice came back over the telephone through a light haze of static. Deal suspected he was on a cellular phone, probably on his way home from dinner somewhere, Mark's Place, Chef Allen's, everything just perfect, here's Deal busting up the night. "Did she say *she* had contemplated suicide?"

Deal took a breath. "No," he said. "But she said it's what people do when they think they're out of choices. Those were her exact words."

There was a dropout on the doctor's line then and Deal fumed helplessly until he heard the voice pop on again, midsentence. ". . . the context of this remark."

"I couldn't hear you," Deal said impatiently. "You'll have to say that over."

"I'm trying to find out what the context of this remark was," the doctor came back, his voice louder. "What were you talking about that might have prompted it?"

Deal hesitated, closing his eyes momentarily. "A friend of ours died last night," he said finally. "The police said it was suicide. I told Janice about it."

There was a pause on the doctor's end of the line, as if Deal were being judged. "Then your wife's response would be perfectly normal, wouldn't it?"

"Well, yes, but . . ."

"Mr. Deal," the doctor cut in, his voice solicitous, "I understand your concern. I've already spoken with the staff on your wife's unit, and they will be sure to exercise every caution. But let me assure you, I have spoken to your wife in great depth, upon several occasions. She is upset, and from your perspective, certainly, she is not herself. She has been under a great deal of stress and she has been undergoing profound self-examination. At times, this has led her to deny old behaviors, and to act out new impulses, to try on new hats, if you will, and this can be quite disconcerting for those who know her only as her old self. But nothing—I repeat, nothing—suggests to me that she is self-destructive."

Deal felt as if he were caught in some time warp, forced to listen to one of his college professors lecture him on something he was supposed to understand but couldn't. The logic was there in the doctor's words, but he hadn't been there, couldn't feel what

Deal felt. And what good was it going to do, running up the meter on this guy's cel-phone?

Deal took a deep breath. "I sure hope you're right, Doctor," he said. "I sure to hell hope you're right."

"I assure you that your wife is receiving the finest care possible," the doctor replied.

"Okay," Deal said. He felt exhausted. "Thanks for calling me back."

"Not at all," the doctor said. And then the line was dead.

All the way home, Deal pondered the doctor's words, running the phrases over and over in his mind until what had seemed to have had a modicum of sense at the time of their phone conversation had become a mantra of meaningless gibberish. *New hats . . . from your perspective . . . not her disconcerting self-destruction . . . "*

"I am losing my wife," he shouted suddenly, banging the wheel of the Hog with the heel of his hand so hard he had to fight to keep from swerving into the oncoming lane. There was a blare of horns as he swung back across the center stripe, realizing he'd climbed past sixty in this residential zone.

"That's what it comes down to," he repeated to himself, gripping the wheel grimly, forcing his foot back off the accelerator. "I am losing my wife and there's not a goddamned thing I can do about it."

The words were so grim, so disheartening, as to shock him into numbness. No thoughts. No images in his mind. Just an awful white blare of nothingness, a roar of noiseless noise in his ears. He glanced about like a man coming out of a dream, having to check just how far he'd driven in his distracted state. Half a block past his usual turnoff, he swung off the busy north-south street onto a narrow lane that led past a neighborhood park for a long couple of blocks, dumping out between a pair of two-story houses across from the fourplex. He swung across the street into an open spot in front of his building, parked, slid out of the Hog, still so distracted that he didn't see the ghostly white limo parked at the curb across the street, didn't register her voice until she called a second time.

"Mr. Deal?" she said.

He turned to see Paige Nobleman moving across the street toward him, the look of distress on her face so great that for a moment, he was pulled up out of his own.

"I'm sorry to bother you," she said, hesitating as he stared at her.

Deal wondered what expression she might have seen on his face. "It's all right," he said. "You surprised me, that's all." He glanced back at the limo, where a burly shape sat motionless in the driver's compartment.

"I've been waiting out here," she said. "Your house-keeper . . ."—she gestured toward the fourplex—". . . she said you'd be back before too long."

Deal nodded, imagining Mrs. Suarez finding a strange woman on his doorstep late at night. It could have been the Queen Mother, she'd have to wait outside, or come back another time.

"You got our message, I guess," he said. "I didn't mean to bring you all the way across town."

"I don't know what you're talking about," she said. "What message?"

He stared at her. "We came by your hotel, the little place down on South Beach." he said. "A couple of hours ago."

She looked at him strangely. "I left there early this morning," she said, shaking her head. "But no one knew I'd moved there. How did you find me there?" She turned back to the limo. "Did you talk to Florentino?"

He followed her gaze. "I don't know any Florentino," he said. He gestured at the south wing of the fourplex, where a light burned in one of Driscoll's windows. "One of my tenants used to be a cop," he said. "He figured out where you'd gone."

"That wouldn't be Vernon Driscoll, would it?" She held up a battered business card. It took him a moment, but then he remembered—it was one of Driscoll's, the only thing he could find to write his number on the night before.

He paused. "Do you mind telling me why you came here tonight, Ms. Nobleman?" he asked.

"Not at all," she said. She gave him a look. "Right after you tell me why you traced me to my hotel."

Deal gave a backward glance at his own apartment. All the

lights shut down, Mrs. Suarez probably in there with her eye at one of the darkened windows, rolling pin in one hand, phone in the other, nine and one already punched in, just give her an excuse to call in some backup.

Finally, he nodded. "Sure," he said. "Let's go inside."

Deal didn't have to knock a second time. Driscoll came to his door in his favorite loungewear, a pair of baggy plaid Bermudas, rubber dime-store flip-flops, and an oversized T-shirt that read "PIG . . . AND PROUD OF IT." There was a picture of a snarling boar wearing a visored patrolman's cap silk-screened just below the lettering.

Deal saw that he'd been sitting at his kitchen table in a nook that opened just off the entryway: There was an open bag of pork skins there, along with a can of Stroh's Light, a tiny television on the counter nearby, tuned to a rerun of *Hawaii Five-0*.

The ex-cop did not seem surprised to find them standing on his doorstep. "This is . . . " Deal got out before Driscoll held up his hand for quiet.

"You don't have to tell me," he said. He turned to Paige, ushered her in with a sweeping motion of his arm. "Come on in, Ms. Nobleman." When he turned, Deal could see the boar's massive behind spread across the back of his shirt.

"How about a beer?" he said, pulling out one of the kitchen chairs for her. He reached over with a meaty fist and banged the switch on top of the television, sending Jack Lord and Danno into oblivion.

"Yes," she said, "A beer sounds fine."

It surprised Deal, but he shrugged his assent as well.

"Beers around, then," Driscoll said. "Help yourselves to the pork rinds," he added as he clapped across the tile floor to the refrigerator.

When he returned with the beer, Deal ran through the conversation he'd had with Paige outside. None of it seemed to surprise Driscoll. Deal went on to recount the course of the day's events, their encounter with the medical examiner, and as brief a discussion of Fenderman's analysis as he could manage.

"I'm sure sorry about your sister," Driscoll said when Deal had finished.

"Thanks," she said. She seemed weary, as if she were unwilling to relive the memory.

"Your mother . . . your sister . . . that's gotta be tough," he continued.

She nodded silently, her eyes glistening.

"Anyway," Driscoll said, his voice uncharacteristically soft, "everything we looked at doesn't mean a whole lot. With there being no apparent reason for anybody to want to do your sister harm, it could have been just the way the police report says. I just thought we ought to talk with you, see if your sister might have said anything that would suggest otherwise."

Paige nodded, her eyes cast down. She had a sip of her beer, and squared her shoulders.

"My sister and I hadn't been close for a very long time, Mr. Driscoll. She had her reasons, I guess. I've been pretty much estranged from the family and she'd built up some strong feelings about me. I saw her for a moment the night our mother died. She said some things to me . . . " Paige broke off, fighting tears again.

Driscoll pushed himself up from the table, went to the counter, tore off a length of paper toweling from a roll that stood on its end beside an empty dispenser. He came back, handed her the toweling, waited while she blotted her eyes dry.

"I didn't know whether to believe her or not," she said when she was able to continue. "I was so stunned by what she said, by what had happened to my mother . . . " She stopped, correcting herself. ". . . to *our* mother, that I couldn't respond. Besides, the way she acted toward me, as if she hated me, as if she wished I were dead . . . " She shook her head at the memory of it. ". . . anyway, it wasn't until the next evening, last evening, that I decided I had to confront her." She stopped and glanced at Deal.

"That's when I drove to her place . . . " She made a hapless gesture. ". . . and you know what happened there."

Deal nodded. "Just what was it she said to you?"

"It's why I came here tonight," she said. She glanced across the table at Driscoll. "I had to talk to someone about what I found, and I had this card that said you were a private detective, and I didn't want to go the police because they'd make things public . . . "

"Whoa," Driscoll said, cutting in. He placed one of his big

hands on her arm. "Take it easy, now. Why don't you tell me what you found."

She glanced up at him, then at Deal, her lips drawn tightly, her eyes as jittery as some cornered creature's. *Who are these humans? Who can I trust?* Deal read the questions in her gaze. He'd seen much the same questions in Janice's gaze when he caught her running down the steps of the Shark Valley observation tower, out in the Everglades, what seemed like eons ago. There was no way to answer those questions. Not with words, at any rate. There was nothing to do but wait.

After a long moment, she let out her breath. She bent and began to rummage in her purse, then withdrew an old black-and-white photograph and placed it on the table before them. Deal picked it up, saw a shapely woman in an old-fashioned halter-top outfit posed on a fishing pier somewhere. He handed it over to Driscoll, who looked at it, then glanced up at Paige.

"I was going through some of the things that were left at my sister's house," she said. She pointed at the photo. "That's my mother."

"A good-looking woman," Driscoll said. "It must run in the family."

If she noticed the compliment, she didn't acknowledge it. "Check the date that's printed on the bottom," she said.

"Yeah?" Driscoll said.

"I was born the next month," she said. "My mother would have been at least seven months pregnant at the time that picture was taken."

Driscoll glanced at the date again, considered things a moment.

"Maybe these photos were taken a long time before, and just developed when it says here," he said.

She shook her head. "It was part of a big trip they took, for months, all across the country. I remember my mother talking about it when I was young—'Our last fling before we had kids.'" She looked from Driscoll to Deal. "There's a whole box of pictures they took along the way. You can trace them, coast to coast, everything developed in order."

Driscoll turned the photo this way and that, as if he might be able to get a different angle on its subject. "Maybe you came along a little premature."

Paige reached into her purse again, produced a copy of a birth certificate. "Eight pounds, two ounces," she said. She smoothed the paper on the table, her eyes moving from Driscoll's to Deal's.

"And this is what your sister spoke to you about?" Deal asked quietly.

Paige nodded. "I was standing at my mother's bedside, watching her die, and my sister was shrieking at me that it wasn't my mother." Her voice was surprisingly even, her chin outthrust as she spoke.

"Jesus," Driscoll said.

"I knew she was upset," Deal said, shaking his head. "But it doesn't sound like Barbara . . . "

"You don't have to apologize for her," Paige said.

"I was just . . . "

"I'm well past that now," she said, cutting him off. Deal didn't think her delivery was very convincing, but she gave him a look that kept him from saying anything else.

She took something else out of her purse then, a yellowed newspaper that she unfolded carefully. "My mother had kept copies of newspapers printed the day my sister and I were born." She looked around at the two of them. "The presumable day, that is."

She took a breath, gathering herself. "I found the two newspapers in the same box as the photos, along with this third paper." She pointed at the date on the paper. "It was printed more than two years after my birth date, but well before my sister was born. I went through every page, looking for something that might refer to me or the family, or anything unusual, but there wasn't a thing that I could see," she said. "But then I noticed this."

She turned the paper around so that they could read the headlines. Problems in Europe with the NATO signatories. A black preacher murdered by a disgruntled parishioner in Overtown. And the piece where Paige's finger rested: "KEFAUVER HEARINGS TO OPEN IN MIAMI—CONGRESSMAN ALLEGES BABY MILL TURNS MAGIC CITY TO SIN CITY."

Deal glanced at Driscoll, then turned back to the story. The story described how crime-busting Senator Estes Kefauver of Tennessee had convened a special hearing of the U.S. Senate subcommittee on juvenile delinquency in Miami to begin the following week in November 1955. The focus of the hearings was to be on baby-selling practices in cities around the country, including Augusta, Georgia; Wichita, Kansas; Phenix City, Alabama: and, chief among them, Miami, Florida, known at the time as "Magic City." The most prominent among the local offenders to be called to testify would be Daniel Vincenzo and Emma Rolle, both naturopathic physicians, referred to as Miami's "evil baby brokers."

"Unwed mothers through the front door," a subhead read, "adopted babies out the back." Dr. Rolle was accused of more than one hundred sales of babies in the years immediately previous to the hearings. Her clients were said to have come from across the United States and Europe, and to have included some of the Social Register's most prominent, both as providers of the infants and as their adopters.

There was also a sidebar about the nature of the naturopathic medical practice: such doctors believed that diet and exercise could cure many ailments; they were easy targets for medical doctors, who had called for legislation to revoke all existing naturopathic licenses; for many naturopaths, delivering babies was the cornerstone of their practice.

There was a photograph of Dr. Rolle on an inside page: wearing a high-necked dress, her hair up in a bun, a stolid expression behind a pair of steel-rimmed glasses, she looked more like Deal's image of a grandmotherly librarian than the fiend the story described. In small type beneath the photo, Dr. Rolle admitted to practicing medicine in Miami since 1925. By her own estimate, she had delivered some 4,000 babies in those thirty years.

"So what does this mean to you, Ms. Nobleman?" Driscoll said, glancing up as he finished the story.

"I think it's pretty obvious," she said, mustering her brave front. "My sister was telling me the truth. I *was* adopted. Someone came to Dr. Rolle to give me up, and my mother . . . " She broke off again. ". . . the woman whom I've always thought of as my mother . . . " Here she hesitated again. ". . . *bought* me."

"That's why you came here," Deal said.

She nodded, turning back to Driscoll. "I need help," she said. "It was just by chance that I saw your card . . . " She gestured aimlessly toward her purse.

"You want to find out who your real mother is," Driscoll said.

"I don't think it should be too difficult," she said, gesturing at the newspaper. "Not if it's as it seems."

Driscoll gave his characteristic shrug. "It's possible. The state generally maintains a sealed record of the original birth certificate," he said. "It'd be easy enough to trace."

"That's what I'd like you to do," she said. "Quietly and quickly, of course."

Driscoll nodded. "What about your sister?" he said.

She stared at him. "What about her?"

"Well," Driscoll said. "You heard what Deal told you, why we wanted to talk to you in the first place."

She hesitated, still puzzled. "Yes, I understood perfectly. And I think I've made it clear. My sister said nothing to me about being in danger, about anyone who might mean her harm." She broke off then, searching for something in Driscoll's imponderable gaze.

"I think my sister was an extremely unhappy person," she said. "And I'm terribly sorry for what she did to herself." She shook her head as if tossing off some invisible burden, her gaze focusing on Deal now. "But I refuse to feel guilty for hating her."

"Excuse me?" Deal said.

"For what she did to me," Paige blurted.

"*Did* to you?"

She stared at him as though she didn't understand. "Did I say that?" She waved her hand as if to wipe the remark away. "For what she *said* to me, that's what I meant." She seemed distracted suddenly. "I don't really mean I hated her. It was just what happened that night at the hospital."

Her face was flushed now, her breath uneven. She looked on the verge of collapse.

Deal glanced at Driscoll, who held up a warning hand.

"Are you all right, Ms. Nobleman?"

She nodded, her lower lip tucked in her teeth so tightly that the skin had turned white.

"I'll get you some water," Deal said, moving quickly from the table.

By the time he brought it back to her, she'd calmed somewhat. She took the glass from him, sipped at it gratefully. "I'm sorry," she said after a moment. "I've been through a lot . . ."

"Just take it easy," Driscoll said.

"I know it must sound strange," she said. "Wanting to look into this at such a time . . . " She took another swallow of the water. "But you've got to understand," she said. "I've lost everything. Not just my mother and my sister . . . " She broke off to stare at them intently. "All of a sudden, I don't know who I am."

Her face was a ruin. "I'm forty years old," she repeated, "and I don't know who I am."

Deal found himself searching for some simpleminded reassurance: But you're Paige Nobleman, you're one terrific actress, you've got a life, a career . . .

. . . but he had the good sense to keep his mouth shut. Here's a woman, he thought, cut off from her family to begin with, who makes a career out of being someone else, one someone after another, a different skin and soul every few months, and as if that weren't enough, she comes home to have her mother die one night, her sister the next, and for a kicker finds out she's been adopted . . . it was enough to make his own problems seem minor.

She was blotting her eyes with the back of her hand. "I've got a number of things to take care of these next few days," she said, still fighting to keep her voice under control. "But this seems very important to me right now." She glanced at Driscoll.

"I don't know how to go about these matters," she said, indicating the birth certificate. "I'd like to engage your services, if you're willing. Whatever you'd charge, I'd be happy to pay . . . "

Driscoll held up his hand to stop her. "Let me look into it first," he said. "We can talk about that part later."

She nodded gratefully. "You know where to reach me, then." She managed a smile. "I guess I should feel like I'm in good hands, as easily as you found me." She finished her water then and stood, glancing at Deal.

"I'm grateful for your concern about my sister," she said. "And I appreciate the trouble you've gone to." She hesitated. "But given what you've told me, perhaps it's best to let things rest as they are. If the police are satisfied, then . . . " she trailed off, shaking her head. "It's painful enough as it is."

He nodded. "I understand," he said. He stood up. "I'll walk you out."

"It's not necessary," she said. "I can find my way."

"I'm going anyway," he said. "It's late, and I've got a little girl who gets up early."

He gave Driscoll a wave, showed her down the hallway and outside. The moon was up now, illuminating a patchwork of clouds moving slowly in from the Atlantic. Far to the north, a bank of thunderheads flickered intermittently, like some huge illuminated sculpture with a shorted-out bulb. The temperature had dropped a few degrees, and he wondered if there might be a front slipping down the peninsula. That would be some small gift, he thought. A little cool weather. A breather. He could use that right about now. It seemed a lot of people could.

The limo still sat across the street, its amber parking lights glowing. As they came down the walk, the motor sprang to life. She stopped at the curb and turned back to him.

"I do want to thank you," she said. "I've been thinking about how it must have been for you to find Barbara . . . and the way I acted . . . "

"Please don't apologize, Ms. Nobleman."

"Paige," she said quietly.

"Paige," he repeated.

"All the things that ran through my mind," she said, shaking her head. "Those assumptions I made about you and Barbara . . . " Again she trailed off.

"She was a good person," Deal said. After a moment he added, "I'm sorry for the way things were between you."

She nodded absently, her eyes pained. "I am too, Mr. Deal." She looked away, her gaze traveling to the north wing of the fourplex. They stood in silence for a moment. When she turned back, her tone was determinedly upbeat.

"You live here, then?"

"I built this place," he said. He noted the touch of unreasoning pride in his voice. Silly, but he'd never gotten over that, the simple pleasure of making something with his own hands.

She was nodding. "With your little girl?"

"Isabel," he nodded. His smile was automatic. "She's three. She's with the housekeeper tonight."

"And your wife?"

It was his turn to look away. "She's in the hospital right now," he heard himself saying.

"I'm *sorry*," she said, her face a sudden mask of concern. "Is she going to be all right?"

He took a deep breath. Had someone told him a week ago that he'd be standing out in front of the fourplex having a little chat with Paige Nobleman, he could imagine how he would have reacted. And in that same imaginary scenario, he would have responded to her question with something on the order of: "Oh, she's fine. Nothing at all to worry about. She'll be up and around in a day or two." But now, with what had happened to her—to them, really—pleasantries seemed impossible. There were only two possibilities, it seemed: to pretend he hadn't heard and stay silent altogether, or . . .

"Janice is in a private clinic," he said, turning to face her. "She's being treated for profound depression."

"Oh," she said. It was as if she'd been struck. "I . . . I'm sorry . . . I didn't mean to . . . " She broke off, throwing up her hands.

"It's okay," he said.

"Jesus Christ," she said, watching him.

After a moment, she turned away. "I think we've had our share." She called up into the patchwork sky. "I think you can take the shitcan somewhere else now," she cried. "We've had our fill."

He found himself smiling despite himself. When she turned back to him, he extended his hand. "It's been good to meet you," he said. "And I never told you how much I liked your movies, either."

She took his hand in both of hers: a surprisingly strong grip, he thought, for someone who was carrying so much pain. "Thanks," she said. "All those disasters."

"Not *all* of them," he said, protesting.

It was her turn to smile. "I meant, what they tend to be about," she said.

He rolled his eyes. "I have a way with words, huh?"

"You're forgiven," she said. "Actually, there *were* a few disasters in there."

"Not in my book," he said. "Not where you were concerned."

"That's nice of you to say." But her smile had turned wan again. "And, really, thanks again." She turned toward the idling limo as a cloud scudded past the moon. The shadow swept over them, then disappeared, as if a great silent plane had just passed over.

Deal nodded. "Don't worry about Driscoll," he said, calling after her. "He'll find whatever there is to find."

"I'm not worried, Mr. Deal," she said over her shoulder.

"It's Deal," he said, "just Deal."

She stopped. "Deal," she agreed. She gave him a long look. "Hang in there, Deal."

"You too," he said, "you too."

She gave a little wave then, and stepped into the waiting limo. He watched the car glide by, got a glimpse of a stolid silhouette behind the wheel, saw nothing but smoked-glass windows and a glint of his own reflection when the passenger compartment whisked by. Still, and not knowing why exactly, he stood watching until the big car was out of sight, its throaty exhaust lost in the hum of the distant traffic on Southwest 8th Street.

"She's one good-looking woman, iddn't she?"

Deal turned. A gust of cool air had rolled down the block in the wake of the limo's departure, bringing with it a fine, misting rain that had covered Driscoll's approach.

"Yes, she is," Deal said finally.

"What do you make of all that talk about her and her sister?" Driscoll said. He nodded back toward the kitchen of his apartment, where the light still burned.

Deal shook his head, puzzled. "You mean, being adopted and all? I don't know. Barbara never said anything to me about it, but why would she?"

Driscoll shrugged. "I was thinking more about the *way* this Paige talked, that business about hating her sister, what Barbara *did* to her."

Deal stared at him. "You're not going to let go of that, are you?" He shook his head. "You really think that woman could have killed Barbara?"

Driscoll shrugged. "We been over that thinking business. What turns out to be, is. What doesn't, isn't."

Deal shook his head. The rain had vanished as quickly as it came, leaving behind the scent of damp pavement and dust driven up in the air. "Maybe she's right," Deal said. "Maybe we've been making something out of nothing. A lot of bad shit goes down, the mind just refuses to accept the most logical explanation."

Driscoll shrugged again. "Maybe I'll go have a talk with Giverty tomorrow, see if he has anything. I wouldn't expect much, though."

Deal nodded glumly. Barbara's fingerprints on the pistol, no evidence of a struggle, no forced entry, her purse on the kitchen counter, all its contents intact . . . then consider all the stress she'd been under, living paycheck to paycheck, taking care of her mother all alone, no man in her life since the time Deal had met her, when Thornton Penfield had gone down in flames, and what kind of relationship had that been, anyway, mistress to a married man who turned out to be a white-collar criminal *par excellence* . . .

. . . all that made his hunch and the suggestions of a whacked-out ex-coroner seem like pretty thin gruel, to be sure. Besides, he had enough troubles of his own to worry about, didn't he? And what business did he have adding more woe to Paige Nobleman's plenty-big-enough burden? Give it up, Deal. Forget about it. Let Barbara rest in peace . . . why was he so reluctant to do that . . .

"I'm sorry to snap at you, Vernon," he said.

But Driscoll waved it away. "I'll go by the County Courthouse first thing, see what I can turn up about Ms. Nobleman or Cooper or whatever you want to call her," he said, "seeing as how she has the potential to be a paying customer and all." He gave Deal a significant glance. "Then I'll ride up to Broward, see if Giverty'll give me a look at his files. If nothing turns up there, pardner . . . " He broke off with his little shrug.

"You're a good guy, Vernon." Deal nodded.

"Hey," he said. "We can say we did our part, right?"

"That's right."

"That's what counts."

"That's what counts."

"You coming in, then?" Driscoll said.

"In a minute," Deal said.

Driscoll clapped him on the shoulder, a light touch that suggested the power of an earth-mover just beneath. "Hang in there, Deal," he said.

"I'm hanging," Deal said. The clouds were scudding in more thickly now. Moments later, with a gust of cool air that took him by surprise, the rain began to fall in sheets.

Gabriel had watched the actress and the tall man talking in the moonlight, aware of an uncharacteristic feeling stealing over him. Perhaps it had something to do with the tropical air, the waving palms silhouetted against the night sky, something to do with the way the woman's voice came softly to him in disconnected bursts like a kind of music from his childhood. Perhaps it was his knowledge of what she had learned of her past, or the fact that the scent of her perfume still lingered in the car with him. These responses he had no name for, but he knew enough to be concerned. It was a way of thinking that he had driven out of himself. That he had no need of. That in fact was dangerous to him, and he forced himself to turn away from the man and the woman in the moonlight and tried to remind himself that this was his work, that he had to think of that and that alone . . .

. . . and yet as he waited, he found his mind drifting, the scent of the woman's perfume transforming itself into the scent of orchids mingled with the exhaust of a million three-wheeled cabs called tuk-tuks, and there were elephants still plodding down narrow streets outside the cell where Gabriel, years after witnessing his grandfather's death, chanced to meet an American GI who knew what had led up to those terrible events.

The GI, a black man who worked for Sergeant Snow in the golden days when the Thai government was even more blind to the heroin trade, had, with the war long gone, finally run afoul of the local authorities. Abandoned by his government, by the people one would laughingly call friends, he had finally exhausted his appeals, and most importantly, his American dollars.

The GI had found himself in Bang Kwang, one of the more notable of the country's dreaded prisons, facing an undetermined number of years in a bamboo cage. The GI spotted English-speaking Gabriel—serving a third sentence for assault and robbery necessary for his own survival—for a brother, and, desperate for any aid and comfort in a place beyond the concept of horrible, had wished to confide in him.

When he learned who Gabriel's mother had been, the GI, a man named Dexter Collins, was astonished. Then he looked again at Gabriel's features. "You look just like the motherfucker," Collins said in amazement.

Gabriel had simply shrugged. He let the man talk about the glory days at Jack's American Style Bar, the tales of the sergeant's import-export acumen honed as a supply master in peacetime Europe, his ruthless tactics—"No offense, but if the slants you're dealing with are cold motherfuckers, you have to be twice as cold, right?"

As the war wound down and business in Thailand began to sag, the sergeant had expanded his horizons. Tons of heroin shipped to the States, kilos at a time, stuffed in the body bags of fallen GIs, jammed into the hollows of bamboo furniture, even packed inside the corpses of babies carried through customs by their "mothers." Untold fortunes made and lost, endless orgies, debaucheries beyond the wildest imaginings.

The stories unfolded over days, and even weeks, Gabriel feigning mild interest, listening to Collins's laments that the sergeant was no longer there to set things straight, his forlorn babblings about the possibility of bribes and crazed escape plots, all this a few minutes at a time when there were no guards nearby to beat them for the momentous offense of talking, until Gabriel finally heard the tale that mattered.

"Your grandfather liked to chase the dragon, you must have known that," the GI told Gabriel. A memorably hot day, the sweet-rotten stink of human waste so thick it seemed to coat the tongue, the whine of the thousand omnipresent varieties of biting insects. Gabriel raised one eyebrow in response.

He and Collins had shed their old cage mates and now shared a cell, a simple matter of a carton of American cigarettes being delivered to the proper guard. There had been a special package of cigarettes included in the smuggled parcel, one that Collins kept for himself.

Collins checked to be sure no keeper was watching, shook a cigarette from the pack, offered it to Gabriel, who declined. Collins lit the cigarette, inhaled deeply, closed his eyes in a beatific pose. From poppy nectar to opium to brown heroin, number three grade, one step shy of the China White that would dissolve in water and send you gently along the rivers, this drug dusted into the tobacco and rolled for smoking.

"He smoked a lot of shit." The GI shook his head, smiling now, as if amused by the immensity of his grandfather's habit. Gabriel did not acknowledge the statement this time. It was true, as the years in Bangkok passed, his grandfather had grown weaker, more and more a shadow of the man who had claimed to have been a fearless pirate. The fishing trips diminished and finally stopped altogether, the long storytelling sessions had become things of the past, and Gabriel had taken to passing the days alone, stealing on the streets, doing anything to stay away from their wretched home.

Still, he could not hold his grandfather responsible, Gabriel thought. Many of the old ones spent their days smoking the opium pipe. The yearning for a lost homeland faded, the aches of aging bodies faded, the many sadnesses of a long life dimmed. And for Gabriel's grandfather, there had surely been more than enough of those.

Gabriel shrugged, glancing out through the rails of their cage into the open courtyard. A guard had clubbed a prisoner to the ground there and now was kicking him methodically, moving this way and that as if to find a more vulnerable target, though the fallen man seemed to be unconscious and barely responded to the blows. It seemed to Gabriel it would be like kicking a bundle of muddy clothes.

Across the narrow passageway, shaded from the sun by a

slanting tin roof, a compactly built Oriental man in a pair of suit pants and a filthy white shirt idled in the corner of a single cell, his legs splayed out on the earthen floor, staring back at Gabriel and Collins.

"The old man came in strung out one day, bugging everybody for a handout, whining for a freebie, pissing everybody off," Collins was saying, savoring his smoke now.

"Your old lady, she was pretty far gone herself by then, she starts screaming at the old man, telling him to get out, and then the sergeant happened upstairs, saw what was going on and whacks your mother a couple of times, and throws the old guy out." Collins shrugged.

"Which would have been the end of it except for the old guy wouldn't go away. He comes back into the place screaming about how he's going to blow the whistle on the sergeant, tell the Commies to blow the place up, all kinds of crazy shit, so Snow tells us to shut him the fuck up."

"Us?" Gabriel said, glancing at Collins.

"Well, not me," Collins said. He hadn't noticed the expression on Gabriel's face.

He was staring instead at the man in the cage across from them. "What the fuck you looking at?" he said to the man, who showed no reaction.

Collins turned back to Gabriel. "I was just sitting at the table. It was a couple of gooks took him away."

"You knew what they would do?"

"Hey," the GI said. He glanced at Gabriel, hit the butt of the cigarette until there was nothing but an ash that he ground in his fingers and licked away. "You think this is my fault or something? I'm just doing you a courtesy, tell you the story, man." His eyes were dreamy now, his movements languid.

"And I appreciate it," Gabriel said solemnly.

Suddenly he lunged forward, grabbed Collins behind his ears, slammed their foreheads together. Threw the man back, ignored the howl of protest and pain, the splashing of blood. Brought him forward again. And again. Until there was only a spongy nothingness that he could barely hold in his hands.

"And I have shortened your sentence in return," he said. He would have bowed to the thing that lay now in his lap, but there was not enough room in the cages to stand.

The guards seemed to find it all amusing and limited their punishment to leaving Collins's body in the cage for several days, until it had begun to bloat. By the time they came to take the corpse away, the powerfully built man across the corridor had disappeared as well.

A week later Gabriel found himself in the office of the prison administrator himself. Expecting punishment at last, he found instead the man who'd watched him kill Collins, the man scrubbed and barbered, impeccably tailored now, sipping tea with a nervous prison administrator and a number of other taciturn Chinese in rippling sharkskin suits.

There had been some terrible mistake that Mr. Huong, such an important member of the Society of the 14K, had ever ended up in Bang Kwang to begin with, but all had been forgotten now. And as was the way of opposites, in accordance with the teachings of the Tao, some good had come of it. Gabriel, for instance, was to have his own sentence commuted forthwith, and he was taken summarily away with those well-dressed men to a place where good work awaited someone with such worthy skills.

Such work as he continued to do, he thought, rousing himself as the actress finished her conversation and began to walk toward the car. And Gabriel watched her carefully, narrowing the field of his vision until he could see the center of the matter, until he could see her once again only in the way that was required.

"They seem like good people," Paige was saying.

As he had since they'd left Barbara's cottage earlier that day, this new driver had left the compartment window down. She could see his massive shoulders move up and down in a shrug.

"I'm glad I spoke to them," she persisted. "I think this Driscoll might be able to help."

"Sometimes it is best to leave sleeping dogs to die," he said.

She stopped for a moment, pondering the way he'd rendered the saying. It made more sense his way, she decided.

"But you can't mean that," she said.

The massive shrug again. "Maybe just as well to never know."

She felt his gaze upon her in the rearview mirror. She shook her head. "But I *do* know."

They drove in silence for a while.

"You don't say anything about your father," Gabriel said finally. They were passing a massive auto dealership now, huge American flags alternating with orangish light standards. She saw his chiseled face in a series of eerie strobe images. He seemed intent, even angry.

"That's right," she said. "I don't like to talk about him."

"But if your mother is not your mother, then very likely your father is not your father."

Could it be? Could it possibly be true? She tried to ignore the urgent voice inside her. They had passed the dealership and Gabriel's face had disappeared into darkness again. "That's right," she said, her voice neutral. *And if her father were not really her father, then perhaps it would be easier to hate him for what he'd done . . .*

"I found my father," Gabriel's voice broke into her reverie. "When I was older."

"Wait a minute," she said. "You were adopted?"

"Not adopted," he said.

"You mean he left your mother?" She shook her head. "When you were very young . . . "

"Too many things," Gabriel said, as if to close the conversation. "Too many things to know."

She shook her head, bewildered by his comments. Something else was bothering her as well, something she couldn't put her finger on. For one thing, she didn't remember passing that huge auto dealership on the way to Deal's apartment, but maybe she hadn't noticed at the time. Or maybe they were simply taking another route back. Still, it didn't seem right that they were traversing such a dark stretch of road. The closer to the beach, the more glitter, right? She saw the glint of water off to the right, felt a jolt as the car dropped off the pavement and began to chew through what sounded like gravel. She could see out the misted windshield through the open driver's compartment: Feathery pine limbs were whipping across the windshield, scraping the sides of the car. There was another crash as the car bottomed out in a swale and a great billowing of dust as they rocketed up the far slope.

"Gabriel," she cried, trying to right herself on the spongy

cushions. Had there been some accident? Why hadn't she bothered to buckle herself in?

The car spun into a tight curve, the force slinging her across the slippery seats against the far door. She felt a jolt of pain as her shoulder crunched against some protruding chunk of metal. Bright lights were pinging behind her eyes as she clutched in vain for the door handle, the arm cushion, anything to anchor her. Then, abruptly, the car righted itself, and she lurched over backward, tumbling onto the floorboards.

"Gabriel!" she cried again, but the car hurtled on. She was struggling to pull herself up when Gabriel mashed the brakes, sending the car to a skidding halt. She knew what was coming before it happened, but there was nothing she could do about it. It was like bouncing around the inside of a cage in a carnival ride, no belt, no safety bar, no hope of appeal to the operator. She flew forward, her cheek cracking off the frame of the Plexiglas divider, felt a bright explosion in her head that sent her tumbling through cool dark space.

She seemed to fall endlessly, spinning and turning as weightlessly as an astronaut, the soft jolt of landing almost unnoticeable. She opened her eyes, blinking at the strange, upside-down images that swam through her vision: the door of the limo opening, Gabriel standing there, looking impassively down at her. Warm air from outside rushed in upon her, so full of humidity and the scent of rotting sea things that she had the sense that she was drowning in it. She opened her mouth to question him, to ask what terrible accident had sent them hurtling to this deserted place, but though she tried, the questions would not come.

Gabriel was shaking his head now, saying something, words that seemed to float down to her in a distorted fashion, as if they were making their way through water. "Better . . . not . . . to . . . know . . . " Each word tolling like a bell.

And then Gabriel had reached into his pocket for something, was holding it up toward the sky, was doing something with his hands . . .

. . . a syringe, she realized, her heart starting to pound—he was holding a syringe up to the dim light of the sky and he was filling it from a tiny bottle . . .

. . . she heard whimpers in her throat as she willed her body to respond . . . pick yourself up, Paige, if you ever did anything in your life, do this one thing now . . .

. . . she saw him toss the bottle aside, depress the plunger of the syringe, felt droplets of something spatter onto her cheek . . .

. . . she gathered all her strength and felt her legs respond at last, was able to twist about, lever one arm onto the seat, lunge for the opposite door.

Her fingers found the cool metal of the handle, and she yanked down. Then pulled again, and again. Locked, her brain was telling her. The goddamned door goddamned fucking locked. Her fingers clawed at the handle, scrambling madly for some button, some lever, then thank God found it, and she pulled, and threw herself forward at the same time, and the door flew open like the gateway to heaven.

She struggled wildly across the leather seats, wriggling snake-like toward the far side of the car when a hand fell heavily upon her ankle. She lashed out with her other foot and felt the satisfaction of her heel thudding solidly into soft flesh—his face, she hoped, let it hurt him, let it hurt him please . . .

She heard a strange cry of pain—some curse in a language she could only guess at—and felt his grip loosen. She kicked again, finding nothing but air this time, but far more important, at last her leg was free.

She was on her hands and knees now, scrambling in a frenzy, was halfway out the opposite door—a glimpse of something out there at the mangrove-shrouded shoreline: *An airplane?? How could there be an airplane??* But there it was, just as impossible as this thing that was happening to her: a seaplane bobbing up and down, tiny red and yellow running lights glowing as bright as the promise of Christmas, maybe someone inside there who could help her—please let there be help, she was thinking, when she felt the stunning blow between her shoulder blades.

The force of it sent her breath from her, sent her down upon the cushion of the seats, paralyzed and gasping. She felt a hand take her by the waistband of her skirt, drag her back. Her eyes were open, unblinking, her mouth opening and closing, her hands vibrating with pain.

She'd read a poem in acting class once: "The Fish." A woman who'd once been to Florida, she seemed to remember, had seen a big one reeled in and was so struck by what she'd seen that she'd had to write something, take up for the victim's point of view. Paige had read it well, she thought, had imbued her performance with honest feeling for the gasping fish and its last moments of life. But she knew now that she'd never understood it quite so fully as she'd thought she had.

She felt herself being drawn inexorably backwards, the fabric of her skirt bunching up under her, felt her shins crack down over the rocker panels of the door, felt her feet and knees thud into the mucky ground. She was half in, half out of the car now, her chin propped up on the seat, her arms outflung like a supplicant's . . .

. . . *oh please,* she thought, with an urgency that she had only known in nightmares: *put a weapon in my hands, a knife, a gun, something sharp and heavy, anything to right this outrage* . . .

. . . but Gabriel's hands were at the band of her panties now. There was a jerking motion, and something gave. There was the sound of tearing fabric, then a hand on one of her buttocks. She felt shame and rage, she felt tears of helplessness and anger gather in her eyes, and finally, she felt the needle plunging home.

In the dream that she knew was not really a dream, Paige saw herself perched on the edge of the bathtub of their family's home in North Miami, her five-year-old little girl's legs swinging back and forth, heels banging time on the tub to some rhythm that only she could hear. Her father stood at the mirror nearby, lathering his face with his shaving brush, smiling when he picked up his razor, reassuring her that this would not hurt, his hand reaching out to stroke her cheek, and she seemed to notice for the first time that he was not wearing clothes, that something in the way he looked at her was . . .

. . . as odd as his breath hot and ragged upon the back of her neck when moments before he'd been telling her a bedtime story, though she sensed she was getting old for those, already eight, in third grade now, and she felt him moving strangely behind her, a muffled cry, and a hand squeezing her shoulder so hard that it . . .

. . . doesn't hurt, it doesn't hurt, you're Daddy's little girl, his voice crooning in her ear, but she was staring up at the ceiling of her room where little stick-on stars glowed in the dark in perfect order, just like she'd placed them to mirror the constellations that she studied in geography, and it *did* hurt, and she wasn't Daddy's little girl anymore, she was twelve and in middle school . . .

215

. . . and she was goddamned old enough now to know better, had picked up a pair of shears from the basket where the costume she was fashioning lay on her sewing table, she would have the part of Laura in *The Glass Menagerie,* the senior play, she had a dinner-theater job promised for the summer, she had somewhere else to go at last, and if he took one more step into her room, she would by God cut his drunken throat wide open . . . and he had stood there staring unsteadily at her and turned and lurched back down the hallway and out of her life.

Six months later paramedics had pried his car from around a pillar that held the newly constructed turnpike extension aloft above his normal route home from the dealership. The car had burned and they'd had to cut their way into the charred hulk to find what was left of him. Her only sadness was that she hadn't been there to see the impact when it happened.

She lay in the back of the plane, still groggy, the tears leaking hotly from her eyes as the memories, loosed by whatever drug she'd been injected with, flooded back upon her. She had no idea how long she'd been unconscious, nor how long she'd lain there, half-aware, the terrible series of images from her childhood, if you could call it a childhood, sweeping back upon her, unchecked.

The knowledge of what her father had done was always there, of course, like some monster thunderstorm that lurks just out of sight, rumbling and threatening and never quite arriving. But she had done such a fine job over the years of forcing the specifics away. Oh yes, awful things had happened, but they were to be put away and forgotten, not to be revisited. She had left all that behind. Her father had been dead for years. Her life had moved on, hadn't it?

She squeezed her eyes shut, clenching her body against the pain of memory that rolled through her with a physical force. She'd read a spate of articles recently, pieces that focused on the parents of children who'd been abused, the parents railing about what they called "false memory syndrome." It was all a hoax, these belated charges of sexual assault filed by long-grown children, the parents—and some therapists—claimed. Bogus accusations planted by suggestion by psychotherapists eager to cash in on their patients' misery. No one could have endured such shocking treatment without remembering it each and every day, went the arguments.

That was rich, Paige thought, biting at the inside of her lip to distract herself from her misery. If she had thought about such things every day of her life, she would not have been able to bear it. She would not have been able to live. Even when she'd read the articles, she had not allowed herself to remember the things that she had gone through, not truly. She'd shaken her head at the absurdity of the parents' position, glanced over her shoulder at the awful unseen storm that was always brooding there, and flipped on through the paper to the entertainment reviews.

Now she lay marveling at the ability of her own mind to erect such barriers, aware how, even as she thought these things, at this very moment, something inside her had gone to work, some indomitable antlike part of her will already busy, lugging the tumbled bricks that sealed off that part of her memory back into place, little antlike thoughts nipping at her . . . *Yes, yes, it was terrible, but you're a big girl now and what's to be done about something that happened so long ago? You've got more pressing problems, young lady, forget what your father did and what your mother must have countenanced—oh dear God, don't bring that up—and see about the mess you're in this moment . . .*

She listened to her mind run on that way until she felt she had passed in and out of some trancelike state, to find herself back on the cool rubber matting again, a person who was the same, and yet who'd been transformed somehow, back into the wakefulness that was life.

The quiet rocking of the plane told her they were back at rest on the water again, but she was certain that they had been traveling. Her body still tingled from the vibration of the engines and her arms and legs ached from the unaccustomed position in which she had been bound. The sky outside was gathering light, and there was a different tang in the air, a bite that told her they'd left the sheltered waters of the South Florida coast behind and were now on open waters somewhere.

She heard the whine of an electric motor or pump from outside the plane, then muffled noises and thumps that echoed along the fuselage, along with the scent of gasoline that seeped into her nostrils from somewhere.

A voice drifted up from below, a nasal whine that sawed

through the suddenly quiet air as the pump shut off: ". . . ain't carryin' any of that wacky tabacky, are you, boys?"

A laugh then—impossible to tell if it could have been Gabriel's—some more conversation, too muffled to hear, and an answering whinny of a laugh from the same person who'd wondered about their cargo. He must have been refueling the plane, she thought, and she strained to raise herself on her elbows, to rub her cheek against the sidewall of the seaplane's frame, dislodge the tape that bound her lips shut, but her arms were wrapped tightly and she could barely raise her head.

She tried to manufacture a scream or groan that might carry outside, but the sounds she made seemed puny even in her own ears. She had given up, and was trying to send a signal by banging her head against the matted floor, when she heard boat engines start up outside. She heard the sucking sound of a fuselage door opening and suddenly a bright beam of light erupted in her eyes.

"Far too early," she heard Gabriel's voice from somewhere above her. "Very much too soon to wake up." Crooning, affecting concern. She tried to twist away from the flashlight beam, but he caught her head in his big hand, lifted her eyelids by turns with his thumb, the light nearly blinding her as he checked her over.

He let her go abruptly and her head dropped back with a thump. She heard the metal latches of some kind of case snapping open, along with the sound of the boat motors receding in the distance.

"Beautiful lady," Gabriel's voice crooned. "Need a lot of beauty sleep," he said, bending over her. She heard the effort of his breathing close to her ear, felt the sting of the needle in her shoulder this time, heard the far-off whine of the boat motors, and soon it was dark again.

The dreams were disconnected this time, as if the drug had multiplied its effects. There was Paul, sitting alongside her father, both of them sprawled in lawn chairs in the backyard of the North Miami house, nodding agreement as Gabriel bound her round and round with strips of tape until she looked like a mummy.

She fought to raise her chin out of the wet St. Augustine grass, saw her mother's feet as she strode past her unconcerned, bearing a tray of drinks for the men. There was a barred window at the back of the house, where Barbara's pale face appeared. Her hands clutched at the bars and her sorrowful gaze was locked on Paige's with the look of a fellow victim who knows her time has come, too.

The vision struck her with a force that seemed beyond what was possible for dreaming. She knew the last of it then, why her sister had resented her so. It wasn't just about leaving her family behind, rising too far, and too fast. It was about leaving your little sister behind in the clutches of a wretched man who'd ruined all their lives.

Oh Barbara, she thought, *he did the same things to you too, and neither one of us had the courage to speak up. We could have confronted our mother, forced her to deal with what went on. Instead we buried our shame, let her do the same, and we spent a lifetime taking it out upon ourselves and each other. The madness of it all. Me sending blood money home, as if cash was what you needed—our guilt-ridden mother able to refuse the money, but never ever to say why. Dear God. If we'd only had the courage to speak. We might have saved something. We might have saved your life.*

She wept in her dream, and knew that when she awoke, she would be soaked with those same tears. Paige knew why Barbara had taken her life now. And Paige also knew why she wanted so desperately to believe Barbara's bitter words, never mind how they were spoken, nor that they came at her mother's deathbed. The thought that she had been adopted offered Paige a kind of reprieve. She did not know how to explain it, but the possibility that it had not been *her* father who'd done those things, nor *her* mother who had let them happen, such a possibility gave her an unreasoning surge of hope.

No sooner had these things occurred to her than the dream turned then, and she saw herself talking earnestly to John Deal outside her sister's house. This time, *she* knew what was inside that cottage, and she was trying to hold *him* back, though he wasn't listening, was pushing past her toward the awful scene, and no sooner had he brushed by than time hurtled forward in a blink and they were standing outside his apartment building and she had the feeling that though terrible things had happened, she could explain everything to him, and if he understood, then maybe, just maybe, the world could be set right after all. But he was shaking his head, holding up his hand in a gesture of peace, a gesture that also told her that her words would do no good . . . and as she watched, his image and his building began to recede, slowly at first, then more rapidly, until it whooshed away into a blackness that engulfed her in sadness altogether.

"Welcome home, Ms. Nobleman." She felt a hand shaking her shoulder, heard the voice in her ear, felt a momentary rush of hope that she might wake to find herself in an airliner with a kindly steward at her side . . .

. . . and then she blinked groggily into consciousness, a desert landscape congealing before her crusted eyes, a debilitating sight that rushed up toward her through the windows of the small plane she'd been in all along. She saw distant peaks, the sky purple behind them, and wondered vaguely if it were night becoming day or the other way around. Her head was splitting and her tongue felt as though it were made of carpeting.

She closed her eyes, then opened them again. It must have been Gabriel who'd awakened her, she thought, realizing as well that she'd been taken off the floor matting and strapped into a seat for their landing. He sat just ahead of her now, buckled in beside the pilot, who stared ahead, silent and intent, as they made their descent: There was a blur of barren peaks, dotted with greasewood and gnarled cacti, a dim Jeep trail, a ridge that rushed up at them fast enough to take her breath away, then a flash of blue that was a vast expanse of desert lake spreading out beneath them.

What she saw might have seemed reassuring, might even have filled her with hope under different circumstances. As it was, the sight only deepened her dread and despair:

There was a dock capped by a familiar boathouse jutting out into the water; there was a similarly familiar car waiting at the end of that dock; and as the plane circled and dipped back toward the calm water, she saw the very worst. It stood on a promontory that overlooked the lake, what Paige knew to be the only habitation for miles and miles, one secluded outpost on thousands and thousands of acres of lonely range and ranchland that stretched south toward Mexico. Fifty miles to the north, beyond those jagged peaks in the distance, lay Palm Springs and the other desert communities, with their swarms of well-tended winter residents golfing and tanning and milling through the artificial splendor. But here there was only the house.

It had been done in mission style, a rambling adobe structure that Rudolph Valentino had commissioned and that Fatty Arbuckle had briefly occupied, twenty-seven rooms and nearly as many baths, tennis courts, pool and stables though there had been no horses for many years, and a mineral hot spring in an outcropping of rock above the lake that Rhonda Gardner had always sworn by as the reason she kept this white elephant, the "desert house."

The desert house. Paradise. It was the place where, not a week ago, Marvin Mahler had suggested she go to rest and sort things out. Dear Marvin, she thought bitterly. Her devoted agent. A shudder rolled through her as the plane kissed down on the water. Marvin Mahler. The man you just couldn't say no to.

 "Cut the shit, Seabiscuit." Buzz Giverty stepped forward, driving an elbow solidly into the ribs of the horse, who took a stutterstep sideways, releasing a slobbery outpouring of breath.

Driscoll thought that the big horse might have been knocked all the way through the spindly-looking rails of the corral they were in if Giverty hadn't been holding onto the cinch so tightly. Giverty yanked on the strap, drawing it tight under the horse's chest, tying it off deftly.

"They're smart bastards," Giverty said, giving Driscoll a look. "They'll hold their breath while you're getting that saddle on, then let it out about the time you mount up. Before you know it, you're flying ass over teakettle."

Driscoll nodded, willing to take Giverty's word for it. He'd intended to start his day down at the Metro-Dade Health Department in Miami, but he'd awakened early, decided to catch Giverty at his house. He'd be dealing with Marie down at Metro-Dade, and he figured it would be best to catch her after she'd had a few cups of coffee. Marie had never been much of a morning person.

Driscoll watched Giverty's hands move deftly about, arranging the rest of the horse's tack. Despite his disinterest in nonhuman creatures, Driscoll was impressed. He'd never imagined that

Giverty, with his drill sergeant's demeanor, would have such an ease with animals. Especially such big animals. "Maybe you ought to put in for the mounted patrol," he said mildly.

Giverty laughed, but the sound didn't really reflect much humor. Giverty was a ruddy-faced man in his late forties, his hair gone steely gray and cut in a flattop, his posture erect, his wrists as thick as the horse's forelegs. There were creases ironed into his Levis, and no visible paunch under his snug-fitting polo shirt. Driscoll found himself sucking in his gut, hiking up his Sansabelts out of reflex. He imagined that he and Giverty would make a pretty good before-and-after ad for a health club.

"Those mounties are a bunch of showboaters," Giverty said disdainfully. "They don't know a damn thing about horses."

Driscoll shrugged. "Maybe they need a new commander over there."

Giverty gave him a sidelong glance. "I'm happy doing just what I'm doing, Driscoll. Five more years of it and I'll be doing what you ought to be doing, taking life easy." He turned and offered the horse something in the palm of his hand. The horse took the treat with a sound like a vacuum hose stuck suddenly in tar, began chewing noisily.

"Never want to hold something out in your fingers," Giverty said. "Good way to lose 'em." He turned back to Driscoll. "You just put it out on the palm of your hand like it was a tray, they'll take it slick as you please."

Driscoll nodded.

"You want to give it a try?" Giverty had what looked like a cube of brown sugar in his hand. The horse was still chewing the first piece he'd given it. It sounded like a handful of marbles had fallen into a set of steel gears. The horse cast one of its doleful eyes on Giverty's outstretched hand and whinnied expectantly, flinging its sizable head about.

"That's okay," Driscoll said. A gob of horse drool had appeared on his coat sleeve.

Giverty gave his humorless laugh and handed whatever he'd been holding to the horse. "What's your interest in this girl's suicide, anyway?" Giverty said, patting the side of the horse's neck.

Driscoll brushed an insistent fly from his ear. He smelled urine, dust, hay, manure, some indefinable odor that must have been the essence of horse. He could only imagine what it would be like around here once the sun cleared the bank of Australian pines bordering the east side of the property and really heated things up.

"She was pushing forty," Driscoll said. "I don't know that I'd call her a girl." He knew it wasn't the right thing, annoying Giverty, but Driscoll couldn't help himself, the guy acting like some know-it-all just because he could give a horse an enema.

"That why you came out here, Driscoll? Give me some sensitivity training?"

"I wouldn't presume," Driscoll said.

"Then what?" Giverty wasn't paying much attention. He jabbed his horse in the ribs with his thumb, got it rearing up while he held it by the reins. "She's a beauty, isn't she," he said.

"I'm just doing a favor for a friend," he said, careful to keep Giverty between himself and the animal. "I just wanted to be sure there wasn't anything I missed in your report."

Giverty brought the horse back down, patted it. He turned to give Driscoll a steely look. "Driscoll, what you read was what there was. Just because the lady had her mouth open when she pulled the trigger doesn't mean jack shit."

Driscoll gave him a look. "I didn't say anything about that."

Giverty snorted. "The problem with you, Driscoll, you think you're the only good cop in South Florida."

Driscoll shrugged. He had to grant Giverty some credit.

"Did you run the serial number on the gun?"

Giverty was about to turn back to his horse, but the question gave him pause. "Yeah, that was one thing," he said.

"What was?" Driscoll said.

"It came right back from the computer," he said. "That number was one of a lot from Colt that never left the factory," he said. "Not in any legitimate way, that is. They manufactured it all right, but according to the records, it was never shipped."

Driscoll nodded. "So she was killed with a stolen gun."

Giverty looked at him. "Yeah, a thirty-eight Special that she could have bought right down the road at the flea market," he said. "Probably ten thousand of them floating around South Florida as we speak."

Driscoll made the gesture with his lips and tilt of his head that was the equivalent of his shrug. What Giverty said about the number of stolen guns might be only a slight exaggeration, but weapons didn't fall off the map at the factory end all that often, not unless serious players were involved. Most of the illicit guns around had been stolen from gun shops or collectors or had been boosted from their rightful owners in the course of garden-variety robberies.

"How about the autopsy?"

Giverty shook his head. "Nothing. No drugs, no hidden trauma, no nothing. Just a healthy thirty-six-year-old woman who blew her brains out with a pistol."

Driscoll was considering Giverty's words when the detective continued. "Course, she might have done herself a favor, according to the doc," he said.

"How's that?" Driscoll said.

"Aluminum," Giverty said.

Driscoll stared at him. "What's that supposed to mean?"

Giverty shrugged. "That's the only thing they found," he said. "She had an elevated concentration of aluminum in her body tissue. What the doc tells me is he helped out on a study while he was in medical school over in England. Some of them over there think there's a direct correlation between aluminum in the body and Alzheimer's. According to Mekhtar, your gal was a prime candidate to develop the disease later in life."

"No shit," Driscoll said.

"I dunno how much stock I'd put in it," Giverty said. "Even Mekhtar thinks it's a stretch."

"Where does it come from, this aluminum?"

"According to the doc," Giverty said, "the most likely source is drinking water." He shrugged. "But there's some thought you oughtn't to cook in aluminum pots and pans . . . " he paused and pointed at Driscoll's gut ". . . or drink a lot of stuff that comes in aluminum cans."

Driscoll gave a mirthless laugh. "That's all it does, this aluminum, prime you for Alzheimer's?"

"What are you talking about?" Giverty said.

"Well, maybe it could predispose you to depression or something, increase the likelihood of suicide in a person."

Giverty shook his head. "The doc didn't say anything about that."

Driscoll nodded, still thoughtful.

"Now was there anything else you wanted," Giverty said, "or would you mind if I gave old Seabiscuit his morning constitutional about now?"

Driscoll glanced up. "Naw, go ahead," he said. "I appreciate the help, Buzz."

"Think nothing of it," Giverty said, swinging deftly up into the saddle. "You were a good cop, Driscoll. I learned a lot from you," he added.

Driscoll nodded, almost embarrassed. Coming from Giverty, it was astounding praise.

"Come on back sometime," Giverty was saying. "I got an old swaybacked mare in the barn, we'll go for a ride."

"I appreciate the offer," Driscoll said, edging back as the horse high-stepped a dust-blowing dance before him. Beer cans and Alzheimer's, he was thinking. The injustice of it all. Pretty soon, you'd get a little card when you were born, "CAUTION: THE SURGEON GENERAL HAS DETERMINED THAT BREATHING WILL PROLONG YOUR LIFE AND CARRY YOU CLOSER TO THE TIME OF YOUR DEATH."

He was still shaking his head about it as Giverty and Seabiscuit cantered off down the graveled lane.

"See if this is okay," Paco said, handing a sheaf of pages to Cross. He tried to adjust the expression on his face, wipe off the impatience he was feeling. He'd heard a joke once, about the starlet so dumb she slept with the writer to get a part, but he'd never really understood it. Not the way he did now.

When he'd heard Mahler and Cross complaining about the changes they needed in the script, Paco had seen his chance. They'd been hesitant at first, but he'd persisted, embroidering on his classwork in the facility, the visiting screenwriter's praise of his efforts until it sounded like Paco was some latter-day Youngblood Hawke, just an unfortunate prison sentence standing between him and an Academy Award. In the end, they'd told him to take a whack at it, and he'd jumped at the chance.

But writing a script for these people, even a script of this dubious type, was like taking a test for which there was no correct answer. He'd been at it the better part of twelve hours now, draft after draft, and he had decided that no matter what he gave them, it wasn't going to be right.

Cross was sitting under some kind of ramada that had been built near the pool of the money man's big house, his gut spilling

221

over the waistband of the Speedo he wore. Paco wondered what on earth would possess a guy with a build like that to wear such a tiny bathing suit. The way Cross looked, he ought to come out to the beach in a barrel.

"I'm sure it's okay now, Paco," Cross said, waving his hand at Paco's rewrites. "Everything'll get dubbed anyway."

Paco stared. "Then why did I have to bother rewriting the god-damned scenes?" he said, his voice rising.

Cross tilted his big shades down, glanced up at Paco over the frames. "Because Mr. Mahler is running a first-class operation here, Paco. Because we have important people watching how we do things."

"Oh," Paco said. He assumed Cross was talking about the old Chinese guy and his entourage. They'd arrived last night by heli-copter, the thing coming down near the unused stables, the blades stirring the sandy soil of the abandoned corral into a regular West Texas dust storm. It had been bad enough to bring tears to Paco's eyes, but whether or not they were the natural effect of grit or the result of some sudden homesickness brought on by this high desert setting, he couldn't say.

The rest of the company had been down at the desert house for a couple of days now: aside from Cross's wife, the actors num-bered four—two men, one a black guy with a vague resemblance to Mr. T., and two dark-haired women with hardened good looks, sizable endowments, and a studied disinterest in Paco's eager gaze. He told himself that they were a pair of dykes, but allowed for the possibility that they simply weren't interested in any guy who lacked a suitcase full of crank.

When the seaplane landed earlier in the day with the mysteri-ous woman who had to be helped to Mahler's wing of the house, Paco had assumed she was going to be the star of this enterprise, but after what he'd heard about the script, he'd had to scotch that assumption.

Still, he had his questions: The working title of the picture was *Dominatrix,* with the concept pretty much contained in the title: a bitched-out college dean, Cherise, recruits a couple of suggestible students to seduce the president and the chairman of the board of trustees, then blackmails them so that her own career might advance. It was essentially an escalating series of sex acts, one every ten pages, which culminated in an all-hands free-for-all at the end. No exteriors, no complicated setups, and, especially, no dialogue that approximated how college-affiliated humans might actually talk.

But there'd been some squabble once the old Chinese guy had arrived at the ranch and taken a look at the script. That's where Paco had come in.

Cross had outlined the changes and thrust the dog-eared script at him. "Primal," he'd said, downing a slug of scotch. "Keep it primal. This is all about fucking, not debating."

After the sixth rewrite, Paco had felt he was getting the hang of it, and even Cross had agreed to show what they had to Mahler, who sent the script back inside of an hour with his own scrawl across the cover: "If I wanted Shakespeare, I'd be paying for him."

Paco had finally gotten the message: He'd reduced the dialogue exchanges to single lines, the language to words rarely exceeding one syllable. Still, though he had long been certain that Cross's wife could handle the title role, he wondered how on earth the others were supposed to approximate their intended characters. The two brunettes looked like their closest brush with higher education had been beautician's college; and as for Mr. T's double playing a university president, well . . . the prospect, even for a porn film, eluded Paco.

Then there was the crew, a bunch of doubtful types who looked more like carnies or oil field roustabouts than people connected with the film industry: There was an alcoholic cameraman and a pair of surly assistants; an enormously obese soundman and his gofer; four long-haired guys who drove around in a step-van with a Zap Comix logo (four muscle-bound likenesses high-stepping under the legend "He-Men Film Services") and who seemed to perform lighting, carpentry, electrical, and general grunt work; and another group of makeup and wardrobe people he hadn't seen much of because they'd set up shop in a big RV down by the dock, where great clouds of smoke and much giggling drifted up at regular intervals. All in all, Paco figured the abused substance tab for this entourage would be equal to whatever they might be drawing in salary. For a while he was sad that he didn't have distributor's rights for this ranch, but then he remembered where he'd been the past couple of years and gave up the thought.

There were also a couple of no-nonsense women from Cross's so-called employment agency who'd be performing the necessary clerical tasks during the actual filming, but they were staying in Palm Springs and wouldn't be back until tomorrow, when the cameras were scheduled to roll. If the script were finally ready, that is.

Cross handed back Paco's freshly typed sheets. "Take them on up to the house," he said. "The big Chink'll get them to Mahler. And don't worry about it. The actors have been prepped. They'll carry you."

Paco considered the prospect of four crank addicts and a nymphomaniac "carrying" him, then shook his head and trudged on up to the house.

He knew that he was simply carrying out an apprenticeship here, that he should be grateful for falling into the setup he had, but it was a tough sell. Here was the bullshitter of the century, trying to bullshit himself. He knew that any number of writers had churned out volumes of such excretions for years just to keep bread on the table. He'd even read an interview in the prison library with that guy who wrote bestsellers about brains being stolen, all that shit, he'd been bragging about writing what he called "schlong and dong" when he first started out, said that he was really writing the same thing now, only it was different body organs going different places.

Also, there was one guy in the joint had a sister who worked for an outfit in New York, she'd go into work Monday morning at nine, sit down in a little cubicle surrounded by a couple dozen other normal-looking people in other little cubicles, pick up her assignment sheet, and start typing out her novel of the week.

"A fuck novel a week," her brother had told Paco, one hand holding up a lurid paperback, the other boosting his balls. "My own little sister."

Given the look on the guy's face, Paco wondered about where she'd picked up some of her ideas, but he'd been more impressed at the time with the sister's ability to manage the system. Here was some little girl from Wichita Falls who wanted to be a poet, live in Greenwich Village, walk around in black stockings and a beret, so what if she had to write a few porno books to keep herself going. She was coping.

Whereas Paco, in his efforts to be his own person, break free of the family money teat, what had he accomplished? He'd ended up sitting in the big house, conversing with sex maniacs and dodging Chicano iron freaks who wanted to roast his *cojones* because he was a white boy with a Mexican nickname.

Therefore, Paco reminded himself as he reached the massive double doors of the ranch house, he should be happy. He was making decent money, was working for people who weren't too concerned about his background, was even getting laid now and then, no matter if Cross's old lady treated him more like a breathing vibrator than a person.

Not much time to work on the novel right now, but what the hey, look at all the material he was storing up. Forget about the fact that the basic moral quotient of the people he was now associating with seemed to be roughly on a par with that in the West Texas Permian Basin. And forget about the sneaking suspicion he had that every day spent working for a guy like Cross was a step deeper into some darkness greater than anything he could comprehend. That was just basic fear of the unknown, the gut-level insecurity that Paco had battled for too much of his life. He was out and he was coping.

Cross and the others might be happy with what they were doing, but Paco was on his way up. That was the important thing. Something was guiding him. The same force that had dropped him into a goldfish pond when he could just as easily have ended up with a broken neck across some rich guy's landscape boulders, that force was going to see him through this little stop along the way.

He rang the bell of the house, feeling a little better, even working up some indignation at having to knock in the first place. Here they were out in the middle of buttfuck and bygone, him staying in the place—the-writer-of-the-film, for Chrissakes—and he had to ring the doorbell of a locked house, stand around and wait in a December heat wave, just to get back inside.

After a moment, he heard the sound of footsteps coming down the hallway, the strides too short and light to be that of the huge guy Cross had referred to as "the big Chink," though to Paco's eyes the guy hardly looked Chinese at all. The door swung open then, and sure enough, it was a normal-sized Asian staring at him, one of the retinue that had descended with the helicopter the night before.

Paco started inside, but the guy put his hand on his chest to

231

hold him back. When Paco tried to keep on going, just steamroll the inscrutable little prick, he felt a searing pain erupt in his rib cage.

"Fuck. Shit. Piss," Paco cried, staggering backward, his hand held to his chest as if his heart had seized.

The little guy stood staring at him implacably, his palm still outstretched to bar the way. He held no weapon, and Paco hadn't seen him make the slightest move. "Asshole," he said, glowering.

The Asian guy regarded him mildly.

"Fuckwad," Paco said.

Not a flicker.

"Look, dickhead," Paco said, holding up the sheaf of pages in his hand. "For Mahler. Mr. Mahler."

The last seemed to register. The Asian guy turned and called something down the hall. After a moment, the huge one came out of the living room and peered toward the entrance. "It is okay," the big guy called down the long hallway. "Open a door."

The little one at the door turned and motioned inside. Paco, however, was finding it hard to move. It wasn't his chest. The pain there had faded almost as quickly as it had come. What had paralyzed him was something in his head, some mind-presence that registered the echoes of the little guy calling down the hallway in what had to be Chinese, the same presence registering the tone of the big guy's response in oddball English: "Open a door."

He'd heard these two before, he realized, and then in the next instant, he was replaying the moment in his mind. "Open a door." The shotgun blasts blowing the California night to smithereens, his grip on the weird-ass tree slipping like something that happens in the worst dream you ever had, the voices calling back and forth above him, the huge orange carp circling below, waiting for the big chunks to come raining down.

Paco swallowed, and he had to force his foot across the sill. *They don't know who you are,* Paco told himself as he stepped inside the cool dark maw of the hallway. *You'd be dead by now if they did.* He forced himself to nod superciliously at the little guy in the doorway: *See, asshole, I told you,* his look said, but the guy seemed unimpressed.

Paco turned then and moved on down the hall, feeling each stride as if he were just learning to walk again after a long convalescence. Every step of the way he pictured himself spinning on

232

his heels, bolting out the big double doors, fleeing wildly across the desert. When the vision turned to include a helicopter swooping down on him, the big guy suddenly become a door-gunner who traced a line up his back with bullets the size of deer slugs, he put that dream aside. Besides, he hadn't been paid yet. Even if he managed to escape, where was he going to go with four dollars in his pocket?

He gave the big guy the you-might-be-able-to-kick-my-ass-but-I'll-hurt-you-in-the-process look he'd worked on for two years in the joint and stepped on into the living room, where Mahler and the old Chinese guy were sitting in high-backed leather chairs, like two guys waiting for lunch in some old-fashioned men's club. Mahler beckoned him forward and took the pages from his hand.

Paco stood quietly, listening to the ceiling fans turn while Mahler flipped rapidly through his changes. The room was big enough for a church, Paco was thinking. Fireplace over there you could park a truck in. Why was it *him* standing there with his thumb up his behind and some jerk like Mahler who owned the place? Mahler finished reading, stacked the papers, sighed, and made a shrugging motion. "Frigging writers," Mahler said to the old guy, who raised his eyebrows in response.

"Okay," Mahler said to Paco then. He held up the pages. "We'll make do."

Maybe it was high praise, coming from Mahler, but Paco didn't trust himself to speak. He nodded in what he hoped was an assured way, then turned and left the room, feeling cold sweat trickling down his back as he went. *What the hell,* he was thinking on the way down the hall. If the writing thing didn't work out, he had one hell of a career waiting for him in acting.

"Hey, Marie," Driscoll called. He had made his way through the crowded reception area in the Vital Statistics Office, waited with his elbows propped on the service counter until he saw her emerge from her inner cubicle, headed toward one of the desks in the sizable clerical bullpen back there.

At first he thought she hadn't heard him over the din—who would have ever expected so many people to be lined up for birth and death certificates, anyway—but the way she kept her head down made him suspect he was being ignored.

"Yo, Marie," he called, louder this time. The young clerk she was talking to glanced up at him and this time his ex-wife had little choice but to follow along. He had his hat off, was giving her his best smile, but he should have saved the energy. Her eyes flashed behind her glasses and her lips compressed into a thin line.

When he motioned urgently for her to come to the counter, she closed her eyes and shook her head silently. The young clerk's eyes were flickering back and forth from Marie to Driscoll, the girl wondering what on earth was going on with her boss and this guy up front.

After a moment, Marie opened her eyes, said something to the clerk. She straightened herself and came toward the counter. She tossed her hair and squared her shoulders like she was getting ready for battle.

"I'm busy, Vernon," she said. "What do you want?"

He was debating how best to begin when he heard a voice behind him. "That man didn't take a number."

Driscoll turned to find a wiry blonde woman taller than he was, glaring down at him. She had an infant on her hip, a pair of toddlers at her knees, and a chin like a hatchet that she used to sight down on him with. She held up a tiny slip of paper in her hand and used it to point at the dispenser affixed to the counter nearby.

"Naw," he said, trying to explain. "I'm not here for that . . . "

"Mister, I been here with these kids all morning and I'm still twenty-six numbers away." Her voice had a piercing twang that suggested roots in Appalachian coal towns and a history of dealing with incautious men who'd tried to dismiss her. She gestured at a computer screen mounted high on the wall at the end of a counter. "Whatever you're doing here, you're holding up my parade."

"You're absolutely correct, ma'am." It was Marie talking now. "This man meant to go to the expedite line."

Driscoll turned to see her pointing at a little window cut into one of the side walls of the room. There was a sign there, swinging from a wrought-iron arm above the frosted glass. "EXPEDITED SERVICE: $5," it read.

"I can take care of you over there," Marie said to him.

Driscoll gave the woman behind him a wary glance and nodded, following Marie along the counter toward the little window. She disappeared around a corner and he stood waiting until the window went up and he found her smiling professionally at him.

"I appreciate it, Marie," he began, but she held up her hand, cutting him off.

"That'll be five dollars," she said.

"You gotta be kidding."

She shrugged, started to close the window again.

"Okay," he said. "Hold on a second." He dug into his pocket, found a crumpled five, passed it through the window. He glanced over his shoulder, saw that the hatchet-jawed blonde was watching the transaction carefully.

"Thank you," Marie said crisply. She made out a receipt for the five dollars, slid it through the window toward him. "Now," she said, in a perfectly disinterested voice, "what can I do for you?"

Driscoll sighed. He'd hoped for a better reception, but he wasn't really surprised. He pocketed the receipt, turned to make sure the blonde woman had not sidled up to listen in. "I heard you were back," he said, trying to ease into things. "So how was California, anyway?"

She gave him an appraising stare, her hands turned over on her hips. "This is my place of business, Vernon," she said. "I don't have time to make small talk with you. If you had something on your mind when you came in here, I'd like to hear it."

He raised his hands in a gesture of peace. After all, he thought, Marie had been the one to walk out on him. Twenty-eight years of marriage, he never had a clue there was anything wrong until the morning he woke up to find her packing, saying she was going to stay with her sister in Costa Mesa. *Stay* as in *vacation,* he'd wondered? As in *moving in with,* she'd answered.

According to Marie, that had been one of the problems, the fact that he'd never had a clue. "Your idea of an in-depth conversation," she'd told him, "is giving someone directions down to the mall."

Okay, aside from the communication thing, he'd wanted to know. "How about sensitivity," she'd fairly screamed at him. According to Marie, his job had made him so cynical to be around that even Rush Limbaugh seemed like a bleeding heart. How could you respond to statements like that, Driscoll had wondered. Almost three years later, Marie back in town, back on her old job, he was still wondering.

He gave her his shrug, and her eyes flashed again as if she were ready to slam the window shut in his face. He didn't mean to communicate indifference, but she always took it that way.

The shame of it was, he found himself still attracted to her. She'd kept herself trim and she still carried a tan despite being cooped up in an office job. She was tall, big-boned, and well-proportioned, had a handsome if not beautiful face; not the petite bombshell that a lot of guys went for, but then Driscoll had never wanted a kewpie doll to set on the shelf.

The fact that she was a sturdy physical specimen had drawn him to her in the first place, that and her capability to move about in the larger world. Here she was, managing thirty or forty people, able to kick ass and take names, including his, that only intrigued him all the more. He stared at her, noted the touch of gray that had crept into her temples, felt a pang of regret. They'd never been able to have children. Maybe that would have made the difference, he thought. They could be Grandpa and Grandma by now, instead of this . . .

"I needed a favor," he managed finally, his eyes dropping from her steady gaze.

"A favor," she repeated. Like maybe he was Judas Iscariot come to ask the old boss for a recommendation.

"That's right," he said, mustering his resolve. He cast a glance back at the reception area, saw that the blonde woman was feeding her baby something out of a jar while the two toddlers pummeled each other by the doorway. "I was hoping you could check into some birth records for me."

"You're doing private investigation work now," she said. It wasn't really a question.

He nodded, wondering how she'd heard about it. Maybe it was a positive sign, though, maybe she'd been asking around about him.

"Then this is something you're getting paid for."

He sensed her hackles rising again, thought maybe she was about to slam the window. She hadn't asked for alimony, but maybe she figured he should have offered. Maybe times had been tough out in the land of milk and honey. That would explain what she was doing back in Miami, at least.

"No," he said, opening his palms. "I'm just doing a favor for a friend."

She nodded, but she didn't seem convinced. "What's this friend need?"

"She found out she was adopted . . . " he began.

"She? How good a friend is this, Vernon?"

He took a breath. Probably a good idea to leave the movie star part out. "She's a friend of a friend, Marie. Somebody who knows John Deal, the builder who got his ass in a crack over the baseball thing with Thornton Penfield, Luis Alcazar, you might remember."

"Maybe," she shrugged.

Despite what she'd said about their lack of communication, he'd always told her about the cases he'd worked on, there was that much at least.

"I rent a place from him now."

That brought no response, but he pressed on, figuring he had to capitalize on anything out of her mouth that wasn't a flat no. "Anyway, this friend of his, she hears from her mother on her deathbed that she was adopted, for Chrissakes. Her old lady croaks, and the next night, when she goes to ask her sister, who happens to be her only surviving relative, about the truth of this matter, she finds that her sister has blown the back of her head off out of grief."

Driscoll realized that he was massaging the truth just a bit, but he rationalized that it was Marie he was dealing with, after all. She'd had a heart once, but the way she looked at him now, you'd never know it.

"You have such an attractive way of putting things," she said.

He started to give her his shrug, but caught himself in time. "Hey, Marie, I'm sorry. It's what happened. That's what I'm talking about here."

She stared at him silently. It was better than the window being closed in his face, he thought. He reached into his pocket, slid the copy of Paige's birth certificate through the passage. She gave him a look that made him imagine the windowsill slamming down on his knuckles. He withdrew his hand quickly, leaving the paper lying there.

She glanced at it, then back at him.

"This is from the fifties," she said. "There wouldn't be anything on the computer."

He nodded. Another good sign, he thought.

Marie picked up the photocopy, examined it more closely. She looked up at him, her eyes softening a bit. "There's a lot of this lately," she said. "Someone in here every week, it seems, convinced they've got another mother and father somewhere." She shook her head. "I'm not surprised. The way people raise their kids these days, I'm not surprised. People *would* like to find a better set of parents."

Driscoll nodded encouragement. Just keep her talking, he thought.

"You and me, for instance," she said. "We'd have had kids, what a disaster that'd have been."

It took him by surprise, like a rabbit punch coming out of a clinch. "You really think that?" he managed.

Her eyes flashed again. "Oh, for Chrissakes, Vernon." She

glanced up at the ceiling in exasperation. "You really don't have a clue, do you?"

He started to say something, but gave it up. Before he realized it, he'd given her his classic response, the shrug that never failed to set her off. But this time, she let it go. Instead, she turned back to the copy of Paige's birth certificate, checked it once again.

"There's no way to tell anything from this," she said. "Not even from our records." She waved a hand in the direction of the vast bank of file cabinets in the bullpen. "If this woman *were* adopted, the doctor who delivered her would have sent the original paperwork straight to Jacksonville."

Driscoll nodded. He knew as much, but it seemed imprudent to say so.

"The true birth record would be sitting up there in a file, with a court order sealing the information, who the real parents were and all."

He nodded again.

"You'd need your own court order to see it. This woman would have to have a good reason, like maybe she'd be worried about passing some genetically linked disease to potential children or something." She glanced at the photocopy again. "Given her age, I don't know the judge would go for that."

"She just wants to know who her real parents are, Marie. You can understand that."

"Yes," she said, giving him her steely look. "Sometimes I used to look at you and wonder where you came from."

Driscoll grunted something between a laugh and a sigh. Let her get her shots in. It didn't matter anymore.

"I wouldn't ask you to do anything that would get you in trouble," he said.

Her eyes widened to show him how preposterous that thought was, but he hurried on before she could come back at him.

"I was just hoping, before this lady goes to all the trouble of getting an attorney, going to a judge and all . . . "

"Hoping what?"

"If maybe you'd find out if there was a sealed record on file, that's all. That'd let her know if it was worth going to all the trouble."

"You mean let you know if it was worth going up to Jacksonville and pulling the same crap with somebody up there that you're pulling with me," she said.

That was it, then. No tack that he could take that she wouldn't turn against him. It saddened as well as frustrated him. And it also seemed that Marie had come to surpass him in the cynicism department.

"I think we'd have been some damn good parents," he blurted suddenly, surprised at the words that came out of his mouth.

"What?" she said.

"We'd have done all right," he said, insistent, almost angry now. "Between the two of us."

She stared at him for a long moment then, and he wondered if he saw moisture brimming in her eyes. It might have just been the reflection of light in her glasses, though. She sighed, giving him a look as if he were a bothersome salesman, and ducked away from the window, out of sight. He was thinking that he had finally driven her away with a vengeance when a door from the inner office opened a few feet away and Marie appeared, beckoning him to follow.

"Come on, Vernon," she said. She'd regained her steely gaze. "You really ache my butt, you know that?"

"Right," Marie was saying into the phone, "uh-huh," nodding along with the buzz of conversation on the other end. Driscoll surveyed her office while he waited: dreary institutional green walls, standard-issue commercial carpet, steel desk, battered file cabinets, groaning bookcases filled with manuals and bound reports. But Marie had overlaid it all with touches of herself: pots of violets here and there, a poster of a train coming out of a mountainside tunnel with the legend "Life is a Journey, Not a Destination" emblazoned on it, a couple of commendations from the County Commission, several framed snapshots scattered atop the flat surfaces: Marie and her sister on a California beach, Marie and her sister in Chinatown, Marie and her sister in Yosemite. He knew it was unreasonable, but he'd have been happy to see one of himself in there, just for old times' sake.

"Okay," Marie said, in a louder voice. "I appreciate the trouble. I owe you one." She hung up the phone and Driscoll turned to her, expectant.

"Nothing," she said.

"What do you mean, nothing?"

"There are no sealed records, Vernon," Marie said. "They checked under Cooper and under the listed mother's maiden name." She gestured at the photocopy of Paige's birth record. "Six months prior, six months following."

Driscoll gave a grunt of surprise, settling back in his chair.

"It's always possible something was filed in the listed parents' birthplace," Marie continued, "but that would be unusual."

"Topeka, Kansas," Driscoll said, dully. "Chillicothe, Ohio."

Marie glanced at the paper again. "You haven't lost your eye for detail," she said. "I could check it out for you, but it might take a couple of days."

Driscoll nodded absently. "It wouldn't hurt, I guess." He glanced up at her. "I don't want to put you to any trouble."

That brought a laugh from her. "Now he says it," she said. She made a couple of notes off the photocopy, handed it across the desk to Driscoll. "This Dr. Rolle," she said, shaking her head.

"What about her?"

"Well, the kind of business she seemed to be in, there might never have been any records filed, did you ever think about that?"

"Sure," he said. "Some poor girl anxious to get rid of a kid comes in, what does she care about the letter of the law as long as there's a good family ready to take her baby?"

Marie nodded. "That's how they feel at the time, maybe. I meet them later, women coming from the other end of where you are, trying to find out what happened to the kids they gave up, thought they'd never want to see again." She nodded at the photocopy. "For all we know this girl could have a real mother wandering around out there wanting to find out where her daughter is. That'd be something, wouldn't it?"

"It would," Driscoll agreed, but his mind was already racing along.

"Life can throw you some real curveballs," Marie said thoughtfully.

He blinked, coming back to her. "It can," he said, folding away the photocopy. "Thanks for checking on this for me, Marie."

She shrugged, and the way she did it seemed familiar. "This

doctor might have kept records of her own," she said. "But who knows what might have happened to them."

Driscoll nodded. "Maybe you should go into this line of work," he said.

She gave him a smile. "I'm just fine where I am, Vernon."

He gave her one back. "Good to see you again, Marie."

"Take care of yourself, Vernon," she said, and rose to let him out.

After he left Marie's office, Driscoll went across the street to the open-air luncheonette he'd noticed on the way in, had a *media noche*—cold cuts and cheese on a hoagie roll—along with a Cuban coffee, and talked the clerk into selling him a roll of quarters for an extra buck. Then he went back to the lobby of the Health Department building, found a pay phone, and went to work.

None of the half-dozen Rolles in the phone book admitted to any relationship or knowledge of the long-deceased Dr. Rolle, and the County Medical Association had no record of any transfer of business or records following Rolle's retirement from practice shortly before her death in 1984.

After a patient half-hour of dialing, Driscoll stumbled onto the right Daniel Vincenzo, the other Miami physician called before the Kefauver Commission back in the fifties. Vincenzo was long retired himself and lived in a condo in West Kendall. He remembered his colleague Dr. Rolle as a "fine individual," unjustly hounded by politicians as he himself had been, but he assured Driscoll that he shared no practice, no patients, no records with her.

"That was one long time ago," he told Driscoll. "Things happened in a more relaxed way. A girl got herself in trouble, you'd want to help her out. A good family wanted a baby, you'd want to help them out, too." Everybody was happy, Vincenzo said, and why should the courts have to get involved. If the paperwork got lost along the way, what did it matter.

"You'd get paid for your trouble, I assume," Driscoll said.

"A modest amount," Vincenzo replied.

"Uh-huh," Driscoll said. "You'd sell somebody's baby, then, not even keep a record of it?" Driscoll heard the accusation in his voice, but he was tired, knew this wasn't going anywhere, and most of all was rankled at the bastard's avuncular pose.

There was a pause on the other end of the line. "I'm an old man," Vincenzo said. "Go bother someone else with your questions." And then the line went dead.

Driscoll checked his watch, stymied for the time being. He'd promised to call Paige Nobleman this afternoon to report what he'd found, and he also meant to hook up with Deal at the fourplex after work, fill him in, maybe ride along down to the clinic in the Gables where Janice was.

He took out the copy of Paige's birth record, stared down at it. What Marie said had stuck with him throughout the afternoon: He had an image of Paige's mother—if there was a *real* mother—wandering through space, her arms outstretched toward the stars, Paige out there in the same cold galaxy, heading in the other direction, her arms in the same forlorn pose. The only thing was, it was a big galaxy, and the two of them were about a million miles apart. Crazy, of course, no reason to suspect there was such a mother hunting for Paige, but the thought haunted him.

He shook himself away from the image, was about to fold the certificate away, when he noticed the address of Rolle's clinic. It was out on 8th Street, or *Calle Ocho* in the local parlance, maybe a mile or so from the fourplex. It was an older part of town, a place where things tended to change far less than you might imagine in a city where change was the order of the day. He could drive by, see what had become of the place, maybe pick up some helpful vibes . . .

Helpful vibes, he thought, bringing himself up. He knew he was down to the short straws now, thinking like that, but what were the alternatives? He scooped up what was left of his pile of quarters from the shelf under the pay phone, dumped the change in his pocket. He stood thinking for a moment, found himself glancing at the building directory, checked his watch again, and hesitated. He could hang around the lobby, wait for quitting time, pretend he'd just happened back into the building, catch Marie on the way out. He could suggest a drink, a little chat—no, a *talk*, a real talk—and maybe she'd go for it. But then a wave of reality swept over him and he laughed at his own lame idea. Maybe another time, he thought, and turned, jingling the lump of change in his pocket all the way to the door.

*　　　*　　　*

All the way out Calle Ocho, Driscoll divided his attention between what he was thinking and what he was seeing out the open window of the Ford. For decades, the east end of 8th Street had really been Main Street for Little Havana, USA, but now, while there were still a lot of Cubans around, many of them had moved out, moved on up, and Little Havana was more like Little Colombia, Little Nicaragua, Little Peru, Little Latin America really, the panoply of flags hanging off the storefronts like something you'd see at the United Nations Plaza.

Of course, the area had started off its life in the thirties as a modest Anglo neighborhood where blue-collar workers, retirees, vets, and others who couldn't stand the taxes in Coral Gables could live in close proximity to the city's center. Driscoll took some pleasure in seeing Deal close the circle, plant his own flag back there by building the fourplex, moving in. That was what America was all about, wasn't it? The melting pot. Everybody gets along. Everybody gets a shot. The way it was supposed to be, anyhow.

And Driscoll was doing his part to keep the tradition alive. He'd rented office space in a tiny strip center that contained, in addition to D&D Investigative Services, a driving school run by a Dominican, an insurance agency managed by a guy and his wife from Cuba, a pet-grooming salon run by an Ecuadorian, and a tattoo parlor owned and operated by a gnarly biker, an ex-con from Talladega, Alabama.

It wasn't the sort of place he'd always dreamed of doing business in, of course, but then in his line of work, there wasn't much walk-in traffic. More important, the location was convenient, both for where he lived and for access to downtown and the freeway system; also, the rent was right; perhaps most important of all, he could eat his way through a series of Latin American cuisines, stay right in the neighborhood every night for two weeks, and never eat fried bananas fixed the same way twice.

All the thinking about food made him conscious of the way his gut strained against the webbing of his normally comfortable Sansabelts. He'd added a bag of chips to the *media noche* he'd eaten earlier, and now found himself thinking that a beer would be good to wash the salt down with. That, of course, was the kind of careless noshing that was going to put him back into whale class if he wasn't careful.

How he envied Deal, a guy who could drink beer all one night, then give it up for a week, clean his plate and go for seconds, never seem to add an ounce to his tennis player's physique. In contrast, big-boned as Driscoll was, solid half-German, half-Polish body frame suited for trench work, he could lard on an extra thirty or forty pounds, hardly even realize it, before the potbelly turned into a considerable orb and ultimately an unstable mountain that would threaten a fatslide that wouldn't stop till it took his stomach down to his toes. He'd been there before, where he had to look in the mirror to make sure he still had all his equipment.

And that was another thing, wasn't it? The old gut surely hadn't done anything to light Marie's fire, had it? Marie looking like she did five miles morning and evening along the beach every day, him looking like Orson Welles's personal trainer, why should she want to be seen next to him?

Also, he realized that putting on weight, generally letting himself go since Marie had left him and he'd left the Department, all that had been a part of him trying to anesthetize himself generally. Become a slob, a potato person, someone a woman wouldn't give a second glance to, maybe his own yearnings would dissipate as well. Life would be easier that way. But the sad fact was, turning to undifferentiated splot hadn't diminished his desires at all.

About nine months ago, he'd finally had enough. He started jogging again, started dropping into a health club up the street from his office (two Salvadorans who bought their equipment from a failed Bally's on the Beach) and hitting the free weights, had switched over to Miller Lite, and cut out the french fries at lunch. Two months later, once he'd shed thirty pounds, he'd worked up the nerve to call a cute little secretary he'd run into down at Baptist Hospital while he was helping Deal out of the jam with Torreno and the right-wing crazies.

She was twenty years his junior, but the way she'd flirted with him, it hadn't seemed to matter. She'd seemed to remember exactly who he was when he called, sounded happy to hear from him, had really helped guide him into asking her for a date. He took her to dinner at Fox's, a white-belt-and-shoes place that was the closest thing to a decent restaurant he felt comfortable in, but she'd loved it. She'd been fascinated by his work with the department, had peppered him with questions about it, laughed at all his jokes. When he'd walked her to her door, wondering whether he should try for a kiss, she'd grabbed him by the tie and yanked him inside the foyer, where it seemed to Driscoll that sexual history had been made. She hadn't let him go home until late the next morning, until after she'd made him promise to ask her out again.

And they *had* gone out, several times since, every evening pleasant enough, every sexual encounter an act of prodigious athleticism. And still, Driscoll could not trust himself to feel fully comfortable in the relationship, could not shed himself of the fear that he was in some way a curiosity to Lisa, some kind of gone-to-seed Sonny Crockett who aroused interests in her that would surely wither one day when she realized just how far apart they were. He knew it was irrational of him, knew he should throw his worries aside and enjoy himself while he could, but once burned, always wary, he thought, cursing himself for his weakness. And, he thought, as his encounter with Marie earlier this day had shown him, perhaps he was just a one-woman kind of guy. Maybe that was the problem. Maybe he'd never get Marie out of his blood.

And of course, no sooner had he considered that possibility than an immediate series of images flew into his mind, Marie indulging herself with an endless series of California lotharios, from surfers to bit-part actors to hotshot entrepreneurs, every one of them bronzed and sculpted, Marie thrashing under and on top of them like she never had with him, and Driscoll nearly groaned with the pang that shot through him.

He gripped the wheel of the Ford tightly, having to mash the brakes to avoid running the light above a crosswalk. A school guard wearing a bright red vest and gloves gave him a suspicious look, then motioned a gaggle of kids across the intersection.

Driscoll felt a wave of shame at his carelessness, something that at least chased away the bolt of despair. Enough introspection, he told himself. Enough of his own troubles. That was one thing about police work, about what he was doing now. You could always find someone in a jam way worse than your own, bury your nose in *their* troubles, whistle your own away.

Deal, for example, look what *he* had to contend with, what was going on with *his* old lady, and a little girl to take care of to boot.

Or this Paige Nobleman. Put yourself in her place. He shook his head. Maybe she'd been adopted, maybe not, maybe they'd never find out, but she had a full plate of problems nonetheless, never mind she got her pretty kisser in the movies. And it *was* a pretty one, all right. He'd also noticed the way she would look straight at him, keep her eyes away from Deal, which probably had Deal thinking, *This broad has no use for me*, but Driscoll figured just the opposite was true. If he had *ever* seen a woman who would welcome a steady shoulder to lean on, Paige Nobleman was the one. And Deal, who radiated composure, concern, capability, no matter where his ass was flapping, he must have been like magnetic north for her fluttering compass. It was something he'd have to bring up with his good buddy, who had enough problems. No need to get life any further complicated.

He was stopped at another light now, saw he had passed Le Jeune, had very nearly reached the address of Rolle's old clinic. Fifty-one years of practice, the last thirty in the same office, he was thinking. The old doc must have been doing something that drew them in.

He eased over into the right lane, behind a Sunbeam bread truck and in front of a battered pickup advertising lawn maintenance. He spotted an ancient Caddy pulling out of a spot just ahead, put on his turn signal. He eased to a stop, waiting for the Caddy to pull away, fully expecting an impatient blast from the horn of the pickup behind him, that being the standard Miami fuck-you for anyone so brazen as to halt the flow of progress, but there was surprising silence from that quarter. He swung straight into the spot, and waved his appreciation as the pickup chugged on by. He thought he saw an answering wave from the driver, but he must have imagined it. That would have constituted road courtesy beyond belief. Maybe the guy had been actually been waving a pistol.

Driscoll got out, checked to make sure he was within a couple feet of the curb, then surveyed the nearby storefronts. He'd pulled up in front of a cafe with a street window and a Brazilian flag draped over the entrance, covering up the numbers. To the east was a plumbing supply house, the numbers a few shy of the doctor's old address. To the west of the cafe was a weed-strewn lot, and beyond that, a smallish strip shopping center about the size of the one Driscoll kept his offices in. There were some interesting-looking pastries piled up in a cake saver on the counter of the cafe, but he forced himself to turn away, head toward the shopping center. Dinner, he told himself, just hold out until dinner.

The builder of the strip had supplied handicapped parking slots, attractive barrel-tile overhangs to shield the various entrances, even some handsome window planters with actual living greenery in them to spruce up the front of the place. What the builder had failed to provide were street numbers. There were letters of the alphabet over each little entryway, A, B, C, and so forth, but nowhere could Driscoll find an address. He considered angling back across the parking lot on to the next building, but he could see the rear of that low-slung place from here: a tall chain-link fence topped with concertina wire surrounded what seemed to be a half-block or more of mainly rusted-out, battered, and blasted automobiles, some of them dating well back into the history of transportation. It might have been a junkyard, or an impound yard, but he doubted it had ever housed a doctor's office.

He turned back to the little center, hoping to find a *clinica* or *medico* or something of the sort, but the closest thing he saw was the Accurso Pain and Chiropractico Centro. The entrance was all the way down at the end of the colonnade, but it was good enough, he thought, ignoring Lilly's Alterations, Fausto's Hair Salon, and something called Cielito Lindo Dos on the way. Two Pretty Something or Others, he managed, then gave up. If he couldn't even puzzle out the meaning of the sign, he thought, passing that doorway, why the hell bother going in?

The Accurso Pain Clinic was open, though there were no customers in the tiny waiting room. There was a wooden plaque hanging on one wall, with the name Dr. A. Agonistes and some strange lettering carved below. On a wall opposite was a life-sized schematic of a fleshless human body, its sinewy muscle groups spiked here and there with red arrows that he supposed were to indicate pain. The whole thing suggested a depiction of some flayed saint to Driscoll.

He saw a button beneath a frosted glass window, several words of Spanish on a card taped nearby. Driscoll stared at the Spanish for a moment. "Push," he translated for himself, and held his thumb to the button. The window shot open almost instantly, startling him.

A handsome, dark-haired woman in a white lab coat looked out the window at him. "Yes?" she said, her eyes luminous, framed by a lustrous mane of hair.

He stared at her for a moment, then remembered why he'd come. "I was looking for Dr. Agonistes," he said.

"Do you have an appointment?" she said, her English precise.

"Oh no," he said, waving his hand in what he hoped was a disarming gesture. "I just wanted to ask him a couple of questions."

"Are you a salesman?" she asked.

"No, no, nothing like that," he smiled. "I'm just trying to find someone."

"A bill collector," she said.

Driscoll paused. He fished around in his jacket pocket, came up with a card. He checked to be sure he hadn't written anything on the back of it, then handed it across the counter to her.

"I'm just trying to track down some information," he said as she studied the card. "I thought maybe the doctor would be able to help."

She glanced up from the card, looked him over carefully. "I am Dr. Agonistes," she said.

"Oh," he said, trying not to stare back. "Uh-huh. A lady chiropractor."

She watched him quizzically. "There were several of us in my school," she said.

"Oh, sure," he said. He pointed to the sign. "Just all the Spanish and all . . . I thought . . . "

"My father was Greek, my mother was from Madrid," she said, a smile playing about the corners of her mouth. "It's a Spanish neighborhood." She cocked her head at him. "Now what was it that you wanted to ask me?"

He nodded, still fighting the urge to step forward, peer over the counter, get a look at her legs. Jesus Christ, he thought, he was such a dinosaur when it came to women.

He cleared his throat, felt himself drawing in his gut. "First thing, I was wondering what your address was."

She laughed. "This is what they send private detectives out for?"

He gave her his shrug. "You ever look outside? There iddn't any numbers."

She raised her chin as if this were news to her. Then she pointed over his shoulder, out the tiny window that flanked the doorway. "You missed it coming in," she said. "The mailbox."

He turned, puzzled. "I looked," he said, turning back to her. "There wasn't any numbers on that mailbox."

She looked at him patiently, as if he were a slow-learning child. "The pole that holds it up," she said. "It's cast in the shape of the address."

He turned and looked again. From this angle it could have been anything supporting the box: a lightning bolt, a pole mangled by a careless driver. "Those are *numbers*?" he said.

"A four, a seven, a four, a seven." She gave him a smile as he turned back to her. "How long have you been at this?" she said.

He paused, calculating, realizing he'd walked too far. He also had the strangest feeling coming over him. He'd spent a career among cops who loved nothing more than busting chops. But this woman? This Dr. Agonistes?

He nodded, gave her her due, then surveyed the empty waiting room. "So how's the chiropracting business?"

She smiled. "Okay," she said. "We're even." She folded her hands in front of her, leaned familiarly on the counter. "This is my first week in business. I think I'm going to have to advertise. What do you think?"

He nodded absently. "They say it pays," he said. Though he'd noticed the absence of a wedding ring, his mind was scooting along now, wondering if was worth trying the Two Pretty What the Hells next door.

"You said you had a couple of questions," she prompted.

"Yeah," he said, drawing a weary breath. "But I think you just took care of it." He had the paper out, checking the numbers just to be sure. "The place I was looking for seems to have been next door, where the empty lot is."

She glanced out the window. "Gee," she said. "I wouldn't know. I think this building is seven or eight years old. Maybe they tore down what was next door the same time they built it."

"Well," he said, "thanks for your trouble." He allowed himself a candid look at her lovely features. The legs would be great, he decided. He didn't have to see. "I get a crick in my neck, I'll come back and see you."

She nodded. "I'm sorry I couldn't help you."

"Are you kidding?" Driscoll found himself saying. "Just looking at you makes me feel better already, Doc."

She laughed and Driscoll gave her his shrug, then let himself out. Maybe he shouldn't wait for his neck to stiffen up, he was thinking as he moved on down the line. Maybe there was such a thing as preventive chiropractic.

The Two Pretty Whatevers had already closed up shop or were not answering his knock, and nobody in Fausto's Hair nor Lilly's seemed willing or able to deal with Driscoll's English or untangle whatever he said to them in Spanish. He stood at the end of the shaded colonnade now, staring forlornly at the vacant lot that had apparently been the site of Dr. Rolle's clinic, thinking that he very well might have come to the end of the road as far as determining Paige Nobleman's true parentage was concerned. Of course, it was always possible that she'd gotten things mixed up in the heat of what had happened to her mother and sister. Maybe Barbara had said something entirely different and Paige had just heard it wrong, or the way she wanted to, whatever. Still, there was the matter of those photographs, and the fact that the infamous Dr. Rolle had been the one to deliver her . . .

. . . he shook his head, thinking he'd call the Nobleman woman and tell her he was still working on some leads, hoping that maybe Marie's efforts up north would bear fruit but not really believing it, and was ready to head back to the cafe, pick up one of those pastries for tonight's dessert, when he heard a popping sound nearby, and glanced over to see a guy at the verge of the vacant lot trying unsuccessfully to start up a string trimmer.

"*Jesu Cristo,*" Driscoll heard as the guy yanked the cord rhythmically. "*Cabron. Pendejo.*" The curses came casually, with no heat, as though it were some kind of litany meant to bring the spirit of the machine to life. The guy noticed Driscoll staring at him and smiled from beneath the broad brim of his straw hat.

"Hello, my friend," the guy said, still pulling on the trimmer cord.

Driscoll saw that the lawn maintenance truck that had waited so patiently for him to park earlier was nosed up at the edge of the lot. Maybe the guy *had* been waving at him. Maybe that's what happened: breathe lawn mower fumes all your life, you finally mellow out.

Driscoll nodded in return. "How you doin', pardner."

The guy took him at his word. "Oh, not so very well," he said.

"This machine . . . " He broke off, shaking his head. He flashed his smile again, leaned the thing against his truck. "Like me, is very old."

Driscoll looked again. Hard to tell, the guy's leathery face shadowed like it was. He could have been fifty-five, maybe. Maybe sixty.

"I am eighty tomorrow," the guy said, as if he'd read Driscoll's mind.

Driscoll turned and glanced in the direction of the Accurso Pain Clinic. Maybe the good doctor was right. Maybe he was in the wrong line of work.

"Well, Happy Birthday," Driscoll said. He'd thought of something else worth mentioning. "And thanks for waiting for me to park out there on the street."

The guy gave him a look. "That was you? Was nothing, my friend."

"Yeah, well, there's a lot of impatient people around these days," Driscoll said.

The guy made a gesture with his hands. "Once you are getting older," he said, "you understand certain things."

Driscoll nodded, then glanced at the guy again. "Eighty, huh? You been working around here long?"

The guy laughed. "How long is long?"

"Since when there was a building here," Driscoll said. "How about that?"

The guy waved it away. "Since long before that," he said.

Driscoll reached into his pocket, pulled out the photocopy of the birth certificate. He pointed out the section where Dr. Rolle had filled in her particulars. "You recognize this?"

The guy shook his head, and Driscoll's hopes evaporated. It had been a long shot anyway. He sighed and was about to fold the paper away when the guy spoke up. "I am not reading English," he said.

Driscoll shook his head. Maybe he was just out of practice. "Okay," he said. "I was wondering if you remember when a doctor used to have her office here. It was a woman . . . "

The old guy's face lit up. "Dr. Rolle," he said. "She was one good woman."

"You knew her?" Driscoll asked.

"Of course," the old guy said. "She own this property. I work for her one very long time."

"Uh-huh," Driscoll said. "Well, you wouldn't have any idea what happened to all the stuff when they tore the building down. All the office equipment, the records, stuff like that."

"Oh," the guy said, shaking his head. "I don't know about that things."

The guy turned to survey the property as if he were able to see what had once stood there. "She help a lot of people, Dr. Rolle."

"So I gather," Driscoll said. He tried to imagine it, too, back in the old days when Miami was just like anyplace else, only hotter, and maybe even sleepier, a place they used to call "Magic City," where a few folks came down for sun and fun, and a little glitter out on the beach . . . and way out here in what would have been the boonies then, some old building that wasn't quite so old, maybe an wood frame house with gables and a high front porch, the kind that looked like your grandmother was inside baking cookies, couldn't wait to sweep you in, put a big arm around you, make your troubles go away.

Except it wasn't Grandma's kisses and cookies, was it? It was what all those girls who came here had in the oven and the good doctor was knocking down a bundle running them in and out and never mind if things got too busy to keep the records straight. All that and more ran through his mind, none of it he saw the point of sharing with the old guy, who seemed to have drifted into the past.

Driscoll was about to give it up, clap the guy on the back and head on home, thinking he could always research the current owner down at County Courthouse, on the distant chance there was a storage room somewhere that still held what he needed, when it occurred to him. Jesus, he thought, it must have been early senility.

"So who do you work for now?" he said, waving his hand about the property. "Who pays you to cut the grass and all?"

"The sister," the old guy said then. "Dr. Rolle's sister." As if it were something that Driscoll should have known all along.

It took him another half-hour of shooting the shit, sharing a cafecito and a couple of pastries at the place next door, but by the time Driscoll drove away, he not only had the address of Dr. Rolle's only living relative, he had a pretty fair set of directions as to how to get to her place in Miami Springs.

The Springs was an older residential area that sat north of

Miami International Airport, squeezed in between that growing, roaring behemoth and another monster of sprawl called Hialeah, a couple miles further north. At one time, The Springs had been a desirable neighborhood, the home of any number of airline pilots, executives, and associated movers and shakers, but like so many other of the older parts of town, it had fallen on hard times as the younger families moved further west and further north, leaving dignity, grace, and charm to fend for themselves.

He spun around the big traffic circle that marked the business district, noting the blank eyes of half a dozen vacant shops, took the turn the old guy said you had to watch closely for, curled down a twisty series of streets that Driscoll suspected had been laid out according to the dictates of a canal or lake that he couldn't see from the street.

The home of Dr. Rolle's sister was well enough tended, but he noted the telltale signs: shingles missing here and there, probably peeled away by Hurricane Andrew a couple years back, the white paint blistered and shaded to a mildewy gray, a couple of panes in the saltbox windows cracked, one of them mended with packaging tape. Only the lawn showed signs of steady maintenance. Apparently the old guy had kept his shoulder to the wheel, doing what he could to stave off the inevitable.

He rang the bell two or three times, then pounded the door for good measure, and was about to give up when he heard a rustling from the side of the house and turned to see an old woman in a flowered hat leaning against a baby carriage and staring at him with a loony smile on her face.

"Who's that? Who's that tapping at my door?" she said as Driscoll gaped back at her. Naked, he thought at first. About a hundred and twenty-seven years old, and naked as a jaybird. Then he realized she was wearing a flesh-colored bikini, some kind of joke-shop bathing suit with breasts and pubic hair painted on the fabric.

"Are you selling something?" she continued. "I don't entertain salesmen, you know."

"No, ma'am," Driscoll shook his head, trying to keep his gaze off the suit. "I'm not a salesman." Thirty years on the force, all the kinds of people he'd seen, you'd think he'd be immune to just about anything. He stepped down off the slab porch and moved her way casually, slowly, as if one sudden move might send her bolting back into the underbrush. "I was looking for Dorothy Kiernan."

"That's me," she said. "Are you from the Publisher's Clearing House?"

"No, ma'am," Driscoll said evenly.

"You look a little like him," she said. "That Ed Whatsisname."

"Thank you," Driscoll said. "I wish I had his money."

It got a laugh from her. "Don't we all," she said.

Driscoll had edged up to within a few feet of her by now. He was about to try explaining himself when he heard something falling through the wild tangle of ficus trees behind them and a thudding sound as whatever it was struck the roof of the house.

"Excuse me," she said, an intense look coming over her features. She turned and wheeled her carriage off around the side of the house, almost sprinting through the thick grass.

By the time Driscoll rounded the corner of the house into the backyard and caught up with her, she was bent beneath the overhang of the roof, pawing through a pile of almond-shaped leaves. "Got you," she said abruptly, and rose to show it to him. It took him a moment to realize: a golf ball, he thought as she turned and tossed it into her baby carriage. From this vantage point he could see that the carriage was very nearly full of the things: white ones, orange ones, lemon-colored ones, even an odd model with two distinctly different-colored hemispheres.

He also saw that the Kiernan house, along with its neighbors, backed up not onto a lake or canal, as he had assumed, but onto a golf course. Right now, two middle-aged men wearing straw boaters, polo shirts, and colorful slacks were edging their electric cart off the neighboring fairway toward the spreading ficus trees of Mrs. Kiernan's backyard.

"This is private property," she shrieked as the cart bumped through the rough into the shade of the trees.

"Did you see a ball come over here?" the man in the passenger seat called, undeterred.

"You darned betcha I did," she said. "It bounced off my roof a minute ago and it's mine now." She pointed at the baby carriage. "I sell golf balls, seventy-five cents apiece, eight dollars a dozen. You can make one of 'em your ball if you want."

"Hey . . . " the guy said, beginning to object, but they were close enough to get a good look at her now.

"Forget it, Earl," the guy's partner said. He put a hand on Earl's arm and swung the cart in a tight circle, back out onto the normalcy of golfdom, Driscoll thought.

"Hah," she said, giving Driscoll a look of satisfaction. "That's the one good thing about this house," she said. "You know what I mean?"

"Not really," Driscoll said.

"We're sitting right on the corner of the dogleg for the four-teenth hole," she said, pointing off in the direction of the golfers. "It's a public course now, and most of those morons can't play worth a nickel. Every time I hear a ball come crashing through those trees, it's just like the sound a cash register makes."

She smiled at him. "I like to wear this suit because it scares the shit out of 'em. Makes 'em think I'm crazy."

Driscoll nodded. The golfer who'd lost his ball was dropping another in the fairway now, pausing to shoot a dark look their way before he took an awkward, slashing swing. Driscoll imagined another homeowner down the way, scurrying out to snatch up another ball. "It must happen a lot," he said.

"You wouldn't believe," she said. "Before the trees grew up, we were always replacing these patio windows back here." She gestured at a bank of sliding glass doors that ran across the back of the house. She shook her head. "I could sell golf balls till the day I die, it'd never make up for what my husband spent on window glass."

"Your husband," Driscoll said. "He's passed away?"

"I like to say 'dead.'" She gave him a smile that had a bit of wistfulness in it. "I'm to the point where I call a spade a spade, Mr. . . . "

"Driscoll," he said, extending his hand. "Vernon Driscoll."

She took it in a grasp that was surprisingly firm. Her palm was worn smooth, the skin on the back of her hand, like that on the rest of her body, a mass of wrinkles. She had to be eighty, maybe more. "I don't suppose you're in the market for any golf balls, are you, Mr. Driscoll?"

"I'm afraid not." Driscoll shook his head. "I came out here because I was talking to Joe Ordones, the fellow who cuts grass for you."

"I'm perfectly happy with him," she said, cutting in, "He's worked for our family since the beginning of time. He'll earn every cent you pay him."

Driscoll smiled. "That's not it, Mrs. Kiernan. I was looking for some information about your sister. Joe Ordones told me where to find you."

Her demeanor changed abruptly. "Are you a reporter?" she asked suspiciously.

"No," he said.

"A policeman?" Her voice had risen.

"I'm a private detective, Mrs. Kiernan." He reached into his pocket, displayed his identification. "I'm helping a woman who wants to find her birth parents," he said. "Your sister apparently brought this woman into the world."

The dreamy look in Mrs. Kiernan's eyes had evaporated, was replaced with a far-off look of sadness. "I don't know anything about that, Mister. My sister was her own person. She had her fair share of trouble and she did a heck of a lot of good. I was just a woman married to a man who sold insurance."

She gave him a glimpse of her loony smile. "And now I've become the crazy lady who sells golf balls. You have to do something to keep life interesting. You know what I mean?"

Driscoll nodded. "I didn't think you'd know about your sister's business," he said. "But Joe Ordones told me you owned the building where she practiced."

She nodded. "Duchess left what she had to me when she died," Mrs. Kiernan said. Her eyes brightened momentarily. "That's what we called her, you know. Duchess."

She stared off, lost in memory for a moment. "Anyway, that's how I came by the property. My husband tore down what was on it, started building a shopping center." She glanced up at Driscoll, clearly disgusted. "Can you imagine? An eighty-year-old man going into the business of building shopping centers?"

He gave her a look meant to show that he understood. "I was wondering if you know what might have happened to your sister's files back when the building was torn down."

She made a snorting sound, as if the idea were preposterous. It wasn't anything he hadn't expected, but that's how this business worked. You ran down every lead. You knocked on every door.

"This woman you're working for," Mrs. Kiernan said after a moment. "Does she have children of her own?"

"No," he said. "None that I know of."

"Me neither," she said. "Me nor Duchess neither one." She shook her head. "At least I got married and gave it a try. Once I'm gone, the Rolle blood is gone. The last of it."

Driscoll nodded absently. He checked his watch, wondering if he might still catch Deal at the fourplex. "Well, Mrs. Kiernan. It's been a real pleasure . . . "

"You sure you don't want any golf balls?" she said.

"I never took up the game," he said.

"That isn't what I asked you," she said.

He heard something in her voice, glanced up. The crazy-lady look in her eyes had gone. The person looking at him now had something to say, was trying to decide the best way to say it.

"We had reporters crawling all over us when they had the Kefauver thing down here."

"I'll bet you did," he said.

"The last years of Duchess's life, she could hardly turn around that there wasn't somebody snooping trying to get something on her."

Driscoll could only nod.

She looked up at the sky, as if she might be seeking advice from some invisible corner. She sighed finally, turned back to him.

"Never mind this bunch," she said, waving her hand at the baby carriage in deprecation. "I keep all the best stuff in the garage."

Driscoll sighed. What the hell, he'd paid less entertaining people a lot more money for even fewer answers. At least she'd been decent enough to wait for her thank you. "Eight bucks a dozen," he said, digging in his pocket. "Is that the going rate?"

"For you I'll make it five," she said, and led him to a boarded-over door in the back wall of the house.

For a golfer, it would have probably seemed like King Solomon's mines. That's what he was thinking at first, once she'd managed to jiggle the moisture-swollen door open, find a dangling light chain. Milk case after old-fashioned milk case filled with golf balls and stacked one on top of the other along one wall. Figure five hundred balls to the case, he had to be looking at easily ten thousand golf balls. Half a dozen sets of clubs, hanging from hooks fixed to the open rafters. A rain barrel full of bent and castoff clubs. A couple of huge mover's cartons overflowing with head covers, golf gloves, hats, and other, unidentifiable golfing paraphernalia.

"Where'd all this come from?" he wondered, finally.

"You'd be surprised what people leave around a golf course," she said. She gestured at the dangling sets of clubs, some of which were twirling like hanged men in the breeze from the open door.

"Once or twice a season somebody'll toss his whole outfit off that little bridge just across the way from me, right into the lake." She grinned. "Cuss, bang, splash. Up until a couple of years ago, I'd take me a little swim most every evening right in that very spot."

Driscoll saw a diver's mask, a snorkel, a set of fins hanging from a series of nails in a support post nearby. He nodded, still shaking his head at the haul. "Until you got too old to dive, is that it?"

"No," she said, affecting indignation. "There's a 'gator got into the lakes right after the hurricane. The way I look at it, there isn't any set of golf clubs worth wrassling an alligator over, is there?"

He laughed. If Dorothy Kiernan were crazy, and by the world's lights, she surely was, it was a form of dementia that he could look forward to in his later years. Even the bizarre bathing suit was beginning to strike him as the reasoned choice of a social critic.

She reached around him to the support post, flipped another light switch.

And then, of course, off in one corner, he saw what she'd actually brought him in to see: a rolltop desk with a banker's lamp and some dusty, taped-up cartons atop it, two leather armchairs, one stacked atop the other, and several old-fashioned oak file cabinets with a painter's cloth draped across their tops to protect them from the dust.

He turned to ask her if the office furniture were indeed what he thought it was, but the silence was interrupted by a loud thump on the roof of the garage. "Gotta get to work," she said, holding up her hand to forestall his question. "It's awful, the kind of pack rat a person becomes later in life. Too much effort to decide what's worth keeping and what isn't and before long, you find yourself holding on to everything." She waved her hand, as if she was tired of hearing herself talk.

"You look around," she told him, "pick out what you want, pay me on the way out." She gave him her crazy lady's grin again, and then was out the door.

It took Driscoll until well past dark, until he had soaked through his shirt with sweat, had breathed in enough dust to get a running start on emphysema, had turned his hands black with the accumulated grime of a dozen years, but once he'd discovered that Dorothy Kiernan had indeed turned over the lifetime repository of her sister's records to his inspection, he had not wavered.

It seemed as though drawers had been shuffled about randomly during the move from the office, and, as well, that whole files had been dumped and replaced randomly, but it was clear that Dr. Rolle had maintained meticulous records. She had also kept her own voluminous files on her opponents, and he noted with some amusement a series of letters calling into question some of the good Senator Kefauver's business practices. If her sister were any gauge, Driscoll thought, you would not go up against Dr. Rolle lightly.

It was nearly seven before he found the records for the last quarter of 1952, a file stuffed, for some reason, at the back of one of the oak cabinets between a fat folder with Eisenhower campaign materials and another labeled "P&L: 1948." As with the other files of that era that he'd glanced at, there was a daily office ledger, with patient names, a brief description of treatment, charges, and outstanding balances, all of that keyed to the master patient files, a series of clothbound volumes that seemed to be recopied and updated every few years. He'd found one such master volume for 1952, but there'd been no listing for the Coopers, nor under Paige's mother's maiden name. This would be the clincher, then, he thought. Were he to find no mention of Paige's mother in the doctor's daily log, he could fold up this tent and move on.

He flipped impatiently through the brittle pages, stopping to be sure he was interpreting the handwriting of the various secretaries correctly, finally found himself in early October. He knew that Paige's certificate listed a birthdate of October 31, but he was curious to see if her mother might not have come in for some kind of examination in the weeks prior. He traced down the crabbed entries without success, noticing four deliveries around mid-month—$75 being the apparent going rate—then nothing but apparently routine office treatments—$5 and $7.50—for the ten days following.

He flipped the page over, found he'd somehow skipped well

into November, had to go back and pry apart two sheets that had stuck together. He went to the top of the preceding page, found October 28 and 29—slow days, apparently—and was beginning to think that the good doctor had either cooked this set of books or the notion that she'd become rich at her game was some reporter's fantasy. He'd almost skimmed through the 30th when something caught him. He stopped and slid his finger back up the page to the last entry for that date, thinking that he'd probably just misread. He blinked his tired eyes, rubbed at them with the back of his hand, then held up the ledger to catch the dim light better. Still, the entry had not changed: "R. Gardner, Pre-Natal, 2,000—" The dollar sign had been omitted, but there was no mistaking that R. Gardner had been charged, and had paid, two thousand some-things, in cash, for her prenatal visit of October 30.

Driscoll shook his head, moved along to the entries for October 31: Rachael Milhauser, Lower Back Pain, $5; Charlotte Weaver, Hemorrhoids, $7.50; etc., etc., was about to go back to the Gardner entry when his gaze traveled to the top of the following page and he found it: "Mrs. Cooper, Delivery, 1,500—" with the sum again set-tled in cash that day. He scanned on through the rest of the day's records, but found nothing else of note. On a hunch, he skimmed over the next couple of weeks, looking for a Gardner delivery or another unusually large transaction, but there was nothing.

He set the ledger aside and looked around for the master files he'd been stacking nearby as he came across them. He flipped through the C's once again, then the R's for Paige's mother's maiden name—Richardson—then tried the G's.

There he had better luck. It was the first entry in the section, in fact: "Last Name: Gardner, First Name: R.," the page was headed. The rest of the information—address, phone, vital statis-tics—was blank. Someone, Dr. Rolle perhaps, had scrawled the words "Private Referral—Jack" across the bottom of the page. It wasn't all that unusual. He'd noticed others in equally cryptic notation among the records already. Young women, ashamed, scared, willing to pay whatever the freight to have Dr. Rolle relieve them of their burden, and to do it with what used to be termed "discretion."

Something was stapled to the back of the sheet on R. Gardner, and Driscoll flipped it over, finding just what he'd expected to find, what he'd found on the backs of the records of other mothers who'd come to be helped by Dr. Rolle: in this case, a carbon copy of the birth certificate for the baby delivered to Miss R. Gardner of Sherman Oaks, California, on October 31, 1952, no street address, no father's name listed, no further particulars. He realized there was another page sandwiched between the certificate and the master sheet, was about to dismiss it as a second copy, but something in his never-leave-a-stone-unturned nature made him take a look anyway.

It was a kind of one-two punch, he realized later, all of it circumstantial, to be sure, but striking him nonetheless with the force of undeniable truth. After a moment, he checked the information on the second birth record again, then flipped back to the one on top. He glanced up into the spiderwork of shadows cast by the bare rafters of the garage and laughed, as much at himself for being so dense and the neatness with which it had finally fallen into place as at the amazing quality of the information he had found.

After a moment, he found the lever that held the master files together, pressed it down hard, and carefully jimmied free the page with the birth records stapled to it. He undid the screws that bound the office ledger and slipped out the page he needed, redid both volumes, and folded what he'd taken into his coat pocket.

He was still oozing sweat when he shrugged back into his jacket, but he didn't care. He dropped his hat on his head. He switched off the light on the post in the middle of the garage, gave a couple of the hanged-man golf bags a twirl as he passed, turned off the dangling bulb with a tug on the chain, and moved out into the balmy Florida night, a grin on his face and a sizable banknote in his hand for Mrs. Kiernan. This was the good part, he was thinking, the fun part, the moment that made it all seem worthwhile. He wasn't sure yet what he should do with what he had just learned, but that was all right. For the moment, he was buoyed by the pure white bubble of light that was knowledge, by that and that alone.

34

"... all the way from Hong Kong," Marvin Mahler was saying, his voice having a crooning quality, or seeming to.

Though his image tended to blur in and out of focus, right now she could see him, standing above her, holding the syringe up to the light, loading something from a tiny bottle. He fiddled around until he seemed satisfied, then bent, plumped up a spot of flesh on her shoulder, jabbed the needle, and squeezed. She tried to twist away, heard him curse, throw himself across her to hold her still. She felt a moment's pain, a rush of something hot invading her arm that soon diminished to a warmth that made her drowsy.

When he raised up from her, she struggled briefly against the restraints that held her down, but her heart wasn't really in it. She wanted to speak to him, ask him why he'd brought her here, why he was doing these things to her, but though she could feel her tongue loll about in her mouth, the actual process of speech seemed a distant dream. She turned her head away from him, felt her cheek touch something on the pillow. Something cool, hard plastic, ridged with what seemed like buttons . . . it must have fallen from his pocket while he struggled with her.

"You don't have to worry, Paige," he said, patting her arm

263

reassuringly. "I'm following exact procedure here. Chinese doctors, British laboratory practices, it's all been worked out to the letter. I'd never do anything to hurt you or Rhonda." She watched from the corner of her eye, using her chin to try and tuck away the thing he'd left on the pillow. He broke off, shaking his head.

"Though now, of course, you've complicated things." He cast a sorrowful look her way. "I don't know, Paige. I just don't know what we'll have to do."

He sat down on the bed beside her, busying himself with something. She dug her chin at the object on her pillow again, and when she felt it slide on down into the tangle of bedcovers at last, she turned her head, saw woozily that he had her purse open, was pawing through the contents. He found a battered business card, held it up to examine it, then turned back to her. "The shame of it is, Gilbert tells me you've involved others." He held the card in front of her nose, waved it about. To Paige's eyes it was simply an undifferentiated oblong of brightness, but in her mind, she knew what it had to be. Vernon Driscoll, she thought. John Deal. Two decent men who'd taken it upon themselves to help her. What had she done to them?

"These are the men, I take it," Mahler continued. "These private investigators." He shook his head again.

"If it were just me, Paige, I'd be willing to do anything to avoid unpleasantness. I'd be willing to take some time, try and find out just where things stand down there in Florida. But you see, I have partners now. The sort of men who don't take chances and who don't tolerate mistakes." He tossed her purse onto a nightstand and stood, with the card held between his fingers. "I'm afraid it's going to take all my powers of persuasion just to keep *you* with us, don't you see?"

He smiled wistfully, bent to pat her cheek. "But don't worry," he said. "I've always tried to do right by you. You were a mediocre talent, I'm afraid, but you were such a lovely person." He gazed off, thinking, then turned back to her.

"That's been the tragedy of my life, Paige. Out there hustling on behalf of so many undeserving egomaniacs." He sighed wistfully. "Even Rhonda," he said, "sweet as she was, what I was selling there was a great head of hair and a big set of headlights." He patted Paige's cheek again. "But she had heart," he said. "And she sure loved you." He gave her another smile, and then he was gone.

Paige lay there wishing she had the capacity for tears, for rage, for any reaction. But, though her thoughts catapulted inside her wildly, her body remained numb. As dumb and unresponsive, she thought with sadness, as Rhonda's. She couldn't even move her hands to find out what he'd left behind. And what did it matter? Even if it were a gun, what could she do, pull the trigger with her tongue?

She heard Mahler's departing footsteps, heard the door to the room open and close, heard someone in the hallway talking to Mahler in a deep Texas drawl.

"Who's the babe in there, Mr. Mahler? She one of ours?"

And then Mahler's voice, reassuring, always in control. "Just one of my clients, Paco. Another one in trouble. She's had to come down to the desert for a little private detox."

There was more, then, something else that Texas Paco wanted to know about her, and Paige wanted to scream, kick, shout out for him to save her, that she'd tell him everything he wanted to know . . . but the very thought of such exertion seemed to exhaust her, empty her even of thought and intention, and what she did, in fact, was go to sleep.

**35**

"Does the name Rhonda Gardner mean anything to you?" Driscoll asked. It was a question he'd rehearsed posing to Paige Nobleman, but he'd considered things on the way back to the fourplex, decided it'd be better to try it out on Deal first.

Deal was on his back on the living room floor of his apartment, his hands and feet up in the air like some circus bear, balancing—or trying to balance, was more like it—his daughter in a hand-to-hand, foot-to-foot position that mirrored his own. Isabel was giggling furiously as one and another of her limbs wiggled and threatened collapse, and at first Driscoll wondered if Deal had heard him.

Then, abruptly, Deal snatched his hands away, sending his daughter into a shrieking tumble onto his chest. He hugged her, let her go, rolled over onto his hands and knees and glanced up at Driscoll.

"Are you kidding?" Deal said. *"African Drums? Wrong Way Street? High, Wide and Lonesome?"*

"I just wondered," Driscoll said.

"Rhonda Gardner was the hottest thing in movies when I was a kid," Deal said. "The way she wore those blouses . . . " He stopped himself, giving a look over his shoulder at Isabel, who was clambering onto his back for a horse ride. He turned back to Driscoll.

"Anyway, what about her? She still alive?"

"She's maybe ten years older than me," Driscoll said dryly.

Deal thought about it. "Kind of funny. You haven't seen her around for years."

Driscoll nodded. "They like a young blouse out there, I guess."

"So what about her?" Deal said. He was bucking and swaying now, sending Isabel into fresh gales of laughter.

Driscoll wasn't sure about the way Deal was behaving. From morose, Eeyore-like Deal to breezy, howyadoing Deal, not a problem in the world in less than twenty-four hours? Or maybe it was just an act he needed to put on for Isabel's sake.

"Look, I can come back in a little while," Driscoll said.

Deal glanced up from the floor where he'd tumbled onto his side. "Horsey's dead!" Isabel shrieked happily.

"It's okay," Deal told him. "It's her bedtime."

Mrs. Suarez, who'd been watching their games from the hall passage, nodded her agreement. "Is late," she said, stepping forward to scoop Isabel up in her arms. "Bath time."

"Noooooo," Isabel wailed, but she brightened when Deal stood, chucked her under the chin, gave her a kiss.

"Daddy'll come and give you a good night kiss," he said. "But you have to mind Mrs. Suarez now, okay?"

Isabel gave him a doubtful look, but after a moment buried her face in Mrs. Suarez's neck. Deal gave her another nudge in the ribs as the two of them went off down the hall, then turned back to Driscoll.

"Okay," he said. "Rhonda Gardner. What about her?"

Driscoll hesitated. There was a brightness in Deal's eyes, a hard quality about his smile. "You all right?" Driscoll asked. "Everything okay over at the clinic?"

"Peachy-keen," Deal said. His smile seemed an eyeblink away from a snarl.

"You taking something? Some kind of pills?"

Deal's mouth opened as if he were about to snap at him, then closed. He rubbed his face with his hands, glanced down the hallway at the splashing sounds that were emanating from the bathroom, then turned back to Driscoll.

"You got any beer at your place?" he asked.

"Sure," Driscoll said.

Deal nodded, then turned to call down the hallway. "I'm going across the hall, Mrs. Suarez."

She poked her head out the bathroom doorway, waved at him, and then the two of them walked out.

"She wants a divorce, Vernon." Deal had drained most of his beer in his first swallow, and was threatening to finish it now, on his second.

Driscoll sat across the kitchen table from him, stunned, trying his best to finish swallowing his beer. "Well, yeah," he managed, finally. "She might say anything right now, but that doesn't mean . . . "

"She means it, Vernon," Deal cut in. "Whoever she is now, anyway. Whoever she's become."

"You make it sound like a science fiction movie," Driscoll said.

Deal shrugged. "That's what it seems like. The scary part is, it's really happening. You live with somebody for fifteen years, you think you know them, then one day you wake up and take a ride to the Everglades . . . " He broke off, shaking his head.

Driscoll rose, went to the refrigerator, brought him another beer. "I wouldn't put too much stock in this, pardner. She'll spend some time down there, mellow out . . . "

Deal shook his head. "She wants to leave the clinic," he said.

Driscoll stared at him. "What's that doctor say?"

Deal shrugged. "The same thing he has from the beginning. She checked herself in, she can check herself out."

"Can't you do anything about that?" Driscoll said.

"Baker Act her?" Deal said. "Baker Act Janice?"

"Whatever it takes," Driscoll said.

"I don't know that I could do that," Deal said. "Besides, what are the grounds? I'm going to go to a judge, say, Your Honor, my wife doesn't love me anymore, I want to lock her up?"

"Yeah, but the thing with the credit cards, running off with Isabel, all that," Driscoll said. "You'd be willing to trust her with your daughter?"

Deal looked at him mournfully. "She doesn't want to take Isabel."

"What?!" Driscoll stared at him, dumbfounded.

Deal threw up his hands. "Janice knows she's confused. She wants to go off somewhere by herself, try to get her head straight. She's got a friend from college, a woman who runs an art and frame shop over on St. Armand's Key. She wants to stay with her, work in the shop . . . "

"You gotta be fucking kidding me," Driscoll said, falling back in his chair.

"She feels it'd be in Isabel's best interest to stay with me," Deal said, weary. "She'd be willing to go over there for a while and defer any precipitous decisions," he said.

"Precipitous decisions? That's the kind of words she used?"

Deal nodded.

"A mother doesn't want her child, that's all you need," Driscoll said, waving his hands about like John Madden diagramming a football play. "You gotta get her locked up, get some real shrinks working on her . . . "

He broke off as the sound of someone knocking on a door outside drifted through the open kitchen window. They looked at each other for a moment, then the knock came again.

"That's your door, pardner."

Deal checked his watch, then rose and moved down the hall, a concerned look on his face. Driscoll was close on his heels.

He swung Driscoll's door open, looked across the breezeway to find two smallish men in dark clothing standing before the entrance to his own apartment. He glanced out toward the street, wondering if he'd see some kind of delivery truck idling, some service van, but there was nothing.

"Can I help you," he called.

One of the men turned toward him, and Deal realized for the first time that they were Asians. "Look for John Deal," he said. He said it more like "John Dear," and it took Deal a moment to respond.

"I'm John Deal," he began . . . and then, in the split second it took for the second man to spin about, raising something in his hands, Deal realized what was about to happen.

Though he'd never felt more urgency, though he willed every fiber of himself to respond, it was as if time had ground to a halt and he were moving in a dream, forcing himself forward through an atmosphere of oil.

He heard Driscoll's footsteps echoing distinctly in the hallway behind him and felt himself turn, shout some unintelligible cry of warning, heard Driscoll's grunt of surprise as his shoulder drove into the big man's chest and sent him over as the explosions roared from the passageway behind them.

They both crashed onto the cold white tile of the foyer, and Deal rolled onto his back in time to see the little man advancing methodically across the breezeway toward them, a strange boxy-looking machine pistol braced at his hip, the muzzle erupting in bright bursts, a strange chuffing sound accompanying the flashes. He saw the tiles of the foyer explode in a brilliant line of fire that traced itself inward from the doorjamb, down the hallway an inch from his cheek, and on into the apartment, where it sounded as if all the kitchen appliances had burst instantaneously into shrapnel.

Deal's vision blurred and he felt a stinging wetness at his face. There was an unexpected silence, and he blinked his eyes back into focus to see the man with the machine pistol dodge past his partner toward the open doorway. Another second or two and he'd be upon them, lacing the two of them with that fire, Driscoll and Deal would be a couple more human hamburger statistics for the morning *Herald*, and what would they say about them anyway . . .

. . . when Deal braced his shoulders against Driscoll's bulk and lashed out with his foot, propelling the entrance door closed. There was a satisfying thud and a cry of pain as the heavy steel door crashed into the little man—something good to say for the revised building code, Deal thought, he might have used wood before the hurricane had changed everyone's attitude.

He scrambled onto his hands and knees, saw that Driscoll was clawing for the pistol he kept holstered at his ankle. No time to discuss the matter, Deal thought, and lunged into the big man once again. Deal, who'd been too slow as a safety and thirty pounds out of his class as a linebacker, had nonetheless kept a spot on the Florida State special teams for a couple years until injuries benched him for good. He'd gotten in his licks from time to time, played respectably if sparingly, but he'd never made a tackle as big as this one.

An inane play-by-play was running in his mind: "Whoa, Nellie, what a lick! The big guy never saw what hit him . . . " as his arms wrapped around Driscoll and rolled them both into the little closet Deal had insisted upon incorporating into each apartment entryway.

"Northerners have foyer closets, Deal," Janice had protested. "That's where they keep their coats and snowshoes. Spend the money on something else." But he had argued that Miamians needed a place for raincoats and so the closets stayed.

And it was fortunate that he had won out, he thought, watching the steel door erupt inward from automatic fire. The hallway went up in a shower of splintered tile. Another burst rattled off the solid steel jambs he'd installed—proof positive against a hurricane prying your door off its hinges, he'd told her during the same conversation—and he heard cries, excited shouts in a language he couldn't understand as fragments ricocheted outside.

There was silence then, and Deal could imagine Mrs. Suarez hearing the strange noises, opening up the doorway across the hall, maybe Isabel in her arms . . . but surely she'd know better, surely she'd be bunkered down, the calls already flying to 911 . . .

. . . Deal was trying desperately to remember if he'd locked his own door on the way out when he saw the shredded door inching slowly open, the snout of another stubby automatic appear in the crevice. Driscoll was still clawing for his pistol, but Deal knew he would never make it in time.

In another instant, the front door was going to swing open and whoever was holding that weapon was going to find them huddled in this thoughtful raincoat closet and blow them into a place where, snow or rain, you could skip along without a care.

Deal didn't really think about what he did next. Outrage, fear, instinct, some blend of all those things took care of it. He just did what it seemed he had to do. His feet were already tucked back under him, and it was a fairly simple move. He lunged forward, springing up out of the closet like some real-life jack-in-the-box. He flew upward, catching hold of the stubby barrel on the way up, driving it toward the ceiling just as the shots exploded again.

He felt pain in the palm of his hand and thought at first that he'd been hit. Then he smelled something bitter and realized it was heat, intense heat that he was feeling, the steel of the muzzle and silencer searing his palm as if he'd pressed it to a griddle.

He cried out as he went on over against the opposite wall, pulling the gunman through the now-open doorway. But his grip on the weapon was giving way, his skin seeming to melt, to grease his hand's slide down the barrel. A slide that would end in oblivion, he was thinking, as he felt the gunman wrench the pistol free.

Deal felt his shoulder crunch into the wallboard, his cheek strike the cool gray tile he'd picked out in that other lifetime, back when the world was still real.

He was waiting for the burst that would take the back of his head off when he heard a shot ring out, this one unsilenced, deafening in the confines of the foyer. There was another blast, and he felt something heavy strike him between the shoulder blades. Surely there'd be more pain than that, he was thinking. And there'd be more than one shot from the guy to take him out.

Then he realized. It was the machine pistol that had fallen upon him, and it was now clattering onto the tile by his cheek. And then, in the next moment, the body of the gunman slumped down upon him. Driscoll, he thought, his ears still ringing from the twin blasts. Driscoll had finally gotten his weapon free, fired at the second man.

He heard the sounds of running footsteps outside in the foyer and struggled up, out from under the inert form of the gunman. The foyer light was out, vaporized by the shots that had shredded the door, but he could hear Driscoll's curses, his raspy breathing beside him as the two of them fought toward the doorway and the receding footsteps of the second assailant.

"Shit," Deal heard then as Driscoll's foot hooked over his own. There was a heavy thud and a great outrush of breath as the ex-cop went down, and a clattering sound as his pistol went skittering out across the breezeway. By the time the two of them made it outside, they heard the sounds of a car door slamming, the shrieking of tires as a car disappeared into the night.

**36** Though the detectives from Metro would turn out to be far more interested in asking questions than answering them, Driscoll had managed to go over the body before the investigating team had arrived. He'd diverted the driver of the first patrol car that had responded back to his unit to put in a lookout for the car they'd heard escaping, then completed his own hasty search. As he would tell Deal later, the dead man hadn't been carrying identification, but his suit held the label of a Hong Kong tailor. There was a half-eaten package of airline peanuts in his jacket, a thousand dollars in fifties and a package of matches from a Los Angeles restaurant in his pants. Once Deal had managed to get Mrs. Suarez calmed down and back inside in case Isabel awoke, Driscoll had beckoned him back to where the body lay. By now several squad cars had arrived, but no one seemed ready to interfere with Driscoll.

The ex-cop was kneeling, holding up the hand of the dead man, nodding for Deal to take a closer look. On the skin between the thumb and palm was a tiny tattoo, something that wouldn't ordinarily be visible unless the hand were splayed open, as Driscoll held it now. At first Deal had thought it was some abstract design, but when Driscoll trained a penlight on the mark, he could see that it was a Chinese hieroglyphic, very intricately done.

"What is it?" Deal asked.

Driscoll had shrugged, dropping the man's hand back to the tile. "Gang bullshit," Driscoll said.

"Gang?" Deal said, disbelieving. "He's part of some street gang?"

Driscoll shook his head. "Gang, as in mob." He glanced up. "*Triad,* to be more exact. You hear about them on the West Coast and New York, for the most part."

"What are you talking about, Driscoll? Chinese mobsters? Why would they come after me?"

Driscoll shrugged. "You must have pissed them off."

"It's not funny, Driscoll."

"Well, what's your explanation, pardner? You think this was some everyday South Florida home invasion? The last I checked, the Chinese down here weren't exactly involved in that." He gestured at the body. "This guy's from L.A., probably from Taiwan before that."

Deal shook his head. "But it doesn't make any sense."

"Oh, it makes sense, all right," Driscoll told him as a white Ford, not unlike the one the ex-cop drove, pulled up to the curb. A pair of detectives got out, pausing as a patrolman filled them in. "The only problem is, we're just not in the place where we can see *how,* as yet."

"So how do we get to that place, Driscoll?" Deal asked.

"Hard to say." Driscoll shrugged again, eyeing the body at their feet. He gestured downward then. "First thing, let's get the mess cleaned up."

"She *what?*" Driscoll said into the phone. "When was this?"

They were in Deal's apartment now, the detectives finally gone, the body of the man who had nearly killed them taken away, though skeins of yellow police-line tape still draped the entrance and breezeway like some huge otherworldly spider had been at work in a place where Deal had just wanted to make a life.

One cruiser remained out at the curb in deference to Driscoll's request. "They're not coming back," Driscoll had said, and Deal wanted to believe him. "But we got a hysterical woman and a little girl in here," he'd pointed out to the investigating officers. And so a car would be staying, at least for the night.

Deal's eyes rested on the amber parking lights of the vehicle, his mind replaying the events of the evening, trying to apply logic to something that seemed essentially illogical. He scarcely paid attention to what Driscoll was saying now. The ex-cop, whose telephone had been blasted into fragments by a stray round from what the detectives assumed was an M-10, had seemed intent upon calling Paige Nobleman, but Deal didn't see why it was so important at this moment.

His mind kept wandering, imagining what might have happened if Mrs. Suarez had opened the door before he and Driscoll had stumbled out. And he kept thinking of Isabel, who had mercifully slept through everything, just as she'd slept through the raging of Hurricane Andrew, without a peep.

He rubbed at his bandaged palm absently, feeling fortunate the burn hadn't been worse than it had turned out. He and Driscoll had debated the wisdom of telling Janice what had taken place—*Yes, things are fine at home, except for the Chinese guys who showed up to kill me for reasons I couldn't begin to explain*—but in the end, they'd settled on letting the detectives confer with the director of the clinic where Janice was staying. Security at the place, already reasonably tight, would be augmented, and patrols in the area would be doubled for the time being. The detectives had listened to what Driscoll had to say about the triads, but had been noncommittal at best.

"You get a lot of street hunters fly in from a lot of places during the tourist season," the lead detective had said. He was a squared-off man in his fifties and looked ready to go in for the night. "Maybe these guys saw your watch."

The detective nodded at the aged Rolex Deal wore—nothing he would have ever bought, it had been a welcome-to-the-partnership gift from his father, fifteen years before. Deal wore it to the job as if it were any other watch; to him, it had long since become too battered to seem anything worth stealing.

"But he asked for me by name," Deal said, idly running his thumb over the crystal of his watch. The thing had become so scratched up, it was getting hard to read the time.

"He could've overhead that somewhere," the detective said. "You were out around town on some jobs today, right?"

"Sure," Deal said, "but . . . "

"These guys see you driving some custom Caddy, figure you're a rich *jefe*, they'll follow you around all day," he said, "just waiting for their chance."

"Rich *jefe?*" Deal echoed, disbelieving. The thought of the Hog as some symbol of status was even more ludicrous.

The detective saw the incredulous look on Deal's face, but that didn't seem to concern him greatly. "Don't worry," the detective had said, apparently as dismissive of any personal motive for the attack as Driscoll was convinced of it. "You're not going to have any more trouble with these scumbags. They'll just move on to the next victim."

Deal was replaying the scene, still marveling at the detective's studied cynicism, when he realized that Driscoll had his hand on his arm, was trying to get his attention.

Driscoll had his other hand clamped over the receiver, had turned to Deal, a look of concern on his face. "They haven't seen Paige Nobleman at her hotel for a day and a half," he said. "Some big guy, they think it was her limo driver, checked her out late Sunday afternoon."

Deal shook his head, trying to focus on what Driscoll was saying. "So what?"

"So that would have been before she came over here," Driscoll said. "Didn't she say she was going back to her hotel?"

Deal sighed. Compared to what had just happened to them, it seemed like some abstract puzzle, some game show question Driscoll had posed. Still, maybe it was worth it, take any excuse to veer away from his own situation for a moment. Finally he nodded. "That's what she said, Vernon."

"I thought so," Driscoll said. He shook his head in puzzlement, then turned back to speak into the phone. "You have any idea who this limo guy worked for?" he asked whoever was on the other end.

Driscoll listened for a minute, made a couple of notes. "Okay, thanks," he added, and hung up.

"You got a phone book?" he said to Deal.

Phone book, Deal was thinking. Is that the answer or the question.

"The hell with it," Driscoll said impatiently. He punched out the number of Information, asked for the number of a limo service. He glanced at Deal's questioning look, and waved his hand. "Turns out that the way she found that shitbox hotel in the first place," he explained, "the first guy driving her was a *compadre* of the person who owns the hotel. This driver works for a service up in Dania."

Deal glanced at his watch as Driscoll began punching in the number. "It's almost midnight," he said idly. He was mildly intrigued suddenly, realizing that his brain could operate on one level, stay numb on so many others.

"So?" Driscoll said. "Who do you think rents limos in this town? The kind of people who go to bed early?"

He motioned Deal quiet abruptly, then spoke into the phone. "Yeah, how you doin'. This is Lieutenant Vernon Driscoll down at Metro-Dade." He waved off Deal's disapproving look.

"Yeah, that's right. I need to talk to one of your drivers, a guy name of Florentino Reyes." He shot Deal his I-know-what-I'm-doing look, but the expression fell away before he got the chance to settle back in his chair.

"Uh-huh," he said. "So how long's this been?" Driscoll moistened the tip of his pencil with his tongue, began writing again.

"How about his replacement," he said after he'd finished. "No, I said *replacement.*" He cut a glance at Deal that could only mean he was talking to someone with a Hispanic accent.

"A big guy. Some kind of Samoan or something," Driscoll said, impatiently."

"*Samoan!*" The ex-cop repeated. "As in a person from the kingdom of Samoa."

He listened for a moment, finally nodding. "Okay, I got it. I see. Sure. I'll follow up on the stolen car report. You bet." He hung up then, sat staring at Deal for a moment.

"It seems this Florentino Reyes has disappeared," Driscoll said finally, "along with the limo he had checked out to drive Ms. Nobleman around in, all of this arranged by a Mr. Marvin Mahler of Los Angeles." Deal gave him a questioning look and Driscoll shrugged. "Must be her manager or whatever.

"Anyway, Reyes was supposed to bring the car back Sunday night," he continued, "leave it off for end-of-the-week servicing, pick up another one." He opened his big palms on the tabletop. "Nobody's seen him since Friday. A coworker went by his house, found the place locked up, his dog inside going apeshit. The company, being the trusting souls they are, guy's only worked for them about twenty years, they filed a stolen car report this morning. They thought maybe I was calling to tell them we found it."

Deal nodded. "What about this Samoan guy?"

Driscoll shrugged. "The fellow who owns the hotel, this Reyes's buddy, he says that's who showed up to check Ms. Nobleman out. He thought maybe it was Reyes's relief. Great big guy wearing a driver's cap and a coat, looked more like he ought to be playing for the Dolphins." Driscoll broke off, jabbed his thumb toward the phone. "But the limo company doesn't know anything about him."

They sat staring at each other for a moment, then Driscoll picked up the phone. He checked his notepad and dialed again. "Yeah. This the Grover Cleveland? Mr. Escobedo? Vernon Driscoll here. Right. This Samoan guy you were talking about who did the checking out for Ms. Nobleman. Yeah, that one. Listen, is there any chance he could have been Chinese? Uh-huh. No, that's Japan, your sumos. Right. Okay, Mr. Escobedo. Thanks for your trouble."

Driscoll turned back to Deal. "It's a definite maybe," he said. "Mr. Escobedo says that all your Orientals look pretty much the same to him." Driscoll raised a finger. "They're very nice people, though."

"So what's the point, Driscoll?"

Driscoll looked at him as if he were brain dead. He opened his mouth to deliver some withering remark, then caught himself. "You're right," he said, holding up his hand in a gesture of apology.

Deal shook his head. "I didn't say anything."

But Driscoll seemed not to be listening. "I never got around to telling you," he said.

"Telling me what, Driscoll?"

"I found out who Paige Nobleman's mother is," he said absently.

Deal stared at him. "Well, who?"

But Driscoll's mind was already elsewhere. "You mind if I call long distance?" he said, already picking up the phone.

Using a contact in the L.A. County Sheriff's office, it took Driscoll less than a half-hour to discover that Rhonda Gardner had a home in Westwood and an unlisted telephone number in her name. After a few more minutes of conversation with a Los Angeles telephone operator, he was talking to someone at the Gardner home.

By then, of course, Deal had figured out who Driscoll believed to be the mother of Paige Nobleman. But it still didn't seem possible. It seemed to be a night of things that did not seem possible. In fact, that's what his life had turned into: a state of affairs that a month ago he could not have ever dreamed possible.

"And exactly why is it Ms. Gardner can't speak to me?" Driscoll was saying.

"Oh," he grunted. He tapped his pencil on the table for a moment. "I'm sorry to hear about that."

He paused, thinking about something, then turned back to the phone. "Let me ask you, does Ms. Gardner have some kind of significant other or personal representative out there, somebody I could get in touch with?"

He stopped, apparently listening to the person on the other end. "Excuse me," he cut in, flipping a couple of pages back in his notepad. "Would that be *Marvin* Mahler?"

Driscoll gave Deal a significant glance, then turned back to the phone. "I see. Now would that be the same Marvin Mahler who's the agent for Paige Nobleman?"

Driscoll was nodding now, his gaze locked with Deal's. "Right. How about if I spoke to Mr. Mahler, then." He held the receiver away from his ear a moment and Deal could hear the buzz of conversation coming from the other end.

"Uh-huh," Driscoll was saying. "I got it," He made another note. "Okay, I appreciate the trouble." Deal thought he was about to hang up, when he raised a finger in the air as if whomever he was speaking to might be able to see it. "One last thing," he said. "I was wondering if you might have received any calls from a Paige Nobleman recently."

He gave Deal a significant glance. "Uh-huh. Right. Not since then, huh."

Driscoll had something approaching a look of satisfaction on his face now. "Well, thanks again, Ms. Retton. You bet."

He hung up then and turned to Deal, his hand up to forestall Deal's questions. He opened his mouth to say something, then thought better of it. He sat back in his chair, massaging his face with his big hands for a moment.

When he looked at Deal again, his expression was intent. "Okay, just one more phone call. Let me give it a shot, then I'll tell you what I think."

Deal threw up his hands. He'd long since learned it was impossible to get Driscoll to explain anything before he was ready. It was like when he first started going out on the jobs and would try to get his father to tell him how to perform some seemingly arcane operation involving carpentry. "I'll explain it to you when I'm damn good and ready," his father would say. "Now bring me that power cord/hammer/box of nails."

Driscoll finished dialing another long-distance-sized series of numbers, then sat waiting for the connection to be made. Deal thought he heard an answering click. After a moment an odd expression came over Driscoll's features.

"Listen," Driscoll said, thrusting the phone at him. "What do you make of this?"

Deal took the phone, puzzled. Brought it to his ear. And then he heard the scream.

The chirring of the tiny phone came to Paige through the thickness of her pillow. It was a sound she sensed more than heard, seeming to reach her from a distance that was greater than space itself could contain. She found herself remembering all the times she'd endured exhausting, disorienting nighttime shoots, would have to sleep days, rise with the sun going down, force herself out of bed like a creature not fully human.

That's what she had become once again, she knew. Whatever Mahler had injected her with had rendered her not fully human. And no way she could move from this bed, not with the restraints that bound her, not with her muscles turned to lead by the drug.

A second ring sounded. It took every bit of her will, focusing on this muscle, then that, until she could nudge the corner of the pillow aside with her chin. She had no idea if the phone had sounded before, no idea if she'd missed other opportunities, how many times it had already rung. Any moment now whoever was calling could ring off, someone would hear the sounds or Mahler would come looking in this room for his misplaced phone . . . but if she could just manage to hit the right button, get a line open and please God let an operator come on, then maybe, some way, she could find help.

The third ring came. She struggled wormlike against the pillow, which in her state was as massive an obstacle as a boulder, felt it buckle and pop up away from the phone. Gasping with effort, she lunged toward the phone before it could ring again, unmuffled.

She felt the side of her face slap down the tiny set. She rolled her cheek blindly back and forth over the buttons, fearing that any moment the phone would blare again or she'd set off some terrible electronic howl that would bring her captors running . . .

. . . and then, mercifully, she heard the connection make. She lay exhausted, thinking that small triumph would have seemed enough, but then she heard the voice on the other end, and that was enough to bring tears to her unfocused eyes.

"This is Vernon Driscoll," the voice said, and for a moment, she believed that she had somehow, miraculously, been saved. But then she tried to speak.

"Who's there?" Driscoll's voice repeated. "Who *is* this?"

Paige listened to the impatience build in Driscoll's voice, willing herself frantically to respond. She could hear her pleas for help echoing inside her mind, a pressure building that seemed enough to blow her head apart. But still, although she fought to cry out with every ounce of strength, although she felt the muscles of her neck and throat quiver with effort, she remained mute:

"Huh . . . huh . . . huh," she managed. "Huh . . . huh . . . huh . . . " Tears were running freely down her face now, all her joy turned in an instant to frustration, rage, and despair. She heard a tiny coughing sound emerge from the back of her throat, wondered for a moment whether it signified the breaking of the dam or if she were simply about to choke and die . . . and then she felt a rough hand clamp down on her shoulder.

It would have taken her far too long to will her gaze upward, so all that happened seemed to come almost by proxy. Someone was shouting in a language she did not understand. She felt the phone being wrenched away from her, felt something hard strike her at the temple, and heard a scream that must have come from her own throat.

Although there was pain, it seemed very far away. She sensed Driscoll's voice swirling away from her as if he, or she, were plunging down a dark, bottomless well. There was another blow then, and the speed of her fall, or was it his, increased into a hurtling, spinning plunge. And finally, one of them struck bottom.

Terrence Terrell himself met Deal and Driscoll at the hangar on the north side of Miami International Airport, where he kept his planes at the ready. The owner of the Florida Manatees, and a man who'd amassed an incalculable fortune as the mastermind of the alternative-to-IBM personal computer, he was accustomed to jetting anywhere on a moment's notice. The call from Deal had not seemed out of the ordinary at all. He hadn't wanted to know the details: it was enough that Deal needed urgently to get to a friend's aid, that the final destination was Palm Springs.

Before Deal made the call to Terrell, Driscoll had laid out what he'd found in Dr. Rolle's records. Still not proof positive, Deal would admit, but he'd be willing to give odds now that Paige Nobleman's real mother had been a pretty fair actress herself; unfortunately, Rhonda Gardner, off in the orbit of Alzheimer's, was in no condition to confirm anything, and the only other person who might shed light on the matter—Marvin Mahler, Rhonda's husband and, significantly enough, Paige's agent—was incommunicado, on the set of a film at the family compound with the unlikely name, somewhere deep in the Southern California desert.

But Deal did know this much: Barbara Cooper had been murdered only hours after telling Paige she'd been adopted. Shortly after Paige came to them for help, he and Driscoll had very nearly been killed. Now Paige herself appeared to be in danger. Impossible to say who was responsible, but Deal was convinced of the why, part of it, at least. Someone was willing to do anything to cover up Paige Nobleman's true identity. Nothing else made sense.

And yet, who could they turn to for help? To the local authorities, there could be no apparent connection between a suicide in Fort Lauderdale and one more garden-variety home invasion in Miami. And as for Paige's disappearance, what would ensue from any complaint? Some bored cop calling another bored cop on the opposite coast, "Hey, would you run down to this hacienda in the desert, see if they have an actress tied up there? Oh, they do that all the time out there?" Sure. Thanks and good night.

And even if their concerns were taken seriously, what if Marvin Mahler—never mind why for the moment—was connected to all this? A phone call, a knock on the door—"Notice any adopted actresses around here, Mr. Mahler?"—what would that accomplish, except to warn him? They had one option, it seemed, the one they were about to take. If it came to nothing, if they found Paige lounging in the desert at poolside—"Oh, that? I must have been dreaming when the phone rang."—then they could come home, accept all that had happened as part of normal life in a place where murder was just another aspect of the landscape: palms, flamingos, and corpses.

But if they did not go, and Paige were never heard from again . . . No, Deal shook his head, hearing the plane's engines whining to life. He would not hesitate this time. They would all be looking over their shoulders for the duration.

"The pilot's ready and the plane's yours, John." Terrell's voice broke into his thoughts. Terrell stepped forward, shook Deal's hand, then Driscoll's. "You're just lucky I was at home, that's all." Home being the twenty-room mansion that sat between Brickell Avenue and the bay, the place that Deal had rebuilt for Terrell after the onslaught of Hurricane Andrew.

Deal nodded his thanks. Typical of Terrell that he wouldn't ask for any explanation. If Deal had made such an unusual request, there had to be good reason. He stood there now, as apparently unconcerned as if Deal had asked to take the family car for a spin around the block.

"We're giving you the Lear Fifty-Five," he said, pointing at the gleaming plane poised before the doors of the hangar. "It'll get you out there with one stop, and quicker than the little one."

Deal glanced back into the shadows where the "little one" sat. This close, both planes seemed as big as the commuter aircraft he'd flown around the state, and either of the sleek-looking craft seemed capable of an around-the-world expedition. He turned to Terrell, nodded his thanks. "I really appreciate this, Mr. Terrell."

Terrell gave the two of them an appraising look. "You sure you two don't need any help?"

"I appreciate the offer," Deal said.

"I have some fellows around, they wouldn't mind whatever came up, you know," Terrell said.

And a part of Deal *was* grateful for that offer, wanted to grab Terrell's sleeve and say, Yes, lend us the whole damned cavalry, but he knew it couldn't work that way. He wasn't sure if it was going to work *any* way, for that matter, but there didn't seem to be much choice. It would have to be Deal and Driscoll, for better or for worse, and Deal gave Terrell a smile that said so.

"We're okay," Driscoll added.

"Good luck, then," Terrell said, giving them his hand once more, and within moments they were strapped in their seats, sinking back as the powerful engines took them into the night, streaking toward California.

 Mahler awoke just before dawn, too groggy to know where he was at first; for a moment he felt only tired, only alive, even good. Then the memory of where he had taken himself swept back and he felt the anxious dread reclaim him.

The filming had gone on until nearly midnight, the old man interrupting the proceedings what seemed like every five minutes to give Mahler and anyone within earshot a lecture on Chinese sexuality. By the time Mahler had called a halt, the actors, already wired to the gills, were ready to kill the old bastard. Even Cross's wife, Cherise, had taken him aside to vent her frustrations in a furious whisper.

"If I hear about the helpless female and the 'sacred square inch' one more time, I'm going to scream," she said. "Let's let the old fart tie me up and stick it in my 'inch.' Maybe that'll quiet him down."

Mahler had cast a glance back off the set, where the old man had ensconced himself in one of the high-backed chairs he'd had Gabriel bring down from the living room. He looked like a gnome back there, like some extra out of a temple scene in a kung fu movie, far too wizened to have a sexual thought. But that hadn't stopped him.

First, when he'd realized what the script's excuse for a story line was about, he'd groused that it had no relevance to the Chinese audience. So they'd given Cherise a geisha outfit and had Paco come up with a couple of lines about her taking over an offshore university for nefarious political reasons. None of it made any sense, but the old guy had been satisfied.

Then, last night, he'd complained that the women playing the roles of college girls came off as too "mature." It had taken wardrobe nearly an hour to get them recoiffed, refitted, and re-made up. Finally, to Mahler's eye, they had two hookers dressed in Barbie clothes, but the old man was content once again.

Hardly had they finished the next setup, however, than the old man had started raving about pigeon eggs. Mahler had to shut everything down again, listen to a discourse that he finally realized was about how virginity was traditionally proven in China.

They'd had to break for another hour while the entirety of He-Men Film Services scavenged about the darkness outside for enough oval river rocks of the appropriate size, then painted them up to the old man's specifications for pigeon eggs.

One of the He-Men had been at Mahler's side watching the ensuing shot. The Mr. T lookalike knelt before one of the spread-eagled Barbies, trying to insert one of the supposed eggs in the crucial spot. His partner stood by, leering, ready to signify his approval through action once this coed's innocence had been established without a doubt.

"Either one of those broads could make an ostrich egg disappear," the He-Man said in Mahler's ear. And though Mahler suspected it was true, he had become philosophical. A couple more days of this insanity, the old guy would get bored, go back to counting his money in Beverly Hills, leave them the hell alone. He'd hoped to average twelve minutes a day, have this piece of shit wrapped in a week, but unless things changed, they'd be rivaling the shooting schedule of *Heaven's Gate*. Patience, he told himself. Have patience. Get this film made, win the old guy's confidence, all the rest of them could be farmed out to the usual players.

He sat on the edge of the bed, rubbing feeling back into his face. There had also been the interruption when he'd sent one of the old guy's minions up to check on Paige and he'd discovered where his cellular phone had been. What a piece of carelessness that had been. While Paige was certainly incapable of making any calls, the very prospect had been enough to stun him.

He shoved himself off the bed, shuddering anew at the thought of what he faced with Paige, staggered into the bathroom. It was true what he'd said—she was just another above-average looker with a mediocre talent, somebody whom he'd had to bust his butt to keep working. But she was a good kid. She'd never begrudged her status, never whined for leads. Downright amazing in their business.

But what were the choices, after all? Keep her loaded up with the meds, move her into the Brentwood house, create a vegetable wing? He didn't think it would wash. The old guy had already told him what to do about the problem, but Mahler had hesitated. The other "corrections," as he'd begun thinking of them, had been abstract, matters taken care of by others, and at some distance. Even Mendanian's death he could rationalize. Mendanian had gone off on his own, crossed the old man as much as Mahler. Mahler wasn't responsible for what had happened. But now there was Paige, and there was no turning from his own responsibility in the matter.

He'd felt a fierce burning at his bladder, but when he tried to relieve himself, what should have been a stream to make a horse envious came out as a pitiful trickle. Probably prostate cancer coming on, he thought. Add it to the list.

He forced himself to the sink, lathered his face, tried to shave without looking himself in the eye. He knew it was a sad picture, all right, one he wasn't anxious to confront. A guy his age doing what he was doing for the sake of money. What the hell, he could have ridden out the string just the way things had been.

But, for all the bullshit about him being Mr. Super Agent, when it came right down to it, he'd been a guy working for wages, it would have meant going to the grave still kissing ass, Rhonda's and everyone else's in the business, and besides, he reminded himself, the way he'd set it up to begin with, it was so simple, no one was going to be hurt, and he'd be able to walk away with a fortune, maybe even nurse Rhonda back to a miraculous recovery— maybe they could reclaim something of the old days, ride out the string together if he were his own man. She'd never be the wiser, after all. No one would, with Paige out of the way.

He closed his eyes on the thought, took a deep breath, forced himself to meet his own gaze in the mirror. All this self-doubt, all the anxiety, it had to be banished. He was too far in now to change course. The old man was responsible for the things that had happened. Mahler had had no choice. And he had no choice now.

The sun would be up soon, he'd have coffee, a decent breakfast, a good piss, and things would be just fine. He'd have a word with the old man, let one of the goons clear out the guest wing. He would steel himself and life would go on. That's the way it would be. And once the money was rolling in, all this weasely thinking would vanish.

That's what he was telling himself, at least, when the old guy's majordomo appeared in the foggy mirror beside his half-lathered face like some vision out of a horror film, scared the living shit out of him.

"How'd you get in here?" Mahler gasped. He held his chest, thinking maybe his heart was going to go, along with the prostate. "I had the door locked. I know I did."

But the big guy shrugged his question away, seemed to glower at him through the mirror.

"Two men," the guy was saying. "Two men from Florida downstairs to see you."

 "We're sorry to trouble you, Mr. Mahler," Driscoll said as he gave him his card. "We understand you're making a movie down here."

"That's true," Mahler said. He glanced at the card, then took a closer look at the two of them. The Chinese man who'd admitted them into the house stood just behind him, his hands behind his back in a casual pose, his eyes missing nothing. Dressed all in black—turtleneck, slacks, even his high-tops—he was the picture of some latter-day palace guard.

Deal noted a speck of shaving cream on Mahler's ear, sensed a wavering in his gaze as their eyes met, but maybe the latter was just a trick of the lighting. They were in the vast living room, the place still gloomy, even with a couple of parchment-shaded floor lamps burning. There were banks of big windows flanking the fireplace on one wall, but the sun had yet to clear the jagged desert peaks visible in the east.

"So what is it, a Western?" Deal asked.

"Actually," Mahler said after a moment, "it's a contemporary piece. We're using one wing of the estate to do some interior shooting."

Driscoll nodded. "Your wife's place, I understand."

Mahler nodded, apparently surprised by what Driscoll knew.

"There's quite a bit of film history connected with this location," he said. *The Devil's Due* was shot in this very room, with Constance MacKenzie and Humphrey Bogart. You remember the famous death scene?" He pointed. "Right over there by the fireplace?"

Driscoll glanced over, shrugged. Deal couldn't tell if that meant he remembered. "You make a lot of films, Mr. Mahler?"

Mahler gave him a look. The man was gathering strength, Deal thought. "It's my first, Mr. . . . "

"Driscoll," the ex-cop said. "Vernon Driscoll. This is John Deal." No one offered to shake hands.

Mahler nodded. "Most of my life I've spent getting people into movies," he said. "I'm really an agent." He waved his hand about. "I'm just down here indulging a whim."

"I've never seen a movie being made," Deal said, letting the suggestion linger.

"Not very exciting, I'm afraid."

"It'd be worth it, just to see what goes on," Deal said.

Mahler gave a shrug of his own. "We're having to keep our sets closed," he said.

"Uh-huh," Deal said, feeling his innate distrust growing. "Why's that?"

Mahler let out his breath with a sigh. "Tell me, Mr. Deal, is that it? Is that why you sought me out? Because you'd like to watch a movie being made?"

Driscoll cut in. "No, Mr. Mahler, it isn't."

Mahler turned back to him then, and the two men faced each other for a moment. Deal noted a movement out in the hallway, saw a familiar hulking shape appear briefly in silhouette, then disappear.

"There's a phone number on the back of the card there," Driscoll said. "I wonder if you'd mind taking a look at it."

Mahler's eyes stayed on Driscoll for a moment, but finally he gave in, turned the card over. Deal watched intently, but if the man had a reaction to what was written there, it was not visible. When Mahler looked up, his gaze went to Deal.

"I owned a portable phone with that number," he said.

"Owned . . . ?" Deal said. He felt menace creeping into his voice, saw Driscoll shoot him a warning glance. He tried to force himself to be patient. What he wanted to do was jack this scum-

bag up by the balls, squeeze him until he sang opera.

"I lost it," Mahler said, still looking at Deal. "Or else it was stolen. I haven't seen it in several days." His face brightened with false cheer. "Maybe you've found it?"

Deal shook his head. "Did you lose it down here?" he asked.

Mahler pursed his lips. "Back in Los Angeles," he said. "I haven't missed it," he said. "I think it's a dead area down here, to tell the truth."

"No," Deal said. "There's cellular service here. We checked." He thought he saw a glimmer of approval on Driscoll's face: Deal the detective, grinding the guy the proper way.

There was a pause as Mahler seemed to gauge Deal's intentions. "Well, that's good to know," Mahler said finally. "But if that's all, gentlemen, I've got a busy day coming up . . . "

"You represent Paige Nobleman?" Driscoll cut in.

Mahler broke off, fairly glaring back at him. "Yes, I do," he said. "Why do you ask?"

"Because, Mr. Mahler," Driscoll said, "that's what we're doing here. She hired me to do some work for her down in Miami, and then she disappeared. I thought you might have heard from her."

Mahler took a moment, then walked over to one of the broad windows and stared out toward the mountains, which had begun to shade from blackness into various purple hues. The very highest of the peaks seemed to glow, backlit now by the sun.

"The last I heard from Paige, she was in Miami," Mahler said. "She'd just returned from the hospital where her mother had died." He turned back to them. "She was extremely distraught. She said she'd had a row with her sister and told me she wouldn't be returning to Los Angeles as planned." He threw up his hands. "She wouldn't say why.

"We've been involved with some tricky negotiations with a British film company concerning a part for her and I told her it was important that she hold to her schedule, but she was too upset to listen. When I tried to get back to her, I found out she'd left her hotel." He shook his head in concern. "I've been worried myself. Paige hasn't been herself lately, and then all these family concerns . . . " He trailed off.

"Was there something specific that was troubling her?" Deal asked.

"Just the usual," Mahler said. "I think she was having troubles with the fellow she'd been seeing . . . and she'd hit the wall for an actress, too old for the obligatory sex interest roles, not quite well enough established to be in the running for the more serious parts, what few there are for women . . . " He shrugged. "That's why these negotiations were so important." He gazed out at the mountains again, the very picture of concern. "Paige just seemed to be losing heart," he said.

"You think she was capable of doing harm to herself?" Driscoll asked.

Mahler turned, looking as if it pained him to consider the possibility. "You know, gentlemen, you and I have jobs," he said. "We have good days and bad days, of course, but we get up every morning knowing we've got an office to go to, calls to make, things to do." He shook his head sorrowfully. "But an actor . . . " He broke off. "It's a terribly tough business," he said. "I've seen so many ruin their lives with drugs, drinking, impossible love affairs. Even the successful ones. So many of them seem to recognize how shifting are the sands their existences are founded upon." He folded his hands in front of him and gave a wistful smile. "I know it must seem like a terribly glamorous life from the perspective of two private detectives from Florida. But the reality is quite otherwise, I can assure you."

Driscoll nodded as if a grave truth had been passed along to him. "Well, I appreciate your concern, Mr. Mahler." He gestured at the card again. "We'll probably be out here in California for a few days, but if you hear anything from Ms. Nobleman, you could leave a message for us at that number."

Mahler glanced at the card again, then stopped. He looked up at Driscoll, puzzled. "Are you sure this is right?" He gave the card back to Driscoll, who held it up to the light, puzzled. "Sorry," Driscoll said, glancing sheepishly at Deal. "One of yours." He showed him the DealCo emblem on the card he'd handed Mahler by mistake. "Always getting these things mixed up," he mumbled, fishing in his wallet. He found one of the D & D Investigative Services cards with the corny hunting cap and magnifying glass logo, handed the card back to Mahler. "You'll let us hear from you?" he repeated.

Deal could only imagine what the man thought. Confronted by

two private detectives who have a sideline in the construction business? Whatever intimidation factor they might have walked in with, it was surely gone.

"Of course," Mahler said, turning the full force of his smile upon them now.

He was about to turn away again when something seemed to occur to him. "I don't suppose I could ask just what sort of work you were doing for Paige, could I?" He'd struck what seemed to be an avuncular pose. "She's like a daughter to me, you know."

"I'm afraid that's privileged information," Driscoll said. "I would like to speak to her, though."

"The moment I hear anything," Mahler assured them.

And then he motioned for the man in black to show them out.

"Sorry about the card," Driscoll said. He was at the wheel of the car that Terrell had had waiting for them at the Palm Springs airport, guiding them back down the driveway toward the farm-to-market road that had brought them through the desert to the isolated compound.

Deal shrugged, still going over what they'd heard from Mahler. "He wasn't going to tell us anything, no matter what."

Driscoll nodded, gave him a look. "You did pretty well in there."

Deal found himself smiling. "I've been studying your technique, Driscoll. Slow but sure."

"That's the ticket, pardner." Driscoll smiled back. "No sign of the big guy?"

Deal shook his head, distracted by something he couldn't put his finger on. "There was somebody in the hallway for a moment, but I couldn't be sure," he said absently.

"So what's your take on Mahler?" Driscoll asked.

"He's full of more shit than a Christmas turkey," Deal said. It would have been the clincher, of course, seeing the big man who'd been driving Paige that night. But all his instincts told him it wasn't necessary. "I don't know why, but he's got her. She's in that house somewhere," he said. "At the very least, he knows where she is."

Driscoll sighed and nodded. "I feel the same way," he said, throwing up his hands. He'd had to stop while a set of electric gates swung open at the end of the lane, allowing them to cross over a cattle guard and back out onto the gravel public road.

"So what are we going to do?" Deal asked.

"We could always try going into town," Driscoll said. He swung the car out through the gates, then turned south, in the opposite direction from the way they'd come. "We could talk to the cops, see if we could get someone to come out and take a look." But the way he said it didn't inspire Deal with much confidence. It might be better than trying the same tactic over the phone, the very prospect of which had sent them flying out here, but just thinking of where to begin the story they'd tell the local authorities made him match Driscoll's doubtful stare: *"Hey, you know the millionaire who lives down the road in Xanadu? We'd like you to go down and bust him for murder and kidnapping. We'll explain it all to you on the way."*

Deal glanced at Driscoll. "Assuming she's there, and even if we could convince somebody to come out," he said, "what's to stop them from moving her someplace in the meantime?"

"What I figure," Driscoll said, "we let everybody wake up and start making their movie or whatever it is they're doing, then I find a way in and have a look around without Kato and his gang watching. Unless you have a better idea."

Deal shook his head. The road was moving through rugged territory, climbing toward the mountains more steeply now, paralleling a high chain-link fence that cut the nearby underbrush. The fence was at least eight feet tall, topped with inward-leaning strands of barbed wire, one course of reinforcement cable running along the bottom. Formidable as it looked, it had been constructed for the purpose of keeping things in, Deal knew. There was no evidence that the thing was electrically charged, no sign of sensors or other electronic devices.

He knew why it had been put there because he'd seen similar fencing at a series of hunting preserves his father had dragged him along to in Central Texas. The idea was to keep the prey of choice—deer, antelope, longhorns, even exotics such as ibex and gazelle—contained in a space just large enough to provide some semblance of sport without leaving the issue of the successful hunt in doubt for the well-heeled patrons.

Deal had once seen a deer, pursued by a hunter in a Jeep accompanying their party, make a magnificent leap toward freedom on a hillside not far from Austin. The deer had come up about a foot shy, however, had hung its hindquarters up on the barbed wire, and the man who thought of himself as a hunter had shot it while it thrashed madly about in the concertina wire.

All his father's reassurances about how much more humane it had been to put the animal out of its misery than to allow it to cut itself to ribbons on the fence fell on deaf ears for Deal, who was twelve at the time. He'd jumped out of their own vehicle and ran at the Jeep, leaping over the side to flail at the so-called hunter, who was readying himself for a second shot at the dying animal, had to be pulled away kicking and screaming by his father. Deal had never gone "hunting" again, and he hadn't seen such a fence since, not in all those years.

Gazing at it now as its posts flashed by, paralleling the rapidly deteriorating road, he could only imagine Paige Nobleman somewhere within its confines, as helpless as that deer, and Marvin Mahler as corrupt and brutal as the hunter he'd wanted to bring down at twelve.

As their car made its way around a steep turn, he caught a glimpse of the red-tiled compound lying behind them. "I'm going in with you," he said.

Driscoll gave him a look. "You've already done your part, you know. You got us out here, you went inside, looked around. I can take it from here."

Deal stared at him. He'd met the man who was responsible for Barbara's death, who'd ordered them killed, who was likely planning the same for Paige, all his instincts told him so. But still, there was that nagging doubt.

He stared down, realized he still held the card Driscoll had handed Mahler: DealCo and the other particulars of his so-called normal life on one side, the cel-phone number Driscoll had scrawled on the other. Runes from two impossibly different dimensions of existence flipping alternately before his eyes as he turned the card idly, over and over. And then he stopped, fixing on something that had been nagging at him since their conversation with Mahler earlier.

"He called us 'two private detectives from Florida,'" Deal said, raising his gaze to Driscoll abruptly.

Driscoll gave him a blank look. "Yeah, so?"

"So how would he get that? The card you gave him says I'm a contractor."

Driscoll shrugged. "Maybe he didn't look close."

"He didn't," Deal insisted. "Not until we were on the way out. That's when he noticed what it said. But he'd already called us a couple of private detectives."

"Maybe he just assumed." Driscoll had to slow down, guide the heavy car around a deep gouge cut in the road by some storm or mountain runoff. "Fucking boat," he grumbled.

But Deal wasn't paying attention. "*That's* how those two guys found us so easily," he said abruptly.

"What are you talking about?" Driscoll said. He was busy wrestling the car around a narrow turn. They had reached the foothills of the mountains now and the road had taken a sudden swing upward. The fence veered away beneath them, following the course of a dry streambed that led off in a nearly opposite direction. "Looks like this is the place," Driscoll was saying.

Deal turned back to him, still distracted. "I gave Paige Nobleman one of the Driscoll & Deal cards," he said, "and I wrote my home number and address on the back of it." He turned to point over the seat, back in the direction they had come. "The sonofabitch sent those guys to kill us, Driscoll," he was saying, and then he broke off, too surprised to register the irony of his words.

The roar that came from behind them drowned out his cry of warning to Driscoll, but Deal doubted it would have done much good. The big black Suburban must have been doing fifty as he watched it come out of the turn behind them, and it was gathering speed—like some four-wheeled shadow of doom, he was thinking—when its massive brush-cutting bumper slammed into them. Deal had one instant of clarity—a flash of steel, the wash of light over the Suburban's windshield, an unobstructed view through glass, and no real surprise to see the hulking man who sat there, staring at them impassively at the moment of impact.

"What the fuck," Driscoll managed as his head snapped back with the force of the blow and the wheel spun out of his hands.

Deal made a lunge for the wheel, but even as he clambered at the blurring spokes, he realized it was a wasted effort. They were over the side and airborne now, and Driscoll, who never listened when Deal nagged at him to wear his goddamned seat belt—a cop, for Chrissakes, and he just wouldn't do it—big, blocky Driscoll seemed to rise in slow motion, like an astronaut in a capsule designed by a car maker, his head crunching into the roof liner at the same moment the nose of the Lincoln finally crashed down for the first time against the side of the cliff. They began to catapult then, end over end, and Deal lost track of what had become of Driscoll. He saw flashes of sky, of rock, of scrub oak and piñon trees, all of it moving faster and faster like an out-of-control film flying off the sprockets, and he was ready for the final launch and free fall that would put them into eternal orbit . . .

. . . when there was a bone-jarring crash and a sudden jolt that ended everything. Deal, momentarily blinded by the whirl of dust stirred up inside the car, felt an intense pressure building in his head, and a similar force pressing against his shoulders and hips. He blinked his eyes into focus, sure, despite the fact that he'd buckled himself in, that he'd suffered some awful nerve damage, was experiencing the onset of paralysis . . . then he stopped as he saw what had happened.

The car had come to a halt upside down, and Deal was dangling like a bat, still held securely by the webbing of the seat belts. His view was straight out one of the side windows—it took him a moment to be sure it was the driver's window—and it took him another moment to realize that they had not plunged to the bottom of the ravine, nor anywhere near it, for that matter. He was staring into a dizzying drop another fifty feet or so, straight down to the rocky streambed below. Were he to fall out of the snarl of strapping that held him, he'd plunge straight to his death.

In the sudden silence, he heard the ticking of the Lincoln's stalled engine and the steady drip of liquid. He smelled burnt oil, unidentifiable fluids cooking themselves on the engine block, the faint hint of gasoline from somewhere. A rock clattered down the slope from above, crashed against the side of the car, then spun off into space. There was a considerable pause before he heard it thud into the streambed below.

He heard a groan from somewhere below him and turned his head carefully, craning his neck until he made out the form of Driscoll crumpled into the shelf space between the shattered rear window and the backseats. There was a gash on the ex-cop's forehead and one of his arms was twisted in what seemed an impossible angle behind his body. Driscoll was half-conscious, his eyes fluttering open and closed, his feet stirring through the shattered window against the rocky slope where they lay.

Deal felt a shudder pass through the car then, and there was a sickening movement—an inch maybe, maybe more—as the big Lincoln responded to the pull of gravity at the precipice.

"Driscoll," Deal said, his voice a fierce hiss. "Driscoll!" he repeated, and the ex-cop's eyes fluttered open.

"Listen to me," Deal said. "You've got to stay still. We're hung up on the side of a cliff, okay? But the goddamn car is ready to go on over the side. Do you understand me?"

Driscoll's eyes blinked a few times. "Fucking boat," he murmured through his swollen lips. "I told you."

"Just lie still," Deal repeated. "Let me get out of here, so I can help."

"I lie still," Driscoll said, suppressing a cough that Deal feared could shake them into oblivion. "And you jump down. I got it, Deal. Send me a postcard from the place you end up, okay?"

"Be quiet," Deal said. He heard another scattering of rocks, smaller ones this time, rattle down upon the undercarriage of the car.

He hooked one hand under the seat above him, found a solid hold, then groped about with the other until he found the catch of the seat belt that was gouging into his hip. He tried to brace himself as he pressed the release button, but one of his feet was waving freely above him and the other slid awkwardly down the inside of the windshield despite anything he could do.

He finished a kind of half-somersault with his feet against the roof liner, balled into a fetal-like crouch. He was sure that his movements had doomed them, but he heard only a creaking of metal, and then there was silence again.

Very carefully, he worked his legs straight out the driver's window, the knowledge that half of him was now waving freely in space sending a brief wave of nausea through him. He fought off the feeling and got himself turned so that he could see Driscoll again. They lay now staring at one another, their noses a couple of feet apart.

"This is another fine mess you've gotten us into, Ollie," Driscoll said, his eyes glassy.

"Be quiet," Deal said. "Come on," he said. "Give me your hand."

"Here," Driscoll said, reaching out toward Deal. "This is the only one I can feel."

Deal took it, brought in one foot and braced it against the door frame, then began half-guiding, half-pushing Driscoll out the opposite window, up the rocky hillside. The ex-cop had nearly cleared the car, had disappeared all the way past his beltline, when there was a pause.

"I'm stuck," he said. "I'm too fucking fat."

"That's not it," Deal said, pushing at Driscoll's rump as hard as he dared. He could see a good inch of clearance between Driscoll's back and the window frame. It didn't make any sense, he was thinking . . . and then he saw it: Driscoll's twisted arm, numb to all feeling apparently, had gotten hung up on the clothes hook above the rear seat. Deal had to maneuver himself over Driscoll's legs, pop the button on the ex-cop's sleeve to get him free.

"Go on," Deal urged frantically. "Go."

Deal didn't have to repeat himself. In seconds Driscoll had vanished, his legs disappearing out the crumpled window frame faster than Deal would have supposed a groggy man his size could move them.

It took Deal a moment to realize what was happening. He hadn't even noticed the fresh grinding sound—roof on stone— from beneath him. But then it struck him.

Driscoll hadn't been leaving the car, the car had been leaving him. The thing was sliding on over the edge, taking Deal with it . . .

So that was it, then. So long, Driscoll. So long, world, he was thinking . . . and was so frozen with fear and despair that he actually had to tell himself to reach out and grasp the meaty hand that had appeared: Driscoll reaching back inside the compartment to save him. He felt Driscoll's firm grasp on his own, prayed they weren't going to be yanked over the side, and then felt himself being pulled free from the sliding car.

He glanced back as his knees dug into the rocky hillside, saw his feet emerge, saw the car grind on another yard, then hang up once again, teetering this time with its crushed nose pointed out into space.

He scrambled to his hands and knees, feeling relief flood into him with a force that made him weak, just in time to hear Driscoll's weary voice.

"Look at that, would you. Every time you get one thing taken care of, something else comes up."

Deal glanced up the slope of the cliff toward the roadway, not sure what Driscoll was talking about. He could see the snout of the big Suburban poised there at the shoulder, saw a couple of pines snapped off where the Lincoln had gone over, saw a trail of debris scattered over the rocks down toward them: wheel covers, chrome strips, the Lincoln's truck deck, even its tiny spare tire.

Then he saw what Driscoll was talking about. The big guy who'd been behind the wheel of the Suburban had seen them emerge from the wreckage. He had jumped down off the roadway and was dodging through the screen of trees toward them, the now-familiar shape of an automatic pistol upraised in his right hand.

"Why did it have to be my shooting hand," Driscoll was saying, clawing awkwardly at his ankle holster with his left.

Deal stared about for cover, but other than the shattered car, teetering at the edge, there was nothing bigger than a wildflower. Then he spotted something. He reached down into a pile of debris dumped by the Lincoln, picked up the jack handle in reflex, held it stupidly aloft as the big man swung passed the last of the stunted pines above and came down with the pistol braced in firing position.

Jack handle and a left-handed .38 against an M-10, at twenty paces, Deal was thinking, noting too that Driscoll, still groggy from the crash, hadn't even straightened up yet.

He saw the look on the big man's face above them, saw the satisfaction that comes when a man knows he has everything he wants from a situation . . . then saw the look replaced by surprise when his feet went out from under him just as he was beginning to fire.

There was a whine as some of the shots tore into the Lincoln's carcass, the explosions continuing as the man slid on down the slope toward them, his finger still locked in reflex on the trigger. He was moving feet first, rocks flying up as he vainly tried to dig his heels in, picking up speed as he came.

He'd stopped firing, was nearly upon them now, trying desperately to lever up off the slope like a skier attempting to right himself in midfall. Driscoll staggered backward across the slope like an awkward crab, still trying to clear his pistol from his ankle holster.

Then, like something rising from a bad dream, the big man

was up, his feet still skidding, but spread beneath him now. He brought the automatic back in front of him, trained it on Driscoll, was ready to fire again, when Deal stepped forward and swung.

He was just trying for the gun, but the big man saw the blow coming and threw up his arm. The barrel of the gun cracked across Deal's wrist with a pain that went from white-hot to numbness in an instant and sent the jack handle flying. That was it, Deal thought, so much for heroism. In the next moment the big man would stitch him and Driscoll into shreds, all this would be over . . .

. . . and then he heard the strangled cry, caught a glimpse of the stunned look on the big man's face and realized what had happened. Deal had been holding the knurled end of the tire iron, leading his swing with the big screwdriverlike point. When he'd lost his grip, the thing had turned into a kind of spear. Some law of physics was involved, Deal thought: physical bulk, angle of incline, speed of slide, not to mention the force of his own desperation. Whatever was to account for it, it seemed a kind of miracle.

It wasn't pain that Gabriel felt, not at first. It was simply something cold and suffocating at his throat, as if he'd swallowed a huge shard of ice. But he knew better. He'd felt the force of the heavy metal bar striking him, felt a moment's stabbing pain, then the sudden impact as whatever it was the man had thrown plunged into him as far as it could go. His fingers were suddenly numb, and he felt his weapon slip from his hands. Although he sensed his feet were still beneath him, he couldn't be sure.

He staggered backward down the rocky slope now, his hands clawing at a strange curved rod that seemed to have wedged itself against his throat. He tried to pull it away, was thinking that if he did, he might be able to breathe, might be able to speak . . .

. . . for a strange calm and clarity had suddenly descended upon him. He wished that he might tell the man whose stunned face swept past him—or was it the other way around—all these things that had occurred to him in an instant: That all was unfolding as it should, that truly Gabriel could wish him no ill will, that what was happening at this very instant was in accordance with some irrevocable web of circumstance . . . *no good, no evil, simply the things that happen,* he thought. *But how to account for the ease, the repose that had come to envelop him . . .*

The vision of the man's face had disappeared. He had a glimpse of sky, a cloud, a swipe of pine bough across it all . . . and felt himself collide with something hard. The point of the bar that had driven through him struck other iron and slung his head sideways.

He saw flashing bursts of light—rockets, pinwheels, the fireworks of some miraculous Bangkok street parade—and there, in the midst of it all, was the image of his grandfather, a young man once more, bandanna at his brow and cutlass in his teeth. He was grinning his pirate's grin, and reaching out to take Gabriel's hand, and finally there was peace.

Deal saw it all happen, though none of it seemed real: the big man clutching dumbly at the rod that had driven itself impossibly deep, its point protruding a foot out his back. He'd staggered past, out of balance, out of luck, his feet plowing drunkenly through the talus, spraying showers of loose rock, his hands clawing awkwardly at the iron bar that pierced his throat. His dazed glance locked momentarily on Deal's, and then he was gone, hurtling on down the slope.

He went over backward, slammed against the side of the Lincoln. Deal thought he would slide off the wreckage, roll on over the edge of the cliff, but he didn't. He stayed where he was, hands outflung against the side of the car, the point of the tire iron piercing the sheet metal of the Lincoln's quarter panel, holding him fast like a specimen on a strange mounting board.

Deal saw the man's pleading gaze come back to his, saw one huge hand reach out for help, felt his own hand start out in reflex. And that was when the car groaned again, a sound that might as easily have come from the big man pinned to its side, and went on over. First the car was gone, then the big man's feet whipped skyward with a speed that seemed impossible, and everything disappeared.

There was a long moment of silence, a terrific sound of impact from below, and finally an explosion—straight from the gates of hell, Deal thought—as a gale of superheated air rushed past him into the cool morning sky.

Mahler was on his way across the wide brick courtyard of the compound, headed toward the east wing, where they were scheduled to shoot some of the innocuous dean-in-the-president's office material in the early hours. As Foxe, the boozehound British cinematographer, had pointed out to him, at this time of day their actors would have a hard time working up a lather for the more physical stuff. They could get some of the bridge scenes out of the way, let the actors ease into a toot, by late afternoon they could break out the leather sheets again.

Mahler had listened to the man, nodded his okay. It had become apparent that he and Cross would more or less rely on Foxe, who'd made a career in this arena, to get them through the project, after all. And they wouldn't be the first producer-director team to take credit for work the cameraman had actually done. Still, it usually worked the other way around: the director had his head down in a mound of coke or soaked in a drum of hootch, the inmates would have to run the show. In this case, Mahler believed himself to be the only clearheaded, sane person within rifle shot of the proceedings, and all he could really do was look on and try to act as if he knew what was important. He shook his head, took a deep draught of the clear desert air. He'd never thought sex could

304

become so tedious, but that was a movie set for you. Clearly, making a movie could turn anything to dreck.

He heard a muffled explosion from somewhere in the hills behind him, nodded with satisfaction. Maybe it was blasting, one of the undying breed of wildcat miners, still combing the hills for the lost mother lode. Better yet, it would be Gabriel, wanting to be sure, taking out the two detectives from Florida with a case of dynamite this time.

He sighed, inured to the necessities by now. The important thing was to focus on where he was headed and to count his blessings that he had associates providing the necessary help. Imagine if there had been no old man, with his cadre of thugs to turn to. What would he have done? Bury the two detectives under a mountain of old scripts?

In any case, what needed to be done would be done. He had more important things to accomplish. He squared his shoulders, moved on across the courtyard. If he were lucky, the old man would prove to be disinterested in the morning schedule, they could get something accomplished without having to listen to a lecture on the superior values of a Chinese higher education.

He heard the sound of a truck engine then, noticed that the He-Men Film Services van was bouncing down the lane away from the compound toward the gates. Odd enough that even one of that crew might be headed off somewhere, since they were short of manpower as it was, but then he noticed another one of the brain-dead group in the passenger seat.

Maybe there'd been some equipment malfunction, and they were headed off to Palm Springs for repairs or replacement parts. But why send two of them? Furthermore, it being a two-hour round trip and likely to cause problems with the shooting schedule, why wouldn't anyone have notified him? He picked up his pace toward the cloister doors on the other side of the courtyard.

He hurried through the entry, down the dimly lit hallway, increasingly concerned at the stillness that gripped this wing of the house. He'd been very explicit at the end of shooting the night before, and even Foxe had weighed in with the crew on the need to start promptly.

He covered the last few steps to the library entrance, where, he and Foxe had determined, the mouse-nibbled volumes on the shelves and neo-Inquisition decor would suggest a college president's office closely enough for their purposes. His concern had built to anger by this time. He burst through the broad double doors of the library, ready to lay into the first of the slackers he encountered . . . then stopped short when he saw what had happened. The set that had been so carefully arranged the night before was in disarray, the "president's" desk swept clean, its banker's lamp toppled over, papers and books littering the floor. The rented camera scaffolding was in a shambles, and all of the lighting equipment that the four He-Men had labored on positioning until well past midnight had vanished. He heard a sound and turned to see Foxe bent over one of his silver camera cases, grunting with effort as he wrestled something into place. The cinematographer snapped the case closed, then stood, his face crimson from strain. When he saw Mahler, his expression darkened another, impossible shade.

"Fuck you," Foxe said. His accent seemed to give the phrase an added, chilling force.

Mahler stared back at him, dumbfounded. "Foxe, what is this?" he managed, sweeping his arm about the room. It occurred to Mahler that a moment ago he was to be the one expressing his outrage, but the best he could now seemed like a whimper.

"Just fuck you altogether," Foxe said, brushing past him toward the door. The heavy case cracked into Mahler's knee, and he yelped with pain.

Foxe seemed not to notice. He paused at the archway and turned to stab a menacing finger back at Mahler, who was bent over, holding his knee. "You pricks want to pull the plug, it's okay with me," Foxe said, his face seeming to glow now, "but I turned down two jobs to truck out into the middle of nowhere for you, Mahler. I'd better see the rest of my money on schedule, or your fucking ass is going to be fucking grass."

Mahler was gasping with pain. He tried to manage some response, but his mouth was still moving soundlessly as Foxe turned and disappeared through the doorway. After a moment, he limped to one of the casement windows, sat down heavily, rubbed his knee until feeling returned to his leg.

A bad dream, he was thinking. In a moment he was going to wake up and see that all this was nothing but the creation of a nocturnal gas bubble, he could stroll down to the real set, the meticulously arranged "Office of the President," where the biggest problem would be coaching Cross's wife through the delivery of her lines according to the generally agreed upon rules of English grammar.

But it wasn't a dream, he knew. His knee throbbed and his stomach sloshed with acids that could surely eat through lead. What in God's name had happened? He glanced out the window, down toward the lake, which still steamed placidly in the vast shadows of the mountains, then got another jolt: The seaplane was still tethered in place, all right, but the wardrobe and makeup RV that had been stationed near the dock had disappeared.

"The ship is sinking, Marvin," that's what the little voice inside was whispering, but he wasn't going to listen. There was a reasonable explanation for what was happening. And an equally good reason why he'd been left out of the loop. He forced his gaze from the pile of litter that had been left by the dock, which was scuttling, piece by Styrofoam piece, into the reeds by the shoreline. The pain in his knee had subsided now. He thought he could make it back to the main house. He could catch Foxe before he got away . . .

"Augh . . . !" The cry escaped him involuntarily.

"Old man need to see you," the wraithlike little man said. He'd appeared at Mahler's side soundlessly once again, startling him so badly that he had to struggle to catch his breath.

"Right," Mahler said, pushing himself up. "Tell him I'll be right there." He started to push himself past, but the little man was instantly in his path.

"Old man say *now*."

Mahler met the little man's gaze. "You going to get out of my way?" he said.

"Say to bring you," the little man replied impassively.

Mahler considered things. The Chinese guy might have been 5'4", weighed possibly a hundred and thirty pounds. Mahler was 6'2" when he remembered to stand up straight, suck in the gut that had pushed him up to about 220. He still worked out with the free weights in the gym, played racquetball twice a week, jogged on the days he didn't.

In the early sixties, a columnist had once written a story about Mahler punching out a noted leading man who'd hit on Rhonda Gardner at a party in the Hollywood Hills. The truth was that the guy, drunk as a lord, had taken a swing at Mahler, whom he'd overheard demeaning his sexual preferences. Rhonda had screamed,

Mahler had ducked, and the leading man took himself through a sliding glass door with the force of his swing. Mahler, who had seen no need to correct the published accounts of the incident, had not had anything resembling a physical encounter since, but, given his frequent verbal pyrotechnics, he had enjoyed the reputation of being a brawler ever after. How could it hurt, he had reasoned. In tough negotiations, he'd perfected a glower that seemed to reach right back to that night in the Hills when he'd duked out the toughest cowboy in filmdom. It was not a tactic he used often, but the other brawlers in the business seemed to appreciate it: He just had to look like he might come unhinged, and as often as not, he'd win his point.

Apparently the Chinese guy had not read any of his press, however. He hadn't moved, stared back through Mahler's glower as if it didn't exist.

"Okay," Mahler said finally. "Where is he?"

"Come," the Chinese guy said, and led him out the door.

"Mmmmm-mmmmmm," the young man said, smoothing Paige's hair back from her brow. "What happened to you anyway, darlin'?"

A nice young man from the country, she thought dreamily. Some odd accent, part hillbilly, part Deep South. It was beyond her to determine things like that, though. And it didn't matter anyway, did it? She drifted along in her separate little dimension, caught occasional glimpses of that other world she'd once belonged to. But there was no possibility of bridging the gap that separated her from that world now, was there? She couldn't speak, she couldn't move. She could only stare out helplessly at what might cross the path of her vision, as if her eyes were windowpanes, her conscious-ness some ghost that had taken up residence behind them.

"Not many of us left," the young man said. "Cutting and run-ning. Everybody cutting and running."

He sat on the edge of the bed beside her, stared off idly as he dipped his fingers into a big Ziploc bag he was holding. He brought his fingertips, now covered in some white powder, up to his nose, inhaled sharply. He sucked his fingertips clean, then turned back to her.

"The He-Men took off so quick they forgot their stash," he said, holding up the bag for her to see. She had no idea who the he-men were, but there must have been a half-pound of whatever powder was inside the bag he was holding, maybe more. Methedrine? Cocaine? She had no idea. Maybe the young man would like some of what Mahler was feeding her.

"You see this?" the nice young man said. He held the bag close to her eyes until she saw some kind of trademark printed in red against a white background: a tiger leaping out of the underbrush, fangs and claws bared at the watcher, Chinese hieroglyphics printed below.

"The best scag in the world," the nice young man said. "China White. All packaged up like it was rice cakes or something." He shook his head. "Makes what I used to bring up out of Mexico look like shit." He shrugged. "It is shit, of course. All of it is, but I could live for a year off what this would bring me back in Austin."

He dangled the bag again. "They were paying those He-Men in scag, you know that? Then the dummies took off and left it. Maybe they think it's still in that little compartment in their truck, but all they've got is flour." He shook his head. "Took me about a minute and a half to find it." He grinned at her. "I had a lot of experience hiding dope, I have to say."

He stared down at her for a bit. "You have a drug of choice, darlin'? Is that what you're doing down here? That's what they told me, but to believe anything those people told you, you'd have to be dumber than dirt."

He sat quietly for a moment, staring off. "I don't want you to get the wrong idea," he said. "I'm not a thief or anything." He shrugged philosophically. "I'm the writer on this picture."

He glanced back at her. "The fact is, the guy who hired me took off already and I'm just trying to make sure I come away with something to show for my trouble." He reached into his shirt pocket, held up another, smaller bag. "Now this crank, I liberated it from the guy's wife. It's got a bit of an edge," he said, "but you hit it with a little scag, it isn't bad." He dropped the smaller bag back into his pocket.

"I mean, it's not like you want to go demanding things from those Chinese guys, I can tell you that." He shook his head.

He gave her his smile again, an expression that was somewhere between a grimace and a dream state. "That's why I wanted to look in on you, darlin'. Make sure everything was okay." He surveyed her face again, shook his head. "Somebody gave you a pretty good lick, didn't they? Mmmm-mmmm. Hit a woman all tied up. That's about as low as it gets," he said. He studied her again. "You look familiar to me, you know that? You ever been to Austin?"

She heard footsteps in the hallway outside then, and a startled look came over the nice young man's face. She felt his weight disappear from her bed, heard scurrying noises, heard a door open and close somewhere. After a moment, the footsteps in the hallway paused and the door to her room swung open. She saw, standing in the doorway, the diminutive Chinese man who'd taken the phone from her in some previous time she could only vaguely remember. But she knew he was the one who'd hit her, who'd done whatever damage the nice young man from the country had seen. She felt a mixture of hatred and helplessness well up in her, then fade away almost as suddenly as it had come, as if even emotion were too difficult to muster.

The man glanced suspiciously about, as if he might have been drawn by the sounds of voices, then entered the room and crossed to her bed. She felt his hands moving about her body, and wondered for a moment what fresh indignities she was about to suffer. After a moment, however, she realized he was simply loosening the restraints that held her fast to the bed. In the next moments, and though she was sure she was very nearly the equal of the small man in size, she felt herself being lifted like a feather and draped over his narrow shoulder. She was being carried off, she thought, but she was no princess being rescued from her prison chamber. No problem figuring that much out. She could feel it in the way he held her. She was just a sack of goods being taken somewhere to dump.

"She will have a most regrettable accident of swimming," the old man said. He was sitting in the same goddamned chair, the high-backed number he'd settled into originally in the library. Now it was perched on the tiles that bordered the indoor pool, the old man sitting comfortably waving at the chlorine-rank water that lapped at its gutters a few feet away. Mahler wondered briefly if the old man had actually left the chair. Maybe he'd just had his bearers—two of whom stood at the doorway nearby—carry him around in it like some ancient emperor.

"She is swimming alone," the old man continued, his voice echoing off the arched ceiling of the room. The air was cloying, the temperature far too hot. Mahler wondered which of the early tenants of the house had thought it a good idea to build such an addition. He'd always hated it. Despite the murals that ringed the walls—Italian gardens, disporting nymphs and satyrs, a view of the Tuscan hills—you couldn't see the outside, you couldn't breathe . . . it was like being in a dungeon with a diving board. But Rhonda had always done her exercising here, never in the outdoor pool, where she claimed the sun got in her eyes.

"And being abusing of drugs and drinking in her distress . . . " The old man trailed off, shrugging. "Not at all a good practice," he said.

Mahler nodded, still uncomfortable. "I don't see why we couldn't have figured something else out, though," he said. "We could have kept her on ice, finished the picture . . . "

The old man held his hands up. "Please," he said. "Trust instincts of mine. Two people come, more may come. Is best send everyone away right now. Start over."

"Sure," Mahler said. "But your instincts are going to cost me about a quarter of a million dollars. You didn't even *ask* me before you started chasing people out of here. I had *relationships* with some of these individuals. This could come back to haunt me."

The old man held up his hands, smiling as if Mahler were making a joke. "Any problem money can cause, not a problem," the old man said.

"Only when it's not your money," Mahler said. He paused as the doors to the pool area opened, and the smallest of the old man's thugs, the one who could move about like smoke, backed in, Paige's form flung over his shoulder like a rug. "Dear God," he said softly, turning away from the sight. There had been a reason he'd started this nightmare. He was sure of it.

Was there some way he could cut his losses, go back to the way things were when China was only something you ate off of? If there was, he'd be ready to accept it.

The little man dropped Paige into a padded chaise longue. Her blank eyes seemed to catch Mahler's gaze for an instant, then her head lolled to the side, and he was spared of that much, at least.

He turned back to the old man. "Can't we get this over with?" he asked.

"Of course," the old man said. And he made a gesture over Mahler's shoulder.

He should have known what was coming, Mahler thought,

even before he felt it: the fingers digging into his hair, someone back there Mahler flailed for but couldn't reach. The person had a thick handful of hair, and was twisting. The pain in his scalp was like fire, so awful it rendered him helpless. And then there was something sharp, stabbing at the base of his skull, the terrible burning sensation, followed by a numbing flood of warmth.

He felt the hand release him, the pain that had turned to mere pressure at his scalp suddenly gone altogether. For an instant he was sure he would be able to run, but then he realized that his legs had turned to rubber beneath him, and he was going down. His cheek cracked off the slick tiles at the poolside, bounced once, and settled. One eye could see nothing but a fiery redness. The other was sighted vaguely toward the ceiling. He saw the visage of the old man wavering above him. He tried to blink, close his eyes, and refocus, but it was as if he had all the volition of a video camera that had been set aside without being turned off.

"Hurting a moment, yes," the old man said. "But pull up on scalp like that, very hard to find needle mark after. Do woman in Florida that way, Work fine. Just hurt a little bit."

Other hands were on him, stripping his clothing away. "Swim around in drug state," the old man was saying. "Fool around with pretty girl. Not a good idea."

Mahler felt a coolness envelop his body, felt his pants sliding over his hips, felt his shorts going after. The few times he'd allowed himself to think about dying, he'd pictured it happening in his sleep, maybe in the midst of a pleasant dream.

One sleeve of his shirt was off, then the next. His arm slapped the cool tile, and he felt a twinge of pain, a slight tremor course through the fingers of one hand.

"Don't worry," the old man said. "Film gonna get made. Your Mr. Cross going to come over to Hong Kong. Better for everybody."

Sure, Mahler thought. Another frigging dagger in the back. First Mendanian. Now Cross. Anybody else want to do him while there was still time? Hurry up now. Last chance!

"Time to go swim now," the old man said. He reached out with his foot, pushed at Mahler's inert shoulder, sent him over the side toward the water. "Don't worry, girl on the way," the old man was saying, but his voice broke off when Mahler's hand caught his pantleg going down.

Two fingers, Mahler was thinking with satisfaction. The last part of himself that worked. And that was all he needed. Two fingers that caught the expensive silk of the old man's cuff like a set of grappling hooks, two fingers that wrapped tight and closed and then locked up like all the rest of his body, now and forever.

His hearing still functioned, and so he had the satisfaction of the old man's cry echoing off the ceiling before the two of them plunged beneath the water. And then, even with hearing gone, he could savor the sight of the scrawny old bastard clawing frantically above him, his face in wild panic as they sank inexorably to the deep end of the pool.

Maybe the old man's bearers would get to him, and maybe not. But it didn't seem important somehow. Mahler saw an explosion of bubbles from his own mouth, saw them merge with a similar burst from the craw of the old man, whose struggles were already weakening.

Mahler heard a muffled explosion from somewhere above, saw a sheet of red cover the glittering surface of the pool above his unwavering, stinging eye. *So this is how it happens,* he was thinking. *Paige,* he thought. *Rhonda,* he thought. And then it all simply stopped.

"Hai-karate!" Paco was shouting. He squeezed off a second blast that cut through the back of the leather chair where another one of the little pricks was trying to hide.

The first one he'd shot in the ass while he was bent over trying to see what had happened to his boss. That one was floating facedown in the water, still kicking feebly, when Paco's second shot sent chair and guy hiding in it cartwheeling into the pool as well, blood, red leather, and splinters spraying everywhere. He didn't really want to kill anyone, but what were the alternatives, really?

The guys would kill him given half a chance, already had tried to, in fact. Would kill him, that woman in there, and anybody else they got a chance to. He'd only done what had to be done. Saved his own ass and that pretty little girl, whatever was wrong with her, and now it was time to go get her and clear out before the big goon they called Gabriel showed up and that's who he was still worrying about when he turned around and saw he'd been worrying about the wrong member of the choir. Paco hardly had the chance to squeeze the trigger again, had only one glimpse of the littlest bastard's face before he caught the first of several blows that had turned his throat to jelly halfway to the ground. *Texas,* he was thinking. A goddamned beautiful place. He never, ever, should have left.

Deal was moving cautiously through the cavernous living room, the automatic pistol raised at his side, when he heard the muffled blasts from somewhere beneath his feet. A shotgun, he thought instinctively. A semiautomatic, a hunter's weapon, judging by the firing interval; either that, or a killer who was picking his shots. He hurried back to the hallway, glanced out through the open door, but Driscoll was still there, propped inside a rear window of the Suburban, pistol at the ready.

They'd had a brief argument about it, but the ex-cop was too woozy and too banged up to move quickly. In the end he'd settled for playing rear guard, ready with his .38 for anyone who might come out behind Deal.

Deal turned and hurried down the hallway in the opposite direction, past the kitchen on his left, dining room and salon on his right. At the end of the hall were three passages: One was a rear staircase that he assumed gave servants access to the upstairs bedrooms. Another doorway led out onto a kind of service porch. The property fell away in back—a broad, emerald lawn running down past a landscaped pool area to a lake that reflected the jagged peaks in the background. There was a seaplane tethered to a dock down there. He paused just long enough to be sure that the props of the plane were quiet, the broad sweep of lawn empty, then turned to try the third door, which he hoped would take him down.

A gust of warm, humid air swept over him as he pushed the door open, and it took him a moment to recognize the chemical odor that came with it. Chlorine, he thought. An indoor pool down there? He ducked his head in and out of the passageway in an instant, but saw nothing except a set of concrete steps leading down to a tiled landing below.

He came around the door frame then and paused again, the strange pistol held in front of him now, finger poised stiffly at the trigger guard. Driscoll had shown him how the thing worked, where the safety was, the switch that toggled the weapon between single-fire and automatic. "Just be careful once it gets going," the ex-cop had said. "Keep it pointed the right way."

Deal didn't doubt his technical abilities with the weapon. His father had him on the firing range from the time he was five, plunking away with pellet guns, then bolt action .22s, and ultimately whatever plaything his father fancied at the time. Deal had fired .45 pistols that bucked straight to the sky unless you were careful, 12-gauge shotguns that numbed his ears and bruised his shoulder blue, even an Uzi, a little bit of a gun that had astonished Deal with its ability to shred a silhouette target in a matter of moments with hardly a tremor of recoil passing through his hands.

What he did wonder about was his ability to fire the weapon he held now should another human being suddenly appear in the passage before him, even with someone else pointing a weapon his way. Deal hadn't so much as shot at a bird since that day when he was twelve, and despite his awareness of what these men were capable of, maybe *because* of that awareness, he was doubly concerned.

Yes, he knew he could will himself to pull the trigger. Self-preservation was a significant motivator. What he worried about was that instant of hesitation, that infinitesimal moment that might have him staring, gaping, *thinking* about what to do, while the other person was turning him into a walking colander. And even as he thought these things, he realized he was wasting valuable seconds. He forced himself on down the stairway, willing himself to focus on the image of the huge man coming down the rocky slope after them, this same weapon poised to blow him and Driscoll into afterthoughts. It was the same man who had killed Barbara, he reasoned, who'd been ready to kill him, and in the next instant there could be others just like him appearing in that wavering rectangle of light below.

His feet moved down the steps as slowly and stiffly as if he had aged fifty years in the past hours, and in some ways he supposed he had. He was nearly at the bottom of the staircase now, and paused when he heard the crash of something, or someone, plunging into water.

He took the last three steps in a rush, skidded on the wet tiles of the landing at the bottom, had to clutch at the open doorway to keep from going down. He realized he had spun out into the room where a sizable indoor pool was housed, had only an instant to take in fragments of the bizarre scene: an upended leather chair bobbed at the surface of the water, one of the black-clad men floating face down near it. On the far side of the pool, the small Chinese man who had let them into the house earlier, dripping wet himself, was struggling to pull an old man up over the side after him.

The little man had one hand on the back of the old man he was trying to drag from the pool, was training another of the automatic pistols on something in the water beneath him. He squeezed off a short burst that seemed to drive the very air from the room, then a second. He was kicking then at whatever it was down there in the water, and still trying to drag the old man out when he noticed Deal.

Their eyes met, and for Deal it was the apotheosis of a nightmare, the very moment that he had dreaded. Deal staring, one hand clutching the door frame, the other holding his weapon upright, watching a little man save another from drowning in the pool. And the little man hesitating not at all.

He slung the old man aside onto the pool apron and began to fire, the tile at Deal's cheek exploding into shrapnel as he tumbled back into the doorway. Deal tucked himself into a ball as the firing continued, fragments of tile and concrete peppering him like buckshot.

There was a lull then, and Deal heard the sounds of a metal door grinding open. He eased his head around the door frame, caught sight of the little man dragging the old man out into a shaft of sunlight, had to duck back as another volley of shots slammed into the wall.

When he heard the door slam shut, he was on his feet and after them, moving as quickly as he dared across the water-slick apron of the pool. He was on the far side of the room, was moving toward the metal doorway, might have missed her altogether. But the sound of someone choking drifted up from the water behind him and he turned to glance in that direction, frozen for the instant it took for Paige Nobleman's face to rise briefly from the cloudy waters, then disappear again.

He didn't have to think this time. He tossed the pistol aside and went into the water in the same motion. He came up under her, cradling her in his arms, realizing the water was just shallow enough for him to stand, keep her afloat as he guided them back to the side. He had to nudge the floating body he'd seen earlier away from the pool gutter before he could boost her inert form up onto the apron.

He vaulted up after her, fearful at first that she might have been shot, his eyes scanning her body until he was reassured she was unmarked. Still, something was wrong. She lay unconscious on her side, water streaming off her in rivulets. Her chest rose and fell in ragged breaths interrupted by involuntary coughs that spewed gouts of pool water from her throat.

He saw the discoloration of a bruise at one eye, then ran his fingertips through her matted hair, wondering if she'd taken a blow there before she'd gone into the water. As he carefully probed, his eyes traveled to the end of the pool where the small Chinese man had been firing at something. He saw something wedged under the rungs of a ladder that curled from the water there: Mahler, he realized finally, a dark stain of blood drifting away from his listlessly bobbing head.

From beneath the leather chair that floated like a dark buoy in the middle of the pool, a motionless arm extended, its black sleeve pushed up, the back of the palm puckered with buckshot wounds. On the side where Deal had entered the room, a young man lay with his legs tangled in fallen lawn furniture, his hands frozen at his throat. A shotgun lay on the wet tiles beside him.

Deal turned from the sight to check on Paige. Her breathing seemed to have steadied now. The water she'd been expelling had become a trickle at the corner of her mouth. Deal heard the sound of footsteps on the stairs he had descended moments before, and remembered the automatic pistol. He lunged across the tiles to where the thing lay, rolled over twice to distance himself from Paige, and came up opposite the doorway, in firing position. There'd be no hesitating this time, he swore it.

He saw movement in the stairwell, feet, a pair of legs. Steadied himself, waiting to be sure, his finger poised at the trigger . . . and then released his breath in a rush when he recognized Driscoll's bulky form emerging into the light.

"Whoa," the ex-cop said, raising his good hand at the sight of Deal with his weapon trained on him.

"They're outside," Deal called. He could already hear the grinding whine of plane engines coming to life.

The sun was just clearing the peaks when he and Driscoll made it through the door. Deal had to shield his eyes from the glare to make out the plane, already taxiing out from the dock into deep water.

Driscoll lumbered a few yards down the pristine lawn until he reached the lingering shadows of the mountains. He raised his pistol toward the receding plane, seemed to gauge the distance, then lowered the weapon helplessly. Deal had reached him by then, and the two watched together as the plane made a whining circle at the far end of the lake, gunned its engines, and began to speed back in the opposite direction.

The skids left the water in twin rooster tails that caught golden shafts of sunlight cutting the water here and there. The plane was up ten feet, twenty, had reached fifty feet perhaps as it cut the air in front of them.

"What are you doing?" Driscoll said, noticing that Deal had braced himself, had raised the automatic, was sighting down its sightless barrel toward the distant plane. "You don't aim that thing," Driscoll was saying. "You take it into a crowded room and yell *surprise.*"

But Deal wasn't paying any attention. He was thinking of Barbara, of Paige, of Isabel, of Janice. He was thinking of the effortless way in which three men had tried to kill him within the past twenty-four hours. And worse, he was thinking of how it was going to be to live the rest of his life wondering when the touch of some stranger might fall upon his shoulder, or that of Driscoll, of any member of his family. How the world is now, Deal thought, how different from what he once believed it might be.

He led the plane what seemed like an appropriate distance and pulled back on the trigger. As the jolts of each shell shook his hands and forearms, melding into an almost indistinguishable roar, he thought of an arcade game he'd favored as a boy, every year a trip to the county fair, find that box the size of an upright freezer with a replica of a machine gun roughly the size of what he held in his hands now mounted on it. He'd stand on a crate to reach the phony gun, squint through a window that gave a view of enemy bombers crossing a made-up sky, pull the trigger until a month's allowance of quarters was gone.

The only thing that had changed when he'd finished back then was that he'd been poorer at the end of it all. There was a score on the counter of the machine, to be sure, but the enemy bombers were still whining across the artificial sky, waiting for the next boy who wanted to imagine he could wipe away evil with a quarter and the bucking of an imaginary gun.

It was the same today, of course. He emptied the automatic pistol into the sky, and the enemy plane whined on, untouched.

"Here," Driscoll said, extending his .38. "You finish with this, we'll find you some rocks to throw."

"It's all right," Deal said. He held up his hand, exhausted. "It's all right."

The plane arrowed on, its engines not flaming, not smoking, but seeming to gain strength and speed as it flashed on across the lake. And it *was* all right. He'd done what he could. He would *do* what he could. That's all you could expect from a life, wasn't it?

He had turned away, back toward the house, to see what they might do for Paige, when he felt Driscoll's hand on his arm.

"Look there," the big man said, and Deal turned in time to see it happen.

He still couldn't believe it. From their vantage point it seemed that the bluff that rose up out of the water was somewhere in the distant background, nowhere near the path of the plane as it roared unwaveringly on.

But it was one of those tricks of perspective, something to do with clear air, distances he wasn't used to gazing across, or maybe it was just the hand of justice that nudged the headlands up another dozen feet or so. He'd never know for sure, would never care to know.

All that mattered was this: The plane did not seem to waver an iota before it slammed into the cliff. There was an instant's pause and then a great fireball erupted where a moment before there had been immutable rock and silence. The huge cloud of flame and black smoke bounded off the rock face and flew skyward like some hideous creature, and finally the sound reached them, sweeping across the vast expanse of lawn in a wave of thunder.

Vaporized, Deal thought. The plane had literally vaporized with the impact. A few boulders tumbled, one piece of flaming metal spiraled down into the water, a fine mist of sand and earth drifted along the cliff, where a black scar was slashed across the rock. It was as if the earth had opened to reclaim some object that should never have been allowed to assemble itself in the first place.

"Fucking A," Driscoll breathed as the shock wave passed over them and the explosion echoed dimly in the distance. "You got him. You fucking blew them right out of the sky."

Driscoll's voice was full of awe by now. But Deal was already on his way toward Paige.

Quite a room, Paige was thinking. Several stories up, broad windows wrapping a corner with a view down over the Palisades to the Pacific, where the sun was setting in a welter of bruised red and purple shadings behind a bank of winter clouds. There was even a balcony with a settee and tiny table where you could go out and breathe in the steady breeze that had washed the entire basin clean this day. A Hockney on one wall, a Miró on another, a huge crystal vase of just-bursting gladioli on a lacquered Chinese table in the corner. If she kept her view just so, there was nothing to suggest she was in a hospital.

But then, Paige thought, Rhonda had always enjoyed the best. Paige turned back to the bed, smiled down wistfully at Rhonda's sleeping form. Given what the woman had been through, she deserved this. This and a hell of a lot more. Paige brushed a tear aside, pulled her gown close around her throat, let her other hand drift down to rest lightly on Rhonda's, careful not to disturb the IV tube that was taped on the back of her palm.

Paige had a room here too, on this very floor, where it was convenient for the team of doctors who were treating them both. Her room was comfortable, too, though nothing quite so grand, of course. No Hockney, no Chinese tables, no balcony. Half the size, and with a view that faced the wooded foothills and the corner of some millionaire's barrel-tiled estate poking out of the trees a few hundred yards away. But she felt safe there, felt her body strengthening every day, had even come to control her impulse to flinch when Dr. Wu, head of the team that had flown from Hong Kong to direct the treatment of the two of them, came in to check on her progress.

It had taken nearly a month, but Paige could walk again, could connect her thoughts with the ability to speak, could sometimes even smile. For the past few evenings, after the meals had been served and cleared, the visitors shooed away, and the floor tended to be quieter, she'd been coming down to Rhonda's room just to talk.

Or unburden herself, was more like it, for Paige was the only one who could speak. There had been no change in Rhonda's condition, in fact. She slept, woke, accepted food, just as she had when she'd been closed away in her Bel Air home. But despite every effort of the doctors, there'd been no reversal in her case, not the slightest sign to date.

"Time," that was all Dr. Wu could counsel. "And love. Let her know how much you want her back," he'd said in his impeccable British accent, encouraging her visits. "This is uncharted territory, medically speaking," he'd continued, gently opening his palms. "We will do everything we can, but we are only scientists. We can address the physical matters, but as to the real engine here, perhaps only you have the capability of reaching that."

And so Paige had come each evening to carry on her monologue, holding Rhonda's hand, praying all the while for some telltale sign, some blink, some twitch, some answering squeeze that would let her know she was getting through. But so far, nothing. As likely as not, Rhonda would simply drift into sleep as Paige talked. She'd been avoiding mention of the more painful details, assuming that the anguish it was sure to cause should Rhonda be able to understand would be even more reason to stay wrapped up in the shell of whatever world she now inhabited.

But when she'd mentioned her fears to Dr. Wu, he had shrugged. "You told me Rhonda Gardner was a strong woman. Tell her the truth, Ms. Nobleman. It's something you Americans like to say, isn't it? 'The truth will set you free.'"

And so this evening she'd decided to go through it all, step by step, as much of it as she had been able to piece together, that is. With Mahler and his cohorts dead, a great deal had been guesswork, of course. But the accounting trail was clear, and the worst of it was undeniable. It had all been about money. Or perhaps what money had signified to Marvin. She shook her head. Maybe she could understand his actions to some degree. She'd once heard a speech by Clifford Irving, the writer who'd been sent to prison for bilking his publisher out of a fortune for a fraudulent "autobiography" by Howard Hughes. Once the contracts for the book had been signed and the advances paid, Irving had said, he'd intended to come clean with his editors, admit the book was a fraud but convince them that it could still be marketed successfully. So why hadn't he done that, a member of the audience wanted to know. "Because," Irving had responded, to thunderous laughter from those assembled, "when someone puts $750,000 in your hand, whole new emotions are born."

So Mahler had sensed the opportunity for a fortune and had been seduced by it. Paige could understand that. There were enough women in the world content to marry a man who would give them a house, along with a checkbook and a budget, women who would trade any real sense of selfhood for the illusion of security. But it was an arrangement that sooner or later bred terrible resentment, and in a way, she supposed, Mahler had come to see himself in the same light, some kind of handmaiden whose fortunes were bound to the well-being of others. And if he had ceased to have any caring, any respect for those others, well . . . perhaps she could understand his desires to become someone other than what he had become. But the fashion in which he had gone about it, that was another matter altogether.

Paige sighed and sat gently on the bedside. Such wearisome thoughts. And what was the difference whether Rhonda slept or not as Paige shared them? The effect seemed to be the same. When she'd described what had happened to Barbara, how she had found her on that awful night, Rhonda's eyes had been staring directly into hers, but there'd been not the slightest flicker. Maybe she had heard, maybe she hadn't.

"The men whom Marvin was dealing with apparently had sources in the research hospital where the Alzheimer's experiments were being conducted," Paige continued, her gaze on the brilliant sunset in the distance. "They'd switch the labels on the two sets of drugs before they were shipped to your doctors. Instead of the experimental antidote, you were receiving the same aluminum solutions they used to induce the symptoms in the lab animals in the first place."

"He needed every cent he had and much more . . . and there was only one ready source. But he knew you'd never stand for this scheme of his," she continued. "So he worked on it until he'd found a way of incapacitating you, but keeping you alive, so he'd still have access to your money. He leveraged everything," she said, "even took out a second mortgage on the Palm Springs property." She paused once more. "He'd found your will, you see." She put her hand on Rhonda's. "He knew what would have happened to everything if you had died."

There was more than one weighty implication in what Paige had just said, of course. *He'd have killed you if he could have.* That's one thing Paige's words implied. The other she still had difficulty articulating, even to herself.

She glanced up at Rhonda's face, was surprised to see that her eyes had flickered open. Usually, once she was out, she was good for a two-hour nap at least. She managed a smile. "You finding this interesting?" she said.

Rhonda's eyes opened a bit wider, blinked. Just a waking-up reflex, Paige knew, but she could pretend otherwise. She gave Rhonda's hand a little squeeze. "It must have driven him crazy, knowing you'd left everything to me," Paige said.

She stared away, thinking for a moment. Searching for the right way to put this. She was angry and resentful, yes, but most of all, she felt a great ache of sadness, for all the years they had missed.

For there had been *some* payoff for this terrible adventure. Something to show for what they'd had to endure. For that much she was grateful.

Finally she turned back to Rhonda. "I just wish you could talk," she said. "There's so much. I wish you could explain it to me. It must have been so hard for you all these years, trying to mother me from a distance, do everything you could, and never let it show."

The clear blue eyes staring steadily back at Paige, the hand so limp in hcrs. "You're my mother," Paige said, her eyes brimming. "I know it now, and I know there's a father somewhere I don't know about and I wish you could tell me about him and I wish you could just say it: 'I'm your mother, Paige.'" She broke off. "I wish you could have come to me twenty years ago and told me. But I want you to know that it doesn't matter. I want you to know it's all right. You've taken care of me all these years and now I'm going to take care of you for as long as it takes." She squeezed her mother's hand tightly.

"I love you. I've always loved you." She swallowed. "And I forgive you."

Paige didn't know where that last statement came from, for it was nothing she'd intended to say. She put her hand to Rhonda's face, searching for words that might explain what she'd meant, then stopped again, drew her hand away. Stared down in wonder at the glistening wetness on her fingertips, then back into that steadfast gaze and the tears that had gathered there, that were streaming down her mother's cheeks like long-awaited rain.

"It's lovely here, isn't it?" Janice was saying. They sat opposite each other in a corner booth of the restaurant, a place on the water that she had directed them to. The windows overlooked a marina where hundreds of sailboats bobbed in their blue rigging blankets, snug as big seabirds settled in for the evening. On a dock outside, Isabel stood with Mrs. Suarez, giggling, dancing back nervously as a freeloading pelican snatched bread scraps from their hands.

"It's pretty," Deal said. His daughter was growing older before his eyes, he thought. Three years old and the spitting image of her mother. "The food was good."

She nodded. "I spoke to Vernon, you know. He told me that you saved that actress's life. He told me everything."

He glanced at her, shrugged. "I lived through it," he said. Then, "I didn't want to worry you."

She stared at him for a moment. "That's the thing about you, Deal. Someone you care about, you'd step in front of a train to save them."

He opened his hands on the table between them. There was nothing he could say to that.

She sighed. "You'd do it for me, for Isabel, I know that." She turned away, her face twisting as if it were knowledge that pained her.

The silence lingered. They'd covered the basics long since. She'd been here in Sarasota for nearly a month, had finally called to arrange this first visit. They'd toured her apartment, a tidy one-bedroom place on the second floor of a building that overlooked the Gulf, as spotless and orderly, to Deal's eye, as a monk's cell. She'd shown them the gallery where she worked, one of several dotting the posh shopping circle on St. Armand's Key. They'd driven out to the beach, watched Isabel chase the waves until she was dizzy with exhaustion. And then it had been time for lunch. Shrimp cocktail and conch fritters for appetizers. A beer for Deal, Shirley Temple for Isabel, Pellegrino for Janice. Excruciating small talk. A fish sandwich for Deal that he'd barely tasted. More small talk, and silences so painful that even Mrs. Suarez had sensed it and fled outside with Isabel.

"So," Deal said finally. "How's this working out for you?"

She stared at him patiently. "This isn't easy for me, Deal. I don't want you thinking I'm over here having a good time."

"All right," he said after a moment.

She stared down at the table for a moment. He noted the ribbon of scar tissue that ran across the back of her left hand, watched her cover it with her right. She looked up, out the window where Isabel was tossing scraps up into the air for the gulls now. "A man came into the gallery the other day," she said.

Deal watched her, steeling himself. "And?"

She shrugged, smiled self-consciously, her eyes still averted. "He pretended to be interested in a painting we'd just hung. It was by a young Brazilian painter. An expensive piece. There was no question this man had the money." She was rattling on a bit now.

"He was hitting on you," Deal said.

"If you want to put it that way," she said. She was toying with her napkin, tearing it into little bits. She turned to him, finally. "It was nearly six and I was closing up." Her eyes on his, steady. He noticed she'd had her hair cut, had swept her bangs to the side, though her ears were still carefully hidden. Was this style more sophisticated? Or less?

She glanced away. "He wanted to know if I'd have a drink with him."

Deal nodded. "What'd you say?"

"I told him I was married," she said. "That I had a daughter who was three."

Deal folded his hands in front of him. "Why are you telling me this, Janice?"

She stared back at him. "It felt good," she said. "It felt very good to know I was attractive to someone, Deal."

He felt his temper rising. "Well of course you're attractive, Janice. You're goddamned beautiful . . . "

She held up her hand to stop him. "I don't want anyone else, Deal. That's not what this is about. I know it's hard for you to understand . . . "

"Then what *is* it about, Janice?"

She looked at him helplessly. "Me," she said simply. She reached across the table to take his hand. "I just need some time, Deal. Can you give me that? You saved Paige Nobleman's life. To me, this is the same thing."

He stared across the table, out the window where a length of tinseled garland still hung, left over from Christmas. Over Janice's shoulder he could see an uncountable flock of gulls, swarming about his daughter as if she were St. Francis incarnate. Mrs. Suarez held the bread sack and shook her head at all the fuss. Inside, Janice stared back at him, waiting.

Men had tried to kill him, that seemed simple compared to this. He felt her hand squeeze his, felt something loosen inside him, some ineffable sadness giving way. *How fragile life is,* he thought. How stupidly taken for granted. How easily taken away. How fortunate he was to have a chance at all.

"Sure," he said, finally. "I can do that." And he raised his hand to Janice's cheek. "I can."

FREE BOOK OFFER—BUY A *DEAL*, GET A *DEAL* FREE!

Get a free copy of the HarperPaperback edition of Les Standiford's *Done Deal* when you send in your receipt from the purchase of *Deal to Die For*.

Praise for *Done Deal*:

"I loved it."

—Stephen King

"Standiford starts this one at high boil and keeps it there. . . . has a sense of rage as old and new clash in the streets of Miami, and that makes for compelling reading."
—*Chicago Tribune*

"Will have readers on the edge of their seats. . . . a smashing good novel."

—*Library Journal*

To receive your free copy of *Done Deal*, mail your original cash register receipt for *Deal to Die For* with your name and address to: HarperCollins Free *Deal*, Box 710, 10 East 53rd Street, New York, NY 10022. Offer expires January 31, 1996.

STA   Standiford, Les.
           Deal to die for.
                6/13

$22.00

DATE			